Practical IT English
实用 IT 英语

王翔　主编

吕英芳　张臻　耿坤　王彦　副主编

清华大学出版社

北京

内 容 简 介

本书依照"教、学、做"一体的 IT 英语课程建设要求，以提高学生在未来工作中实际使用 IT 英语的技能水平为目的，根据高职高专学生特点，较为系统地讲述 IT 英语知识和基本技能，强调实用性、基础性及 IT 英语学习的可持续性。

全书共有 32 单元，每单元除专业课文及难度不大的配套练习外，还大量引用了知名企业当今主流产品英文的介绍和使用说明书，为学生提供与未来实际工作接轨的仿真环境。全书内容涵盖计算机软硬件基础知识、多媒体技术、网络技术、电子商务及嵌入式技术等专业英语知识；并将课文参考译文、练习参考答案等内容作为共享电子资源。

本书可作为高职高专学生的 IT 英语或计算机英语教材，也可供从事 IT 相关专业的工作人员或关心、爱好 IT 业的朋友们学习参考。

图书在版编目（CIP）数据

实用 IT 英语 / 王翔主编. —北京：清华大学出版社，2011.9
ISBN 978-7-302-26136-0

Ⅰ.①实⋯　Ⅱ.①王⋯　Ⅲ.①IT 产业 – 英语 – 高等职业教育 – 教材　Ⅳ.①H31

中国版本图书馆 CIP 数据核字（2011）第 135322 号

责任编辑：闫红梅　李　晔
责任校对：焦丽丽
责任印制：王秀菊

出版发行：清华大学出版社	地　　址：北京清华大学学研大厦 A 座
http://www.tup.com.cn	邮　　编：100084
社　总　机：010-62770175	邮　　购：010-62786544
投稿与读者服务：010-62795954，jsjjc@tup.tsinghua.edu.cn
质　量　反　馈：010-62772015，zhiliang@tup.tsinghua.edu.cn

印　刷　者：北京市清华园胶印厂
装　订　者：三河市李旗庄少明印装厂
经　　销：全国新华书店
开　　本：185×260　印　张：16.5　字　数：391 千字
版　　次：2011 年 9 月第 1 版　印　次：2011 年 9 月第 1 次印刷
印　　数：1～3000
定　　价：26.00 元

产品编号：037530-01

前　言

在 IT 知识与技能迅速更新和 IT 产业不断升级的信息时代背景下，IT 英语在计算机类专业学生的技能培训方面，正在扮演着越来越重要的角色。特别是随着我国在面向全球的计算机软硬件外包领域所取得的长足发展，IT 企业对具有较高专业英语应用水平的应届 IT 类专业毕业生的需求人数急剧增加。具备良好的 IT 英语应用技能，已成为求职者进入 IT 企业、行业的"敲门砖"。

本书在教学要求上，强调 IT 领域的专业术语及相关技术的英语表述和阅读方法，不将公共英语方面的内容作为教学重点，从而避免与《大学英语》、《实用英语》等教材的重叠；在编写内容上，强调广泛地讲述和介绍 IT 英语知识与技能，力求使读者能较为全面地掌握使用 IT 英语的思想和方法，并对以后继续深入学习 IT 英语奠定基础，不对某一知识或某一技术细节着太多笔墨，从而避免与 IT 类其他中文专业教材的重叠。

培养高素质、技能型人才已经成为高职高专类院校的人才培养目标。因此，学习企业和行业工作者需要的 IT 英语知识和技能，避免今天所学内容与明天工作需求不相吻合的情况，是本书编写的出发点。本书大量引用国内外知名 IT 企业当今主流产品的介绍和使用说明书，力求为读者提供一个仿真的工作环境，全面提升学生在未来实际工作中使用 IT 英语的技能水平和职业素养。

本书在编写过程中，参考了大量的文献资料，其中部分内容来自互联网，特别是 IT 领域一些知名厂商和机构官方网站，在此向这些文献资料的作者深表谢意。来自 IT 行业和企业界的专家、学者也对本书的编写提出了宝贵建议，编者在此一并表示感谢。

本书由王翔任主编，吕英芳、张臻、耿坤、王彦任副主编。本书第 1～12 单元由王翔编写，第 13～16 单元由耿坤编写，第 17～20 单元由吕英芳编写，第 21～28 单元由张臻编写，第 29～32 单元由王彦编写。孙慧芹、李宏力、李勤、郝玲、赵家华、贾海瀛、李莉、王炯、张林中、艾艳锦、薛继霜、傅春、王晓星参与了本书的译文、专业词汇整理等部分的编写工作。

我们愿意为使用本书的教师、学生、IT 业工作人员及计算机爱好者提供该领域的帮助，请通过电子邮箱 pingfan6699@163.com 与我们联系。为更好地服务于教学，编者已将本书课文部分的译文、专业词汇缩写及习题参考答案作为共享资源供大家下载使用。

尽管我们依照"教、学、做"一体的 IT 英语课程建设要求，在 IT 英语教材建设突破方面做出了许多努力，但由于编者的水平有限，加之时间仓促，书中内容难免有错误、不足和疏漏之处，恳请各教学单位、行业和企业的工作人员及广大读者不吝赐教、批评指正。

编　者
2011 年 6 月

Table of Contents Contents

Computer and Internet

Multimedia

Programming Languages

Operating Systems

Database and Data Warehouse

Computer Networks

E-commerce

Embedded Technology

Computer and Internet

Unit 1   The Development of Computer Technology

WORDS AND EXPRESSIONS

manipulate [mə'nipjuleit]   操作

Maryland ['mɛərilænd]   马里兰州

Pennsylvania [pensil'veinjə]   宾夕法尼亚州

semiconductor ['semikən'dʌktə]   半导体

transistor [træn'zistə]   晶体管

fingernail ['fiŋgəneil]   手指甲

Harvard ['hɑːvəd]   美国哈佛大学

Dartmouth ['dɑːtməθ]   美国达特茅斯

enthusiasts [in'θjuːziæst]   热心家，狂热者

fledgling ['fledʒliŋ]   无经验的人

unprecedented [ʌn'presidəntid]   空前的

kilobyte ['kiləubait]   千字节，1,024 字节

automate ['ɔːtəmeit]   使自动化，自动操作

novice ['nɔvis]   新手，初学者

underestimated ['ʌndər'estimeit]   低估，看轻

abruptly [ə'brʌpt]   突然地，唐突地

dub [dʌb]   授予…以称号；给…起（绰号）

prestige [pres'tiːʒ]   声望，威望

fad [fæd]   时尚

productivity [ˌprɔdʌk'tiviti]   生产力

drop-out ['drɔpˌaut]   中途退学的人

vacuum tube   电子管，真空管

ENIAC   Electronic Numerical Integrator And Calculator Computer   电子数字积分计算机

Ballistics Research Laboratory   弹道学研究工作实验室

large-scale integrated ['intigreitid] (LSI) circuit   大规模集成电路

very large-scale integrated (VLSI) circuit   超大规模集成电路

International Business Machines (IBM)   美国国际商用机器公司

Intel   美国英特尔公司

Microsoft   美国微软公司

QUESTIONS AND ANSWERS

1. Do you think that computers have become one of the **most important helpful "partners"** of human beings? Why?

2. What did engineers develop in the late 1960s and early 1970s?

3. What is the phylogeny of Microsoft?

4. Who designed and developed Apple?

5. What is the difference between IBM and Apple?

6. What were the first generation programs?

7. Can you tell us something about Bill Gates?

8. What is the relationship between Computers and Internet?

9. When did many application packages begin to appear?

10. When did IBM introduce its own microcomputer IBM PC?

TEXT

As is known to all that computers have played an important **role in the modern society.** High up in space and deep down in oceans, they are used to make **the scientific discoveries;** on farms and in factories, they help us to do difficult work and take the **place of routine jobs.** Computer to human being is like food to our bodies, without food we cannot survive; without **computers the** world would not be what it is today.

The first electronic computers were built in the 1940s**.** At that time, John Louis von Neumann announced the famous stored program concept which says that the program is stored as data in the computer's memory and the computer is able to manipulate it as data—to load it from disk, store it back on disk, and move it in memory. This concept became a fundamental of modern computing. Meanwhile, the Ballistics Research Laboratory in Maryland decided to build a high-speed electronic computer to assist in the preparation of firing tables for artillery. It was built at the University of Pennsylvania's Moore School of Electrical Engineering. This machine became known as ENIAC (Figure 1-1).

Figure 1-1   ENIAC

ENIAC covered an area of 1,800 square feet, weighted 30 tons. This machine was so huge, because it used 18,000 vacuum tubes. The use of the transistor in computers in the late 1950s meant more powerful, more reliable, and less expensive computers that would occupy less space and give off less heart than did vacuum tube powered computers.

In the late 1960s and early 1970s, engineers made great strides in reducing the size of electronic components. They developed the semiconductor chip, which was about the size of a fingernail and could contain hundreds of transistors. The semiconductor chips enabled engineers to miniaturize the circuits contained in all electronic devices. Most importantly, it produced a new generation of mainframes and minicomputers with increased capability, greater speed, and smaller size.

The microprocessor became a reality in the mid-1970s with the introduction of the large-scale integrated (LSI) circuit and the very large-scale integrated (VLSI) circuit (microchip), with many thousands of interconnected transistors etched into a single silicon substrate. In late 1970 Intel introduced a 1k RAM chip and the 4004, a 4-bit microprocessor. Four years later came the 8080, an 8-bit microprocessor. The earliest microcomputer, the Altair 8800, was developed in 1975 by Ed (Edwin) Roberts; this machine used the Intel 8080 microprocessor and had less than 1 kilobyte of memory.

In order for microcomputers to become problem-solving tools, a number of hurdles needed to be overcome. The first was to simplify the program for the machines. One step in this direction was taken by a young Harvard drop-out named Bill Gates, who wrote a version of the programming language BASIC for one of the earliest microcomputers. BASIC had been introduced at Dartmouth College in the mid-1960s by John Kemeny and Kenneth Kurtz. Thus it was a popular programming language on mainframe computers. Gates founded a computer company called Microsoft, which has become one of the major producers of software for microcomputers.

In 1977, Steven Jobs and Stephen Wozniak, two microcomputer enthusiasts, working in a garage, designed their own microcomputer. This was to be named the Apple II (Figure 1-2). And their fledgling business was to become the Apple Computer Corporation. Business grew at an unprecedented rate. In no time, Apple was selling hundreds and then thousands of machines per month.

Figure 1-2　Apple II

One reason behind Apple's success was the availability of number of useful application programs. The most important of these was spreadsheet VISICALS, which allowed accountants and financial planners to automate many of the calculations that they were accustomed to doing on adding machines, or with pencil and paper. Hours of calculations were thus completed in a matter of seconds. Such raw power did much to convince peoples that microcomputers were real problem-solving tools, not toys.

At about the same time as the introduction of the Apple Ⅱ, a number of the microcomputers appeared on the market. One of the most popular computers was Tandy Corporation's TRS-80. Apple and Tandy were the two largest manufacturers, each with about a 25 percent share of the market.

Early microcomputer users banded together into groups to exchange ideas and to share solutions to problems. A strong spirit of adventure encouraged users to feel they were participating in a major intellectual turning point in computer use. Part of the excitement was created by the unusual mixture of people who participated. In addition to computer scientists and engineers, physicians, business people, and students become microcomputer enthusiasts, at work as well as at home. All were interested in the same goal: using microcomputers to solve problems.

So many application packages began to appear around 1980. The first generation programs for word processing, data management, spreadsheets, and communication allowed novice users to experience the power of microcomputing.

However, most corporations underestimated the significance of bringing computing power down to the level of the individual users. This view abruptly changed in 1981 when International Business Machines (IBM), the largest computer company in the world, introduced its own microcomputer, dubbed the IBM PC ("PC" being the abbreviation for personal computer). The fact that IBM, a company of such corporate prestige, would enter this market convinced businesses that the microcomputer was more than a passing fad. Within a short time, the microprocessor was recognized as a productivity tool to be used by workers at all levels to process, store, retrieve, and analyze information. Almost every business could find a legitimate place for the microcomputer (Figure 1-3).

Figure 1-3   IBM 386

Now, there is a light-weight, notebook computer, or portable computer (Figure 1-4), designed to be moved easily.

Figure 1-4   HP Compaq 2510p

EXERCISES

1. Judge whether the following given statements are true or false. If correct, write T in parentheses; otherwise, write F.

(1)   (   ) The first electronic computers were built in the 1950s.

(2)   (   ) ENIAC used 18,000 transistors.

(3)   (   ) Intel 8080 is an 16-bit microprocessor.

(4)   (   ) In 1977, Steven Jobs and Stephen Wozniak designed their own microcomputer in a garage.

2. Complete the following note-taking with the information mentioned in the text.

(1)   John Louis von Neumann announced the famous _____concept which says that the program is stored as data in the computer's memory and the computer is able to manipulate it as data.

(2)   The use of the _____ in computers in the late 1950s meant more powerful, more reliable, and less expensive computers.

(3)   In addition to computer scientists and engineers, physicians, business people, and students become _____, at work as well as at home.

(4)   IBM, a company of such corporate prestige, would enter this market convinced businesses that the _____ was more than a passing fad.

READING MATERIALS

Product Description 1: Lenovo G Series Laptop (Figure 1-5)

Figure 1-5   Lenovo G560

All the tools you need for everyday computing in a worry-free, easy-to-use notebook with stunning good looks—at equally attractive prices!

Smart and affordable never looked so good

➤ Sleek finishes, including hairline or textured (depending on model).

➤ Thin design for great portability.

➤ Full-sized ergonomic keyboard.

➤ Convenient right-side numeric keypad on G550, G555 and G560 models.

For your viewing pleasure

Select G Series models let you enjoy high-definition, widescreen movies without the black horizontal bars thanks to a 16:9 aspect ratio. Plus LED backlight technology is thinner, lighter and minimizes energy consumption.

Supercharged graphics and gaming

Jump into games and video. The latest high-definition, 3-D and audio technologies on select G Series models give your multimedia experience a boost:

➤ High-definition graphics.

➤ Enhanced video playback.

➤ Fast applications.

➤ Wider sound stage.

Get more done in less time

The latest multi-core processor technologies help speed computing tasks, even when you're working in more than one application simultaneously, so you can do more and do it faster. High-performance memory makes applications more responsive, lets you quickly burn DVD and lets you easily compress and open large documents.

Worry-free security features

➤ G Series laptops give you something priceless: peace of mind. Protect your PC and its important data with state-of-the-art security technology.

➤ OneKey™ Rescue System lets you restore your system and recover valuable data from a virus attack or crash with the touch of a button.

➤ VeriFace™ controls access to your notebook by using your face as your logon password and recording the faces of others who try to log on or leave you a message.

➤ Lenovo Energy Management, our advanced power and battery-management software, helps you easily control your laptop's energy usage with a simple interface and a quiet mode for studying or working.

➤ Multimedia features like the integrated camera, integrated microphone, HDMI connector and optical disc drive provide a great multimedia experience at home or on the go.

➤ Lenovo offers a wide variety of systems preloaded with the newest Windows® 7 operating system.

Product Description 2: Dell XPS Laptop (Figure 1-6)

Figure 1-6   Dell XPS Laptop

Movies, games, music and Web chat come to life with leading-edge graphics, 3D capabilities, high-definition (HD) video chat and sound that can fill a room.

➢ Leading-edge NVIDIA® performance graphics bring your media to life.

➢ Get high-fidelity JBL® speakers with Waves MaxxAudio® 3.

➢ Get the first Skype™-certified laptop — video chat with HD Webcam.

➢ Enjoy 3D on the big screen2 with integrated NVIDIA 3DTV Play™ software. Check out the Dell 3D Learning Center.

➢ Turbocharge your performance with Intel® Core™ i5 Processors with four-way multitask processing and Intel® Turbo Boost Technology.

Feel the Rush

Powerful graphics. Powerfully smart. The XPS™ 14 laptop has what it takes to take you to new levels of performance.

Razor-Sharp Graphics Come Standard

The XPS 14 comes with standard leading-edge NVIDIA® performance graphics3 (available up to 2 GB) for powerful photo and video editing and high-resolution gaming with breathtaking detail.

Smart Power Management

➢ Long media marathons are no problem with smart power management that helps extend battery life when you need it.

➢ Optimus™ technology automatically optimizes your battery life while maintaining the graphics performance you expect (completely, seamlessly and transparently) whether you're watching an HD movie, surfing the Web or playing a 3D game (available with Core i5 configurations only).

Mind-Blowing Audio

➢ XPS laptops are designed to be the loudest, clearest and cleanest laptops on the planet with built-in high-fidelity JBL speakers and Waves MaxxAudio® technology. Together they produce rich, full sound that delivers booming bass and razor-sharp clarity to your favorite movies, music and games.

➢ Treat your ears to peak audio performance with the XPS's 6W JBL speakers. Then, layer in the Waves algorithms — designed to deliver better dynamic range, frequency response and imaging — with maximum transparency, clarity and natural sound.

➢ Together, these technologies enable you to take the surround-sound experience of your home theater with you wherever you go.

Your Life in Hi-Def

XPS laptops have the tools that bring your world to you, wherever you are.

Ultra-Clear. Ultra-Flexible.

Connect with your loved ones across the globe in stunning high definition using the internet and XPS 14's HD Webcam. It's the first Webcam to offer HD video streaming for ultra-clear 720p resolution. The extreme flexibility of the new XPS also enables you to record video using different bit rates, depending on the application you use.

Connect to the World

Video conferencing is now even easier with Dell and Skype™4. The new XPS 14 is one of the first laptops to be certified by Skype and offers preinstalled Skype software standard on every XPS 14.

Movies, Games and 3D Videos Come to Life

➢ XPS laptops are the first Dell laptops to offer integrated NVIDIA 3DTV5 Play technology. This enables you to leverage the 3D processing power of GeForce® graphics to create an immersive 3D experience in your own home, on the big screen.

➢ Simply connect your laptop to your 3D-enabled TV and effortlessly project your favorite Blu-ray6 3D movies and 3D photo slideshows for a real-life theater experience. Then, bring your best games7 to life. Using the power of your laptop and your 3D TV, you can step into an eye-popping 3D gaming experience right in your living room. All you need to harness the 3D power of your XPS 14 is a high-definition multimedia interface (HDMI) cable, optional Blu-ray Disc™ drive, approved 3D-enabled TV and 3D media2.

Smarter, faster Intel Core i5 processors come standard

➢ Experience solid performance for everyday applications and additional speed when you need it most with the Intel® Core™ i5 Processor.

➢ Get more done with Intel Turbo Boost Technology that automatically adapts processing speed to accommodate what you are doing.

➢ Four way multitasking with Intel® Hyper-Threading Technology enables each core of the processor to work on two tasks at the same time.

Simple and Smart Support

Dell DataSafe Online

Our online backup service offers data protection by enabling customers to back up data to a safe, remote storage site using a broadband connection. Dell DataSafe Online Backup is easy, flexible and secure. After setup, it will automatically back up data to help protect your data from software, hardware and catastrophic failure.

Dell Support Center

Our centrally located, easy-to-use application provides personalized support resources. Conveniently located on your PC's desktop with quick links to service, support and system resources. Helps keep your system up-to-date and running efficiently through automated fixes for common configuration issues.

The Characteristics of IT English

科技英语（Science and Technology English）是在自然科学和工程技术领域中的使用及随着科学技术的迅速发展而逐渐形成的一种英语文体。我国著名科学家钱三强同志曾指出："科技英语在许多国家已经成为现代英语的一个专门的新领域。"IT 英语属于科技英语范畴，相对于公共英语（General English），IT 英语中的复杂长句、被动语态和非谓语动词等语言形式出现的比较频繁；此外，在 IT 技术迅猛发展的过程中，IT 专业英语中的新术语和新的知识描述语言也在不断出现。

1．复杂长句使用实例

System software, which consists of programs that control the operations of the computer and its devices, serves as the interface between a user and the computer's hardware.

复杂长句在 IT 英语中是比较常见的，此类长句中往往包含若干个从句和非谓语动词短语，而从句和短语间又相互制约和依附，从而形成从句中含短语、短语中带从句的复杂语言现象。此例句中有一个主句和两个定语从句，剖析句意时，应首先抓住主句，再研究定语从句与主句之间如何衔接的问题。

例句译文：系统软件作为用户与计算机硬件之间的接口，是由控制计算机及相关设备操作的程序所构成。

2．被动语态使用实例

The procedure by which a computer is told how to work is called programming.

在 IT 英语中，着重说明客观事物和过程，被动语态有助于将事物的过程和结果置于句子的中心地位，突出讨论的对象，从而有利于 IT 英语实现着重演绎论证的目的；被动语态的表达较主动语态相对客观，回避了人的主观感觉及其体现的个人感情色彩，从而满足科技作品在描述现象、论证推理时对于客观公正性的要求；此外，被动语态可使句子更为紧凑、简短，符合科技文章严谨、精炼的标准。

例句译文：告诉计算机如何工作的过程称为程序设计。

3．非谓语动词使用实例

In communications, the problem of electronics is how to convey information from one place to another.

英语每个简单句只允许使用一个谓语动词，其余动作须使用非谓语动词形式，这也是为什么英语特别是科技英语中非谓语动词使用频繁的原因。

例句译文：在通讯系统中，电子学要解决的问题是如何把信息从一个地方传递到另一个地方。

4．派生词、缩略词、复合词、混成词和借用词使用实例

IT 英语的专业性集中体现在它的特殊专业内容和特殊专业词汇，尤其是伴随着 IT 新技术的不断涌现，都会产生大量复杂的新术语，而这些新术语又往往通过派生词和缩略词的形式呈现出来。缩略词（Acronym）是指由某些词组的首字母所组成的新词；派生词（Derivation）是根据已有的英语词汇，通过对词根加上各种前缀和后缀而构成的新词；复合词（Compound Word）通常是以连字符"-"连接单词构成或者采用短语构成的；混成词（Blending）是将两个单词的前部拼接、前后拼接或将一个单词的前部与另一个词拼接构成新的词汇；借用词（Loanword）往往来自厂商名、商标名、产品代号名、发明者姓名、地名等，是将普通英语单词演变为具有 IT 专业含义的一类词汇。

派生词：

multimedia　多媒体

interface　接口

hypertext　超文本

teleconference　远程会议

缩略词：

ROM　（Read Only Memory）只读存储器

COBOL　（Common Business Oriented Language）面向商业的通用语言

CAD　（Computer Aided Design）计算机辅助设计

HTTP　（Hypertext Transfer Protocol）超文本传输通讯协议

复合词：

object-oriented　面向对象的

point-to-point　点到点

plug-and-plug　即插即用

front-user　前端用户

混成词：

codec (coder+decoder)　编码译码器

compuser (computer+user)　计算机用户

syscall (system+call)　系统调用

modem (modulate+demodulate)　调制解调器

借用词：

flag　标志、状态

bug　程序漏洞

cache　高速缓存

firewall　防火墙

Unit 2   Computer Hardware

WORDS AND EXPRESSIONS

synchronous ['siŋkrənəs]   同时的

combinatorial [ˌkɔmbinə'tɔːriəl]   组合的

multiplexed ['mʌltipleks]   多元的

thumb [θʌm]   拇指

etched ['etʃid]   被侵蚀的，被蚀刻的

Pentium['pentiəm]   Intel 公司"奔腾"CPU 芯片

quadrillion [kwɔ'driljən]   千的五次方，百万之四次方

architecture ['ɑːkitektʃə]   体系机构

multitask ['mʌltiˌtɑːsk]   多任务

mainstream ['meinstriːm]   主流

parallel ['pærəlel]   并行的

video ['vidiəu]   视频

audio ['ɔːdiəu]   音频

optical ['ɔptikəl]   光学的

multidrop ['mʌltidrɔp]   多支路

protocol ['prəutəkɔl]   协议

gigabyte   十亿字节

CPU (Central Processing Unit)   中央处理器

ALU (Arithmetic Logical Unit)   算术逻辑单元

CISC (Complex Instruction Set Computers)   复杂指令集计算机

RISC (Reduced Instruction Set Computers)   精简指令集计算机

AMD   美国 AMD 公司，主要生产计算机的 CPU 芯片

RAM (Random-Access Memory)   随机存取存储器

SRAM (Static RAM)   静态随机存取存储器

DRAM (Dynamic RAM)   动态随机存取存储器

CD-ROM (Compact Disc-Read-only memory)   光盘驱动器

DVD (Digital Versatile Disc)   数字化视频光盘

USB (Universal Serial Bus)   通用串行总线

ISA (Industry Standard Architecture)   工业标准结构

PCI (Peripheral Component Interconnect)   外设组件互连接口

AGP (Accelerated Graphics Port)   图形加速接口

QUESTIONS AND ANSWERS

1. What is the heart of a computer device?
2. What are the two main types of microprocessors for PCs?
3. What is main memory?
4. What is RAM?
5. What is ROM?
6. What is the relationship between BIOS and ROM?
7. What is secondary storage? Please give several examples.
8. What are four I/O buses in the modern PC architecture?

TEXT

A computer system consists of four basic components. An input device provides data. The data are stored in memory, which also holds a program. Under the controls of the program, the computer's processor processes the data. The results flow from the computer to an output device. Another important concept of computer architecture is that most machines nowadays are synchronous, which means they are controlled by a clock. Registers and combinatorial logic blocks alternate along the data-paths through the machine. Let us come closer to the system components one by one, beginning with the processor.

CPU

A very simple processor structure—such as might be found in a small 8-bit microprocessor has the following components: ALU, Register File, Instruction Register, Control Unit, Clock, Program Counter, Memory Address Register, Address Bus, Data Bus, and Multiplexed Bus.

The microprocessor or CPU (Central Processing Unit), is the heart of a computer. It is the CPU that in fact processes or manipulates data and controls all the rest parts of the computer. Modern processors contain millions of transistors which are etched onto a tiny square silicon called a die, which is about the width of a standard thumb. There are two main types of microprocessors for PCs: Complex Instruction Set Computers (CISC) based processors and Reduced Instruction Set Computers (RISC) based processors. The famous example of CISC based processor is Pentium 4, which is Intel's powerful processor for the desktop. RISC based processors are also very important and popular; we can find their way to cable—modems, PDAs, and even our mobile phones.

The Pentium 4 processor improves performance on today's high-end applications and emerging Internet demands.

Based on the same technology as the popular desktop Pentium 4 processor, the Mobile Pentium 4 processor features similar architecture optimized for battery life and other mobile computing needs. The highest-performance processors are available in the mobile space, Mobile

Pentium 4 processor-based systems help provide the same powerful computing experience desktop users have come to expect. Unequaled in 3D tasks, Mobile Pentium 4 processor also offers excellent performance for emerging web-based activities and multitask-oriented users. Mobile Pentium 4 processors also boast a 400 MHz Processor Support Bus.

The newest thing in processor design is 64-bit processors, and people are expected to have these processors in their home PCs in the next decade. 64-bit processors have been with us since 1992, and in 21st century they have started to become mainstream. Both Intel and AMD have introduced 64-bit chips, and Mac G5 supports a 64-bit processor. 64-bit processors have 64-bit ALUs, 64-bit registers, 64-bit buses and so on. One reason why the world needs 64-bit processors is because of their enlarged address spaces. 32-bit processors are often constrained to a maximum of 4GB of RAM access. However, a 64-bit RAM address space is quadrillion gigabytes of RAM.

Memory

The CPU is controlled by program and data that is from storage. We usually divide the storage devices into two types: the main memory and the secondary storage. A CPU can only execute the instructions of a program which has already been in the main memory.

When we talk about main memory, we mean physical memory that is internal to the computer. The word "main" is used to distinguish it from external mass storage devices such as disk drives. Another term for main memory is RAM. RAM is short for random access memory, a type of computer memory that can be accessed randomly; that is, any byte of memory can be accessed without touching the preceding bytes.

RAM (Random Access Memory)is the workhorse behind the performance of your computer. Working as a foot soldier for your processor, RAM temporarily stores information from your operating system, applications, and data in current use. This gives your processor easy access to the critical information that makes your programs run. The amount of RAM you have determines how many programs can be executed at one time and how much data can be readily available to a program. It also determines how quickly your applications perform and how many applications you can easily toggle between at one time. Simply put, the more RAM you have, the more programs you can run smoothly and simultaneously.

There are two basic types of RAM: static RAM (SRAM) and dynamic RAM (DRAM). The two types differ in the technology they use to hold data, DRAM being the more common type. SRAM keeps data in the main memory, without frequent refreshing, for as long as power is supplied to the circuit. SRAM is very fast and fits better with the speed of the CPU. DRAM can hold its data if it is refreshed by special logic called the refresh circuit. Though DRAM is slower than SRAM and requires refresh circuit, it is much cheaper and takes much less space, about one fourth of SRAM.

Hard Drive

On the other hand, secondary storage devices are also very important for computers. As we all known that the hard drive is the primary device that a computer uses to store information.

Most computers have one hard drive located inside the computer case. If a computer has one hard drive, it is called "drive C". If a computer has additional hard drives, they are called "drives D, E, F", and so on. And the hard drive light is on when the computer is using the hard drive. Do not move the computer when the light is on. The hard drive is also called the hard disk, hard disk drive or fixed disk drive.

Video Card

A video card is the part of your computer that transforms video data into the visual display you see on your monitor. The video solution plugs into your computer's motherboard, and is responsible for decoding and processing the video signal. The quality of video you see on your monitor depends on both the video card and the monitor you choose. More video card memory and faster graphics processors can result in more stunning and enjoyable visual effects when running games and programs with detailed graphic design.

Today's video cards provide all the capabilities and features you need for basic home and office use. A high quality video card will further enhance the images you see in games, video, and movies, and will provide smooth, life-like reproductions of actual characters and scenes. If you're a serious gamer or a graphics designer, you'll need the 3D enhancements and higher refresh rates.

Sound Card

In order to hear sound playback from your computer, your system must contain an integrated audio solution or a sound card, as well as speakers. A sound card or integrated audio solution gives your computer the ability to send sound through speakers, record sound from a microphone connected to your computer, or even manipulate sound stored on a disk. A high quality sound card can turn your computer into an exciting multimedia entertainment system. When choosing which audio solution is right for you, consider the impact sound will have on your overall computing experience.

Sound cards allow you to listen to music CD, enjoy the intense sound effects in your DVD movies, and record & edit audio files. Higher-end cards also support 3D sound enhancements and joystick/MIDI support for the ultimate gaming adventure. Your choice of sound card and speaker system can greatly enhance your computer's sound quality and your overall audio experience.

Optical Media Drive

You can customize your PC's optical media drives, depending upon the model you choose. Most come with a CD-ROM or DVD-ROM drive as standard equipment and many also have a second drive bay for additional media. These media drives can be used to store and transport data, to play music and movies and to create music CD.

A CD-ROM provides a low cost way to read data files and load software onto your computer. CD-ROMs are modified to support the highest quality readability. A DVD-ROM allows you to enjoy the crystal clear color, picture and sound clarity of DVD video on your notebook. It will also prepare you for future software and large data files that will be released on

DVD-ROM. A DVD-ROM drive can also read CD-ROM disks effectively providing users with full optical read capability in one device.

A CD-RW will allow users to easily create their own custom data CD for data back-up or data transfer purposes. It will also allow you to store and share video files, large data files, digital photos, and other large files with other people that have access to a CD-ROM drive. This drive will also do anything your CD-ROM will do. It reads all your existing CD-ROMs, Audio CD and CDs that you have created with your CD burner. A DVD-RW Drive brings you the leading-edge rewritable DVD solution, built around the emerging DVD+RW standard. Use it to store your favorite original video or to archive up to 4.7 GB of your personal data.

Speaker

Speakers connect to your computer and allow you to hear sound from your computer. The combination of a quality sound card with high-end speakers will turn your computer into a multimedia powerhouse and allow you to make the most of your sound experience. If you're looking for a premium quality sound experience, opt for a speaker system with satellite speakers and a separate subwoofer.

Computer Bus

Many computational science applications generate huge amounts of data that must be transferred between main memory and I/O in this text since the devices such as disk and tape. Computer buses play an important role in finishing this task.

A bus is an important subsystem in computer architecture which transfers data or power between computer components inside a computer or between computers. Unlike a point-to-point connection, a bus can logically connect several peripherals over the same set of wires. At the very beginning computer buses meant literally parallel electrical buses with multiple connections, but the term is now used for any physical arrangement that provides the same logical functionality as a parallel electrical bus. Modern computer buses can use both parallel and bit-serial connections, and can be wired in either a multidrop (electrical parallel) or daisy chain topology, or connected by switched hubs, as in the case of USB.

There are four I/O buses in the modern PC architecture and each of them has several functions. They may lead to internal and external ports or they lead to other controlling buses. The four buses are: ISA, which is old, slow, and limited, compared to the alternatives listed below; PCI, which is the newer high speed multifunction I/O bus; AGP, which is only used for graphics adapter; USB, which is the new low speed I/O bus to replace ISA.

Now "Third generation" computer buses are in the process of coming to market, including Hyper Transport and InfiniBand. They typically include features that allow them to run at the very high speeds needed to support memory and video cards, while also supporting lower speeds when talking to slower devices such as disk drives. They also tend to be very flexible in terms of their physical connections, allowing them to be used both as internal buses, as well as connecting different machines together. This can lead to complex problems when trying to service different requests, so much of the work on these systems concerns software design, as opposed to the hardware itself. In general these third generation buses tend to look more like a network than the original concept of a bus, with a higher protocol overhead needed than early systems, while also allowing multiple devices to use the bus at once.

EXERCISES

1. Judge whether the following given statements are true or false. If correct, write T in parentheses; otherwise, write F.

(1) (　) Most computers nowadays are synchronous, which means they are controlled by a clock.

(2) (　) The famous example of RISC based processor is Pentium 4, which is Intel's powerful processor for the desktop.

(3) (　) The quality of video you see on your computer depends on the monitor you choose.

(4) (　) USB is the new low speed I/O bus to replace PCI.

2. Complete the following note-taking with the information mentioned in the text.

(1) Modern processors contain millions of ＿＿＿ which are etched onto a tiny square silicon.

(2) CPU is controlled by ＿＿＿ and data that is from storage.

(3) Use ＿＿＿ to store your favorite original video or to archive up to 4.7 GB of your personal data.

(4) ＿＿＿ transfer data or power between computer components inside a computer or between computers.

READING MATERIALS

Product Description 1: Intel® Core™ i7 Processor Extreme Edition (Figure 2-1)

Figure 2-1   Intel® Core™ i7 Processor Extreme Edition

The Intel® Core™ i7 processor Extreme Edition is the perfect engine for power users who demand unparalleled performance and unlimited digital creativity. Experience Intel's fastest, smartest PC processor. You'll get maximum PC power for whatever you do, thanks to the combination of smart features like Intel® Turbo Boost Technology³ and Intel® Hyper-Threading Technology, which together activate full processing power exactly where and when you need it.

Gear up for extreme processing power

➢ Hardcore multitaskers rejoice. Fly through everything you do on your PC - from playing intense 3D games to creating and editing digital video, music, and photos. With the high performance platform capabilities of Intel® X58 Express Chipset-based motherboards, along with faster, intelligent multi-core technology that applies processing power dynamically when its needed most, PCs based on the Intel® Core™ i7-980X processor Extreme Edition deliver incredible performance with a rich feature set.

➢ Wield the ultimate gaming weapon for greater performance in 3D gaming applications. Experience smoother and more realistic gaming made possible by distributing AI, physics, and rendering across six cores and 12 threads, bringing 3D to life for the ultimate gaming experience. And take digital content creation to a whole new level for photo retouching and photo editing. Unlock your full potential with Intel's top-of-the-line desktop processor and experience total creative freedom that's limited only by your imagination.

Intel® Core™ i7-980X processor Extreme Edition

➢ 3.33GHz core speed.

➢ Up to 3.6GHz with Intel® Turbo Boost Technology.

➢ 6 cores and 12 processing threads with Intel® Hyper-Threading Technology.

➢ 12MB Intel® Smart Cache.

➢ 3 Channels DDR3 1066MHz memory.

➢ 32nm manufacturing process technology.

Intel® Core™ i7-975 processor Extreme Edition

➢ 3.33GHz core speed.

➢ Up to 3.6GHz with Intel® Turbo Boost Technology.

➢ 4 cores and 8 processing threads with Intel® Hyper-Threading Technology.

➢ 8MB Intel® Smart Cache.

➢ 3 Channels DDR3 1066MHz memory.

➢ 45nm manufacturing process technology.

Get extreme with your gaming and advanced multimedia.

➢ Intel® Core i7 processors deliver an incredible breakthrough in six-core performance and feature the latest innovations in processor technologies:

➢ Intel® Turbo Boost Technology maximizes speed for demanding applications, dynamically accelerating performance to match your workload-more performance when you need it the most.

➢ Intel® Hyper-Threading Technology enables highly threaded applications to get more work done in parallel. With 8 threads available to the operating system, multi-tasking becomes even easier.

- Intel® Smart Cache provides a higher-performance, more efficient cache subsystem. Optimized for industry leading multi-threaded games.
- Intel® QuickPath Interconnect is designed for increased bandwidth and low latency. It can achieve data transfer speeds as high as 25.6GB/sec with the Extreme Edition processor.
- Integrated memory controller enables three channels of DDR3 1066MHz memory, resulting in up to 25.6GB/sec memory bandwidth. This memory controller's lower latency and higher memory bandwidth delivers amazing performance for data-intensive applications.
- Intel® HD Boost significantly improves a broad range of multimedia and compute-intensive applications. The 128-bit SSE instructions are issued at a throughput rate of one per clock cycle, allowing a new level of processing efficiency with SSE4 optimized applications.
- AES-NI Encryption/Decryption Acceleration provides 6 new processor instructions that help to improve performance for AES encryption and decryption algorithms.

Product Description 2: Kingston HyperX Genesis DDR3 Memory (Figure 2-2)

Figure 2-2   Kingston HyperX Genesis DDR3 Memory

HyperX DDR3 memory adopts the latest generation of DDR memory technology. Like all Kingston HyperX products, DDR3 modules are specifically engineered and designed to meet the rigorous requirements of PC enthusiasts. DDR3 memory offers faster speeds, lower latencies, higher data bandwidths and lower power consumption than DDR2. HyperX DDR3 modules are available in single, dual and triple-channel memory kits.

HyperX DDR3 features

- 1.7V-1.95V voltage range for dual-channel applications for AMD based systems and Intel chipsets older than X58.
- 1.65V voltage for triple-channel Intel Core i7 9xx series applications.
- 1.65V voltage for dual-channel Intel Core i5 7xx series and Core i7 8xx series applications.
- Currently available in speeds up to 2000MHz and kits capacities of 8GB dual-channel, and 12GB triple-channel configurations.

DDR3 memory modules are not backward compatible to DDR2 based motherboards, due to incompatible module connections (number of pins), voltage and DRAM technology. DDR3 memory modules have a different key or notch than the same-sized DDR2 modules to prevent their insertion into an incompatible memory socket. HyperX DDR3 modules are available in single, dual and triple-channel memory kits

Notice: All Kingston products are tested to meet our published specifications. Some system or motherboard configurations may not operate at the published HyperX memory speeds and timing settings. Kingston does not recommend that any user attempt to run their computers faster than the published speed. Overclocking or modifying your system timing may result in damage to computer components.

Product Description 3: Barracuda XT SATA 6Gb/s 2TB Hard Drive (Figure 2-3)

Figure 2-3   Barracuda XT SATA 6Gb/s 2TB Hard Drive

Perfect for desktop PC and Mac® computers, Barracuda hard drives deliver the technology, speed, efficiency and large capacities needed by today's computer enthusiasts. The Barracuda XT is the performance leader in the Barracuda family, offering maximum capacity, maximum cache and maximum SATA performance for the ultimate in desktop computing power.

Highlights
- ➤ The combination of SATA 6Gb/s interface and 7200 RPM spindle speed delivers top notch performance needed by today's high-end computers.
- ➤ 64MB cache optimizes burst performance and reduces data throughput bottlenecks.
- ➤ 2TB drive capacity provides plenty of room for space-hungry PC games and high-definition video.
- ➤ Native Command Queuing dramatically increases performance by organizing incoming commands in the most efficient order.
- ➤ Perpendicular recording technology increases performance and reliability by aligning the data bits vertically on the disk.
- ➤ Works with both PC and Mac® desktop computers.
- ➤ Fully compatible with legacy SATA 1.5Gb/s and SATA 3Gb/s interfaces.

Perfect for
- ➤ High-end computers.

- Gaming rigs.
- Multi-media workstations.
- Entry-level servers.

What's in the box

- Barracuda XT 3.5" internal hard drive.
- Interface cable.
- Power adapter.
- Mounting screws.
- CD with software and manual.
- Quick installation guide.

System requirements

- Windows Vista®, Windows® XP, Windows® 2000 Pro, Windows® 7.
- Power Mac® G5 and newer with Mac® OS X 10.2 or later.
- Can be used with Linux.
- SATA interface connector on motherboard or add in SATA card.

Product Description 4: ATI Radeon™ HD 5870 Graphics (Figure 2-4)

Figure 2-4   ATI Radeon™ HD 5870 Graphics

Prepare to experience a riveting high-definition gaming experience with ATI Radeon™ HD 5870 graphics processor.

- 2.15 billion 40nm transistors.
- TeraScale 2 Unified Processing Architecture.
  - 1600 Stream Processing Units
  - 80 Texture Units
  - 128 Z/Stencil ROP Units
  - 32 Color ROP Units
- GDDR5 interface with 153.6GB/sec of memory bandwidth.
- PCI Express 2.1 x16 bus interface.
- Speeds & Feeds.
  - Engine clock speed: 850MHz
  - Processing power (single precision): 2.72 TeraFLOPS

- Processing power (double precision): 544 GigaFLOPS
- Polygon throughput: 850M polygons/sec
- Data fetch rate (32-bit): 272 billion fetches/sec
- Texel fill rate (bilinear filtered): 68 Gigatexels/sec
- Pixel fill rate: 27.2 Gigapixels/sec
- Anti-aliased pixel fill rate: 108.8 Gigasamples/sec
- Memory clock speed: 1.2GHz
- Memory data rate: 4.8Gbps
- Memory bandwidth: 153.6GB/sec
- Maximum board power: 188Watts

Product Description 5: Creative Sound Blaster X-Fi Titanium HD (Figure 2-5)

Figure 2-5   Creative Sound Blaster X-Fi Titanium HD

The Sound Blaster X-Fi Titanium HD provides the highest quality audio playback of any other sound card Creative has ever introduced. This sound card includes THX TruStudio PC audio technology, bringing together two of the most respected names in sound quality to provide an unparalleled audio experience on the PC. The Sound Blaster X-Fi Titanium HD features audiophile-grade components for high-quality playback of music, games and movies, including 122db SNR Digital-to-Analog Converters (DACs), the highest signal-to-noise ratio sound card ever produced by Creative. Replaceable OP-amps provide the flexibility to further customize your audio experience through different sound coloration. If you are serious about how your PC sounds, this is the ultimate Sound Blaster experience.

Premium Sound Blaster quality

Featuring High-Fidelity audio performance with the Digital-Analog (D/A), Analog-Digital (A/D) converters, together with a signal-to-noise ratio (SNR) of 122dB with 0.001% (THD) distortion, the Sound Blaster X-Fi Titanium HD is the ideal choice for the demanding audiophile.

Audiophile components

The Sound Blaster X-Fi Titanium HD features high quality components offering audiophile-grade performance, designed to eliminate noise, while dramatically improving sound field dynamics in the high and mid tones.

Superior headphone experience

Enjoy pristine audio in private anywhere with the superlative headphone output featuring an amazing 115dB, 24-bit/96kHz support in High-Definition (HD) quality sound for original playback.

Personalize your sound with upgradeable components

For the discerning music listener, you can personalize your listening experience with the swappable OP-amp sockets on the sound card to tailor sound to the way you want it.

THX TruStudio PC for unprecedented audio realism

The ground-breaking THX TruStudio PC sound effects will transform your experience into a true High-Definition (HD) multimedia emotional journey.

Hardware accelerated EAX 5.0 for ultimate gaming audio

Hardware-powered 3D positional audio and EAX 5.0 effects provide stunning audio realism over both headphones and speakers without affecting your frame-rates.

Pristine audio recordings with ultra low latency

ASIO recording support with latency as low as one millisecond and minimal CPU load for precise audio recordings.

Immersive digital home entertainment

Dolby Digital and DTS encoding enable a simple one-step single-cable connection to home entertainment systems with included optical cables, for compelling surround sound.

Optimized for Windows Vista and Windows 7

In order to achieve the ultimate Sound Blaster performance, the Sound Blaster X-Fi Titanium HD has been optimized to work on PCs with Windows Vista or Windows 7 only.

Product Description 6: ASUS P6T Deluxe V2 (Figure 2-6)

Figure 2-6   ASUS P6T Deluxe V2

The Best Intel® Core™ i7 Platform

➤ Intel LGA1366 Platform / X58 chipset.

➤ Triple-channel DDR3 2000(O.C.) / 1866(O.C.) / 1800(O.C.) / 1600(O.C.) / 1333 / 1066 Memory.

➤ True 16+2 phase Power Design.

➤ TurboV - New OC Records with Real-Time Super-precise Tunings.

➤ EPU - System Level Energy Saving.

➤ Express Gate SSD - 0 to Internet in Seconds.

> SLI and CrosFireX on Demand.
> 100% High-quality Japan-made Conductive Polymer Capacitors.

CPU, Chipset and Graphics features

> This motherboard supports the latest Intel® Core™ i7 processors in LGA1366 package which has memory controller integrated to support 3-channel (6 DIMMs) DDR3 memory. Supporting Intel(R) QuickPath Interconnect (QPI) with system bus up to 6.4GT/s and a max bandwidth of up to 25.6GB/s, the Intel® Core™ i7 processor is one of the most powerful and energy efficient CPU in the world.

> The P6T Deluxe Series breaks the boundaries to bring you the multi-GPU choice of either Nvidia® SLI™ or ATI® CrossFireX™. Get ready to change your gaming style with faster frame rates!

> This motherboard supports the latest PCIe 2.0 devices for double speed and bandwidth which enhances system performance.

Memory Features

> The motherboard supports DDR3 memory that features data transfer rates of 2000(O.C.)/ 1866(O.C.) / 1800(O.C.) / 1600(O.C.) /1333 / 1066MHz to meet the higher bandwidth requirements of the latest 3D graphics, multimedia, and Internet applications. The triple-channel DDR3 architecture enlarges the bandwidth of your system memory to boost system performance.

ASUS Exclusive Features

> The groundbreaking 16+2 phase VRM design is brrought to the ASUS motherboards. 16+2 phase power design, 16-phase for vCore and extra 2-phase for QPI/Memory controller inside CPU, can provide the highest power efficiency, and hence generates less heat to effectively enhance the overclocking capability. With the high quality power components such as low RDS (on) MOSFETs, Ferrite core chokes with lower hysteresis loss and 100% Japan-made high quality conductive polymer capacitors, ASUS 16+2 phase VRM design also ensure longer component life and minimum power loss.

> Feel the adrenaline rush of real-time OC-now a reality with the ASUS TurboV. This extreme OC tool lets you set new ambitions on the OC stage with an advanced and easy-to-use interface - allowing you to overclock without exiting or rebooting the OS. With micro adjustments of the CPU PLL, NB, NB-PCIe, and DRAM voltages in 0.02v intervals, there are no limits - only extreme results to break new OC records.

> Express Gate™ is an ASUS exclusive OS that provides you with quick access to the Internet and key applications before entering Windows®.

ASUS Power Saving Solution

> The ASUS EPU providing total system power savings by detecting current PC loadings and intelligently moderating power in real-time. It automatically provides the most appropriate power usage for the CPU, VGA card, memory, chipset, hard drives, and system fan- helping save power and money.

➤ With AI Nap, users can instantly snooze your PC without terminating the tasks. System will continue operating at minimum power and noise when user is temporarily away. It keeps downloading files or running applications in quietest state while you're sleeping. Simply click keyboard or mouse, you can swiftly wake up the system in few seconds.

ASUS Quiet Thermal Solution

➤ Enjoy a super cool and quiet PC environment with the innovative Wind Flow Thermal Design. With specifically-engineered copper pipes, this thermal design effectively manages the airflow of the CPU fan and directs system heat away from the PC - resulting in efficient heat dissipation to lower overall system temperature and prolong system lifespans.

➤ Stack Cool 2 is a fanless cooling solution offered exclusively by ASUS. It effectively and noiselessly transfers heat generated by the critical components to the other side of the specially designed PCB (printed circuit board) for effective heat dissipation-making temperatures cooler by up to 20℃.

➤ ASUS Fan Xpert intelligently allows users to adjust both the CPU and chassis fan speed according to different ambient temperature, which is caused by different climate conditions in different geographic regions and system loading. Built-in variety of useful profiles offer flexible controls of fan speed to achieve a quiet and cool environment.

ASUS Crystal Sound

➤ This feature detects repetitive and stationary noises like computer fans, air conditioners, and other background noises then eliminates it in the incoming audio stream while recording.

ASUS EZ DIY

➤ Easy and Comfortable Installations—The specially designed ASUS Q-Shield does without the usual "fingers" - making it convenient and easy to install. With better electric conductivity, it ideally protects your motherboard against static electricity and shields it against Electronic Magnetic Interference (EMI).

➤ Simply update BIOS from a USB flash disk before entering the OS—EZ Flash 2 is a user-friendly BIOS update utility. Simply launch this tool and update BIOS from a USB flash disk before entering the OS. You can update your BIOS only in a few clicks without preparing an additional floppy diskette or using an OS-based flash utility.

➤ Make connection quick and accurate! —The ASUS Q-Connector allows you to connect or disconnect chassis front panel cables in one easy step with one complete module. This unique adapter eliminates the trouble of plugging in one cable at a time, making connection quick and accurate.

➤ Conveniently store or load multiple BIOS settings—Freely share and distribute favorite overclocking settings The motherboard features the ASUS O.C. Profile that allows users to conveniently store or load multiple BIOS settings. The BIOS settings can be stored in the CMOS or a separate file, giving users freedom to share and distribute their favorite overclocking settings.

SAS onboard

➤ Dual Gigabit LAN—The integrated dual Gigabit LAN design allows a PC to serve as a network gateway for managing traffic between two separate networks. This capability ensures rapid transfer of data from WAN to LAN without any added arbitration or latency.

➤ S/PDIF-out on Back I/O Port—This motherboard provides convenient connectivity to external home theater audio systems via coaxial and optical S/PDIF-out (SONY-PHILIPS Digital Interface) jacks. It allows to transfer digital audio without converting to analog format and keeps the best signal quality.

➤ Enjoy high-end sound system on your PC—The onboard 8-channel HD audio (High Definition Audio, previously codenamed Azalia) CODEC enables high-quality 192KHz/24-bit audio output, jack-sensing feature, retasking functions and multi-streaming technology that simultaneously sends different audio streams to different destinations. You can now talk to your partners on the headphone while playing a multi-channel network games. All of these are done on one computer.

➤ SATA on the Go—The motherboard supports the next-generation hard drives based on the Serial ATA (SATA) 3Gb/s storage specification, delivering enhanced scalability and doubling the bus bandwidth for high-speed data retrieval and saves. The external SATA port located at the back I/O provides smart setup and hot-plug functions. Easily backup photos, videos and other entertainment contents on external devices.

➤ IEEE 1394a interface—IEEE 1394a interface provides high speed digital interface for audio/video appliances such as digital television, digital video camcorders, storage peripherals & other PC portable devices.

Green ASUS

➤ The motherboard and its packaging comply with the European Union's Restriction on the use of Hazardous Substances (RoHS). This is in line with the ASUS vision of creating environment-friendly and recyclable products and packaging to safeguard consumers' health while minimizing the impact on the environment.

Product Description 7: Samsung FX2490HD LED Series 90 (Figure 2-7)

Figure 2-7   Samsung FX2490HD LED Series 90

This Samsung HDTV monitor flaunts head-to-stand style with a chrome-coated, mystic brown finish and Touch of Colour's design. And thanks to its built-in digital tuner this monitor transforms into a TV - right on your desk. A unique, quadruple stand makes sure it stays firmly put while you watch your favourite programs. Plus the 1080p high definition LED images keeps it all rich, realistic and sharp while stunning surround sound adds the finishing touch.

A monitor that's also a digital TV

Experience the best of both worlds with a monitor that's also a TV. This versatile monitor boasts a built-in digital TV tuner so you can watch your favourite television programs without a computer. Use your monitor as a PC and a TV, and you'll not only save money, you'll also save space. Or use it as a standalone TV in your kitchen or bedroom. The series 90 HDTV monitor is truly a multifunction monitor.

A movie-worthy monitor

This monitor's 1080p high-definition technology will mesmerise you. Enjoy realistic images bursting with rich details and eye-popping colour. Plus LED technology creates an ultra-high MEGA dynamic contrast ratio which keeps everything crystal-clear and incredibly vivid. Thought this monitor would sacrifice picture quality.

Immerse yourself in crystal-clear audio

Your experience doesn't end with amazing picture quality - this monitor also features superior surround sound. Sit back, relax and enjoy a home theatre experience with up to 7.1 channel Dolby Digital Plus sound, 5.1 channel DTS sound and SRS theatre sound. Position the speakers throughout your space to bring your favourite movies to life with true cinematic sound. Now sound is just as stunning as picture quality.

Multitasking made fun

Hard at work but need a break with some playtime? No problem-the Samsung HDTV monitor features Picture in Picture (PIP) support. You can watch TV while working on a spreadsheet during commercials. Eliminate the need for a second monitor, additional connectors and power cords. The series 90 HDTV monitor is the one monitor you need for all your multitasking.

PC-free media sharing

Simply plug your USB directly into the series 90 HDTV monitor, and you can instantly share music, movies and photos from your MP3 player or digital camera-without even turning on your PC. With ConnectShare, it's true plug-and-play convenience.

Reduce eyestrain Enhance your viewing experience

How do you like to watch movies? Do you like lying down on the couch? Sitting in your favourite chair? Cooking or exercising? Whether you're standing, sitting or lying down, Samsung's Magic Angle makes sure that the movie always takes centre stage. And that you're always comfortable. Wherever you place the series 90 HDTV monitor, its 5-mode angle management allows you to extend its viewing angle so the screen always appears as if viewed face-on. So stop craning your neck and start enjoying the movie.

Product Description 8: Canon i-SENSYS LBP7750Cdn (Figure 2-8)

Figure 2-8   Canon i-SENSYS LBP7750Cdn

This robust colour and mono print solution offers outstanding performance and reliability – with the flexibility, security and control that busy corporate and business workgroups require.

Features

➢ 30 ppm colour and mono laser printing.

➢ Up to 9,600×600 dpi printing.

➢ Fast 10.4 sec First Print Out Time.

➢ No waiting with Quick First-Print technologies.

➢ Automatic double-sided printing.

➢ Network ready.

➢ PCL5c/6 and optional PostScript support.

➢ Energy efficient.

Save time

There's no waiting for your urgent print jobs with rapid 30 ppm colour and mono printing, a fast First Print Out Time of just 10.4 seconds and quick wake-up from sleep mode thanks to Quick First-Print technologies. Save even more time with productive automatic double-sided printing as standard.

Outstanding colour

Produce impressive colour documents on demand. Canon's colour imaging technologies give you a competitive edge, delivering professional quality colour and sharp black text. Automatic Image Refinement (AIR) for up to 9600×600 dpi printing and superior S-Toner provide the finest detail for presentations, brochures and all your colour material.

Cut costs, save energy

Save paper and cut costs with automatic double-sided printing. Save energy and reduce running costs with this Energy Star certified printer that uses as little as 1.7 watts in sleep mode. Canon Authentic Laser Cartridges provide cost effective colour and mono printing, plus an optional high capacity Canon black cartridge can cut print costs even further.

Complete connectivity

Thanks to PCL5c/6 support, optional PostScript Level 3 emulation and PDF direct print; this network ready printer can be integrated seamlessly into existing corporate IT workflows and systems. The optional Wireless Network Interface Board NB-W2 provides a secure and convenient alternative to wired connectivity.

Maximum uptime, minimum maintenance

The i-SENSYS LBP7750Cdn is perfect for high volume printing as it has a durable design and maximum 850-sheet paper capacity for uninterrupted output (with optional 500-sheet cassette). Canon's All-in-One cartridge system provides maintenance-free operation, consistently high quality output and the convenience of fewer consumables.

Simple to setup and operate

A 5-line display with intuitive menus and animated troubleshooting makes this high performance printer simple for staff to operate, right from the start.

Workgroup security and control

The Remote User Interface allows users and administrators to remotely monitor and manage printer status effortlessly, directly over the network. Control access to the machine and manage it securely thanks to Department ID management and Simple Network Management Protocol version 3 (SNMPv3). Optional encrypted and secure printing protects sensitive information, making sure that confidential material remains in the right hands.

Product Description 9: Founder Scanner Z3600 (Figure 2-9)

Figure 2-9   Founder Scanner Z3600

Ideal solution for hyper- speed & exceptional quality large format scanning

➢ Any Scan Z3600 is the workhorse for large format scanning. It is a USB 2.0 device that can scan an A3 size document with high quality resolution as high as 600dpi×1200dpi and scanning area as large as 12×17 (304.8 mm×431.8 mm). When it comes to speed, it has one of the highest in the industry for it can scan an A3 page in just 2.4 seconds (color at 300dpi). Often, large format scanning is considered to be complex but Founder Any Scan Z3600 takes the pain out of the process.

➢ It features advanced networking capabilities, rich functionality and comes bundled with valuable yet easy-to-use document management software. Not to forget the reliability and cost efficiency it has on offer for users. Founder Any Scan Z3600 is an imperative for finance, insurance, law, healthcare, transport and education verticals.

➢ Users can personalize the settings and then access them at the press of a button. It has one-touch functions buttons for routine operations like scan, OCR, copy, fax and email. For further ease and convenience, its graphical user interface (GUI) is available in multiple languages.

Product Description 10: LG GE24LU20 DVD and Blu-Ray™ Drive (Figure 2-10)

Figure 2-10   LG GE24LU20 DVD and Blu-Ray™ Drive

Drive24x External Super-Multi DVD RewriterWith an LG 24x internal DVD burner, you can boost your computing capabilities with a 24x writing speed. SecurDisc™ technology keeps your media safe from tampering, and LightScribe technology allows you to create silkscreen-quality labels right inside the drive, with just a flip of the disc.

Key Features
➢ Double/Dual Layer Compatible: Double/Dual discs give desktop users the ability to store the maximum amount of data on their DVDs, including up to 4 hours of high-quality video, bonus content, and other large media.

➢ Lightscribe Technology: LightScribe is a laser-printing technology that allows users to create silkscreen-quality labels right inside LG optical drives with a simple clip of the disc.

➢ USB 2.0 Connection: An advanced USB interface transfers raw data at rapid speeds. Compatible with USB version 2.0 and 1.1.

➢ SecurDisc™ Technology: SecurDisc™ is an innovative technology giving users the means to protect and share data securely, via data protection and content access-control of your media.

Product Description 11: Microsoft Wireless Laser Desktop 6000 (Figure 2-11)

Figure 2-11   Microsoft Wireless Laser Desktop 6000

Microsoft Hardware brings performance, style and comfort to your desktop with a new keyboard and perfectly portable mouse. Whether you're at home or on the go, enjoy desktop comfort and style.

Extended Battery Life
Maximum efficiency--most users average more than six months of battery life; status

indicator tells you when your battery is running low.

Device Stage

Quickly and easily access common tasks, including product information, registration, settings and more for popular devices such as cell phones, cameras, printers, and mouse, keyboard and webcam products.

Inspired by Windows Aero

Bring translucent beauty to your desktop with design inspired by Windows® Aero™.

Wireless Freedom

Give yourself room to move with a wireless mouse and keyboard that lets you work without worrying about tangled wires.

Magnifier

Point and click to enlarge and edit details using the Magnifier.

3-Year Limited Hardware Warranty

Mouse Features

➢ Snap-in Transceiver: Connects the keyboard and mouse right out of the box with virtually no interference, and provides up to a 30-foot wireless range.

➢ Laser Technology: Microsoft Laser Mouse products are more precise, more responsive, and deliver smoother tracking.

➢ 4-way Scrolling: Scroll four ways for greater efficiency and comfort with Tilt Wheel Technology.

➢ Five Customizable Buttons: The mouse has five buttons that can be programmed to do a variety of functions.

➢ Rubber-sided grip: The rubber grip provides a more intimate, tactile feel.

Keyboard Features

➢ Soft-Touch Palm Rest.

➢ Comfort Curve with Quiet Touch Keys: Type more comfortably with this ergonomist-approved keyboard.

➢ Windows Flip: Easily switch between open windows with the click of a button.

➢ Taskbar Favorites: Easily access programs in the taskbar with convenient keyboard hot keys. Applications can be easily rearranged by clicking and dragging, and the keys will automatically adapt to the new location.

➢ Multimedia Keys: With the touch of a button you can easily access your favorite music, video clips, and media programs.

➢ Thin Profile Keys: The notebook-like, sleek design of these keys feels and looks great.

The Quality Criteria and Basic Method of IT English Translation

IT 英语是对 IT 领域某个科学问题的介绍和讨论，其本身具有结构严谨、行文规范、技术术语使用准确和艺术性修辞较少等特点。IT 英语承载的是科学技术内容，而科学技术关心的不是个人情感因素，而是客观事实及其普遍规律。因此，IT 英语的翻译过程，既不能逐字逐句地机械翻译，使文体呆板；也不能刻意追求文艺作品中的艺术感染效果，使文体花哨；更不能单凭主观臆断对原文随意篡改和增删，以至于译文背离原文。只有在忠实于原文的原则下，使译文客观、准确、精炼、逻辑关系正确并且符合汉语习惯才是高质量 IT 英语翻译工作标准。

深刻理解 IT 英语原文含义是做好翻译工作的根本点和出发点。此外，还要根据原文的文体形式、句式结构、主从句辨别及其语法关系，采用分组归纳的方法辨明主语、谓语、宾语以及它们的修饰语，联系上下文并结合 IT 专业知识理解主句与从句、句与句之间的关系。IT 英语中长句多、难句多、修饰语多、语态和时态变化多、各类短语和从句间相互搭配和相互修饰的情况多。因此，我们须重视对于原文语法结构的剖析，准确找到长句主干，采用逐层推进的翻译策略。同时为了避免译文失真或晦涩，译者应充分考虑到在 IT 英语中，词义的引申、词序的变动、词性和句式成分的转换以及词语的增删。

1．复杂长句翻译实例

The interface board physically can control the disk drive, accepting seek, read and write commands from the processor, positioning the access mechanism, and the main memory.

原文是一个较为复杂的长句，我们可以采用分解归类的语法分析方法来翻译。首先，该句的谓语是"can control"，不会是非谓语动词，如"accepting"、"positioning"，而"seek"、"read"、"write"在本句中是名词充当"commands"的形容词，意思是"寻找指令""读取指令"和"写入指令"。谓语找到了，接下来主语就很明显是"The interface board"了。至于分词短语"accepting seek, read and write commands from the processor"和"positioning the access mechanism, and the main memory"实际上充当着非限定性定语从句的作用，用来作为主句"The interface board physically can control the disk drive"的补充。

例句译文：这个接口面板能够控制磁盘驱动器，以此接收来自处理器的寻找、读取和写入指令，或者操控磁盘表面和主存之间的数据流动。

2．词义引申使用实例

Both Intel and AMD have introduced 64-bit chips.

此例句中的"introduce"一词，直译为"介绍，传入，引进，提出"，根据我们的专业知识，直译"introduce"一词在本句中显然是不合适的，考虑到 Intel 公司和 AMD 公司在 64 位芯片方面的科技行为和商业行为，还是将"introduce"译为"推出"为好。

例句译文：Intel 和 AMD 公司都推出了 64 位芯片。

3．词序变动使用实例

A floppy disk is portable, inexpensive storage medium that consists of a thin, circular, flexible plastic disk with a magnetic coating enclosed in a squares-shaped plastic shell.

此例句中如果不对原文词序进行调整，而是逐词地机械翻译，那么译文就无法符合汉语言使用习惯。事实上，该句可分为三部分进行翻译，从而使译文结构清晰、句意精确。

例句译文：软盘时一种移动式的廉价存储介质，由盘片和方形塑料外套构成，盘片是一种具有磁性涂层的既薄又圆的软塑料片。

4．词性和句式成分使用实例

The paper aims at discussing new technologies in computers.

此例句中 "aims" 一词在原文中是谓语动词，如果我们在翻译时依然将其译为谓语动词词性，则不符合汉语言特点，如果我们将其词性转译为名词，翻译效果就会很好。

例句译文：本文的目的在于讨论计算机方面的新技术。

Electronic computers must be programmed before they can work.

此例句中，主句为 "Electronic computers must be programmed"，从句为 "before they can work."，如果我们翻译时将主句译为从句，从句译为主句，就会使译文更加流畅。

例句译文：必须先为电子算计设计程序，它才能工作。

5．词语的增删使用实例

The runtime system initializes fixed variables only once, whereas dynamic variables, if they are declared with an initializer, are re-initialized each time their block is entered.

在此例句中，讲的是系统运行期间，固定变量只被进行一次初始化，而动态变量则不然，原文中 "are re-initialized each time their block is entered" 是指动态变量 "dynamic variables" 会被重新初始化，我们在翻译时应将此明确，即相当于增加了词汇 "dynamic variables"。

例句译文：运行期间，系统只初始化一项固定变量，而对于动态变量，若用初始程序说明，则每当进入动态变量模块时，动态变量就被重新初始化。

With an Intel$^{@}$ Celeron$^{@}$ processor-based desktop PC, you get a useful tool for the most common applications—from finance management to the Internet and interactive games—at a terrific value.

此例句中出现了单词 "you"，但是 IT 英语中的 "you" 往往是泛指的，并非针对某人，在翻译时一般不直接译出较为妥当。

例句译文：Intel Celeron 处理器的桌面 PC 是常用的工具——从财务管理到因特网交互游戏，其价值惊人。

Unit 3　Computer Software

WORDS AND EXPRESSIONS

analogous [ə'næləgəs]　类似的

tournaments ['tuənəmənt]　锦标赛

gargantuan [gɑː'gæntjuən]　巨大的，庞大的

scary ['skɛəri]　引起惊慌的

cognitive ['kɔgnitiv]　认知的，认识的，有感知的

ledger ['ledʒə]　分类帐

virus ['vaiərəs]　病毒

warehouse ['wɛəhaus]　仓库

intriguing [in'triːgiŋ]　迷人的

mechanism ['mekənizəm]　机械装置，机构，机制

EXE (executable ['eksikjuːtəbl])　可执行程序的扩展名

host [həust]　主机

bootstrap ['buːtstræp]　引导程序

fragment ['frægmənt]　碎片

MBA (Master of Business Administration)　工商管理硕士

Windows XP (Windows Experience)　微软公司生产的"视窗"操作系统

Novell [nən'vel]　美国网络产品公司

Oracle ['ɔrəkl]　美国 ORACLE 公司，主要生产数据库产品

Sybase　美国赛贝斯公司，主要生产数据库产品

DBMS (Database Management System)　数据库管理系统

DB2　IBM 出口的一系列关系型数据库管理系统

CIH　台湾大同工学院学生陈盈豪编写的以其名字拼音缩写 CIH 命名的病毒

PE (Portable ['pɔːtəbl] EXE)　在 Windows 9x 和 Windows NT 下运行的可执行文件

Mac OS (Mackintosh ['mækintɔʃ] Operating System)　Mac 操作系统（苹果操作系统）

MVS (Multiple Virtual Storage)　多虚拟存储器

ERP (Enterprise Resource Planning)　企业资源计划

HR (Human Resource)　人力资源管理

EPROM (Erasable Programmable ROM)　可擦除可编程 ROM

BIOS (Basic Input Output System)　基本输入输出系统

DOS (Disk Operating System)　磁盘操作系统

QUESTIONS AND ANSWERS

1. Simply speaking, what is system software?
2. Simply speaking, what is application software?
3. Is Windows XP a system software or an application software? Why?
4. What is the meaning of ERP?
5. Can you give us some examples about "ERP"?
6. Why is a simple virus dangerous?
7. What has aroused the interest of the virus research?
8. What separates CIH from other viruses?

TEXT

As we all know, a computer can do nothing without the support of software. If we describe a computer as a person, we usually say that the hardware is like a person's body, while the software is like the soul. Just as a person has a lot of ideas, there are several kinds of software, each of which does different jobs.

System Software and Application Software

You've been around information technology and computers for a while, you have probably run into these two terms: system software and application software. Without the former, your computer won't run. And without the latter, your computer (no matter how powerful) won't do much to help run your business.

System software is the stuff that makes your computer work. It's roughly analogous to the stem of the human brain—you have got to have it to keep breathing; but with just the stem you aren't likely to win any chess tournaments or earn an MBA degree. System software includes the computer's basic operating system, whether that's Windows XP or Mac OS on your home computer or something like MVS on à gargantuan mainframe in the data center. The term also usually encompasses any software used to manage the computer and network, which includes diagnostic software and anything used to tune up the computer's performance. Novell Netware and other network management packages thus fall under system software. In the mainframe world, system software would include all kinds of utility packages with scary names like "Disk Defragmenter".

Application software trains the PC's brain for higher cognitive functions rather than just keeping the PC alive and connected to other computers. Think of it this way: Applications apply the computer's thinking power to business tasks such as tracking the general ledger or billing your customers.

Software that clearly falls on the application side of the line includes manufacturing, financial and human resources software and the enterprise resource planning (ERP) packages. Other examples of application software include CAD and various engineering packages, groupware like Lotus Notes, supply chain management software and a raft of industry-specific programs for everything from routing railcars to tracking clinical trials for pharmaceuticals.

So system software runs your computer while application software runs your business.

The line between the two kinds of software is somewhat blurry, depending on who's doing the talking. In the gray zone between them, you might include database management software like Oracle 8, Sybase or DB2, which handle a very general sort of task—storing and manipulating data and records—and often must be further programmed in order to perform a specific application. Some operating systems incorporate basic database management functionality, so some people call DBMS system software, which others simply call it application software.

Windows XP users might wonder which category Solitaire belongs to. Sorry, we will have that up to Microsoft.

ERP Software

Enterprise resource planning software, or ERP, doesn't live up to its acronym. Forget about planning (it doesn't do much of that, and forget about resource, a throwaway term. But remember the enterprise part. This is ERP's true ambition. It attempts to integrate all departments and functions across a company into a single computer system that can serve all those different department's particular needs.

That is a tall order, building a single software program that serves the needs of people in finance as well as it does the people in human resources and in the warehouse. Each of those departments typically has its own computer system optimized for the particular ways that the department does its work. But ERP combines them all together into a single, integrated software program that runs off a single database so that the various departments can more easily share information and communicate with each other. That integrated approach can have a tremendous payback if companies install the software correctly.

ERP vanquishes the old standalone computer systems in finance, HR, manufacturing and the warehouse, and replaces them with a single unified software program divided into software modules that roughly approximate the old standalone systems. Finance, manufacturing and the warehouse all still get their own software, except now the software is linked together so that someone in finance can look into the warehouse software to see if an order has been shipped. Most vendors' ERP software is flexible enough that you can install some modules without buying the whole package. Many companies, for example, will just install an ERP finance or HR module and leave the rest of the functions for another day.

Virus

Most viruses can replicate themselves. All computer viruses are manmade. A simple virus that can make a copy of itself over and over again is relatively easy to produce. Even such a simple virus is dangerous because it will quickly use all available memory and bring the system to a halt. An even more dangerous type of virus is one capable of transmitting itself across networks and bypassing security system.

The technical details of CIH's infection mechanism are intriguing for the virus researcher, and its payload is what sets it apart from other viruses. The payload consists of two parts, both of which are triggered when the right conditions are met. As the payload is part of the infection mechanism, it is not triggered until the virus is resident in memory. The trigger condition is met when a file which has an EXE extension, but which is not a suitable host, is opened on the trigger date.

The first part of the payload code to trigger is what has given CIH the world's sudden attention. Flash ROM technology has existed for several years. Having the BIOS "flashable", by storing it in such a chip, has allowed the basic bootstrap procedure and I/O routines of the PC to be rewritten by software. Early EPROM technologies allowed reprogramming the BIOS, but required the chip to be removed, erased under ultraviolet light and reprogrammed in dedicated hardware.

The second part of the payload is common. It overwrites the first 2,048 sectors (1MB) of each hard disk in the system with random data from memory. Anything overwritten in such a manner will be difficult or impossible to recover. The virus looks for further disks indefinitely and the machine—despite running the hard disk continuously—is unresponsive to user input.

PE files are executables used by Windows 9x and Windows NT. A PE file consists of a DOS executable, usually just a stub that indicates the program should be run under Windows, a PE header section and several data objects. These objects can contain executable code, information on imported and exported functions, data or relocation information. Each object following the PE header must be aligned within the file to start on a boundary that is an even power of two, between 512 bytes and 64kB.

Any difference between the length of useful code or data in an object and the chosen section alignment is normally padded with nulls by the linker. Information on the alignment of the objects and the size of each object is stored in the PE header and in a series of object tables just after the header. Typical PE files contain five or six objects, all of which have some space that is effectively wasted. It is in these areas that CIH stores its code, thus infecting a file without increasing its length.

CIH breaks its code into chunks that it uses to fill "slack space" at the end of the sections in its hosts. It checks for files with insufficient slack space, refusing to infect them. However, this is unlikely, since all known variants are just under 1kB along and most PEs will have at least that much free space. A peculiarity of the Borland Linker means files produced by it are uninfectible.

When infecting a file, CIH builds a table of data about the length and location of its code fragments. This, and the minimal code to allocate memory for itself and to piece its code fragment back together, is stored between the PE header and the first object of the host. If there is insufficient space in the header to take this crucial data and code the file is also deemed uninfectible.

CIH sits in the file system API chain waiting for EXE files to be opened. On receiving such a call, it checks whether the file is a PE that is not already infected. Files with a nonzero value in the byte immediately before the PE signature are considered infected. The virus itself writes the first byte from the Ring0_File IO routine into this location when infecting files. This is usually 55h("U")—the PUSH EBP opcode. When a potential target is found, its header and object table are processed to determine how much of the virus can be placed at the end of each object. There is no lower limit to the code fragment size CIH will place at the end of each object. In testing, it readily inserted a one-byte fragment into a specially modified PE, using eight bytes of its fragment table space to record the fact.

EXERCISES

1. Judge whether the following given statements are true or false. If correct, write T in parentheses; otherwise, write F.

(1)　(　) Application software includes system software.

(2)　(　) The line between application software and system software is clear.

(3)　(　) Most viruses can't replicate themselves.

(4)　(　) CIH infects a file without increasing its length.

2. Complete the following note-taking with the information mentioned in the text.

(1)　Without _____ software, your computer won't run. And without application software, your computer won't do much to help run your business.

(2)　_____ trains the PC's brain for higher cognitive functions rather than just keeping the PC alive and connected to other computers.

(3)　Some _____ incorporate basic database management functionality, so some people call DBMS system software, which others simply call it application software.

(4)　Most vendors' ERP software is _____ enough that you can install some modules without buying the whole package.

READING MATERIALS

Product Description: Microsoft Office 2007

When planning the release of the 2007 Microsoft Office system we took on the challenge of making the core Microsoft Office applications easier to work with. Taking into account extensive usability data and recent advancements in hardware and software, the team has delivered the most significant update to the Microsoft Office user interface in more than a decade. The result of these efforts is the Microsoft Office Fluent user interface—a user interface that makes it easier for people to get more out of Microsoft Office applications so they can deliver better results faster.

Microsoft Office Word 2007, Office Excel 2007, Office PowerPoint 2007, Office Outlook 2007, and Office Access 2007 will feature a streamlined, uncluttered workspace that minimizes distraction and enables people to achieve the results they want more quickly and easily.

Design Goal and Approach

In previous releases of Microsoft Office applications, people used a system of menus, toolbars, task panes, and dialog boxes to get their work done. This system worked well when the applications had a limited number of commands. Now that the programs do so much more, the menus and toolbars system does not work as well. Too many program features are too hard for many users to find. For this reason, the overriding design goal for the Office Fluent user interface is to make it easier for people to find and use the full range of features these applications provide. In addition, we wanted to preserve an uncluttered workspace that reduces distraction for users so they can spend more time and energy focused on their work. With these goals in mind, we developed a results-oriented approach that makes it much easier to produce great results using the 2007 Microsoft Office applications.

Key Features

While the overall look of the redesigned applications is new, early testing indicates that people quickly feel at home in the Office Fluent user interface and rapidly become accustomed to the new way these applications work. The ease with which people use the Office Fluent interface is due to the simplicity of the interface features.

The Ribbon

In the Office Fluent UI the traditional menus and toolbars have been replaced by the Ribbon—a device that presents commands organized into a set of tabs. The tabs on the Ribbon display the commands that are most relevant for each of the task areas in the applications. For example, in Office Word 2007, the tabs group commands for activities such as inserting objects like pictures and tables, doing page layout, working with references, doing mailings, and reviewing. The Home tab provides easy access to the most frequently used commands. Office Excel 2007 has a similar set of tabs that make sense for spread-sheet work including tabs for working with formulas, managing data, and reviewing. These tabs simplify accessing application features because they organize the commands in a way that corresponds directly to the tasks people perform in these applications.

The Microsoft Office Button

Many of the most valuable features in previous versions of Microsoft Office were not about the document authoring experience at all. Instead, they were about all the things you can do with a document: share it, protect it, print it, publish it, and send it. In spite of that, previous releases of the Microsoft Office applications lacked a single central location where a user can see all of these capabilities in one place. File-level features were mixed in with authoring features.

The Office Fluent user interface brings together the capabilities of the Microsoft Office system into a single entry point in the UI: the Microsoft Office Button. This offers two major advantages. First, it helps users find these valuable features. Second, it simplifies the core authoring scenarios by allowing the Ribbon to focus on creating great documents.

Contextual Tabs

Certain sets of commands are only relevant when objects of a particular type are being edited. For example, the commands for editing a chart are not relevant until a chart appears in a spreadsheet and the user is focusing on modifying it. In current versions of Microsoft Office applications, these commands can be difficult to find. In Office Excel 2007, clicking on a chart causes a contextual tab to appear with commands used for chart editing. Contextual tabs only appear when they are needed and make it much easier to find and use the commands needed for the operation at hand.

Galleries

Galleries are at the heart of the redesigned user interface. Galleries provide users with a set of clear results to choose from when working on their document, spreadsheet, presentation, or Access database. By presenting a simple set of potential results, rather than a complex dialog box with numerous options, Galleries simplify the process of producing professional-looking work. The traditional dialog box interfaces are still available for those wishing a greater degree of control over the result of the operation.

Live Preview

Live Preview is a new technology that shows the results of applying an editing or formatting change as the user moves the pointer over the results presented in a Gallery. This new, dynamic capability streamlines the process of laying out, editing, and formatting so users can create excellent results with less time and effort. These elements are just a few of the new technologies that combine to create the Office Fluent user interface.

Benefits

The goal of the Office Fluent user interface is to make it easier for people to use Microsoft Office applications to deliver better results faster. We've made it easier to find powerful features by replacing menus and toolbars with a Ribbon that organizes and presents capabilities in a way that corresponds more directly to how people work. The streamlined screen layout and dynamic results-oriented Galleries enable users to spend more time focused on their work and less time trying to get the application to do what they want it to do. As a result, with the Office Fluent user interface, people will find it much easier and quicker to produce great looking documents, high-impact presentations, effective spreadsheets, and powerful desktop database applications.

Participle, Gerund, Adjective Clause and Adverbial Clause in IT English

在 IT 英语文章中，特别是在复杂长句中，分词、动名词、定语从句和状语从句是非常多见的语言现象。

1. 分词

有现在分词和过去分词两种类型，在句子中具有形容词词性或副词词性，可以充当句子的定语、表语、状语和补足语。现在分词所表示的动作具有主动意义，并且表示该动作正在进行，相对于谓语动词具有同时性；及物动词的过去分词所表示的动作具有被动意义，并且表示的动作已经完成，相对于谓语动词具有先时行。

Once talking about the computer, we have to think of the birth of ENIAC.

例句译文：每当讨论计算机的时候，人们就必然会想到 ENIAC 的问世。

In the late 1960's and early 1970's, engineers made great strides in reducing the size of electronic components.

例句译文：20 世纪 60 年代末 70 年代初，工程师们在缩小电子元件方面取得了很大进展，他们研制了半导体芯片。

Based on the same technology as the popular desktop Pentium 4 processor, the Mobile Pentium 4 processor features similar architecture optimized for battery life and other mobile computing needs.

例句译文：Intel Pentium 4 芯片改进了当今高端应用性能并突显了因特网需求。基于与流行的桌面型 Pentium 4 处理器的相同技术，Mobile Pentium 4 处理器具有类似的体系结构，它延长了电池寿命并满足了其他移动计算的需求。

Most computers have one hard drive located inside the computer case.

例句译文：大多数计算机都在机箱内设置一个硬盘驱动器。

2．动名词

具有动词词性和名词词性，在句子中充当主语、表语、定语和宾语。

Applications apply the computer's thinking power to business tasks.

例句译文：应用软件提供计算机思考商业任务的能力。

That is a tall order, building a single software program that serves the needs of people in finance as well as it does the people in human resources and in the warehouse.

例句译文：要建立一个既满足财务部门的需要，又要同时满足人事部和仓库管理的需要的软件程序，是一个很高的要求。

3．定语从句

修饰某一名词或代词的从句时，被定语从句修饰的词叫先行词，定语从句往往跟在先行词之后。定语从句通常由置于先行词和定语从句之间并承担联接作用的关系代词：that、which、who、whom、whose 或关系副词 when、where、why、how 引导。定语从句一般被分为限定性定语从句和非限定性定语从句。

Any program that remains in memory while the computer is running is called memory resident.（限定性定语从句）

例句译文：计算机运行期间任何保存在内存的程序被称做驻留内存。

In this step you will be given instructions for uploading your new website to a server where it makes your information available to any web surfer in the world wide. （限定性定语从句）

例句译文：这步操作将指导你将新建的网站上传到服务器系统上，上传后就可以使全世界的浏览者访问到你的网站。

Internet is a giant global and open computer network, which is a collection of interconnected networks.（非限定性定语从句）

例句译文：因特网是一个巨大的全球性开放式计算机网络，它由众多网络互联而成。

JPEG stands for Joint Photographic Experts Group, which is also sometimes abbreviated JPG.（非限定性定语从句）

例句译文：JPEG 代表联合图像专家组，有时也缩写成 JPG。

4. 状语从句

起副词作用，在句子中做状语，用以修饰谓语动词和非谓语动词。状语从句通常可分为时间状语从句、地点状语从句、原因状语从句、目的状语从句、结果状语从句、条件状语从句、让步状语从句、比较状语从句和方式状语从句。

While using 24 bits per pixel limits the number of colors to about 16 million, the human eye cannot even distinguish so many colors.（时间状语从句）

例句译文：当采用 24 比特/像素时，颜色可达 1,600 万种，人眼已无法分辨如此多的颜色。

Light pens are used in applications where space is limited.（地点状语从句）

例句译文：在空间受限制的地方，使用光笔来运行应用程序。

Understanding programming languages is crucial for those engaged in computer science because today all types of computation are done with computer languages.（原因状语从句）

例句译文：理解程序语言对于今天的计算机科学的从业者是至关重要的，因为今天所有的计算都是通过计算机语言完成的。

Tabs for each open document are displayed at the top of the workspace so that users can quickly locate and switch between open documents.（目的状语从句）

例句译文：每一个打开的文档的选项卡显示在工作区的顶部，以便用户可以快速找到打开的文档以及在这些文档之间切换。

Mobile users have notebook computers so that they can work on the road.（结果状语从句）

例句译文：因为移动用户有笔记本电脑，所以他们可以在路途中工作。

If you're familiar with regular audio/music CDs, then you will know what a VCD looks like.（条件状语从句）

例句译文：如果你熟悉一般的声音/音乐光盘，那你就可以想象一张 VCD 是什么样子的了。

The object-oriented database often returns results more quickly than the same query of a relational database.（比较状语从句）

例句译文：面向对象的数据库比关系数据库作相同查询时更快地返回结果。

Although there have been several attempts to make a universal computer language that serves all purposes, all of them have failed.（让步状语从句）

例句译文：尽管人们试图去设计服务于各种目的的通用的计算机语言，但是都失败了。

You can transfer files as though both computers' hard disks were in the same system.（方式状语从句）

例句译文：你可以传输文件，就像两个计算机硬盘在一个系统中一样。

Unit 4　The Introduction of Internet

WORDS AND EXPRESSIONS

giant ['dʒaiənt]　庞大的，巨大的

protocol ['prəutəkɔl]　协议

dial-up ['daiəlʌp]　拨号（上网）

via ['vaiə]　经，通过，经由

modem ['məudəm]　调制解调器

repository [ri'pɔzitəri]　贮藏室

nonlinear ['nɔn'liniə]　非线性的

grammatically [grə'mætikəl]　遵循语法规则的

Gopher ['gəufə]　基于菜单驱动的 Internet 信息查询工具

icon ['aikɔn]　图标

retrieve [ri'tri:v]　重新得到

prior ['praiə]　优先的

tutorial [tju:'tɔ:riəl]　指南

template ['templit]　模板

concise [kən'sais]　简明的，简练的

surfer ['sɜ:fə(r)]　冲浪运动员

vista ['vistə]　狭长的景色，街景，展望，回想

stationery ['steiʃ(ə)nəri]　文具，信纸

ARPANET (Advanced Research Projects Agency Network)　ARPA 计算机网

TCP/IP (Transmission Control Protocol/Internet Protocol)　传输控制协议/因特网协议

NSF (National Science Foundation)　国家科学基金会

LAN (Local Area Network)　局域网

MAN (Metropolitan Area Network)　城域网

WAN (Wide Area Network)　广域网

HTML (Hypertext Markup Language)　超文本标记语言

URL (Uniform Resource Locator)　统一资源定位符

FTP (File Transfer Protocol)　文件传输协议

WWW (World Wide Web)　万维网

HTTP (Hypertext Transfer Protocol)　超文本传输协议

Telnet ['telnet] (teletype network)　远程登录（协议）

DNS (Domain Name Server)　域名服务器

BBS (Bulletin Board System)　电子公告板

QUESTIONS AND ANSWERS

1. What is the history of Internet?
2. What is the Internet according to the text?
3. What main functions does the E-mail have on the Internet?
4. What is the meaning of BBS?
5. How do you get to the Internet?
6. How to put your new site on the Web?

TEXT

Today, the Internet has become a widespread medium for entertainment, information acquisition, electronic commerce, and interaction between individuals. Scientists and programmers will continue to introduce new applications that make the Internet easier to use and navigate. The Internet is now available to everyone who owns a computer and has a phone line connected to a network. A growing number of people are spending increasing amounts of time in cyberspace at the expense of other media. In fact, Internet has been a giant global and open computer network, which is a collection of interconnected networks. It is also a way to realize worldwide information exchanging and resource sharing between international computers.

By the mid-1970's, many U.S. government agency networks had been linked by ARPANET (the original Internet that was established by the U.S. Department of Defense in 1969), because the networks were of a disparate nature, a common network protocol called TCP/IP was developed and became the standard for inter-networking military computers. So the U.S. Department of Defense Advanced Research Program Management Bureau asked all hosts connected with ARPANET to adapt TCP/IP to be their protocol in 1983. In 1985, the U.S. NSF established a specially used net which connected six super computing centers—NSFNET. This is the basic of Internet. With the network developing in all society, a lot of institutes and universities established their LANs, and connected them to NSFNET. In 1989, the ARPANET had been dismissed and the NSFNET had been opened to the public and became the most important backbone of Internet.

When the U.S. developing their national net, the other countries were developing, too. At the end of 1980's, interlink age of different countries' computer net appears. After that there were countries joining in every year and getting to form the present Internet. The word "Internet" became the common term for referring to the worldwide network of military, research and academic computers. Now, there are 86 countries directly connected with Internet and 150 countries can access it by E-mail. It is growing so quickly that nobody can say exactly how many users are "On the Net".

First, let us see how to access the Internet.

Access to the Internet falls into two broad categories: dedicated access and dial-up access. With dedicated access, a computer is directly connected to the Internet via a router, or the computer is part of a network linked to the Internet. With dial-up access, a computer is connected to the Internet with a telephone line using a modem.

Internet makes all kinds of physical net connection be a whole one. All computers that adopt TCP/IP protocol can communicate with any computer of Internet and can be looked as a part of Internet. Host is the computer that directly connects with Internet. All the hosts are in equal class in Internet, no matter they belong to LAN, MAN or WAN. They are all in equal class in communicating data and sharing resources.

Once your computer enters into a connection with the Internet, you will find that you have walked into the largest repository of information. The two most popular Web browsers are Microsoft Internet Explorer and Netscape Navigator. A Web browser presents data in multimedia on Web pages that use text, graphics, sound and video.

The Web pages are created with a formal language called Hypertext Markup Language (HTML). The term "hypertext" is used to describe an interlinked system of documents in which a user may jump from one document to another in a nonlinear way. Hyperlink makes the Internet easy to navigate. It is an object (work, phrase, or picture) on a Web page that , when clicked, transfers you to a new Web page. The Web page contains an address location known as Uniform Resource Locator (URL). When hypertext pages are mixed with other media, the result is called hypermedia.

The following are the important service functions that Internet provides.

E-mail

The most widely used tool on the Internet is electronic mail or E-mail. E-mail enables you to send messages to Russia, Japan and so on, no matter how far between individuals. E-mail messages are generally sent and received by mail servers—computers that are dedicated to processing and directing E-mail. Once a server has received a message, it directs it to the specific computer that the E-mail is addressed to. To send E-mail, the process is reversed. As a very convenient and inexpensive way to transmit messages, E-mail has grammatically affected scientific, personal, and business communications. In some cases, E-mail has replaced the telephone for carrying messages.

File Transfer Protocol

File Transfer Protocol (FTP) is a method of transferring files from one computer to another over the Internet, even if each computer has a different operating system or storage format. FTP is designed to download files (e.g. receive from the Internet) or upload files (e.g. send to the Internet). The ability to upload and download files on it is one of the most valuable features the Internet offers. This is especially helpful for those people who rely on computers for various purposes and who may need software drivers and upgrades immediately. Network administrators can rarely wait even a few days to get the necessary drivers that enable their network servers to function again. The Internet can provide these files immediately by using FTP. FTP is a client-server application just like E-mail and Telnet. It requires server software running on a host that can be accessed by client software.

The World Wide Web

The World Wide Web (WWW), which Hypertext Transfer Protocol (HTTP) works with, is the fastest growing and most widely used part of the Internet. It provides access to multiple services and documents as Gopher does but is more ambitious in its method. A jump to other Internet service can be triggered by a mouse click on a "hot-linked" word, image, or icon on the Web pages. One of the main reasons for the extraordinary growth of the Web is the ease in which it allows access to information. One limitation of HTTP is that you can only use it to download files, and not to upload them.

Telnet

Telnet allows an Internet user to connect to a distance computer and use that computer as if he or she were using it directly. To make a connection with a Telnet client, you must select a connection option:"Host Name" and "Terminal Type". The host name is the IP address (Domain Name Server, DNS) of the remote computer to which you connect. The terminal type describes the type of terminal emulation that you want the computer to perform.

BBS

Another interesting application for Internet is the Electronic Bulletin Board which is also called Bulletin Board Service, BBS for short. It allows users to post and retrieve messages that are not directed to a specific user, much like announcements are posted on an office bulletin board. BBS has been used for everything from dating services and want ads to highly specialized applications such as the exchange of research data in a narrow scientific field.

The Internet has many new technologies, such as global chart, video conferencing, free international phone and more. The Internet becomes more and more popular in society in recent years. So we can say that Internet is your PC's window to the rest of the world.

Website Design

Many people wish to create a flashy website. But creating a great website doesn't happen at the tips of the fingers, it happens in the depths of the brain. Outstanding websites result from extensive planning. Prior preparation saves time and avoids frustration both during page creation and when updates and additions are required. The 3-step design tutorial will show you how to create high-end attractive websites.

➢ Determine Who Use Your Site and Their Information Needs

Successful websites know who their customers are and why they visit, and they provide a responsive and attractive display to those viewers. Customers don't visit our site because we spend time creating it; customers deserve maximum benefit from the time they allocate to us.

➢ Editing Your Web Pages

- Establish an Identity and Use It Consistently on All Pages. Viewers of our Web pages, should know exactly who we are, and after being linked, should know if they're still on one of our site's pages. It doesn't mean every page looks the same, but the colors and graphics we use should be consistent throughout the website. Establish a theme or identifying characteristic for your website.

- Create User-friendly Navigation. On a well-planned website it's quick and easy to get to information pages—that's navigation. Plan navigation before pages are created. Establish navigation plan to ensure that viewers quickly get what they need and that new pages of content can be quickly inserted and located.
- Page Layout. What's the difference between a webpage and a GREAT webpage catches our attention—that "Oh, Wow!" reaction—and gives information as expeditions as possible—the key is planning and creativity.

To begin layout, analyze the information to be displayed and decide how it will be most readable. Pick the template that best accommodates that display. As your templates were created, page layout may have been anticipated.

There are three methods to create balanced page layout: block quote margins, tables, and frames. Each method has pros and cons; it can be advantageous to use all these three to build a website.

- Focus on Text. Viewers come to website for information and if they don't get what they need, flash and glitz won't bring them back. The best websites pack essential information into well-organized and well-written text. Web pages should not, however, be too heavily written text. Surveys show that Web users will not read long paragraphs of information. They prefer concise, bite-sized sections, clearly delineated so they can scan for the information they need. You should write essential content as clearly and concisely as possible with brief topic headers.
- Use Graphic Images to Enhance, Not Overpower. Graphics are a special challenge for web designers, requiring balance between overuse and skimpiness. A site filled with graphic images can have charm and impact. The secret for effective graphics is to stick to the theme and identity of the website.

➢ Putting Your New Site on the Web

- Domain Name Registration. The domain name is the address that users type into their web browsers (Internet Explorer or Netscape) to view your website. You select one or more proposed domain names such as Amazon.com or Buy.com. Your domain name that best reflects your business, products or services.
- Publish the Website. In this step you will be given instructions for uploading your new website to a computer known as "server" where it makes your information available to any web surfer in the world wide. You will need an FTP client in order to upload files to your web server. CuteFTP (www.cuteftp.com) are highly recommended.

Once a host has been selected, we will "publish" your new website for accessibility to everyone on the World Wide Web.

- Promote Your Website. Website promotion involves submitting your site address and search words to the top 12 search engines, which are Netscape, Yahoo, Microsoft, Alta

Vista, Ask Jeeves, AOL, Excite, Google, Goto, HotBot, Looksmart and Lycos. These engines represent over 98% of all U.S. web searches. We can create special "headers" on your website that include all the necessary search engine friendly information. Other website promotion you may establish is: placing your web address on all stationery, business cards, and all broadcast and printed advertising media. You can begin as soon as your domain name is registered.

Creating and publishing your website is just "Tip of the Iceberg". The remaining 90% is unseen below the surface. These unseen features are important to the success of your website. They include meta tag creation, regular search engine submission, marketing exchange programs and many other promotional programs.

EXERCISES

1. Judge whether the following given statements are true or false. If correct, write T in parentheses; otherwise, write F.

(1)　(　) By the 1960's, many U.S. government agency networks had been linked by ARPANET.

(2)　(　) With dedicated access, a computer is connected to the Internet with a telephone line using a modem.

(3)　(　) FTP is designed to download files or upload files.

(4)　(　) The host name is the TCP address of the remote computer to which you connect.

2. Complete the following note-taking with the information mentioned in the text.

(1)　In 1989, the _____ had been opened to the public and became the most important backbone of Internet.

(2)　All computers that adopt _____ protocol can communicate with any computer of Internet.

(3)　When hypertext pages are mixed with other media, the result is called _____.

(4)　The _____ describes the type of terminal emulation that you want the computer to perform.

READING MATERIALS

Internet Explorer Applies to All Editions of Windows Vista

Here are some of the ways that Internet Explorer makes browsing the web easier, safer, and more enjoyable.

Increased Security and Privacy

New security and privacy features allow you to browse the web more safely. Phishing Filter can help protect you from phishing attacks, online fraud, and spoofed websites.

Internet Explorer Address bar with phishing warning. Protected mode can help protect your computer from websites that try to install malicious software or to save files on your computer without your consent.

Higher security levels can help protect you from hackers and web attacks.The Security Status bar displays the identity of secure websites to help you make informed decisions when using online banking or merchants. Internet Explorer now supports Extended Validation (EV) certificates to help make a more positive identification of website owners and organizations.

Internet Explorer's add-on disabled mode lets you start Internet Explorer without toolbars, ActiveX controls, or other add-ons that might slow your computer or prevent you from getting online.

New Features

Tabbed browsing is a new feature in Internet Explorer that allows you to open multiple websites in a single browser window. If you have a lot of tabs open, use Quick Tabs to easily switch them.

The new Instant Search box lets you search the web from the Address bar. You can also search using different search providers to get better results.

Internet Explorer now lets you delete your temporary files, cookies, webpage history, saved passwords, and form information from one place. Delete selected categories, or everything at once.

Click the Favorites Center button ☆ to open the Favorites Center to manage favorites, feeds, and history in one place.

Printing now scales webpages to fit the paper you're using. Print Preview gives more control when printing, with manual scaling and an accurate view of what you're about to print.

The Zoom feature lets you enlarge or reduce text, images, and some controls.

Read and Subscribe to Feeds (Figure 4-1)

Figure 4-1

A feed, also known as RSS feed, XML feed, or syndicated content, is website content that can be automatically delivered to your browser. By subscribing to a feed, you can get updated content, such as breaking news or your favorite blog, without having to visit the website. The Feeds button 🔲 in the Internet Explorer toolbar will light up when a feed is available for a webpage you're viewing. Click the button to display the feed or to subscribe.

Help prevent online attacks by keeping Windows and Internet Explorer up to date is one of the best ways to prevent trouble online. Microsoft periodically issues updates which can help prevent online attacks. These updates are available free of charge through Windows Update.

If your computer is not set up to automatically receive updates, you can manually request these updates by using Internet Explorer. Click the Tools button, and then click Windows Update. Follow the prompts on the screen to check for updates.2 Multimedia.

Introduction to IT English Reading

IT 英语的阅读过程，就是对于来自英语语言及 IT 专业两个方面的专业知识与技能的综合运用。其中，词汇（特别是 IT 领域的特殊专业词汇）和语法结构是 IT 英语阅读的基础。此外，具备灵活运用英语语言技巧、辨认文章主题与细节、理清文章段落之间和句式之间的逻辑关系以及根据上下文确定生僻单词准确词义等方面的能力，也是 IT 英语阅读过程中所不可或缺的。

1．阅读方法

IT 英语的阅读方法一般可分为精读（Intensive Reading）、略读（Skimming Reading）和查询性阅读（Scanning Reading）等。

1）精读

要求对文章有全面和深入的理解，对难句、长句，要根据语法知识和 IT 专业内容对其进行分析，以便于获取详细信息。并要做好以下几项工作：

➢ 掌握原文的主题和产生的背景；
➢ 领会原文作者的观点、意图和态度；
➢ 了解原文体系结构和逻辑关系；
➢ 根据上下文，判断某些词汇和短语的含义；
➢ 对 IT 英语文章所述内容与同类技术文档相比较；
➢ 找出原文在科技论述方面所采用的事实根据、科学原则、实验数据、研究方法和具体操作步骤；
➢ 分析原文内容的科学指导意义、可应用的工作领域和应用途径；
➢ 依据原文内容进行一定的判断、推理、引申和应用实践；
➢ 找出原文存在的局限性和不足。

2）略读

是在了解原文主旨、结构的前提下，以较快的速度进行粗略阅读。略读时既要精力集中找准文章大意，又要注意文中各技术细节描述的分布情况。略读时，不必对某一技术细节或个别生僻词汇花费太多时间，而应着眼于做好以下几项工作：

➢ 关注原文的起始和结束部分，力求抓住文章的主题大意；
➢ 关注原文各节的主题句和结论句，力求摸清文章技术细节的叙述情况；
➢ 关注原文的题材和文体特征，力求了解原文整体结构；
➢ 关注支撑文章主旨的信息，其他细节予以忽略。

3）查询性阅读

是指在对文章有所了解的基础上，在文章中查找某一个问题的解决方案、某一观点的描述或某一专业词汇的含义。在进行查询性阅读时，要以很快的速度扫视文章，确定所查询的信息范围、注意所查信息的特点，并且准确略过与所要查询信息无关的内容。特别需要指出的是，能够很好地进行略读和查询性阅读的前提是大量的 IT 英语精读训练，没有在精读过程中积累的阅读体验和阅读能力，就谈不上进行略读和查询性阅读。

2．阅读技巧

为了提高 IT 英语阅读能力，可以采用无声阅读法、鉴别阅读法和段落阅读法等阅读技巧。

1）无声阅读法

是指大脑直接通过视觉接受文字信息，而不必通过发音过程将文字转换为声音。在进行 IT 英语无声阅读的过程中，视觉不受发音的影响，而能用较大的视角，以句、行甚至段落位单位进行阅读，还可以根据阅读任务的需要，对原文进行浏览或跳读。在进行无声阅读时，我们还可以用手指、铅笔等作为视觉引导物，指点着单词、句子和段落，以利于实现流畅的阅读节奏，进行快速阅读训练。

2）鉴别阅读法

是一种快速提炼文章的段意、主要内容和主旨思想的阅读方法。采用鉴别阅读法需要注意以下三个环节：

➢ 迅速找出原文段落中心句、重点句，或用自己的语言概括出段意；

➢ 将原文各段段意相连接，以便找到全文主旨；

➢ 关注文章题目、开头段、结束段以及文章的讨论部分，从中寻求文章中心思想。

鉴别阅读法实际上是通过以上三个环节来掌握文章的重要信息，不需逐字逐句地阅读全文，但需要注意力高度集中，大脑要处于积极思维状态，以此来保证较高的阅读质量。

3）段落阅读法

是指充分利用 IT 英语原文中的段落结构和它们在文中的位置，提高阅读效率。一般的 IT 类英语文章，往往在开头和结尾的几段内容中，包含有大部分的关键信息。IT 英语文章中的各个段落，可基本归纳为解释性段落、描述性段落和连接性段落。

➢ 解释性段落的起始部分通常会指出所要解释的论点，结束句为结论，而中间部分为详细描述，阅读者可根据此规律对该类型段落的不同部分进行详、略选择。

➢ 描述性段落往往是设置 IT 场景或扩展前文的内容，除非该段中包含对重点人物和事物的描述；否则，在对全文进行略读时，一般可以忽略。

➢ 连接性段落中通常会对前后的某些段落进行概括或总结，甚至是全文的主旨段落，因此会包含一些关键信息，需要重点阅读。

良好的 IT 英语阅读能力是学好 IT 英语这门专业课程的基础。在培养自身 IT 英语阅读能力的过程中，除了对于 IT 英语特点的了解、IT 英语翻译技巧的掌握和 IT 英语阅读方法的科学使用以外，阅读者还须夯实英语语言基础并坚持强化 IT 英语阅读训练。提升 IT 英语的阅读能力必须扩大词汇量，特别是 IT 专业词汇；必须能够熟练地掌握英语语法和惯用法；必须在大量的 IT 英语文章的阅读实践中，培养语感、寻求培养适合自己的阅读习惯，从而最终提高阅读的质量和速度。希望广大读者朋友，在 IT 英语阅读中，提高自身的专业英语阅读水平，巩固 IT 专业知识，了解 IT 领域的发展方向。

Multimedia

Unit 5　An Introduction to Multimedia

WORDS AND EXPRESSIONS

multimedia [ˈmʌltiˈmiːdjə]　多媒体

resolution [ˌrezəˈljuːʃən]　分辨率

coprocessor [kəʊ ˈprəʊsesə]　协处理器

sampling [ˈsɑːmpliŋ]　取样

analogical [ˌænəˈlɔdʒikəl]　模拟的

rectangular [rekˈtæŋgjulə]　矩形的

grid [grid]　格子

interlacing [ˌintə(ː)ˈleisiŋ]　隔行

compression [kəmˈpreʃ(ə)n]　压缩

code [kəud]　代码

encode [inˈkəud]　编码

decode [ˌdiːˈkəud]　解码

algorithm [ˈælgəriðəm]　算法

asymmetry [æˈsimətri]　不对称

extension [iksˈtenʃən]　扩展名

platform [ˈplætfɔːm]　平台

synchronize [ˈsiŋkrənaiz]　同步

dominate [ˈdɔmineit]　支配

ADC (Analog Digital Converter)　模数转换器

MIDI (Musical Instrument Digital Interface)　乐器指令数字化接口

MPEG (Motion Picture Experts Group)　运动图像专家组

NTSC (National Television Systems Committee)　全国电视系统委员会制式

JPEG (Joint Photographic Experts Group)　联合图像专家组

GIF (Graphics Interchange Format)　可交换的图像文件

BMP (Bitmap-File)　位图文件

AVI (Audio Video Interleaved)　音频视频交错格式

WAV (wave)　微软和 IBM 联合开发的用于音频数字存储的标准

AU(ADOBE AUDITION)　早期 UNIX 下的一种音频文件格式

SND (sound)　是苹果公司开发的音频文件标准

QUESTIONS AND ANSWERS

1. What is the multimedia conception?
2. Can you tell us something about Audio and Video?
3. What's the difference between MPEG and JPEG?
4. Briefly describe the basic function of multimedia computers.
5. How can you make multimedia computers display different kinds of image formats?
6. How can external images be displayed on Web browsers?
7. Who can hear the sound from your Web pages linked to AU files?
8. Can they hear the sound of higher quality? If not, why?
9. Give some examples to illustrate the way to play movies by browsers.

TEXT

Multimedia Devices

Multimedia PC is used in various aspects. Its appearance is a revolution in computer field. Multimedia is the combination of sound, graphics, animation, video and text. It makes the computer play an important role in developing application. Multimedia PC can run multimedia application, normally equipped with a sound card, a CD-ROM drive and a high-resolution color monitor. In addition, there are also scanner, digital camera and so on.

Especially, video capture board is a high speed digital sampling circuit which stores a TV picture in memory so that it can then be processed by a computer; graphics accelerator board is a specialized expansion board containing a graphics coprocessor as well as all the other circuitry found on a video adapter. Sometimes it is called a video accelerator board. Transferring most of the graphics processing tasks from the main processor to the graphics accelerator board improves system performance considerably, particularly for Microsoft Windows users.

Multimedia Conception

Multimedia is the audio, graphics, animation, video and text within an application.

Audio is referring to sound or to things which can be heard; usually, the human ear can hear a range of frequencies between around 20 Hz-20kHz. But some animals can hear higher frequencies.

Audio waves can be converted to digital form by an ADC (Analog Digital Converter). To represent this signal digitally, we can sample it every ΔT seconds; sampling more often is of no value.

Audio CDs are digital with a sampling rate of 44,100 sample/sec, enough to capture frequencies up to 22,050Hz, which is good for people, bad for dogs.

Computers in software can easily process digitized sound. Virtually all professional sound recording and editing are digital nowadays. MIDI (Musical Instrument Digital Interface) is a representation of many musical instruments now.

Video can be divided into two patterns: analogical system and digital system.

Analogical system: To represent the two-dimensional image in front of it as a one-dimensional voltage as a function of time, the camera scans an electron beam rapidly across the image and slowly down it, recording the light intensity as it goes. The exact scanning parameters vary from country to country. The system used in North and South America and Japan has 525 scan lines, a horizontal to vertical aspect ratio of 4 : 3, and 30 frames/sec. The European system has 625 scan lines, the same aspect rate of 4 : 3, and 25 frames/sec.

Digital system: The simplest representation of digital video is a sequence of frames, each consisting of a rectangular grid of picture elements, or pixels. Each pixel can be a single bit, to represent either black or white. To use 8 bits per pixel represent 256 gray levels. This schedule gives high-quality black-and-white video. For color video, good systems use 8 bits for each of the RGB colors. While using 24 bits per pixel limits the number of colors to about 16 million, the human eye cannot even distinguish so many colors, let alone more.

To produce the smooth motion, digital video, like analog video, must display at least 25 frames per sec. However, since good quality computer monitors often rescan the screen from images stored in memory at 75 times per second or more, interlacing is not needed and consequently is not normally used. Just repainting the same frame three times in a row is enough to eliminate flicker.

Data Compression: Transmitting multimedia material in uncompressed form is completely out of the question. The only method is that massive compression is possible. All compression systems require two algorithms: one for compressing the data at the source (encoding), and the other for decompressing it at the destination (coding). These algorithms have certain asymmetries, that is to say, a multimedia document will be encoded once but will be decoded thousands of times.

On the other hand, for the real-time multimedia, such as video conferencing, slow encoding is unacceptable. Encoding must happen on the fly in real time. A second asymmetry is that the encode/decode process need not be invertible, that is, when compressing a file, transmitting it, and then decompressing it. When the decoded output is not exactly equal to the original input, the system is said to be lossy. If the input and output are identical, the system is lossless. Lossy systems are important because accepting a small amount of information loss can give a huge payoff in terms of the compression ration possible.

The MPEG (Motion Picture Experts Group) standards: These are the main algorithms used to compress video and have been international standards since 1993. Because movies contain both images and sound, MPEG can compress both audio and video. The goal of MPEG-1 (International Standard 11172) was to produce video recorder-quality output (352×240 for NTSC) using a bit rate of 1.2Mbps. At this lower resolution, MPEG-1 can be transmitted over twisted pair transmission lines for modest distances. MPEG-1 is also used for storing movies on CD-ROM in CD-Video format. MPEG-2 (International Standard 13818) was originally designed for compressing broadcast quality video into 4 to 6 Mbps. MPEG-2 was expanded to support higher resolutions, including HDTV. It is likely that in the long run MPEG-1 will dominate for CD-ROM movies and MPEG-2 will dominate for long-haul video transmission.

JPEG: JPEG stands for Joint Photographic Experts Group, which is also sometimes abbreviated JPG. An image-compression standard and file format define a set of compression methods for high-quality imagers such as photographs, single video frames, or scanned pictures. JPEG does not work very well when compressing text, line art, or vector graphics. JPEG uses lossy compression methods that result in some loss of the original data. When you decompress the original image, you don't get exactly the same image that you started with, although JPEG was specifically designed to discard information not easily detected by the human eye. JPEG can store 24-bit color images in as many as 16 million colors; files in Graphics Interchange Format (GIF) form can only store 256 colors.

Multimedia Principle

Multimedia is not a new word. In fact, the concept of multimedia has been around for years. However, it appears that multimedia has finally started to play an increasingly important role in today's computer world. Because of ever more powerful computer systems and the experience of creative programmers, multimedia is truly changing the way people are using computers.

Multimedia is a kind of computer technology. Essentially, it is the integration of text, static images, audio sound, animations, and full-motion video. The followings are the three formats of them.

Image files come in a variety of formats, so Web browsers must either be able to deal with many formats, or you must have the capability to convert easily among these formats.

Browsers generally display images in two different ways: (1) in-line, using the browser itself, and (2) externally, in a separate window, often with the aid of a "Helper Application".

The popular browsers support only a limited number of graphics file formats for in-line images, with the most common being GIF and JPEG. You don't need to worry about the technical differences between BMP and JPEG and GIF formats; you only need to know that there are programs available that will convert from the BMP format to either GIF or JPEG. So if you are using graphics software on a PC to create artwork that you want to put on a Web page, you will probably also need access to one of these format conversion programs.

Web browsers are more flexible in the formats. They can display as external images because these are often displayed using separate "Helper Applications" that can be tailored to deal with a particular format. Provided a program exists that can display the format and runs on your computer, it is likely that the browser can be configured to display that format by launching the helper application.

For example, it is very common in scientific and technical settings to encounter images written in Postscript format (Postscript files commonly have a .ps or .eps extension in their names). A browser like Explorer cannot display Postscript directly, but it can be configured such that when it encounters a Postscript file it launches a helper application that displays the file in a separate window.

Like images, sound files also come in a variety of formats, not all of which can be used on every platform. AIFF is a native audio format for the Macintosh; WAV is native for Windows.

Both platforms also can play and save sounds in AU, SND, and MPEG audio formats. Both also use the MIDI format, but only for music.

AU is a Sun Microsystems format that is popular in the UNIX world and has the advantage of being available on a wide variety of systems. So if you choose to link to AU files in your Web pages, people visiting your pages from PCs, Macs, and UNIX machines should all be able to hear the sounds. On the other hand, AU files have comparatively rather poor sound quality.

If you are only concerned with other Windows users hearing your audio files, you can treat them too much higher quality sound with the WAV format.

MIDI is a very efficient format for many kinds of music and certain kinds of sounds. However, it is less well supported on the Web than the other formats and doesn't work well for things like voice (unless you want to sound like a computer).

Generally browsers do not have sound playing capabilities built-in, but can be easily configured to use other programs to play sounds which are sent to the browser. Modern browsers increasingly incorporate sound plug-ins in the default installation.

QuickTime and MPEG are two of the most common Cross platform movie formats currently in use. Of these, QuickTime is perhaps more popular for Windows and Macintosh because of the wide availability of its plug-ins for browsers on these systems, and because of its ability to synchronize multiple media streams. Players for QuickTime multimedia are freely available for the Macintosh, Windows 3.1, and Window 95/NT/XP from http://quicktime. apple.com.

Actually, QuickTime is not really a movie format, but is a software development package that allows the synchronization of video, text, sound, and music. But the name "QuickTime" has come to be popularly applied to movies files that are produced using the package. Such files general have either a .MOV or .QT extension. (Note that while the QuickTime players are free, the developer's package is a commercial product from APPLE.)

QuickTime VR is recent addition to the QuickTime technology. QTVR is designed to provide a sense of virtual reality by giving a user a 360-degree view, allowing him to move through scenes and around objects.

Many movies that originate on Windows systems are instead in AVI format (and have an .AVI extension). This is the format of movies created by Microsoft's Video for Windows; Windows 95 users can view these movies with Media Player that is included with their systems. AVI does not use a single common timeline for playing images and sounds so these movies may sometimes exhibit some audio/video synchronization problems.

As was the case with sound, browsers themselves do not play movies that they receive from a server. Instead, they can be configured either to save a movie to a disk file, to pass the movie to a "helper" program that can play the movie, or to use a special plug-in to play the particular format. For the Macintosh, the freeware program Sparkle can be used to play both MPEG and QuickTime movies, and can also be used to convert between the two formats. The newer versions of QuickTime will do the same. For Windows, the QuickTime plug-in can be used to play QuickTime and QTVR.

EXERCISES

1. Judge whether the following given statements are true or false. If correct, write T in parentheses; otherwise, write F.

(1)　(　) The human ear can hear a range of frequencies between around 10 Hz-20kHz.

(2)　(　) Virtually all professional sound recording and editing are analog nowadays.

(3)　(　) To produce the smooth motion, digital video, like analog video, must display at least 25 frames per sec.

(4)　(　) AVI does not use a single common timeline for playing images and sounds so these movies may sometimes exhibit some audio/video synchronization problems.

2. Complete the following note-taking with the information mentioned in the text.

(1)　Transferring most of the graphics processing tasks from the main processor to the _____ improves system performance considerably.

(2)　A multimedia document will be encoded once but will be _____ thousands of times.

(3)　Because movies contain both_____ and sound, MPEG can compress both audio and video.

(4)　Modern browsers increasingly incorporate sound _____ in the default installation.

READING MATERIALS

Product Description 1: Windows Media Player 12 (Figure 5-1)

Figure 5-1　Windows Media Player 12

The features of Windows Media Player 12

Designed by media lovers, for media lovers. Windows Media Player 12 (available only in Windows 7) plays more music and video than ever, including Flip Video and unprotected songs from your iTunes library!

➤ Plays more media...

Windows Media Player 12 has built-in support for many popular audio and video formats—including 3GP, AAC, AVCHD, MPEG-4, WMV, and WMA. It also supports most AVI, DivX, MOV, and Xvid files.

➤ ...in more places

The new Play To feature streams music and video to other PCs running Windows 7 or compatible devices around the home. With Remote Media Streaming, you can enjoy music or videos on your home PC from the road.

➤ New playback modes

The new Now Playing mode is a study in minimalism: It shows only the controls you need, so nothing comes between you and your music or video. A new taskbar thumbnail with playback controls makes previewing easier and fun.

➤ Easier, more fun

Enjoy smarter DVD playback, 15-second song previews, Jump Lists for fast access to favorite media. And that's just for starters.

➤ Note

Available only in Windows 7. Windows Media Player 12 comes as part of Windows 7 and is not available as a separate download. Check out the Top 10 reasons to buy Windows 7.

Getting started with Windows Media Player

Windows Media Player provides an intuitive, easy-to-use interface to play digital media files, organize your digital media collection, burn CD of your favorite music, rip music from CD, sync digital media files to a portable device, and shop for digital media content from online stores.

➤ Start Windows Media Player

To start Windows Media Player, click the Start button ⬤, click All Programs, and then click Windows Media Player.

➤ Two ways to enjoy your media: the Player Library (Figure 5-2) and Now Playing mode (Figure 5-3)

Windows Media Player allows you to toggle between two modes: the Player Library, which gives you comprehensive control over the Player's many features; and Now Playing mode, which gives you a simplified view of your media that's ideal for playback. From the Player Library, you can go to Now Playing mode by clicking the Switch to Now Playing button ⠿ in the lower-right corner of the Player. To return to the Player Library, click the Switch to Library button ▦ in the upper-right corner of the Player.

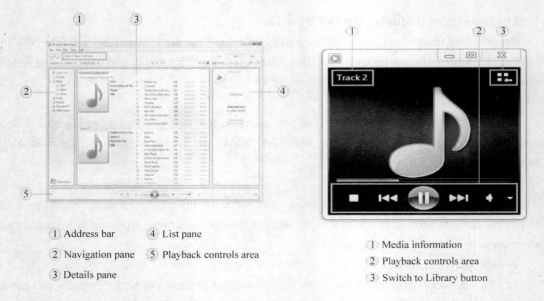

① Address bar   ④ List pane
② Navigation pane   ⑤ Playback controls area
③ Details pane

① Media information
② Playback controls area
③ Switch to Library button

Figure 5-2   The Player Library   **Figure 5-3   Now Playing mode**

In the Player Library, you can access and organize your digital media collection. Within the navigation pane, you can choose a category, such as Music, Pictures, or Videos, to view in the details pane. For example, to see all of your music organized by genre, double-click Music, and then click Genre. Then, drag items from the details pane to the list pane to create playlists, burn CD or DVD, or sync to devices, such as portable music players. As you move between the various views in the Player Library, you can use the Back and Forward buttons in the upper-left corner of the Player to retrace your steps.

➢ Use the Player Library to do any of the following

- Play an audio or video file
- Find items in the Windows Media Player Library
- Add items to the Windows Media Player Library
- Remove items from the Windows Media Player Library
- Create or change an auto playlist in Windows Media Player
- Add or edit media information in Windows Media Player

In Now Playing mode, you can view DVDs and videos or see what music is currently playing. You can decide to view only the currently playing item, or you can right-click the Player, and then click Show list to view a selection of available items.

Use Now Playing mode to do any of the following:

- Play a CD or DVD in Windows Media Player
- Shuffle and repeat items in Windows Media Player
- Change volume settings in Windows Media Player
- Switch between display modes in Windows Media Player

➢ Play from the taskbar

You can also control the Player when it's minimized. You can play or pause the current item, advance to the next item, and go back to the previous item using the controls in the thumbnail preview. The thumbnail preview appears when you point to the Windows Media Player icon on the taskbar.

➢ Build a media library

Windows Media Player looks for files in specific Windows libraries on your computer to add to the Player Library: Music, Videos, Pictures, and Recorded TV. To build your media library, you can include folders in the libraries from other locations on your computer or external devices, such as a portable hard drive.

➢ Rip CDs to create digital music files (Figure 5-4)

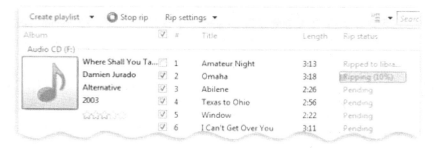

Figure 5-4   Ripping a music CD

You can add music to the Player Library by using your computer's CD drive to copy CDs and store them on your computer as digital files. This process is known as ripping.

➢ Use tabs to complete key tasks (Figure 5-5)

Figure 5-5   Play, Burn, and Sync tabs

The tabs at the top right of the Player open the list pane in the Player Library, making it easier for you to focus on specific tasks, such as creating playlists of your favorite songs, burning custom song lists to a recordable CD, or syncing playlists in your media library to a portable media player.

To get started, click the tab that corresponds to the task you want to perform in the Player Library. To hide the list pane, click the tab that is currently open.

To find out what you can do on each tab, click the links under the following sections:

- Play. The list below the Play tab reflects the items currently playing and the items you've selected to play in the Player Library. For example, if you selected a specific album to play, the entire album will appear in the Play tab. You can also use the Play tab to create and save custom playlists.

- Burn (Figure 5-6). If you want to listen to a mix of music while you're away from your computer, you can burn CDs containing any combination of music. For example, you can burn audio CDs with the Player and play them in any standard CD player. Use the Burn tab to do any of the following:
  ✧ Burn a CD or DVD in Windows Media Player
  ✧ Change settings for burning a CD or DVD in Windows Media Player

Figure 5-6　Burning a CD

- Sync. You can use the Player to sync music, videos, and pictures to a wide range of portable devices, including portable media players, storage cards, and some mobile phones. To do this, just connect a supported device to your computer and the Player will select the sync method (automatic or manual) that is best for your device. Then, you can sync files and playlists in your Player Library to your device. Use this tab to do any of the following:
  ✧ Set up a device to sync in Windows Media Player
  ✧ Sync manually in Windows Media Player

Unit 6　Storage of Multimedia

WORDS AND EXPRESSIONS

studio ['stjuːdiəu]　工作室

bandwidth ['bændwidθ]　带宽

stereo ['stiəriəu]　立体的，立体感觉的

unprecedented [ʌn'presidəntid]　空前的

blurry ['blɜːri]　模糊的，不清楚的

bi-level image　二值图像

DAT (Digital Audio Tape)　数字录音带

JBIG (Joint Bi-level Image Experts Group)　联合二值图像专家组

ISO (International Organization for Standardization)　国际标准化组织

ITU (International Telecommunications Union)　国际电信联盟

ITU-T (ITU-Telecommunication Standardization Sector)　国际电信联盟管理下的专门制定远程通信相关国际标准的组织

M-JPEG (Motion JPEG)　运动静止图像（或逐帧）压缩技术

FourCC (Four-Character Codes)　一种独立标示视频数据流格式的四字符代码

VHS (Video Home System)　家用录像系统

DivX (Digital Video Express)　一种 MPEG4 编码格式

VCD (Video Compact Disc)　视频高密光盘

DVD (Digital Video Disc)　数字化视频光盘

VCR (Video Cassette Recorder)　盒式磁带录像机

QUESTIONS AND ANSWERS

1. Please name a few common multimedia storage facilities covering sound video and mobile technology.

2. Can a VCD be played on a standard DVD player?

3. Discuss the different types of storage media including hard disks and optical disks.

4. Describe ways to improve hard-disk operations: disk caching, redundant arrays of inexpensive disks, data compression and decompression.

5. Describe the different types of optical disks.

6. Describe other kinds of secondary storage including solid state storage, Internet drives, and magnetic tape.

TEXT

Modern multimedia data storage comes in different format and varying quality. The medium in which they are stored determines to a large extent the quality of the information retrieved during usage.

Data storage on disk and tape became popular after Valdema Poulseu developed magnetized recording in which data was recorded on a magnetized steel tap. In the early 1990's, a digital video system capable of capturing full-screen video images would have cost several thousands of pounds. The biggest cost element was the compression hardware, needed to reduce the huge files that result from the conversion of an analogue video signal into digital data, to a manageable size. Less powerful "video capture" cards were available, capable of compressing quarter-screen images (330×240 pixels) but even these were far too expensive for the average PC user. The consumer end of the market was limited to basic cards that could capture video, but which had no dedicated hardware compression features of their own. In this text we will discuss in brief some of the common multimedia storage facilities covering sound video and mobile technology, which include GIF, MPEG, JBIG, AVI, VHS, VCD and DVD.

MPEG

MPEG (Moving Pictures Expert Group) is the name of the ISO committee which is working on digital color video and audio compression, and by extension the name of the standard they have produced.

MPEG defines a bit-stream representation for synchronized digital video and audio, compressed to fit into a bandwidth of 1.5Mbit/s. This corresponds to the data retrieval speed from CD-ROM and DAT, and a major application of MPEG is the storage of audio visual information on this media. MPEG is also gaining ground on the Internet as an interchange standard for video clips.

The MPEG standard is the three parts—video encoding, audio encoding, and "systems" which includes information about the synchronization of the audio and video streams. The video stream takes about 1.15Mbit/s, and the remaining bandwidth is used by the audio and system data streams.

JBIG

JBIG is short for the "Joint Bi-level Image Experts Group". This was (and is) a group of experts nominated by national standards bodies and major companies to work to produce standards for bi-level image coding. The "joint" refers to its status as a committee working on both ISO and ITU-T standards. The "official" title of the committee is ISO/IEC JTC1 SC29 Working Group 1, and is responsible for both JPEG and JBIG standards.

AVI

AVI stands for "Audio Video Interleave". This is a container video format that specifies certain structure how the audio and video streams should be stored within the file. AVI itself doesn't specify how it should be encoded, so the audio/video can be stored in very various ways. Most commonly used video codes that use AVI structure are M-JPEG and DivX.AVI contains code called FourCC which tells what code it is encoded with.

VHS

VHS stands for "Video Home System". This was the most common format for coding and playing a video tape for video cassette recorder.

VHS delivers around 240 lines of resolution, which is why a tape never looks as good as live broadcast. There are also differences in contrast, color saturation, etc. The bottom line is that VHS is a poor representation of what NTSC can deliver. VHS is an analog format developed in the 1970's.

VCD

VCD stands for "Video Compact Disc" and basically it is a CD that contains moving pictures and sound. If you're familiar with regular audio/music CDs, then you will know what a VCD looks like. A VCD has the capacity to hold up to 74/80 minutes on 650MB/700MB CD respectively of full-motion video along with quality stereo sound. VCD use a compression standard called MPEG to store the video and audio.A VCD can be played on almost all standard DVD Players and of course on all computers with a DVD-ROM or CD-ROM drive with the help of a software based decoder/player. It is also possible to use menus and chapters, similar to DVD, on a VCD and also simple photo album/slide shows with background audio. The quality of a very good VCD is about the same as a VHS tape based movie but VCD is usually a bit more blurry.

DVD

DVD (Digital Video Disc) is the new generation of optical disc storage technology. DVD is essentially a bigger, faster CD that can hold cinema-like video, better-than-CD audio, still photos, and computer data. DVD aims to encompass home entertainment, computers, and business information with a single digital format. It has replaced laserdisc, is well on the way to replace videotape and video game cartridges, and could eventually replace audio CD and CD-ROM. DVD has widespread support from all major electronics companies, all major computer hardware companies, and all major movie and music studios. With this unprecedented support, DVD became the most successful consumer electronics product of all time in less than three years of its introduction. In 2003, six years after introduction, there were over 250 million DVD playback devices worldwide, counting DVD players, DVD PCs, and DVD game consoles. This was more than half the numbers of VCR, setting DVD up to become the new standard for video publishing.

EXERCISES

1. Judge whether the following given statements are true or false. If correct, write T in parentheses; otherwise, write F.

(1)　(　) In the early 1990's, a digital video system capable of capturing full-screen video images would have cost several thousands of pounds.

(2) (   ) MPEG defines a bit-stream representation for synchronized digital video and audio.

(3) (   ) VCDs use a compression standard called MPEG to store the video and audio.

(4) (   ) The quality of a very good VCD is about the same as a VHS tape based movie but VHS is usually a bit more blurry.

2. Complete the following note-taking with the information mentioned in the text.

(1) MPEG is the name of the ISO committee which is working on _____ and audio compression.

(2) The video stream takes about 1.15Mbit per second, and the remaining bandwidth is used by the _____ and system data streams.

(3) _____ is a container video format that specifies certain structure how the audio and video streams should be stored within the file.

(4) DVD can encompass home entertainment, computers, and business information with a single _____ format.

READING MATERIALS

Product Description 1: QuickTime Player (Figure 6-1)

Clearer picture with H.264 Video

Volume   Player Controls   Progress Bar   Live Resize

Figure 6-1   QuickTime Player

Just launch QuickTime Player, and there's no telling where you're likely to land. The Player may whisk you to the Moon or perhaps to an exotic location on this planet. Take you on a virtual field trip to the National Baseball Hall of Fame and Museum. Or treat you to the latest news, movie trailers, music videos, HBO series or PBS specials.

When you hop aboard QuickTime 7 Player, you're assured of a truly rich multimedia experience.

That's because QuickTime 7 Player takes advantage of the latest video compression technology. It's called H.264, and it's an important new industry standard that's quickly garnered widespread support. Chosen as the industry-standard codec for 3GPP (mobile multimedia),

MPEG-4 HD-DVD and Blu-ray, H.264 represents the next generation of video for everything from mobile multimedia to high-definition playback.

Ultra-efficient, the H.264 codec compresses video tightly—resulting in much smaller files—without sacrificing any quality. So you can watch video of astonishing quality—crisp, clear and brilliantly saturated—in a window up to four times the size you are currently used to seeing.

Full Screen Playback

Tired of pillar bars and letterboxes? Full screen playback, now included in the free QuickTime Player, has been enhanced to allow you to take full advantage of your computer's widescreen display. Select from three different modes to fit your content to any size screen.

Just Open It and It Works

The new QuickTime 7 Player not only delivers startling quality, but it's easier to use than ever. It requires no set up for content that streams over the network. Instead, QuickTime 7 Player automatically determines your system's connection speed and chooses the highest quality stream for the amount of bandwidth you have available. And if you ever lose a connection while watching streaming video, QuickTime 7 Player automatically reconnects. Now, that's convenience.

You also have the option of using the Player's new audio and video playback controls. With them, you can easily adjust balance and volume or make changes to bass and treble response. If you're running Mac OS X Tiger or later with a capable video card, you can adjust brightness, color, contrast and tint with sliders in the same control palette, too. Want to speed through a movie? Or really slow things down? A handy slider lets you set playback speed from 1/2x to 3x normal speed. And by using the new Jog Shuttle, you can adjust the speed at which you search through individual movie frames.

Sounds Really Good, Too

Do you think great video deserves great audio? We do, too. And QuickTime 7 Player delivers truly outstanding multi-channel audio. In fact, it provides you with up to 24 channels of audio. So if you watch a movie that offers surround sound, you'll be amazed at the heightened audio experience you'll enjoy from your Mac or PC and your surround-sound speakers. A really good sport, QuickTime 7 Player supports a wide-range of industry-standard audio formats, including AIFF, WAV, MOV, MP4 (AAC only), CAF and AAC/ADTS.

Unit 7　Flash

WORDS AND EXPRESSIONS

deploy [di'plɔi]　配置
hybrid ['haibrid]　复杂的
accessibility [ˌækəsesi'biliti]　辅助功能
presentation [ˌprezen'teiʃən]　演示文稿
symbol ['simbəl]　符号
previous ['pri:vjəs]　先前的
drag-and-drop　拖放
built-in　内置的
Action Script　动作脚本
SWF (Shock Wave Flash)　是 Macromedia 公司（现已被 ADOBE 公司收购）的动画设计软件 Flash 的专用格式
Timeline Effects　时间轴特效
Updated Templates　更新模板
third-party　第三方
XML (Extensible Markup Language)　可扩展标记语言
HTTPS (Hypertext Transfer Protocol over Secure Socket Layer)　安全超文本传输协议
ECMA (European Computer Manufacturers Association)　欧洲计算机厂商协会

QUESTIONS AND ANSWERS

1. Did you use Flash?
2. Can you tell us something about Flash?
3. What do you think of Flash?
4. What's the difference between Flash MX 2004 and Flash MX Professional 2004?
5. What are the new features available in both Flash MX 2004 and Flash MX Professional 2004?
6. Do you have a plan to create and deliver rich web content by Flash now? What's it?

TEXT

Flash provides everything you need to create and deliver rich web content and powerful applications. Whether you're designing motion graphics or building data-driven applications, Flash has the tools necessary to produce great results and deliver the best user experience across multiple platforms and devices.

Flash is an authoring tool that allows you to create anything from a simple animation to a complex interactive web application, such as an online store. You can make your Flash includes many features that make it powerful but easy to use, such as drag-and-drop user interface components, built-in behaviors that add Action Script to your document, and special effects that you can add to objects.

When you author in Flash, you work in a Flash document, a file that, when saved, has the file extension .fla. When you are ready to deploy your Flash content, you publish it, creating a file with the extension .swf. The Flash Player runs the SWF file.

Macromedia Flash Player 7, which runs the applications that you create, installs by default along with Flash. The Flash Player ensures that all SWF content is viewable and available consistently and across the broadest range of platforms, browsers, and devices.

Let's talk about two editions of Flash: Flash MX 2004 and Flash MX Professional 2004.

➢ Flash MX 2004 is the perfect tool for the web designer, interactive media professional, or subject matter expert developing multimedia content. Emphasis is on creation, import, and manipulation of many types of media (audio, video, bitmaps, vectors, text, and data).

➢ Flash MX Professional 2004 is designed for advanced web designers and application builders. Flash MX Professional 2004 includes all the features of Flash MX 2004, along with several powerful new tools. It provides project-management tools for optimizing the workflow between the members of a web team made up of designers and developers. External scripting and capabilities for handling dynamic data from databases are some of the features that make Flash particularly suitable for large-scale, complex projects deployed using the Flash Player along with a hybrid of HTML content.

New features available in both Flash MX 2004 and Flash MX Professional 2004 provide greater productivity, enhanced rich media support, and streamlined publishing.

Timeline Effects

You can apply Timeline effects to any object on the stage to quickly add transitions and animations such as fade-ins, fly-ins, blurs, and spins.

Behaviors

With behaviors, you can add interactivity to Flash content without writing a line of code. For example, you can use behaviors to include functionality that links to a website, loads sounds and graphics, controls playback of embedded videos, plays movie clips, and triggers data sources.

Accessibility Support in the Authoring Environment

Accessibility support in the Flash authoring environment provides keyboard shortcuts for navigating and for using interface controls, letting you work with these interface elements without using the mouse.

Updated Templates

Flash includes updated templates for creating presentations, e-learning applications, advertisements, mobile device applications, and other commonly used types of Flash documents.

Document Tabs

Tabs for each open document are displayed at the top of the workspace so that you can quickly locate and switch between open documents.

Find and Replace

The Find and Replace feature locates and replaces a text string, a font, a color, a symbol, a sound file, a video file, or an imported bitmap file.

Flash Player Detection

You can now publish SWF files with associated files that detect if a user has a specified Flash Player version. You can configure your published files to direct users to alternate files if they don't have the specified Flash Player.

Accessibility and Components

New accessibility features and a new generation of components offer tab ordering, tab focus management, and improved support for third-party screen readers and closed-caption programs.

Strings Panel

The new Strings panel makes it easier to publish Flash content in multiple languages. With the clock of a few buttons, Flash creates external XML files for each specified language.

Security

The Flash Player 7 enforces a stricter security model than previous versions of the Flash Player. Exact domain matching requires that the domain of the data to be accessed match the data provider's domain exactly in order for the domains to communicate. HTTPS/HTTP restriction specifies that a SWF file using non-secure (non-HTTPS) protocols cannot access content loaded using a secure (HTTPS) protocol, even when both are in exactly the same domain.

Other Improvements

Flash Player performance has been greatly improved, and ActionScript has been enhanced to comply with ECMA script language specifications. Also, Flash now tracks interactions so that they can be converted to reusable commands.

EXERCISES

1. Judge whether the following given statements are true or false. If correct, write T in parentheses; otherwise, write F.

(1)　(　) When you author in Flash, you work in a Flash document, which has the file extension .swf.

(2)　(　) If you want to add interactivity to Flash content, you must write codes.

(3)　(　) You may work with some Flash interface controls without using mouse.

(4)　(　) You can create presentations through updated templates which are included in

Flash.

2. Complete the following note-taking with the information mentioned in the text.

(1)　Flash includes many features, such as drag-and-drop user interface components, built-in behaviors that add ＿＿＿ to your document.

(2)　The Flash Player runs the ＿＿＿ file.

(3)　You can apply ＿＿＿ to any object on the stage to quickly add transitions and animations.

(4)　You can configure your published files to direct users to alternate files if they don't have the specified ＿＿＿.

READING MATERIALS

Product Description 1: Adobe® Flash® Professional CS5 (Figure 7-1)

Figure 7-1   Adobe® Flash® Professional CS5

Adobe® Flash® Professional CS5 software is the industry standard for interactive authoring and delivery of immersive experiences that present consistently across personal computers, mobile devices, and screens of virtually any size and resolution.

➢ Flash Professional for web design

Create web designs and online experiences complete with interactive content, exceptional typography, high-quality video, and smooth animation for truly engaging web experiences.

● Text engine. Take complete control over your text with print-quality typography via the new Text Layout Framework.

● XML-based. FLA source files Collaborate on projects more easily with a new XML-based implementation of the FLA file format. Uncompressed projects appear and act like folders, allowing you to quickly manage and modify assets such as images.

- Code Snippets panel. Speed project completion by using convenient prewritten code snippets for common actions, animation, audio and video insertion, and more. Also discover an easier way to learn the ActionScript® 3.0 language.

- Creative Suite integration. Enhance productivity when using Flash Professional together with Adobe Photoshop®, Illustrator®, InDesign, and Flash Builder™.

- Wide content distribution. Publish content virtually anywhere, using Adobe AIR® for desktop applications and mobile platforms including the iPhone®, or Adobe Flash Player for browser-based experiences.

- Spring for Bones. Add expressive, lifelike animation properties like spring and bounce with new motion attributes added to the Bones tool. An improved inverse kinematics engine provides more realistic and complex physics movements within a simple, familiar interface.

- Deco drawing tools. Add advanced animation effects with a new comprehensive set of brushes for the Deco tool. Quickly create movement for particle phenomena like clouds or rain, and draw stylized lines or patterns with multiple objects.

- ActionScript editor. Speed up the development process with an improved ActionScript editor, including custom class code hinting and code completion. Quickly grasp the fundamentals of ActionScript, and efficiently reference your own code or external code libraries.

- Video improvements. Streamline video embedding and encoding processes with on-stage video scrubbing and a new cue points property inspector. See and play back FLV components directly on the stage.

- Flash Builder integration. Work more closely with developers who can use your Flash project files with Flash Builder to test, debug, and publish your content more efficiently.

➢ Flash Professional for web application development

Efficiently develop cross-platform web applications and content with an integrated development environment that offers intelligent ActionScript® coding tools and powerful integration with other Adobe tools.

- XML-based FLA source files. Manage and modify projects using source control systems and collaborate on files more easily. An XML-based nonbinary implementation of the FLA format allows projects and associated assets to function as items in a directory or folder.

- ActionScript editor. Speed the development process with an improved ActionScript editor, including custom class code hinting and code completion. Start projects and grasp the fundamentals of ActionScript more quickly, or reference your own code or external code libraries efficiently.

- Wide content distribution. Publish content virtually anywhere, using Adobe AIR® for desktop applications and mobile platforms including the iPhone®, or Adobe Flash Player for browser-based experiences.
- Code Snippets panel. Quickly include functional code for things like timeline navigation, actions, animation, audio and video, and event handlers. Reduce the ActionScript 3.0 learning curve and enable greater creativity by injecting prebuilt code into projects.
- Spring for Bones. Create more realistic inverse kinematic effects with new motion attributes added to the Bones tool. Strength and Damping settings provide more realistic and complex physics movements within a simple, familiar interface.
- Text engine. Get global bidirectional language support and a set of advanced print-quality typography APIs via the new Text Layout Framework. Format text in columns and maintain layout and formatting with greater fidelity when importing content from other Adobe products.
- Video improvements. Streamline video embedding and encoding processes with on-stage video scrubbing and a new cue points property inspector. See and play back FLV components directly on the stage.
- Creative Suite integration. Enhance productivity when using Flash Professional together with Adobe Photoshop®, Illustrator®, InDesign®, and Flash Builder.
- Deco drawing tools. Add advanced animation effects with a new comprehensive set of brushes for the Deco tool. Quickly create movement for particle phenomena like clouds or rain, and draw stylized lines or patterns with multiple objects.

➤ Flash Professional for interactive and video projects

Wow your audience with engaging FLV video content and interactivity that contains expressive, lifelike motion and animation. Fully control the playback experience, and easily integrate content from Adobe video editing and motion software.

- Video improvements. Streamline video embedding and encoding processes with video scrubbing directly on the stage and a new way to work with cue points. See and play back FLV components directly on the stage.
- XML-based FLA source files. Collaborate on projects more easily with a new XML-based implementation of the FLA file format. Uncompressed projects appear and function like folders, allowing you to quickly manage and modify assets such as images.
- Creative Suite integration. Enhance productivity when working with Adobe® Creative Suite® components such as Adobe Photoshop®, Illustrator®, InDesign®, and Flash® Builder™.
- Code Snippets panel. Quickly include functional code for things like audio and video control, timeline navigation, actions, animation, and more. Reduce the ActionScript® 3.0 learning curve and enable greater creativity by injecting prebuilt code into

projects.

- Text engine. Take complete control over your text with print-quality typography via the new Text Layout Framework. Work with columns and bidirectional text, and maintain layout and formatting with greater fidelity when importing from other Adobe products.

- Wide content distribution. Publish content virtually anywhere, using Adobe AIR® for desktop applications and mobile platforms including the iPhone®, or Adobe Flash Player for browser-based experiences.

- Deco drawing tools. Add advanced animation effects with a new comprehensive set of brushes for the Deco tool. Quickly create movement for particle phenomena like clouds or rain, and draw stylized lines or patterns with multiple objects.

- Spring for Bones. Add expressive, lifelike animation properties like spring and bounce with new motion attributes added to the Bones tool. An improved inverse kinematics engine provides more realistic and complex physics movements within a simple, familiar interface.

- Flash Builder integration. Work more closely with developers who can use your Adobe Flash Professional project files with Flash Builder to test, debug, and publish your content more efficiently.

- ActionScript editor. Speed the development process with an improved ActionScript editor, including custom class code hinting and code completion. Quickly grasp the fundamentals of ActionScript, and efficiently reference your own code or external code libraries.

Unit 8   Multimedia Application

WORDS AND EXPRESSIONS

animation [ˌæuiˈmeiʃən]   动画片，卡通
evaluate [iˈvæljueit]   评价，估计
reliability [riˌlaiəˈbiliti]   可靠性
transformation [ˌtrænsfəˈmeiʃən]   变化，转换
pseudocolor [ˈsju:dəuˌkʌlə]   伪彩色
exaggerated [igˈzædʒəreitid]   夸大的
storyboard [ˈstɔ:ribɔ:d]   （电影、电视以及其他视频节目）情节串连图板
digitize [ˈdidʒitaiz]   将资料数字化
synchronization [ˌsiŋkrənaiˈzeiʃən]   同步
soundtrack [ˈsaundˌtræk]   声道
rough [rʌf]   粗糙的，粗略的
sketch [sketʃ]   略图，草图
playback [ˈpleibæk]   重放
SMPTE (Society of Motion Picture and Television Engineers)   电影与电视工程师学会
EDL (Editorial Determination List)   编辑决策列表
physical quantity   物理量
time sequence   时序
time interval   时间间隔

QUESTIONS AND ANSWERS

1. Can you give us some examples of the typical applications of computer-generated animation? What are they?

2. Describe the design of animation sequences.

3. Describe video editor and video editing.

4. Describe video conferencing.

5. What's the meaning of Key-frame specifications?

6. What's the meaning of generation of in-between frames?

TEXT

Computer Animation

Some typical applications of computer-generated animation are entertainment studies, training and education. Although we tend to think of animation as implying object motions, the term "computer animation" generally refers to any time sequence of visual changes in a scene. In addition to changing object position with translations or rotations, a computer-generated animation could display time variations in object size, color, transparency, or surface texture. Advertising animations often transform one object shape into another. And we can produce computer animations by changing lighting effects or other parameters and procedures associated with illumination and rendering.

Many applications of computer animation require realistic displays. An accurate representation of the shape of a thunderstorm or other natural phenomena described with a numerical model is important for evaluating the reliability of the model. Also, simulator for training aircraft pilots and heavy equipment operators must produce reasonably accurate representations of the environment. Entertainment and advertising applications, on the other hand, are sometimes more interested in visual effects. Thus, scenes may be displayed with exaggerated shapes, unrealistic motions and transformations. These are many entertainment and advertising applications that do require accurate representations for computer-generated scenes. And in some scientific and engineering studies, realism is not a goal. For example, physical quantities are often displayed with pseudocolors or abstract shapes that change over time to help the researcher understand the nature of the physical process.

Design of Animation Sequences

In general, an animation sequence is designed with the following steps:

- Storyboard layout;
- Object definitions;
- Key-frame specifications;
- Generation of in-between frames.

This standard approach for animated cartoons is applied to other animation applications as well, although there are many special applications that do not follow this sequence. Real-time computer animations produced by flight simulators, for instance, display motion sequences in response to setting on the aircraft controls. For frame-by-frame animation, each frame of the scene is separately generated and stored. Later, the frames can be recorded on film or they can be consecutively displayed in "realtime playback" mode.

The storyboard is an outline of the action. It defines the motion sequence as a set of basic events to take place. Depending on the type of animation to be produced, the storyboard could consist of a set of rough sketches or it could be a list of the basic ideas for the motion.

An object definition is given for each participant in the action. Objects can be defined in terms of basic shapes, such as polygons or splines. In addition, the associated movements for each object are specified along with the shape.

A key frame is a detailed drawing of the scene at a certain time in the animation sequence. With each key frame, each object is positioned according to the time for that frame. Some key frames are chosen at extreme positions in the action; others are spaced so that the time interval between key frames is not too great. More key frames are specified for intricate motions than for simple, slowly varying motions.

In-betweens are the intermediate frames between the key frames. The number of in-betweens needed is determined by the media to be used to display the animation. Film requires 24 frames per second, and graphics terminals are refreshed at the rate of 30 to 60 frames per second. Typically, time intervals for the motion are set up so that there are three to five in-betweens for each pair of key frames. Depending on the speed specified for the motion, some key frames can be duplicated. For a 1-minute film sequence with no duplication, we would need 1 440 key frames. With five in-betweens for each pair of key frames, we would need 288 key frames. If the motion is not too complicated, we could space the key frames a little farther apart.

There are several other tasks that may be required, depending on the application. They include motion verification, editing, and production and synchronization of soundtrack.

Video Editor and Video Editing

Video editor is a computer that controls two videotape recorders to allow an operator playback sequences from one and record these on the second machine; it synchronizes the sequences using SMPTE time codes or by counting frames or by using an EDL that has been produced with an off-time editing software package. Video is digitized and stored in a computer; the editor can then cut and move frames in any order before outputting the finished sequence. The finished sequence can either be recorded directly from the computer output (but this is normally at a lower quality than the original due to compression loss) or the computer can output time code instructions that can be then used with an editing suited to edit the original video tape.

Video Conferencing

This is a method used to allow people at remote locations to join in a conference and share information. Originally, done with analog video and expensive satellite links, video conferencing is now performed with compressed digital video transmitted over a local-area network or the Internet. From an application standpoint, video conferencing has gone way beyond looking at a picture of a person; users can look at and update charts, make drawings, and so on, all online. A video camera and a speakerphone are linked to a PC which in turn is linked to the network.

EXERCISES

1. Judge whether the following given statements are true or false. If correct, write T in parentheses; otherwise, write F.

(1)　(　) Advertising animations never transform one object shape into another.

(2)　(　) These are many entertainment and advertising applications that do require accurate representations for computer-generated scenes.

(3)　(　) For frame-by-frame animation, each frame of the scene isn't separately generated and stored.

(4)　(　) From an application standpoint, video conferencing has gone way beyond looking at a picture of a person.

2. Complete the following note-taking with the information mentioned in the text.

(1)   We can produce computer animations by changing lighting _____ or other parameters and procedures.

(2)   Objects can be defined in terms of _____ shapes, such as polygons or splines.

(3)   Depending on the speed specified for the motion, some key _____ can be duplicated.

(4)   Video conferencing is now performed with _____ transmitted over a local-area network or the Internet.

READING MATERIALS

Product Description 1: Autodesk® 3ds Max® 2011 (Figure 8-1)

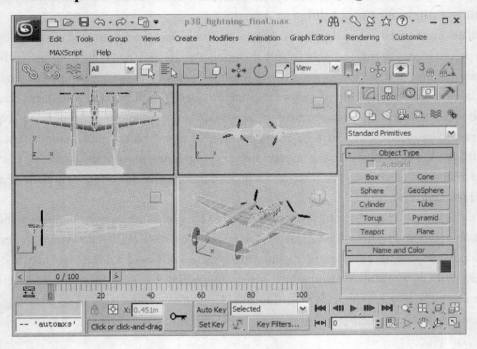

Figure 8-1   Autodesk® 3ds Max® 2011

Autodesk® 3ds Max® 2011 software delivers compelling new techniques for helping create and texture models, animate characters, and produce higher-quality images in less time.

Whether you're looking to create differentiated 3D assets for games, compelling broadcast graphics for television, or stunning visual effects for the latest box-office attraction, Autodesk® 3ds Max® 2011 software provides a comprehensive, integrated 3D modeling, animation, rendering, and compositing solution that enables you to more quickly ramp up for production.

Accelerate Everyday Workflows

Model and texture characters, props and environments more efficiently in 3ds Max 2011, with expanded Graphite and Viewport Canvas toolsets that deliver intuitive new brush-based interfaces for 3D painting, texture editing, and object placement. Meanwhile, a new in-context direct manipulation UI helps make polygon modeling faster and helps you maintain focus on the creative task at hand, while customized user interface (UI) layouts keep your choice of frequently used actions and macro scripts readily accessible. And, for projects where collaboration is critical, a significantly enhanced workflow with Containers enables multiple users to work in parallel, helping to meet tight deadlines.

Create Believable Movement Faster

Achieve higher-quality results in less time when creating animations and simulations in 3ds Max 2011. With the flexible, approachable Character Animation Toolkit (CAT) now fully integrated, you can use default settings to more quickly create working rigged characters or customize rigs for more demanding set-ups.

Polish Your Image

Whether an image sequence is the final, reined product of a production, an animatic for review, or part of an interactive experience, 3ds Max 2011 offers new tools to help you create it more easily. An intuitive new node-based material editor, Slate, helps make it easier to create and edit complex material networks, while   the innovative Quicksilver hardware renderer can render at incredible speeds and it supports advanced lighting effects.

Meanwhile, the new ability to view 3ds Max texture maps and materials in the viewport means that you can make interactive decisions in a higher-fidelity context, helping to reduce errors. Finally, the inclusion of 3ds Max Composite, a fully featured HDR-capable compositor based on technology from Autodesk® Toxik® software, provides a powerful toolset that incorporates keying, color correction, tracking, camera mapping, raster and vector paint, spline-based warping, motion blur, depth of field, and tools to support stereoscopic productions.

Slate Material Editor

More easily visualize and edit material component relationships with Slate, a new node-based editor that helps significantly improve workflow and productivity for creating and editing complex material networks.

Quicksilver Hardware Renderer

Create higher-fidelity pre-visualizations, animatics, and games-related marketing materials in less time with Quicksilver, an innovative new hardware renderer that uses both the CPU and the GPU to help produce higher-quality images at incredible speeds.

Local Edits to Containers

Collaborate more efficiently with significantly enhanced workflows for Containers that enable you to meet tight deadlines by working in parallel: multiple users can layer local edits nondestructively on top of referenced content, working simultaneously on different aspects of the same container.

Viewport Display of Autodesk 3ds Max Materials

Develop and refine scenes in a higher-fidelity interactive display environment that enables you to help make better decisions in context with the new ability to view most 3ds Max texture maps and materials in the viewport.

3ds Max Composite

Enhance rendered passes and incorporate them into live action footage with 3ds Max Composite: a fully featured, high-performance, HDR-capable compositor, based on technology from Autodesk® Toxik® software.

In-Context Direct Manipulation UI

Save time when modeling and maintain focus on the creative task at hand with a new in-context UI for polygon modeling tools that enables you to more interactively manipulate properties and enter values directly at the point of interest in the viewport.

CAT Integration

More easily create and manage characters, and layer, load, save, remap, and mirror animations with CAT. Now fully integrated into 3ds Max, CAT provides an out-of-the-box advanced rigging and animation system.

UI Customization

Focus on the features that matter most for specialized workflows with customizable UI layouts that enable you to store personalized configurations that include frequently used action items and macro scripts.

Save to Previous Release

Manage the transition to the Autodesk 3ds Max 2011 release with the option to save scene files in a format compatible with the 2010 version*. This enables you to take advantage of the new features in 2011 before your entire studio, pipeline, or client base is ready to upgrade.

Autodesk® 3ds Max® Entertainment Creation Suite 2011

3ds Max 2011 is part of the Autodesk® 3ds Max® Entertainment Creation Suite 2011, which also includes Autodesk® Mudbox™ 2011 and Autodesk® MotionBuilder® 2011 software — offering you more creativity at a reduced price.

Programming Languages

Unit 9   The Development of Programming Languages

WORDS AND EXPRESSIONS

recognizable ['rekəgnaizəbl]   可认识的，可辩认的
subsequent ['sʌbsikwənt]   后来的，并发的
breakthrough ['breik'θruː]   突破
flexibility [ˌfleksə'biliti]   适应性
sequence ['siːkwəns]   序列
binary [bainəri]   二进制，二进制的
PHP (PHP:Hypertext Preprocessor)   超文本预处理语言
BCPL (Basic Combined Programming Language)   基本组合程序设计语言
O-code   BCPL 使用的一种中间语言
P-code   由 Pascal 编译器产生的代码
high-level language   高级语言
Procedural Programming   面向过程的程序设计
Object-Oriented Programming (OOP)   面向对象的程序设计

QUESTIONS AND ANSWERS

1. What language has been widely used for the development of operating system and compilers?

2. What are two mechanisms used to translate a program written in a programming language into the specific machine code of the computer being used?

3. What is the difference between the two mechanisms?

4. What's machine language?

5. What's the differences between machine language and assembly language?

6. C++ is now the most common application programming language on the Microsoft Windows operating system, where does C remain more popular?

TEXT

Introduction to the History of Programming Languages

The development of programming languages, unsurprisingly, follows closely the development of the physical and electronic processes used in today's computers.

In the 1940s the first recognizably modern, electrically powered computers were created, requiring programmers to operate machines by hand. Some military calculation needs were a driving force in early computer development, such as encryption, decryption, trajectory calculation and massive number crunching needed in the development of atomic bombs. At that time, computers were extremely large, slow and expensive. The advances in electronic technology in the post-war years led to the construction of more practical electronic computers. At that time only Konrad Zuse imagined the use of a programming language (developed eventually as Plankalkul) like those of today for solving problems.

Subsequent breakthroughs in electronic technology (transistors, integrated circuits, and chips) drove the development of a variety of standardized computer languages to run on them. The improved availability and ease of use of computers led to a much wider circle of people who can deal with computers. The subsequent explosive development has resulted in the Internet, the ubiquity of personal computers, and increased use of computer programming, through more accessible languages such as Python, Visual Basic.

A primary purpose of programming languages is to enable programmers to express their intent for a computation more easily than they could with a lower-level language or machine code. For this reason, programming languages are generally designed to use a higher-level syntax, which can be easily communicated and understood by human programmers. Programming languages are important tools for helping software engineers write better programs faster.

Understanding programming languages is crucial for those engaged in computer science because today all types of computation are done with computer languages.

During the last few decades, a large number of computer languages have been introduced, have replaced each other, and have been modified/combined. Although there have been several attempts to make a universal computer language that serves all purposes, all of them have failed. The need for a significant range of computer languages is caused by the fact that the purpose of programming languages varies from commercial software development to hobby use; the gap in skill between novices and experts is huge and some languages are too difficult for beginners to come to grip with; computer programmers have different preferences; and finally, acceptable runtime cost may be very different for programs running on a microcontroller and programs running on a supercomputer.

There are many special purpose languages, for use in special situations: PHP is a scripting language that is especially suited for Web development; Perl is suitable for text manipulation; the C language that has been widely used for development of operating systems and compilers (so-called system programming).

Programming languages make computer programs less dependent on particular machines or environments. This is because programming languages are converted into specific machine code for a particular machine rather than being expected directly by the machine. One ambitious goal of FORTRAN, one of the first programming languages, was this machine-independence.

There are two mechanisms used to translate a program written in a programming language into the specific machine code of the computer being used.

If the translation mechanism used is one that translates the program text as a whole and then runs the internal format, this mechanism is spoken of as compilation. The compiler is therefore a program which takes the human-readable program text (called source code) as data input and supplies object code as output. The resulting object code may be machine code that will be executed directly by the computer's CPU, or it may be code matching the specification of a virtual machine.

If the program code is translated at runtime, with each translated step being executed immediately, the translation mechanism is spoken of as an interpreter. Interpreted programs run usually more slowly than compiled programs, but have more flexibility because they are able to interact with the execution environment. Although the definition may not be identical, these typically fall into the category of scripting programming languages.

Most languages can be either compiled or interpreted, but most are better suited for one than the other. In some programming systems, programs are compiled in multiple stages, into a variety of intermediate representations. Typically, later stages of compilation are closer to machine code than earlier stages. One common variant of this implementation strategy, first used by BCPL in the late 1960s, was to compile programs to an intermediate representation called "O-code" for a virtual machine, which was then compiled for the actual machine. This successful strategy was later used by Pascal with P-code and Smalltalk with byte code, although in many cases the intermediate code was interpreted rather than being compiled.

Machine Language

Computer programs that can be run by a computer's operating system are called executables. An executable program is a sequence of extremely simple instructions known as machine code. These instructions are specific to the individual computer's CPU and associated hardware. For example, Intel Pentium and Power PC microprocessor chips each have different machine languages and require different sets of codes to perform the same task. Machine code instructions are few in number (roughly 20 to 200, depending on the computer and the CPU). Typical instructions are for copying data from a memory location or for adding the contents of two memory locations (usually registers in the CPU). Machine code instructions are binary—that is, sequences of bits (0 s and 1 s). Because these numbers are not understood easily by humans, computer instructions usually are not written in machine code.

Assembly Language

Assembly language is easier for programmers to understand than machine language. Each machine language instruction has an equivalent command in assembly language. For example, in assembly language, the statement "MOV A, B" instructs the computer to copy data from one location to another. The same instruction in machine code is a string of 16 0 s and 1 s. Once an assembly-language program is written, it is converted to a machine-language program by another program called an assembler. Assembly language is fast and powerful because of its correspondence with machine language. It is still difficult to use, however, because assembly language instructions are a series of abstract codes. In addition, different CPUs use different machine languages and therefore require different assembly languages. Assembly language is sometimes inserted into a high-level language program to carry out specific hardware tasks or to speed up a high-level program.

High-level Language

The improvement of machine language to assembly language set the stage for further advances. It was this improvement that led, in turn, to the development of high-level languages. If the computer could translate convenient symbols into basic operations, why couldn't it also perform other clerical coding functions?

A high-level programming language is a means of writing down, in formal terms, the steps that must be performed to process a given set of data in a uniquely defined way. It may bear no relation to any given computer but does assume that a computer is going to be used. The high-level languages are often oriented toward a particular class of processing problems. For example, a number of languages have been designed to process problems of a scientific-mathematic nature, and other languages have appeared that emphasize file processing applications.

Procedural Programming and Object-oriented Programming

There are two popular approaches to writing computer programs: procedural programming and object-oriented programming.

➤ Procedural programming involves using your knowledge of a programming language to create computer memory locations that can hold values and writing a series of steps or operations that manipulate those values. For convenience, the individual operations used in a computer program are often grouped into logical units called procedures. A procedural program defines the variable memory locations and then calls or invokes a series of procedures to input, manipulate, and output the values stored in those locations. A single procedural program like C language program often contains hundreds of variable and thousands of procedure calls.

➤ Object-oriented programming is an extension of procedural programming in which you take a slightly different approach to writing computer programs. Thinking in an object-oriented manner involves envisioning program components as objects that are similar to concrete objects in the real world. Then you manipulate the objects to achieve a desired result. Writing object-oriented programs involves both creating objects and creating applications that use those objects.   Object-oriented programming (OOP) languages like C++ are based on traditional high-level languages, but they enable a programmer to think in terms of collections of cooperating objects instead of lists of commands.

EXERCISES

1. Judge whether the following given statements are true or false. If correct, write T in parentheses; otherwise, write F.

(1)　(　) Computers were extremely large, slow and expensive in the 1940s.

(2)　(　) Programming languages make computer programs more dependent on particular machines or environments.

(3)　(　) Machine code instructions are hexadecimal sequences.

(4)　(　) For convenience, the individual operations used in a computer program are often grouped into logical units called procedures.

2. Complete the following note-taking with the information mentioned in the text.

(1)　Subsequent breakthroughs in _____ drove the development of a variety of standardized computer languages to run on them.

(2)　Programming languages are generally designed to use a higher-level _____, which can be easily communicated and understood by human programmers.

(3)　The resulting object code may be machine code that will be executed directly by the computer's _____.

(4)　A single procedural program often contains hundreds of variable and thousands of _____ calls.

READING MATERIALS

Product Description: Installation and Setup of Visual Studio.NET

As you install Visual Studio.NET, you will have the opportunity to choose among several different installation and setup options. This topic will help you familiarize yourself with these options, and direct you to appropriate help.

You also can refer to the Readme files, located in the root of the installation CD or DVD. The Readme files contain detailed information on installation issues for all of the products in Visual Studio.NET. The Readme files are in HTML format and can be viewed with an Internet browser such as Microsoft Internet Explorer 4.0 or later. For information on locating Readme files, refer to the topic Locating Readme Files.

Side-by-Side Installations of Visual Studio.NET

Visual Studio supports installation of versions 2002 and 2003 on the same machine, which allows you to evaluate the latest version of Visual Studio and upgrade gradually.

You should be aware of the following conditions.

➤ If you open a solution created with Visual Studio.NET 2002 in Visual Studio.NET 2003 and save the solution, you can no longer open the solution in Visual Studio.NET 2002.

➢ Visual Studio.NET 2002 shipped with version 1.0 of the Microsoft.NET Framework SDK; Visual Studio.NET 2003 shipped with version 1.1. If you have both versions of the .NET Framework installed, Visual Studio.NET 2003 allows you to choose which version your projects support. Visual Basic, Visual C#, and Visual J# projects use a new property, Supported Runtimes. Visual C++ provides a way to manually specify runtime support.

➢ You can copy certain Options dialog box settings from Visual Studio.NET 2002 to Visual Studio.NET 2003.

➢ Changes in how ProgIDs are handled in the Visual Studio.NET 2003 Automation model can cause errors with add-ins written in Visual Studio.NET 2002. Also, invoking new instantiations of the Visual Studio.NET IDE now requires a version-dependent ProgID.

Side-by-Side Installations of Help

If you install Visual Studio.NET 2002 and Visual Studio.NET 2003 on the same machine, you also install two different versions of Help for Visual Studio.

You should be aware of the following conditions:

➢ The Help that installs with Visual Studio.NET 2003 includes corrections and additional information that also applies to Visual Studio.NET 2002 as well as new information for the features and updates provided in Visual Studio.NET 2003.

➢ To save space on your machine, you can specify that Visual Studio.NET 2002 use the version of Help included with Visual Studio.NET 2003 and then uninstall the Visual Studio.NET 2002 Help files.

➢ If you attempt to view the topics you included in your Favorites from Visual Stu-dio.NET 2002 in the Help for Visual Studio.NET 2003, the topic titles will appear, but the links will be broken.

➢ If you open a Visual Basic project that was upgraded from Visual Basic 6.0 in Visual Studio.NET 2003, any Help links in the project will be broken.

User Permissions

You must have Administrator permissions for the computer on which you are installing the product. You do not, however, need Administrator permissions to use Visual Studio after installation. Most tools require only the basic permissions provided by the Users group. Visual Studio has its own user groups, such as Debugger Users or VS Developers, for certain tools. For example, you must be a member of the VS Developers group to create Web projects on your local machine. If you do not have the correct permissions to use a certain tool, Visual Studio provides an alert to notify you.

Advanced Setup Options

Visual Studio.NET setup provides two specialized installations modes: Administrator and Remote components.

➢ Administrator Setup. This mode of setup allows network administrators to silently deploy to client computers. Administrator setup allows you to create custom installation files for Visual Studio.NET Prerequisites and the main Visual Studio.NET installation.

For more information on Administrator setup for Visual Studio.NET Prerequisites, see adminreadme.htm in the \Help folder in the Visual Studio.NET Prerequisites CD or on the Visual Studio.NET DVD in the \wcu\Help folder.

For more information on Administrator setup for the main Visual Studio.NET installation, see adminreadme.htm in the Setup folder in the Visual Studio.NET CD or DVD.

➢ Remote Components Setup. This mode of setup allows you to install select components, such as debugging and analysis components, on remote computers. For more information, see RemoteComponents.htm at the root of Visual Studio.NET CD or DVD.

Service Releases

You can check for service releases applicable to your installation directly from within the integrated development environment (IDE).

Note: Your computer must be able to connect to the Internet to check for available service releases online, or you must have a service pack CD.

If an update is available, you will be prompted to close the IDE and install the service release.

You can check for available service release using Add/Remove programs as well.

Registering the Product

If you choose not to register the product at the end of setup, you can register the product using other methods.

Repairing Your Product Installation

If you are experiencing problems or unexpected behavior while using this product, you can easily repair your current installation by using the Add/Remove Programs dialog box; choose the product you have installed, such as Visual Studio.NET, and then choose Change/Remove. Setup allows you to repair both Visual Studio.NET Prerequisites and the main product installation.

Unit 10　Object-oriented Programming Concepts

WORDS AND EXPRESSIONS

variable ['vɛəriəbl]　变量

models ['mɔdl]　模型

superclass ['sju:pə,klɑ:s, -klæs]　超类

subclass ['sʌbklɑ:s]　子类

function ['fʌŋkʃən]　函数

subroutine [ˌsʌbru:'ti:n]　子程序

instance ['instəns]　实例

encapsulation ['instəns]　封装

inheritance [in'heritəns]　继承

gear [giə]　车辆排档，传动装置

pedal ['pedl]　踏板

clip [klip]　剪辑

blueprint ['blu:,print]　蓝图

tandem ['tændəm]　双人自行车

penny-farthing ['peni] ['fɑ:ðiŋ]　19 世纪末的前轮大后轮小的老式自行车

GUI (Graphical User Interface)　图形用户界面

protective custody　置于保护之下

rpm (revolutions per minute)　转数 / 分

QUESTIONS AND ANSWERS

1. What's the characteristic of Object?

2. What does information hiding mean?

3. What are the components that comprise a message?

4. What can subclasses do besides inheriting state from the superclass?

5. Compared with the traditional method, what is the main advantage of Object-oriented technology?

TEXT

What Is an Object?

Objects are key to understanding object-oriented technology. You can look around you now and see many examples of real-world objects: your dog, your desk, your television set, your bicycle.

These real-world objects share two characteristics: they all have state and behavior. For example, dogs have state (name, color, breed, hunger) and behavior (barking, fetching, and wagging tail). Bicycles have state (current gear, current pedal cadence, two wheels, number of gears) and behavior (braking, accelerating, slowing down, changing gears).

Software objects are modeled after real-world objects in that they, too, have state and behavior. A software object maintains its state in one or more variables. A variable is an item of data named by an identifier. A software object implements its behavior with methods. A method is a function (subroutine) associated with an object.

Definition: An object is a software bundle of variables and related methods.

You can represent real-world objects by using software objects. You might want to represent real-world dogs as a software objects in an animation program or a real-world bicycle as a software object in the program that controls an electronic exercise bike. You can also use software objects to model abstract concepts. For example, an event is a common object used in GUI window systems to represent the action of a user pressing a mouse button or a key on the keyboard.

Everything that the software object knows (state) and can do (behavior) is expressed by the variables and methods within that object. A software object that modeled your real-world bicycle would have variables that indicated the bicycle's current state: its speed is 10 mph, its pedal cadence is 90 rpm, and its current gear is the 5th gear. These variables are formally known as instance variables because they contain the state for a particular bicycle object, and in object-oriented terminology, a particular object is called an instance.

In addition to its variables, the software bicycle would also have methods to brake, change the pedal cadence, and change gears. (The bike would not have a method for changing the speed of the bicycle, as the bike's speed is just a side effect of what gear it's in, how fast the rider is pedaling, whether the brakes are on, and how steep the hill is.) These methods are formally known as instance methods because they inspect or change the state of a particular bicycle instance.

The object's variables make up the center, or nucleus of the object. Methods surround and hide the object's nucleus from other objects in the program. Packaging an object's variables within the protective custody of its methods is called encapsulation. This conceptual picture of an object() a nucleus of variables packaged within a protective membrane of methods() is an ideal representation of an object and is the ideal that designers of object-oriented systems strive for. However, it's not the whole story. Often, for practical reasons, an object may wish to expose some of its variables or hide some of its methods. In the Java programming language, an object can specify one of four access levels for each of its variables and methods. The access level determines which other objects and classes can access that variable or method. Encapsulating related variables and methods into a neat software bundle is a simple yet powerful idea that provides two primary benefits to software developers.

Modularity

The source code for an object can be written and maintained independently of the source code for other objects. Also, an object can be easily passed around in the system. You can give your bicycle to someone else, and it will still work.

Information hiding

An object has a public interface that other objects can use to communicate with it. The object can maintain private information and methods that can be changed at any time without affecting the other objects that depend on it. You don't need to understand the gear mechanism on your bike to use it.

What Is a Message?

A single object alone is generally not very useful. Instead, an object usually appears as a component of a larger program or application that contains many other objects. Through the interaction of these objects, programmers achieve higher-order functionality and more complex behavior. Your bicycle hanging from a hook in the garage is just a bunch of titanium alloy and rubber; by itself, the bicycle is incapable of any activity. The bicycle is useful only when another object (you) interacts with it (pedal).

Software objects interact and communicate with each other by sending messages to each other. When object A wants object B to perform one of B's methods, object A sends a message to object B.

Sometimes, the receiving object needs more information so that it knows exactly what to do; for example, when you want to change gears on your bicycle, you have to indicate which gear you want. This information is passed along with the message as parameters.

➢ The three components comprise a message:

➢ The object to which the message is addressed;

➢ The name of the method to perform;

➢ Any parameters needed by the method.

These three components are enough information for the receiving object to perform the desired method. No other information or context is required.

Messages provide two important benefits.

➢ An object's behavior is expressed through its methods, so (aside from direct variable access) message passing supports all possible interactions between objects.

> Objects don't need to be in the same process or even on the same machine to send and receive messages back and forth to each other.

What Is a Class?

In the real world, you often have many objects of the same kind. For example, your bicycle is just one of many bicycles in the world. Using object-oriented terminology, we say that your bicycle object is an instance of the class of objects known as bicycles. Bicycles have some state (current gear, current cadence, two wheels) and behavior (changing gears, braking) in common. However, each bicycle's state is independent of and can be different from that of other bicycles.

In object-oriented software, it's also possible to have many objects of the same kind that share characteristics: rectangles, employee records, video clips, and so on. Like the bicycle manufacturers, you can take advantage of the fact that objects of the same kind are similar and you can create a blueprint for those objects. A software blueprint for objects is called a class.

Classes can define class variables. A class variable contains information that is shared by all instance of the class. For example, suppose that all bicycles had the same number of gears. In this case, defining an instance variable to hold the number of gears is inefficient; each instance would have its own copy of the variable, but the value would be the same for every instance. In such situations, you can define a class variable that contains the number of gears. All instances share this variable. If one object changes the variable, it changes for all other objects of that type. A class can also declare class methods. You can invoke a class method directly from the class, whereas you must invoke instance methods on a particular instance.

You probably noticed that objects and classes look very similar. And indeed, the difference between classes and objects is often the source of some confusion. In the real world, it's obvious that classes are not themselves the objects they describe: A blueprint of a bicycle is not a bicycle. However, it's a little more difficult to differentiate classes and objects in software. This is partially because software objects are merely electronic models of real-world objects or abstract concepts in the first place. But it's also because the term "object" is sometimes used to refer to both classes and instances.

What Is Inheritance?

Generally speaking, objects are defined in terms of classes. You know a lot about an object by knowing its class. Even if you don't know what a penny-farthing is, if I told you it was a bicycle, you would know that it had two wheels, handle bars, and pedals.

Object-oriented systems take this a step further and allow classes to be defined in terms of other classes. For example, mountain bikes, racing bikes, and tandems are all kinds of bicycle. In object-oriented terminology, mountain bikes, racing bikes, and tandems are all subclasses of the bicycle class. Similarly, the bicycle class is the superclass of mountain bikes, racing bikes, and tandems.

Each subclass inherits state (in the form of variable declarations) from the superclass. Mountain bikes, racing bikes, and tandems share some states: cadence, speed, and the like. Also, each subclass inherits methods from the superclass. Mountain bikes, racing bikes, and tandems share some behaviors: braking and changing pedaling speed, for example.

However, subclasses are not limited to the state and behaviors provided to them by their superclass. Subclasses can add variables and methods to the ones they inherit from the superclass. Tandem bicycles have two seats and two sets of handle bars; some mountain bikes have an extra set of gears with a lower gear ratio.

Subclasses can also override inherited methods and provide specialized implementations for those methods. For example, if you had a mountain bike with an extra set of gears, you would override the "change gears" method so that the rider could use those new gears.

You are not limited to just one layer of inheritance. The inheritance tree, or class hierarchy, can be as deep as needed. Methods and variables are inherited down through the levels.

The object class is at the top of class hierarchy, and each class is its descendant (directly or indirectly). A variable of type Object can hold a reference to any object, such as an instance of a class or an array. Object provides behaviors that are required of any object, running in the Java Virtual Machine. For example, all classes inherit Object's to String method, which returns a string representation of the object.

Subclasses provide specialized behaviors from the basis of common elements provided by the superclass. Through the use of inheritance, programmers can reuse the code in the superclasses many times.

Programmers can implement superclasses called abstract classes that define "generic" behaviors. The abstract superclass defines and may partially implement the behavior, but much of the class is undefined and unimplemented. Other programmers fill in the details with specialized subclasses.

EXERCISES

1. Judge whether the following given statements are true or false. If correct, write T in parentheses; otherwise, write F.

(1) (   ) A software object maintains its state in only one variable.

(2) (   ) Packaging an object's variables within the protective custody of its methods is called inheritance.

(3) (   ) Object-oriented systems forbid classes to be defined in terms of other classes.

(4) (   ) A variable of type Object can hold a reference to any object.

2. Complete the following note-taking with the information mentioned in the text.

(1) A software object that modeled your real-world bicycle would have _____ that indicated the bicycle's current state.

(2) Subclasses can add variables and methods to the ones they inherit from the _____.

(3) Software objects are merely electronic _____ of real-world objects or abstract concepts.

(4) Subclasses provide specialized _____ from the basis of common elements.

READING MATERIALS

Product Description: ASP.NET

The History of ASP.NET

ASP.NET is a web application framework developed and marketed by Microsoft, which programmers can use to build dynamic web sites, web applications and web services. It was first released in January 2002 with version 1.0 of the .NET Framework, and is the successor to Microsoft's Active Server Pages (ASP) technology. ASP.NET is built on the Common Language Runtime (CLR), allowing programmers to write ASP.NET code using any supported .NET language.

After the release of Internet Information Services 4.0 in 1997, Microsoft began researching possibilities for a new web application model that would solve common complaints about ASP, especially with regard to separation of presentation and content and being able to write "clean" code. Mark Anders, a manager on the IIS team, and Scott Guthrie, who had joined Microsoft in 1997 after graduating from Duke University, were tasked with determining what that model would look like. The initial design was developed over the course of two months by Anders and Guthrie, and Guthrie coded the initial prototypes during the Christmas holidays in 1997.

The initial prototype was called "XSP"; Guthrie explained in a 2007 interview that, "People would always ask what the X stood for. At the time it really didn't stand for anything. XML started with that; XSLT started with that. Everything cool seemed to start with an X, so that's what we originally named it." The initial development of XSP was done using Java, but it was soon decided to build the new platform on top of the Common Language Runtime instead. Guthrie described this decision as a "huge risk", as the success of their new web development platform would be tied to the success of the CLR, which, like XSP, was still in the early stages of development, so much so that the XSP team was the first team at Microsoft to target the CLR.

With the move to the Common Language Runtime, XSP was re-implemented in C# (known internally as "Project Cool" but kept secret from the public), and renamed to ASP+, as by this point the new platform was seen as the successor to Active Server Pages, and the intention was to provide an easy migration path for ASP developers.

Mark Anders first demonstrated ASP+ at the ASP Connections conference in Phoenix, Arizona on May 2, 2000. Demonstrations to the wide public and initial beta release of ASP+ (and the rest of the .NET Framework) came at the 2000 Professional Developers Conference on July 11, 2000 in Orlando, Florida. During Bill Gates's keynote presentation, Fujitsu demonstrated ASP+ being used in conjunction with COBOL, and support for a variety of other languages was announced, including Microsoft's new Visual Basic .NET and C# languages, as well as Python and Perl support by way of interoperability tools created by ActiveState.

Once the ".NET" branding was decided on in the second half of 2000, it was decided to rename ASP+ to ASP.NET. Mark Anders explained on an appearance on The MSDN Show that year that, "The .NET initiative is really about a number of factors, it's about delivering software as a service, it's about XML and web services and really enhancing the Internet in terms of what it can do ... we really wanted to bring its name more in line with the rest of the platform pieces that make up the .NET framework."

After four years of development, and a series of beta releases in 2000 and 2001, ASP.NET 1.0 was released on January 5, 2002 as part of version 1.0 of the .NET Framework. Even prior to the release, dozens of books had been written about ASP.NET, and Microsoft promoted it heavily as part of their platform for web services. Guthrie became the product unit manager for ASP.NET, and development continued apace, with version 1.1 being released on April 24, 2003 as a part of Windows Server 2003. This release focused on improving ASP.NET's support for mobile devices.

The Characteristics of ASP.NET

ASP.NET pages, known officially as "web forms", are the main building block for application development. Web forms are contained in files with an ASPX extension; in programming jargon, these files typically contain static HTML or XHTML markup, as well as markup defining server-side Web Controls and User Controls where the developers place all the required static and dynamic content for the web page. Additionally, dynamic code which runs on the server can be placed in a page within a block "<% -- dynamic code -- %>" which is similar to other web development technologies such as PHP, JSP, and ASP, but this practice is generally discouraged except for the purposes of data binding since it requires more calls when rendering the page.

Sample web form.(Note that this sample uses code "inline", as opposed to code behind.)

```
<%@ Page Language="C#" %>
<!DOCTYPE html PUBLIC "-//W3C//DTD XHTML 1.0 Transitional//EN"
"http://www.w3.org/TR/xhtml1/DTD/xhtml1-transitional.dtd">
 <script runat="server">
    protected void PageLoad(object sender, EventArgs e)
    {
        Label1.Text = DateTime.Now.ToLongDateString();
    }
</script>
<html xmlns="http://www.w3.org/1999/xhtml" >
<head runat="server">
    <title>Sample page</title>
</head>
<body>
    <form id="form1" runat="server">
    <div>
        <asp:Label runat="server" id="Label1" />
    </div>
```

```
    </form>
</body>
</html>
```

➢ Code-behind Model. It is recommended by Microsoft for dealing with dynamic program code to use the code-behind model, which places this code in a separate file or in a specially designated script tag. Code-behind files typically have names like MyPage.aspx.cs or MyPage.aspx.vb based on the ASPX file name (this practice is automatic in Microsoft Visual Studio and other IDEs). When using this style of programming, the developer writes code to respond to different events, like the page being loaded, or a control being clicked, rather than a procedural walk through the document.

ASP.NET's code-behind model marks a departure from Classic ASP in that it encourages developers to build applications with separation of presentation and content in mind. In theory, this would allow a web designer, for example, to focus on the design markup with less potential for disturbing the programming code that drives it. This is similar to the separation of the controller from the view in model-view-controller frameworks.

➢ User Controls. ASP.NET supports creating reusable components through the creation of User Controls. A User Control follows the same structure as a Web Form, except that such controls are derived from the System.Web.UI.UserControl class, and are stored in ASCX files. Like ASPX files, a ASCX contains static HTML or XHTML markup, as well as markup defining web control and other User Controls. The code-behind model can be used.

Programmers can add their own properties, methods, and event handlers. An event bubbling mechanism provides the ability to pass an event fired by a user control up to its containing page.

➢ Rendering Technique. ASP.NET uses a visited composites rendering technique. During compilation, the template (.aspx) file is compiled into initialization code which will build a control tree (the composite) representing the original (static) template. Literal text goes into instances of the Literal control class, and server controls are represented by instances of a specific control class. The initialization code is combined with user-written code (usually by the assembly of multiple partial classes) and results in a class specific for the page. The page doubles as the root of the control tree.

Actual requests for the page are processed through a number of steps. First, during the initialization steps, an instance of the page class is created and the initialization code is executed. This produces the initial control tree which is now typically manipulated by the methods of the page in the following steps. As each node in the tree is a control represented as an instance of a class, the code may change the tree structure as well as manipulate the properties/methods of the individual nodes. Finally, during the rendering step a visitor is used to visit every node in the tree, asking each node to render itself using the methods of the visitor. The resulting HTML output is sent to the client.

After the request has been processed, the instance of the page class is discarded and with it the entire control tree.

➢ State Management. ASP.NET applications are hosted in a web server and are accessed over the stateless HTTP protocol. As such, if the application uses stateful interaction, it has to implement state management on its own. ASP.NET provides various functionality for state management in ASP.NET applications.

- Application State. Application state is a collection of user-defined variables that are shared by all invocations of an ASP.NET application. These are set and initialized when the ApplicationOnStart event fires on the loading of the first instance of the applications and are available till the last instance exits. Application state variables are accessed using the Applications collection, which provides a wrapper for the application state variables. Application state variables are identified by names.

- Session State. Session state is a collection of user-defined session variables, which are persisted during a user session. These variables are unique to different instances of a user session, and are accessed using the Session collection. Session variables can be set to be automatically destroyed after a defined time of inactivity, even if the session does not end. At the client end, a user session is identified either by a cookie or by encoding the session ID in the URL itself.

ASP.NET supports three modes of persistence for session variables.

InProc—The session variables are maintained within the ASP.NET process. However, in this mode the variables are destroyed when the ASP.NET process is recycled or shut down.

StateServer—In this mode, ASP.NET runs a separate Windows service that maintains the state variables. Because the state management happens outside the ASP.NET process, this has a negative impact on performance, but it allows multiple ASP.NET instances to share the same state server, thus allowing an ASP.NET application to be load-balanced and scaled out on multiple servers. Also, since the state management service runs independent of ASP.NET, variables can persist across ASP.NET process shutdowns.

SqlServer—In this mode, the state variables are stored in a database server, accessible using SQL. Session variables can persist across ASP.NET process shutdowns in this mode as well.

- View State. View state refers to the page-level state management mechanism, which is utilized by the HTML pages emitted by ASP.NET applications to maintain the state of the web form controls and widgets. The state of the controls are encoded and sent to the server at every form submission in a hidden field known as_VIEWSTATE. The server sends back the variable so that when the page is re-rendered, the controls render at their last state. At the server side, the application might change the view state, if the processing results in updating the state of any control. The states of individual controls are decoded at the server, and are available for use in ASP.NET pages using the ViewState collection.

➢ Template Engine. When first released, ASP.NET lacked a template engine. Because the .NET framework is object-oriented and allows for inheritance, many developers would define a new base class that inherits from "System.Web.UI.Page", write methods here that render HTML, and then make the pages in their application inherit from this new class. While this allows for common elements to be reused across a site, it adds complexity and mixes source code with markup. Furthermore, this method can only be visually tested by running the application—not while designing it. Other developers have used include files and other tricks to avoid having to implement the same navigation and other elements in every page.

ASP.NET 2.0 introduced the concept of "master pages", which allow for template-based page development. A web application can have one or more master pages, which can be nested. Master templates have place-holder controls, called ContentPlaceHolders to denote where the dynamic content will go, as well as HTML and JavaScript that will be shared across child pages.

Child pages use those ContentPlaceHolder controls, which must be mapped to the place-holder of the master page that the content page is populating. The rest of the page is defined by the shared parts of the master page, much like a mail merge in a word processor. All markup and server controls in the content page must be placed within the ContentPlaceHolder control.

When a request is made for a content page, ASP.NET merges the output of the content page with the output of the master page, and sends the output to the user.

The master page remains fully accessible to the content page. This means that the content page may still manipulate headers, change title, configure caching etc. If the master page exposes public properties or methods (e.g. for setting copyright notices) the content page can use these as well.

Unit 11　C++ and Java

WORDS AND EXPRESSIONS

polymorphism [ˌpɔli'mɔːfizəm]　多态性
reference ['refrəns]　参考文献
Simula　一种早期的面向对象的计算机语言
BCPL (Basic Combined Programming Language)　基本组合程序设计语言
CFront　第一个 C++编译器，源自 Bell 实验室
ANSI (American National Standards Institute)　美国国家标准协会
ISO (International Organization for Standardization)　国际标准化组织
IEC (International Electro technical Commission)　国际电工委员会
Ph.D. (Doctor of Philosophy)　哲学博士（理学博士）

QUESTIONS AND ANSWERS

1. How many major compilers does C++ have? And what are they?
2. Of different C++ compilers what are the similarities and differences?
3. What is the function of the part between /* and */?
4. What are the basic types of C++?
5. What is the function of the symbol "++" in C++?
6. C++ is now the most common application programming language on the Microsoft Windows operating system, where does C remain more popular?

TEXT

The Basics of C++

C++ is a programming language. It is a programming language of many different dialects, just like each language that is spoken has many dialects. There are about four major ones: Borland C++, Microsoft Visual C++, Watcom C/386, and DJGPP. You can download DJGPP from http://www.delorie.com/djgpp/ or you may already have another compiler.

Each of these compilers is a little different. The library functions of one will have all of the standard C++ functions, but they will also have other functions. At times, this can lead to confusion, as certain programs will only run under certain compilers.

C++ (pronounced "see plus plus") is a general-purpose computer programming language. It is a statically typed, free-form, multi-paradigm language supporting procedural programming, data abstraction, object-oriented programming and generic programming. During the 1990's, C++ became one of the most popular commercial programming languages.

Stroustrup began work on C with Classes in 1979. The idea of creating a new language originated from Stroustrup's experience programming for his Ph.D.thesis. Stroustrup found that Simula had features that were very helpful for large software development but was too slow for practical uses, while BCPL was fast but too low-level and unsuitable for large software development. When Stroustrup started working in Bell Labs, he had the problem of analyzing the UNIX kernel with respect to distributed computing. Remembering his Ph.D. experience Stroustrup set out to enhance the C language with Simula-like features. C was chosen because it is general-purpose, fast and portable. At first, class (with data encapsulation), derived class, strong type checking, inlining, and default argument were features added to C.

As Stroustrup designed C with Classes, he also wrote Cfront, a compiler that generates C source codes from C with Classes source codes. The first commercial release occurred in October 1985.

In 1982, the name of the language was changed from C with Classes to C++. New features were added to the language including virtual functions, function name and operator overloading, references, constants, user-controlled free-store memory control, improved type checking, and a new comment style (//). In 1985, the first edition of The C++ programming Language was released, providing an important reference to the language, as there was not yet an official standard yet. In 1989 Release 2.0 of C++ was released. New features included multiple inheritance, abstract classes, static member functions, const member functions, and protected members. In 1990, the Annotated C++ Reference Manual was released and provided the basis for the future standard. Late addition of features included templates, exceptions, etc.

As the C++ language evolved, a standard library also evolved with it. The first addition to the C++ standard library was the stream I/O library which provided facilities to replace the traditional C functions such as printf and scanf. Later, among the most significant additions to the standard library, was the Standard Template Library.

After years of work, a joint ANSI-ISO committee standardized C++, in 1998 (ISO/IEC 14882—1998).

Three important features of C++ are encapsulation, inheritance and polymorphism.

Encapsulation

C++ fulfills the requirement of encapsulation by allowing all members of a class to be declared as either private, public, or protected. A public member of the class will be accessible to every other class. A protected member will only be accessible to the class in which it is in and the classes that inherit said class. A private member will only be accessible within that class. (Also, those functions declared as friends in the class will be able to access private members.) Obviously, it is possible to bypass encapsulation completely and declare all members of the class public, but these defeat the purpose of encapsulation which is that there are functions which will be able to control the modification of the data.

In general, this is what is generally thought of as "good Practice". One should make all data in a class private and the functions public only if they will be accessed outside the class.

Inheritance

As stated earlier, the Inheritance used in C++ is one that allows multiple inheritance and so therefore has sparked much debate. Many newer languages, such as Java, do not allow multiple inheritances. However, it is still a powerful feature in C++. This allows a base class to "be" as many classes as it is. For example, if you create a "Flying Cat" class it can inherit from both a "Cat" and "Flying Mammal". Also, in C++, a class must mention whether it will inherit the public members of the class or the protected members.

Polymorphism

Polymorphism is a bit complex, if you are interested in its special knowledge, you can get more help from your teacher.

An Introduction to Java Programming

Based on the enormous amount of press Java is getting and the amount of excitement it has generated, you may get the impression that Java will save the world or at least solve all the problems of the Internet. Not so. Java's hype has run far ahead of its capabilities, and while Java is indeed new and interesting, it really is another programming language with which you write programs that run on the Internet. In this respect, Java is closer to popular programming languages such as C, C++, Visual Basic, or Pascal, than it is to a page description language such as HTML, or a very simple scripting language such as JavaScript.

More specifically, Java is an object-oriented programming language developed by Sun Microsystems, a company best known for its high-end UNIX workstations. Modeled after C++, the Java language was designed to be small, simple, and portable across platforms and operating systems, both at the source and at the binary level, which means that Java programs (applets and applications) can run on any machine that has the Java virtual machine installed.

Java is usually mentioned in the context of the World Wide Web, where browsers such as Netscape's Navigator and Microsoft's Internet Explorer claim to be "Java enabled". "Java enabled" means that the browser in question can download and play Java programs, called "applets", on the reader's system. Applets appear in a Web page much the same way as images do, but unlike images, applets are dynamic and interactive. Applets can be used to create animation, figures, forms that immediately respond to input from the reader, games, or other interactive effects on the same Web pages among the text and graphics.

To create an applet, you write it in the Java language, compile it using a Java compiler, and refer to that applet in your HTML Web pages. You put the resulting HTML and Java files on a Web site in the same way that you make ordinary HTML and image files available. Then, when someone using a Java-enabled browser views your page with the embedded applet, that browser downloads the applet to the local system and executes it, allowing your reader to view and interact with your applet in all its glory. (Readers using other browsers may see text, a static graphic, or nothing.)

While applets are probably the most popular use of Java, the important thing to understand about Java is that you can do so much more with it than create and use applets. Java was written as a full-fledged general-purpose programming language in which you can accomplish the same sorts of tasks and solve the same sorts of problems that you can in other programming languages, such as C or C++.

The Java language was developed at Sun Microsystems in 1991 as part of a research project to develop software for consumer electronics devices—television sets, VCRs, toasters, and the other sorts of machines you can buy at any department store. Java's goals at that time were to be small, fast, efficient, and easily portable to a wide range of hardware devices. Those same goals make Java an ideal language for distributing executable programs via the World Wide Web and also a general-purpose programming language for developing programs that are easily usable and portable across different platforms.

The Java language was used in several projects within Sun (under the name Oak), but did not get very much commercial attention until it was paired with HotJava. HotJava, an experimental World Wide Web browser, was written in 1994 in a matter of months, both as a vehicle for downloading and running applets and also as an example of the sort of complex application that can be written in Java. Although HotJava got a lot of attention in the Web community, it wasn't until Netscape incorporated HotJava's ability to play applets into its own browser that Java really took off and started to generate the excitement that it has both on and off the World Wide Web. Java has generated so much excitement, in fact, that inside Sun the Java group spun off into its own subsidiary called JavaSoft.

Versions of Java itself, or, as it's most commonly called, the Java API, correspond to versions of Sun's Java Developer's Kit, or JDK. As of this writing, the current version of the JDK is 1.6.004. Previously released versions of the JDK (alphas and betas) did not have all the features or had a number of security-related bugs. Most Java tools and browsers conform to the features in the 1.6.004 JDK.

Currently, to program in Java, you'll need a Java development environment of some sort for your platform. Sun's JDK works just fine for this purpose and includes tools for compiling and testing Java applets and applications. In addition, a wide variety of excellent Java development environments have been developed, including Sun's own Java Workshop, Symantec's Café, Microsoft's Visual J++(which is indeed a Java tool, despite its name), and Natural Intelligence's Roaster, with more development tools appearing all the time.

What's in store for Java in the future? A number of new development have been brewing.

➢ Sun is developing a number of new features for the Java environment, including a number of new class libraries for database integration, multimedia, electronic commerce, and other uses. Sun also has a Java-based Web sever, a Java-based hardware chip (with which you can write Java-specific systems), and a Java-based operating system.

> Sun is also developing a framework called Java Beans, which will allow the development of component objects in Java, similarly to Microsoft's ActiveX (OLE) technology. These different components can then be easily combined and interact with each other using standard component assembly tools.

> Java capabilities will be incorporated into a wide variety of operating systems, including Solaris, Windows Vista, and Mac OS. This means that Java applications (as opposed to applets) can run nearly anywhere without needing additional software to be installed.

> Many companies are working on performance enhancements for Java programs, including the aforementioned Java chip and what are called just-in-time compilers.

EXERCISES

1. Judge whether the following given statements are true or false. If correct, write T in parentheses; otherwise, write F.

(1)   (   ) C++ is a dynamicly-typed language.

(2)   (   ) BCPL was suitable for large software development.

(3)   (   ) A public member of the class will be accessible to every other class.

(4)   (   ) Java programs can run on any machine that has the Java virtual machine installed.

2. Complete the following note-taking with the information mentioned in the text.

(1)   C was chosen because it is general-purpose, fast and _____.

(2)   The first addition to the C++ standard library was _____.

(3)   Applets can be used to create interactive effects on the same Web pages among _____.

(4)   Java Beans is similar to Microsoft's _____.

READING MATERIALS

Product Description: Java Technology

Java technology was created as a computer programming tool in a small, secret effort called "the Green Project" at Sun Microsystems in 1991.

The secret "Green Team", fully staffed at 13 people and led by James Gosling, locked themselves away in an anonymous office on Sand Hill Road in Menlo Park, cut off all regular communications with Sun, and worked around the clock for 18 months.

They were trying to anticipate and plan for the "next wave" in computing. Their initial conclusion was that at least one significant trend would be the convergence of digitally controlled consumer devices and computers.

A device-independent programming language code-named "Oak" was the result.

To demonstrate how this new language could power the future of digital devices, the Green Team developed an interactive, handheld home-entertainment device controller targeted at the digital cable television industry. But the idea was too far ahead of its time, and the digital cable television industry wasn't ready for the leap forward that Java technology offered them.

As it turns out, the Internet was ready for Java technology, and just in time for its initial public introduction in 1995, the team was able to announce that the Netscape Navigator Internet browser would incorporate Java technology.

Now, nearing its twelfth year, the Java platform has attracted over 5 million software developers, worldwide use in every major industry segment, and a presence in a wide range of devices, computers, and networks of any programming technology.

In fact, its versatility, efficiency, platform portability, and security have made it the ideal technology for network computing, so that today, Java powers more than 4.5 billion devices:

> over 800 million PCs;
> over 1.5 billion mobile phones and other handheld devices (source: Ovum);
> 2.2 billion smart cards;
> plus set-top boxes, printers, web cams, games, car navigation systems, lottery terminals, medical devices, parking payment stations, etc.

Today, you can find Java technology in networks and devices that range from the Internet and scientific supercomputers to laptops and cell phones, from Wall Street market simulators to home game players and credit cards—just about everywhere.

The best way to preview these applications is to explore java.com, the ultimate marketplace, showcase, and central information resource for businesses, consumers, and software developers who use Java technology.

Why Software Developers Choose Java Technology?

The Java programming language has been thoroughly refined, extended, tested, and proven by an active community of over five million software developers.

Mature, extremely robust, and surprisingly versatile Java technology has become invaluable in allowing developers to:

> Write software on one platform and run it on practically any other platform;
> Create programs to run within a web browser and web services;
> Develop server-side applications for online forums, stores, polls, HTML forms processing, and more;
> Combine Java technology-based applications or services to create highly customized applications or services;
> Write powerful and efficient applications for mobile phones, remote processors, low-cost consumer products, and practically any device with a digital heartbeat.

GDI Graphics in Delphi

GDI stands for Graphics Device Interface, and is the interface that Windows uses for drawing 2D graphics. It is also, unfortunately, the slowest method around, but is useful for basic graphics. This tutorial will introduce you to some of the jargon and terms in the GDI.

The first point to note is that you should not attempt to use the GDI for any fancy graphical effects, like cross-fading pictures, as it is a bit primitive. For professional-looking graphics try using DirectX, OpenGL, or a graphics library (e.g. any of these, among others: DelphiX, FastLib, DIBUltra, Graphics32...). However, you can use the GDI for some neat effects, with a little creativity.

One common acronym you will find with GDI is DC ("Device Context"). This is what you draw on, and is represented in Delphi by TCanvas. The idea behind device contexts is to abstract the output device details, so you can use the same drawing functions for (e.g.) a screen or a printer.

Another (pretty important) note is that you will start by using the standard Delphi graphics functions, as these are wrappers for the GDI functions of Windows.

Unit 12 Fourth-generation Programming Language

WORDS AND EXPRESSIONS

frustrating [frʌs'treit] 枯燥的

prone [prəun] 易于

Mathematica [ˌmæθə'mætikə] 一款科学计算软件

hierarchy ['haiərɑ:ki] 层次

FORTRAN ['fɔ:træn]FORTRAN 语言，公式翻译程序语言

outsourcing ['aut.sɔ:siŋ] 外包

oracle ['ɔrəkl] 美国 ORACLE 公司主要生产数据库产品

non-procedural [nɔŋ][prə'si:dʒərəl] 非过程化

macro ['mækrou] 宏

stagnate ['stægneit] (使)停滞

limelight ['laim.lait] 引人注目的中心

Report generator 输出发生器

ad hoc ['æd'hɔk] 特别的，专设的

New Jersey [nju: 'dʒə:zi] （美国）新泽西州

Princeton ['prinstən] 普林斯顿（美国新泽西州中部的自治镇）

CT（Connecticut）[kə'netikət] （美国）康涅狄格州的缩写

Stamford ['stæmfəd] 斯坦福德（美国康涅狄格州西南部城市）

COBOL ['kəubəul] COmmon Business-Oriented Language 面向商业的通用语言

time-sharing 分时

RAMIS Rapid Access Management Information System 快速访问的信息管理系统

NOMAD 美国 NCSS 公司的一种数据库管理系统

high-level 高级的

IBI. (Information Builders, Inc) 美国 IBI 公司

Computer Associates 电脑联盟

PeopleSoft 网络软件供应商，2005 年 1 月被 Oracle 收购

SAP (Systems Applications and Products in Data Processing) SAP 既是公司名称又是其产品（企业管理解决方案）的软件名称

royalty payments 专利使用费

turn-key solutions 完全解决方案

DP (Data processing) 数据处理

inelegant and unmentionable code 杂乱而且不可维护的代码

QUESTIONS AND ANSWERS

1. What's the meaning of 4GL?
2. What's the difference between 3GL and 4GL?
3. What is the background of the generation of 4GL?
4. What are all 4GLs designed to? Is it successful?
5. What do the more ambitious 4GLs attempt to do?
6. What are the basic principles of 4GLs?

TEXT

A fourth-generation programming language (or 4GL) is a programming language designed with a specific purpose in mind such as the development of commercial business software.

The process of software development had been much improved with modern block structured third-generation programming languages but it was still frustrating, slow, and error prone to program computers. This led to the first "programming crisis", in which the amount of work that might be assigned to programmers greatly exceeded the amount of programmer time available to do it. Meanwhile, a lot of experience was gathered in certain areas, and it became clear that certain applications could be generalized by adding limited programming languages to them.

In 1969, a product called RAMIS from a group of people at Mathematica Products Group in Princeton, New Jersey was among the first of the languages dubbed a 4th Generation Language, or 4GL. It was available commercially, exclusively, on the time-sharing service provided by National CSS Inc. of Stamford, CT, on a version of IBM's CP-67/CMS known as VP/CSS. The authors included Dick Cobb and Gerry Cohen, with help from some NCSS folks, including Harold Feinlieb and Nick Rawlings. It had its own database structure, which was essentially a single path hierarchy, a powerful REVISE command for importing data, and a powerful reporting verb PRINT.

One could say PRINT ACROSS MONTH SUM SALES BY DIVISION and receive a report that would have taken many hundreds of lines of COBOL to produce. The product grew in capability and in revenue, both to NCSS and to Mathematica, who enjoyed increasing royalty payments from the sizable customer base.

In 1973, NCSS decided to fund the development of an alternative product, which in October of 1975 was released under the name NOMAD. That same month, Gerry Cohen left Mathematica and released a product called FOCUS, which he made available on Tymshare Inc's competing time-sharing system, with the promise to RAMIS users that their applications could run unmodified, and at a significant discount over NCSS's charges for RAMIS applications.

NOMAD from NCSS, later D&B Computing Services, became quite successful under the

VP/CSS operating system, generating some $100M per year by the mid 1980's. As NOMAD2, it became available under IBM's VM in 1983 and MVS in 1984. When the NOMAD software business was sold to Thomson, CSF in 1987, the customer base included over 800 of the Fortune 5000. In addition to providing its own relational database, NOMAD by 1984 had interfaces to IBM's SQL/DS and DB2, as well as VSAM and IMS, and Teradata's database computer. Software sales approached $30M annually. The importance of the 4GL language replaced the importance of its native database.

FOCUS from Information Builders, Inc. (IBI), did even better, with revenue approaching a reported $150M per year. RAMIS moved among several owners, ending at Computer Associates in 1990, and has had little limelight since NOMAD's owners, Thomson, continue to market the language from Aonix, Inc. While the three continue to deliver 10-to-1 coding improvements over the 3GL alternatives of Fortran, Cobol, or PL/1, the movements to object orientation and outsourcing have stagnated acceptance.

The owners of the three now count on maintenance and support revenues to remain profitable. Few new sales are made, as prospects look to PeopleSoft, SAP, Oracle, and others, to provide the turn-key solutions to their data warehousing and reporting requirements.

The term 4GL was according to James Martin first used in his 1982 book Applications Development Without Programmers to refer to non-procedural high-level specification languages. Nevertheless, the great majority of users of 4GLs would describe themselves as programmers and most 4GLs allowed for (or required) system logic to be written in a proprietary macro language of 3GL.

All 4GLs are designed to reduce programming effort, the time it takes to develop software and the cost of software development. They are not always successful in this task and sometimes result in inelegant and unmentionable code. However, given the right problem the use of an appropriate 4GL can be specially successful.

A number of different types of 4GLs exist:

Report generators take a description of the data format and the report to generate and from that they either generate the required report directly or they generate a program to generate the report.

Similarly forms generators manage online interactions with the application system users or generate programs to do so.

The more ambitious 4GLs (sometimes termed fourth generation environments) attempt to automatically generate whole systems from the outputs of CASE tools, specifications of screens and reports, and possible also the specification of some additional processing logic.

Some 4GLs have integrated tools, which allow for the easy specification of all the required information. Next we will list some examples.

James Martin's won Information Engineering systems development methodology was automated to allow the input of the results of system analysis and design in the form of Data Flow Diagrams, Entity Relationship Diagrams, Entity Life History Diagrams etc., from which hundreds of thousands of lines of COBOL would be generated overnight.

More recently Oracle Corporation's Oracle Designer and Oracle Developer 4GL products could be integrated to produce database definitions and the forms and reports programs.

The basic Principles of 4GLs includes:

➢ The Principle of Minimum Work;
➢ The Principle of Minimum Skill;
➢ The Principle of Avoiding Alien Syntax and Mnemonics;
➢ The Principle of Minimum Time;
➢ The Principle of Minimum Errors;
➢ The Principle of Minimum Maintenance;
➢ The Principle of Maximum Results.

And 4GLs have many unique properties. Some of them are:

➢ User Friendly;
➢ A nonprofessional programmer can obtain results with it;
➢ It employs the database management system directly;
➢ Programs for most applications can be created with 10 times fewer instructions than in a Third Generation Language.

Finally, to distinguish 4GLs from other languages, we have the following criteria:

➢ Is it intended for routine computing of ad hoc decision making?
➢ Is it intended for end users or DP professionals (many 4GLs are appropriate for both)?
➢ Does it require the skills of a programmer, or can an analyst who does not program in a 3GL use it?
➢ Is it on-line or off-line?
➢ Does it run on mainframes, minicomputers or personal computers?
➢ Can it access mainframe or remote databases?
➢ Is it genuinely easy to use?
➢ Can results be obtained with it very quickly?

EXERCISES

1. Judge whether the following given statements are true or false. If correct, write T in parentheses; otherwise, write F.

(1)　(　) RAMIS was the first of the languages dubbed a 3rd Generation Language.

(2)　(　) In November of 1975, Gerry Cohen released a product called FOCUS.

(3)　(　) NOMAD2 became available under IBM's VM in 1983 and MVS in 1984.

(4)　(　) Most 4GLs required system logic to be written in a proprietary macro language of 3GL.

2. Complete the following note-taking with the information mentioned in the text.

(1)　Programmers had been much improved the process of software development through modern block _____ 3GL.

(2)   RAMIS was available commercially, exclusively, on the _____ service provided by National CSS Inc. of Stamford, CT.

(3)   RAMIS moved among several owners, ending at _____ in 1990.

(4)   Sometimes 4GLs result in inelegant and unmentionable _____.

READING MATERIALS

Product Description: PowerBuilder

PowerBuilder, sometimes abbreviated PB, is a computer application development system created by Powersoft, which was later purchased by Sybase. Marketed as a Rapid Application Development (RAD) system, it includes tools for drawing the user interface and reports, and accessing database content. The tools are provided in an integrated development environment that is the application developer's interface to the capabilities of the system.

PowerBuilder has a native data-handling object called a DataWindow, which can be used to create, edit, and display data from the database. This object gives the programmer a number of tools for specifying and controlling user interface appearance and behavior, and also provides simplified access to database content. To some extent, the DataWindow frees the programmer from considering the differences between Database Management Systems from different vendors.

PowerBuilder also includes a scripting language, PowerScript, which is used to specify the application behavior when events occur. Events usually correspond to user actions, such as clicking on an element of the user interface, or closing a window.

As of July 2007, the latest release of PowerBuilder is version 11. It includes DataWindow.NET, which is a .NET-enabled version of PB's DataWindow control. It includes ASP.NET 2.0 Web Forms application capability.

PowerBuilder 10 and above use Unicode internally. This allows the use of characters from multiple languages concurrently. This affects the coding of API calls, however, the upgrade from PowerBuilder 9 to 10 automatically converts your existing API calls for you. Therefore, in PB10, you have a choice of making ANSI or Unicode API calls at the call level. PowerBuilder 10 supports reading and writing to flat files larger than 2GB. PB9.0 supports the TRY CATCH FINALLY syntax of error handling. PB10 has a built-in date-picker control.

PowerBuilder is used primarily for building business applications. There are also versions of PowerBuilder that can be used to build applications to run on mobile devices such as cell phones or PDAs.

PowerBuilder is used commonly by companies in the financial sector, in the United States, Canada, and the United Kingdom. It is also used by many government agencies. PowerBuilder remains in use at thousands of organizations around the world.

The PowerScript language supports Object-oriented features of Inheritance, Polymorphism, and Encapsulation, but does not support importing from DataWindow, which is the main window that applications use. Powerscript does not require the use of these features, however—this gives developers the power of OO with the flexibility to develop using one's own strategy. Some developers use a framework, such as PowerBuilder Foundation Classes (PFC), and from it inherit all objects such as windows.

The DataWindow is the key component which makes PowerBuilder so powerful. The DataWindow offers a powerful, visual SQL painter which supports outer joins, unions and subquery operations. It can convert SQL to Visual representation and back, so the developer can use native SQL if desired. DataWindow updates are automatic—it produces the proper SQL at runtime based on the DBMS to which the user is currently connected. This feature saves the developer from a very tedious chore.

The DataWindow also has the built-in ability to both retrieve data and update data via Stored Procedures. The user picks the Stored Procedure from a visual list.

In fact, the DataWindow itself is so powerful, many PowerBuilder applications have no framework, or only use inheritance in a limited way, because it is not necessary.

Another key strength is its database connectivity. PowerBuilder offers native interfaces to all major databases, as well as ODBC and OLE-DB, in the Enterprise version. PowerBuilder applications tend to support multiple databases with relative ease. There are many sophisticated connectivity options, such as:

> Asynchronous operations (so a long-running query won't "lock up" the application);
> Static Binding on or off;
> Integrated Security;
> Tracing of all SQL;
> Isolation Level;
> Password Expiration Dialog;
> Blocking Factor;
> Number of SQL statements to Cache;
> Use Connection Pool;
> Thread Safe;
> Trace ODBC API Calls.

As a result of its sophisticated connectivity, and the efficiency of the DataWindow, PowerBuilder applications have been observed to outperform many other competing applications in terms of the number of seconds it takes to retrieve data from a database and display it to the user. Updates are also trivial to code in most cases (1 to 4 lines of code), and run extremely quickly. Here is a sample PowerBuilder update script.

dw_1.AcceptText()

dw_1.Update()

PowerBuilder supports the following ways of interacting with a database.

DataWindow—This is the simplest, most powerful, and usually the fastest at run time.

Embedded SQL—This is a standard which, surprisingly, is not supported by some big-name development environments. Embedded SQL supports SELECT, INSERT, UPDATE, DELETE and cursors. It is a convenient way to do a simple update. Example:

UPDATE myemployee SET STATUS = 'A';

IF sqlca.sqlcode<>0 THEN ...

Dynamic SQL—This is offered in 4 formats. The user builds a string which may optionally have bind variables. Dynamic SQL may be used to create cursors as well.

PowerBuilder supports Active-X and OCX controls, both visible and non-visible. It also can use OLE Automation as a client. However, PowerBuilder supports only late binding, not early binding. Therefore, when using OLE Automation, a dropdown of possible actions is not provided. PowerBuilder can be a DDE client or server. This allows it to interoperate with other applications.

PowerBuilder can make Windows and third-party API calls, and, in general, works well with third-party libraries in DLL files, however it does not directly support callback functions.

PowerBuilder offers a "/pbdebug" runtime switch, which creates a log file. This can help track down a bug "in the field", as the user simply emails this log file to the deve-loper. It has another feature which can log all SQL statements to a file. It also has built-in performance profiling, an integrated debugger, context-sensitive help, and an active newsgroup to provide support.

PowerBuilder applications are typically compiled to p-code, which is then interpreted by the PowerBuilder runtime. Although it can be compiled to machine code (called c-code), a typical business application does not run any faster. Only applications which do an unusually large amount of computations with little I/O are likely to benefit from compiling to machine code.

Although PowerBuilder can work well for quickly developing very large applications with enterprise-level databases, the deployment to machine code for such application might take a considerable amount of compilation time by the developer. However, there is rarely a need for a developer to compile a PowerBuilder application to machine code, as PowerBuilder applications are typically deployed as interpreted code (p-code). The developer will ordinarily choose to deploy compiled p-code libraries (.pbd files) as separate files from the executable. Much like .dll's, this allows for application updates to consist of migrating only a single affected library. Even if it is desired to deploy an application to machine code, the compile only needs to be done once right before deployment and will not affect the development lifecycle of the application.

Extensibility of the language is also rather limited. The technologies provided to overcome this (ex. PowerBuilder Native Interface, or PBNI) are still rather tricky. To develop a solution that includes external C++ code may not only require a competent C++ developer, but also a PowerBuilder expert to guide the developer through the myriad of subtleties of the language and the PowerBuilder Virtual Machine.

Operating Systems

Unit 13   Windows

WORDS AND EXPRESSIONS

subsequently [ˈsʌbsikwəntli]   后来

compatible [kəmˈpætəbl]   兼容的

applications [æpliˈkeiʃəns]   应用程序

release [riˈliːs]   发布

vigor [ˈvigə]   活力

overhaul [ˌəuvəˈhɔːlˈəuvəhɔːl]   彻底检查

vendor [ˈvendɔː]   供应商

pre-emptive [priˈemptiv]   优先购买的

multitask [ˌmʌltiˈtaːsk]   多任务处理

revised [riˈvaizd]   改进的

specs [speks]   规格

convert [kənˈvəːt]   转换……

integrate [ˈintigreit,ˈintigrit, -greit]   集成

monitor [ˈmɔnitə]   显示器

navigate [ˈnævigreit]   定位

intranet [ˈintrənet]   内联网

consistent [kənˈsistənt]   一致的

plumb [plʌm]   管道

reliability [riˌlaiəˈbiləti]   可靠性

kernel [ˈkəːnəl]   核心

codebase   代码库

PageMaker   专业排版软件

Multiple Display Support   多显示支持

Active Desktop   活动桌面

GUI(Graphical User Interface)   图形用户界面

Disk Defragmenter Wizard   磁碟重组向导

Distributed File System   分布式文件系统

Millenium Edition   千禧版

Encrypted   加密的

QUESTIONS AND ANSWERS

1. When did Microsoft first begin to develop the Interface Manager?
2. When did Microsoft announce the development of Windows?
3. What are the characteristics of the Windows 2.0?
4. When did Microsoft release the Windows 95?
5. What does take over from the start of the DOS?
6. What interface did the Windows 98 integrate?
7. Which use was increased in the Windows 98?
8. Can you tell us something about the Windows NT 5.0?
9. When did NT5.0 is called Windows 2000?
10. When did Microsoft release the Windows XP?

TEXT

Microsoft first began development of the Interface Manager (subsequently renamed Microsoft Windows) in September 1981.

In 1983, Microsoft announced the development of Windows, a graphical user interface (GUI) for its own operating system (MS-DOS, see Figure 13-1), which had shipped for IBM PC and compatible computers since 1981. The product line has changed from a GUI product to a modern operating system over two families of design, each with its own codebase and default file system.

Figure 13-1　MS-DOS

Microsoft released Windows 2.0 in the fall of 1987, provided significant useability improvements to Windows. With the addition of icons and overlapping windows, Windows became a viable environment for development of major applications (Excel, Word for Windows, PageMaker and Micrografx Designer), and the sales were spurred by the runtime ("Single Application Environment") versions supplied by the independent software vendors.

Windows 3.0, released in May, 1990, was a complete overhaul of the Windows environment. With the capability to address memory beyond 640K and a much more powerful user interface, independent software vendors started developing Windows applications with vigor. The powerful new applications helped Microsoft sell more than 10 million copies of Windows, making it the best-selling graphical user interface in the history of computing.

Figure 13-2　Windows 95

Windows 95(Figure 13-2), released in August of 1995. A 32-bit system providing full pre-emptive multitasking advanced file systems, threading, networking and more. Includes MS-DOS 7.0, but takes over from DOS completely after starting. Also includes a completely revised user interface.

Windows 98, released in June of 1998. Integrated Web Browsing gives your desktop a browser-like interface. You will "browse" everything, including stuff on your local computer. Active Desktop allows you to setup your desktop to be your personal web page, complete with links and any web content. You can also place active desktop items, such as a stock ticker, that will update automatically. Internet Explorer 4.0 New browser that supports HTML 4.0 and has an enhanced user interface. ACPI supports OnNow specs for better power management of PCs. Multiple Display Support can expand your desktop onto up to 8 connected monitors. New Hardware will support the latest technology such as DVD, Firewire, USB, and AGP. Win32 Driver model uses same driver model as Windows NT 5.0 Disk Defragmenter Wizard enhanced hard drive defragmenter to speed up access to files and applications.

Windows NT 5.0 will include a host of new features. Like Windows 98, it will integrate Internet Explorer 4.0 into the operating system. This new interface will be matched up with the Distributed File System, which Microsoft says will provide a logical way to organize and navigate the huge volume of information an enterprise assembles on servers, independent of where the servers are physically located.

As of November 1998, NT 5.0 will be known as Windows 2000, making NT a "mainstream" operating system.

Feb. 17 2000, Windows 2000(Figure 13-3) provides an impressive platform of Internet, intranet, extranet, and management applications that integrate tightly with Active Directory. You can set up virtual private networks—secure, encrypted connec-tions across the Internet—with your choice of protocol. You can encrypt data on the network or on disk. You can give users consistent access to the same files and objects from any network-connected PC. You can use the Windows Installer to distribute software to users over the LAN.

Figure 13-3   Windows 2000 Professional

Thursday Sep. 14, 2000 Microsoft released Windows Me, short for Millenium Edition, which is aimed at the home user. The Me operating system boasts some enhanced multimedia features, such as an automated video editor and improved Internet plumbing. But unlike Microsoft's Windows 2000 OS which offers advanced security, reliability, and networking features Windows Me is basically just an upgrade to the DOS-based code on which previous Windows versions have been built.

Microsoft officially launches Windows XP(Figure 13-4) on October 25th. 2001. XP is a whole new kind of Windows for consumers. Under the hood, it contains the 32-bit kernel and driver set from Windows NT and

Figure 13-4   Windows XP Professional

Windows 2000. Naturally it has tons of new features that no previous version of Windows has, but it also doesn't ignore the pastold DOS and Windows programs will still run, and may even run better.

EXERCISES

1. Judge whether the following given statements are true or false. If correct, write T in parentheses; otherwise, write F.

(1)   (   ) Microsoft first began development of the Interface Manager in September 1981.

(2)   (   ) In late 1987 Microsoft released Windows 2.0.

(3)   (   ) Active Desktop allows you to setup your desktop to be your personal web page, complete with links and any web content.

(4)   (   ) Microsoft officially launches windows XP on October 25th. 2001.

2. Complete the following note-taking with the information mentioned in the text.

(1)   In 1983, Microsoft announced the development of Windows, ＿＿＿＿＿＿ for its own operating system (MS-DOS), which had shipped for IBM PC and compatible computers since 1981.

(2)   Windows 3.0, released in ＿＿＿＿＿, was a complete overhaul of the Windows environment.

(3)   Feb. 17 2000, ＿＿＿＿＿ provides an impressive platform of Internet, intranet, extranet, and management applications that integrate tightly with Active Directory.

(4)   Naturally it has tons of new features that no previous version of Windows has, but it also doesn't ignore the past--old DOS and ＿＿＿＿＿ will still run, and may even run better.

READING MATERIALS

Product Description: Features New To Windows 7(Figure 13-5)

Windows 7 is the latest release of Microsoft Windows, a series of operating systems produced by Microsoft for use on personal computers, including home and business desktops, laptops, net books, tablet PCs, and media center PCs. Windows 7 was released to manufacturing on July 22, 2009, and reached general retail availability on October 22, 2009, less than three years after the release of its predecessor, Windows Vista. Windows 7's server counterpart, Windows Server 2008 R2, was released at the same time.

Figure 13-5   Windows 7 system

Windows 7 includes a number of new features, such as

advances in touch and handwriting recognition, support for virtual hard disks, improved performance on multi-core processors. Windows 7 adds support for systems using multiple heterogeneous graphics cards from different vendors (Heterogeneous Multi-adapter), a new version of Windows Media Center, a Gadget for Windows Media Center, improved media features, the XPS Essentials Pack and Windows PowerShell being included, and are designed Calculator with multiline capabilities including Programmer and Statistics modes along with unit conversion. Many new items have been added to the Control Panel, including ClearType Text Tuner, Display Color Calibration Wizard, Gadgets, Recovery, Troubleshooting, Workspaces Center, Location and Other Sensors, Credential Manager, Biometric Devices, System Icons, and Display. Windows Security Center has been renamed to Windows Action Center (Windows Health Center and Windows Solution Center in earlier builds), which encompasses both security and maintenance of the computer. Readyboost on 32bit editions now supports up to 256 Gigabytes of extra allocation. The default setting for User Account Control in Windows 7 has been criticized for allowing untrusted software to be launched with elevated privileges without a prompt by exploiting a trusted application. Microsoft's Windows kernel engineer Mark Russinovich acknowledged the problem, but noted that malware can also compromise a system when users agree to a prompt. Windows 7 also supports images in the RAW image format through the addition of Windows Imaging Component-enabled image decoders, which enables raw image thumbnails, previewing and metadata display in Windows Explorer, plus full-size viewing and slideshows in Windows Photo Viewer and Window Media Center.

The taskbar has seen the biggest visual changes, where the Quick Launch toolbar has been replaced with the "Superbar" allowing applications to be pinned to the taskbar. Buttons for pinned applications are integrated with the task buttons. These buttons also enable the Jump Lists feature to allow easy access to common tasks. The revamped taskbar also allows the reordering of taskbar buttons. To the far right of the system clock is a small rectangular button that serves as the Show desktop icon. This button is part of the new feature in Windows 7 called Aero Peek. Hovering over this button makes all visible windows transparent for a quick look at the desktop. In touch-enabled displays such as touch screens, tablet PCs, etc., this button is slightly wider to accommodate being pressed with a finger. Clicking this button minimizes all windows, and clicking it a second time restores them. Additionally, there is a feature named Aero Snap, that automatically maximizes a window when it is dragged to the top of the screen. Dragging windows to the left/right edges of the screen allows users to snap documents or files on either side of the screen for comparison between windows. When a user moves windows that were maximized using Aero Snap, the system restores their previous state automatically. This functionality is also accomplished with keyboard shortcuts. Unlike in Windows Vista, window borders and the taskbar do not turn opaque when a window is maximized with Windows

Aero applied. Instead, they remain translucent.

Although the direct quote from Ballmer was not released, a transcript from the White House quoted Obama raising the concerns from Steve Ballmer.

Microsoft has been battling piracy for years in America, and has gained tremendous ground in the market.

Unit 14　Mac OS

WORDS AND EXPRESSIONS

compatibility　兼容性

Internally　国内的

compression　压缩

adware　广告

shimmering　闪耀的

bundle ['bʌndl]　捆绑

conscience ['kɔnʃəns]　良心

malicious [mə'liʃəs]　恶意的

directory [di'rektəri, dai-]　目录；工商名录；姓名地址录

essence ['esəns]　本质，实质；精华；

representation [ˌreprizen'teiʃən]　表现；陈述；表示法；代表

integrated ['intireitid]　综合的；完整的；互相协调的

assembler [ə'semblə]　汇编程序；汇编机；装配工

Motorola　摩托罗拉（美国主营电子的公司）

Macintosh　Apple 公司于 1984 年推出的一种系列微机

Power PC　IBM 和 Apple 公司联合生产的个人台式机

QUESTIONS AND ANSWERS

1. Have you used MAC before?

2. What is the classic desktop is designed as?

3. When the System software 7.6 the name was changed to Mac OS?

4. What is the disadvantage of the optimization of the operating system to the hardware?

5. What is Mac Os X? How many versions of Mac Os are there?

6. Why does so many people use Mac Os X?

7. What's the diference between Windows and Mac Os X?

8. What are the advanced features of Mac Os X?

9. What are the most famous programs of Mac Os X?

10. What are there reasons make you become a Mac fan?

TEXT

Mac OS was named by the company Apple as "Mac System Software" in the beginning, a specially designed operating system only for 68K first Motorola processors. With own Macintosh hardware, Mac OS takes up a special role in the world of desktop systems. The first version was "System 1" and appeared bundled with the Mac in 1984. The classic desktop is designed as a single user operating system and almost completely hides the full path to files and directories. The graphic representation is reduced to the essence. Overall the interface is very easy to use and does not need the right mouse button for user interaction. Mac OS does not include a command line in_ terface.

Starting with System 3.0, the used file system HFS was used officially, which does not different between uppercase and lowercase letters. System 5.0 was the first release to run several programs with the integrated MultiFinder at the same time. The operating system was programmed up to system 6.0 mostly in assembler and partially in Pascal and used a 24-bit addressing mode. Cooperative Multi-tasking could optionally be enabled in System 6. System 7.0 first supported 32-bit addressing. Thus allow the operating system can use more memory and more powerful programs. Since 1994 System 7.5 supported for the first time the PowerPC architecture. With System software 7.6 the name was changed to Mac OS in January 1997.

The optimization of the operating system to the hardware has the disadvantage that the system software can not be installed on every Mac.

In 2006 ,Mac OS X was presented for the first time publicly on x86 hardware, Apple allows the use of Mac OS X only on specific intel-Macintosh systems. According to Steve Jobs Mac OS X have been developed since 2000 internally parallel for Intel and PowerPC processors. The version of Mac OS X 10.6.0 raised the optimization to Intel-based processors further, the new operating system is no longer available for PowerPC Macintosh or pure 32-bit intel processors. In return the user receives a pure 64-bit operating system optimized for performance on multiple processors. Even the GPU computing power itself can be used with specific applications.

The selection of software is focused on the creative industry and enables such as the professional graphic, audio and video editing. Office applications such as MacWrite, Microsoft Office, OpenOffice and 3D games are also available. The choice of browsers is large with iCab, Microsoft Internet Explorer, Netscape, Opera and Mozilla Firefox. Stuffit is the standard software for file compression.

These days, a key attraction of the Mac—at least as far as switchers are concerned—is its security features. There isn't yet a single widespread Mac OS X virus. "Even Microsoft Word macro viruses don't run in Mac OS X." For many people, that's a good enough reason to move to Mac OS X right there.

Along the same lines, there have been no reported sightings of adware software that displays annoying ads when you use your Web browseror spyware (malicious software that tracks your computer use and reports it back to a shady company) for Mac OS X. Mail, Mac OS X's built-in E-mail program, deals surprisingly well with spam—the unsolicited junk E-mail that's become the scourge of the Internet.

If you ask average people why the Mac isn't overrun by viruses and spyware, as Windows is, they'll probably tell you, "Because the Mac's market share is too small for the bad guys to write for."

That may be true. But there's another reason, too: Mac OS X is a very young operating system. It was created only a few years ago, and with security in mind. (Contrast with Windows, whose original versions were written before the Internet even existed.) Mac OS X is simply designed better. Its built-in firewall makes it virtually impossible for hackers to break into your Mac, and the system insists on getting your permission before anything gets installed on your Mac. Nothing can get installed behind your back, as it can in Windows.

But freedom from gunkware and viruses is only one big-ticket item. Here are a few other joys of becoming a Mac fan:

Stability. Underneath the shimmering, translucent desktop of Mac OS X is UNIX, the industrial strength, rock-solid OS that drives many a Web site. It's not new by any means; in fact, it's decades old, and has been polished by generations of programmers. That's precisely why Apple CEO Steve Jobs and his team chose it as the basis for the NeXT operating system, which Jobs worked on during his 12 years away from Apple and which Apple bought in 1997 to turn into Mac OS X.

No nagging. Unlike Windows, Mac OS X isn't copy-protected. You can install the same copy on your desktop and laptop Macs, if you have a permissive conscience. When you buy a new Mac, you're never, ever asked to type in a code off a sticker. Nor must you "register," "activate," sign up for ".NET Passport," or endure any other friendly suggestions unrelated to your work. And you won't find any cheesy software demos from other companies clogging up your desktop when you buy a new Mac, either. In short, Mac OS X leaves you alone.

Sensational software. Mac OS X comes with several dozen useful programs, from Mail (for email) to a 3-D, voice-activated Chess program. The most famous programs, though, are the famous Apple "iApps": iTunes for working with audio files, iMovie for editing video, iPhoto for managing your digital photos, GarageBand for creating and editing digital music, and so on. You also get iChat (an AOL-, Jabber-, and Google Talk-compatible instant messaging program that also offers videoconferencing) and iCal, a calendar program.

Simpler everything. Most applications in Mac OS X show up as a single icon. All of the support files are hidden away inside, where you don't have to look at them. There's no Add/Remove Programs program on the Macintosh; in general, you can remove a program from your Mac simply by dragging that one application icon to the Trash, without having to worry that you're leaving scraps behind.

Desktop features. Microsoft is a neat freak. Windows XP, for example, is so opposed to your using the desktop as a parking lot for icons, it actually interrupts you every 60 days to sweep all your infrequently used icons into an "Unused" folder. The Mac approach is different. Mac people often leave their desktops absolutely littered with icons. As a result, Mac OS X offers a long list of useful desktop features that will be new to you, the Windows refugee.

Advanced graphics. Mac programmers get excited about the set of advanced graphics technologies called Quartz (for two-dimensional graphics) and OpenGL (for three-dimensional graphics). For the rest of us, these technologies translate into a beautiful, translucent look for the desktop, smooth-looking (antialiased) on screen lettering, and the ability to turn any document on the screen into an Adobe Acrobat (PDF) file. And then there are the slick animations that permeate every aspect of Mac OS X: the rotating-cube effect when you switch from one logged-in person to another, the "genie" effect when you minimize a window to the Dock, and so on.

Advanced networking. When it comes to hooking up your computer to others, including those on the Internet, few operating systems can touch Mac OS X. It offers advanced features like multihoming, which lets your laptop switch automatically from its cable modem settings to its wireless or dial-up modem settings when you take it on the road. If you're not so much a switcher as an adder (you're getting a Mac but keeping the PC around), you'll be happy to hear that Macs and Windows PCs can "see" each other on a network automatically, too. As a result, you can open, copy, and work on files on both types of machines as though the religious war between Macs and PCs had never even existed.

Voice control, keyboard control. You can operate almost every aspect of every program entirely from the keyboard—or even by voice. These are terrific timesavers for efficiency freaks. In fact, the Mac can also read aloud any text in any program, including Web pages, email, your novel, you name it.

What it all adds up to is that Mac OS X is very stable; that a crashing program can't crash the whole machine; that the Macintosh can exploit multiple processors; and that the Mac can easily do more than one thing at once—downloading files, playing music, and opening a program, for example—all simultaneously.

EXERCISES

1. Judge whether the following given statements are true or false. If correct, write T in parentheses; otherwise, write F.

(1) (　) More than an operating system, Mac OS X is a collection of very cool applications..

(2) (　) Macintosh(mac) computer is a popular model of computer made by Inter Computer..

(3) ( ) Mac OS X have been developed since 2000 internally parallel for Intel and PowerPC processors.

(4) ( ) Like Windows, Mac OS X is copy-protected.

2. Complete the following note-taking with the information mentioned in the text.

(1) Mac programmers get excited about the set of advanced graphics technologies called Quartz and _____ (for three-dimensional graphics).

(2) Apple leads the industry in innovation with its award-winning _____ computers, OS X operating system, and consumer and professional applications software.

(3) There isn't yet a single widespread Mac OS X _____.

(4) Today's Mac is powered by the latest _____ processors..

READING MATERIALS

Product Description: Mac OS X 10.6 Snow Leopard（Figure 14-1）

Figure 14-1   Mac OS X 10.6 Snow Leopard

Different technologies like the Mach Kernel, NEXTSTEP and tools from NetBSD and FreeBSD found influence in Mac OS X to merge the previous Apple technology with UNIX features. The operating system core Darwin is open source and can be used also on x86 computers standalone. Mac OS X works with preemptive multi-tasking and includes beside the new GUI Aqua the classic GUI from Mac OS 9.

Mac OS X 10.0 came out in March 2001. To install are 128MB RAM (256MB RAM starting from Mac OS X 10.3.9) and 1.5GB hard disk space (3.0GByte starting from Mac OS X 10.2) provided. Mac OS X 10.5 requires at least 512MB RAM and 9GByte of free disk space.

- 32-bit or 64-bit processing
- SMP with up to 32 CPUs
- needs a PowerPC G3, G4 or G5
- POSIX compatible
- HFS+ file system
➢ Field of Application

- digital photography
- 2-D and 3-D animations
- video processing, streaming
- audio processing
- platform for DTP, web design
- office applications
➢ Structure Information
- supports QuickTime/VR
- monolithic Kernel
- Read/Write FAT, FAT32, ISO 9660, UDF
- well proven TCP/IP Stack
- graphical user interaction with the finder
- graphical representation by Quick draw
- central password administration (Keychain)

Considerable performance and comfort improvements were carried out in version Mac OS X 10.1. The surface reacts quicker at user interaction, the system start was accelerated and the OpenGL performance increased noticeable.

Mac OS X 10.3 has now a GUI in metallic scheme and the optimized Finder. The use and access in heterogeneous networks was further simplified. Files can be provided with etiquettes, the compression format ZIP is now directly supported. 12 million Mac OS X user were counted in October 2004.

According to Apple Mac OS X 10.4 brings more than 200 new features. Features are the fast, system-wide and index-based search function named Spotlight, the Dashboard for easy access to small programs (Widgets), the Automator for the simplified composition of Apple scripts for the automation of tasks. The Web browser Safari in version 2.0 now contained RSS support, the QuickTime software was updated to version 7 with support for the H.264 video codec. Further novelty is the delivery at a DVD medium, an installation of CD-ROM is no longer possible.

First since the 10th January 2006 is Mac OS X 10.4.4 next to the PowerPC version available for Intel based Macs. On the 6. June 2005 , Steve jobs announced at the WWDC the switch to Intel processors. As further details became known that Apple had developed Mac OS X since 2000 internally also for the Intel platform.

Apple released the successor Mac OS X 10.5, Leopard at the 26.10.2007. With more than 300 innovations Mac OS offers the user an enhanced user interface with virtual desktops, a fast file preview and Dock with 3D effect. The Finder was revised, the expansion "Boot Camp" for the installation of Windows on Intel-Macs is an official component now. As a file system ZFS is optionally available. For the surfing on the Internet the Apple Safari 3 Web browser is included. Backups can be made, managed and restored in a simple way with "Time Machine". Time Machine makes every hour the day automatically a file backup and every day a snapshot for the duration of a complete month. Lost files are recovered easily over the display of a dynamic time line of those snapshot. The security of the operating system and applications is improved by 11 enhancements. This are beside others the application-based firewall, signed applications, the use of ASLR (Address Space Layout Randomization) and Sandboxing for applications.

Open Group certified Mac OS X 10.5 according to the standard UNIX 03 in November 2007. Mac OS X is the first free BSD derivative with such certificate to bear the name UNIX officially. The certification guarantees the use of UNIX standard implementations to porting UNIX applications easily.

The first update with bug fixes was released with Mac OS X 10.5.1 by Apple on November 15th, 2007. It contains general bug fixes for the operating system to improve stability, better compatibility and safety. Mac OS X 10.5.2 cames with 125 bug fixes and smaller optimizations on January 24th, 2008.

Mac OS X 10.6 is a Mac computer with Intel Core 2 Duo processor with at least 1GB memory and 5GB free space ahead. This operating system no longer exists as PowerPC execution. Apple placed the focus development on performance and stability. It supports up to 16 TByte memory, it is optimized for multi core processors, and is a pure 64-bit operating system. With the technology OpenGL graphics processor can speed up in specific applications calculations.

Unit 15   Linux

WORDS AND EXPRESSIONS

flexibility [ˌfleksiˈbiliti]   柔韧性，机动性，灵活性，适应性

available [əˈveiləbl]   可利用的；有效的，可得的；空闲的

distribution [ˌdistriˈbjuːʃən]   分布；分配，发行

maintain [meinˈtein]   维持；维修；供养；继续；主张

versatile [ˈvəːsətail]   多才多艺的；通用的，万能的；多面手的

massive [ˈmæsiv]   大量的；巨大的，厚重的；魁伟的

upgrade [ˈʌpgreid, ʌpˈgreid]   提升；使升级；改良品种

Acronym [ˈækrəunim]   首字母缩略词

Hewlett-Packard   惠普（美国计算机公司）

proxy [ˈprɔksi]   代理人；代用品；委托书

norm [nɔːm]   规范，基准；定额，分配之工作量

stable [ˈsteibl]   稳定的；坚定的；牢固的

institution [ˌinstiˈtjuːʃən]   制度；（社会或宗教等）公共机构；习俗；建立

Macintosh [ˈmækintɔʃ]   苹果公司生产的一种型号的计算机

GUI　（Graphical User Interfaces）图形用户界面

Free Software Foundation   免费软件基金会

UNIX [ˈjuːniks]   一个强大的多用户、多任务操作系统，支持多种处理器架构，最早由 KenThompson、DennisRitchie 和 DouglasMcIlroy 于 1969 年在 AT&T 的贝尔实验室开发。

GNU   GNU 计划，又称革奴计划，是由 Richard Stallman 在 1983 年 9 月 27 日公开发起的。它的目标是创建一套完全自由的操作系统。

GNOME   GNOME 即 GNU 网络对象模型环境 (The GNU Network Object Model Environment)，GNU 计划的一部分，开放源码运动的一个重要组成部分。 是一种让使用者容易操作和设定电脑环境的工具。

QUESTIONS AND ANSWERS

1. What is the Linus Operating System?

2. What are the distinguished features of the Linus?

3. How many versions of Linus are there?

4. What is consist of Linus Operating System?

5. What did develop the source software?

6. How many servers of Linus are there?

7. Why Linus can become an operating system of choice as a network server?

8. What is the developed background of Linus?

9. Why is Linus so successful?

10. What's the difference between Linus and UNIX operating system?

TEXT

Linux is a fast, stable, and open source operating system for PC computers and workstations that features professional-level Internet services, extensive development tools, fully functional graphical user interfaces (GUIs), and a massive number of applications ranging from office suites to multimedia applications. Linux was developed in the early 1990s by Linus Torvalds, along with other programmers around the world. As an operating system, Linux performs many of the same functions as UNIX, Macintosh, Windows, and Windows NT. However, Linux is distinguished by its power and flexibility, along with being freely available. Most PC operating systems, such as Windows, began their development within the confines of small, restricted personal computers, which have only recently become more versatile machines. Such operating systems are constantly being upgraded to keep up with the ever-changing capabilities of PC hardware. Linux, on the other hand, was developed in a different context. Linux is a PC version of the UNIX operating system that has been used for decades on mainframes and minicomputers and is currently the system of choice for network servers and workstations. Linux brings the speed, efficiency, scalability, and flexibility of UNIX to your PC, taking advantage of all the capabilities that personal computers can now provide.

Technically, Linux consists of the operating system program, referred to as the kernel, which is the part originally developed by Linus Torvalds. But it has always been distributed with a massive number of software applications, ranging from network servers and security programs to office applications and development tools. Linux has evolved as part of the open source software movement, in which independent programmers joined together to provide free quality software to any user. Linux has become the premier platform for open source software, much of it developed by the Free Software Foundation's GNU project. Many of these applications are bundled as part of standard Linux distributions. Currently, thousands of open source applications are available for Linux from sites like the Open Source Development Network's (OSDN) sourceforge.net, the software depositories rpmfind.net, rpm.livna.org, freshrpms.net, KDE's www.kde-apps.org, and GNOME's www.gnome.org.

Along with Linux's operating system capabilities come powerful networking features, including support for Internet, intranets, and Windows networking. As a norm, Linux distributions include fast, efficient, and stable Internet servers, such as the Web, FTP, and DNS servers, along with proxy, news, and mail servers. In other words, Linux has everything you need to set up, support, and maintain a fully functional network.

Linux does all this at the right price. Linux is free, including the network servers and GUI desktops. Unlike the official UNIX operating system, Linux is distributed freely under a GNU General Public License as specified by the Free Software Foundation, making it available to anyone who wants to use it. GNU (the acronym stands for "GNU's Not UNIX") is a project initiated and managed by the Free Software Foundation to provide free software to users, programmers, and developers. Linux is copyrighted, not public domain. However, a GNU public license has much the same effect as the software's being in the public domain. The GNU general public license is designed to ensure Linux remains free and, at the same time, standardized. Linux is technically the operating system kernel—the core operations—and only one official Linux kernel exists. People sometimes have the mistaken impression that Linux is somehow less than a professional operating system because it is free. Linux is, in fact, a PC, workstation, and server version of UNIX. Many consider it far more stable and much more powerful than Windows. This power and stability have made Linux an operating system of choice as a network server.

To appreciate Linux completely, you need to understand the special context in which the UNIX operating system was developed. UNIX, unlike most other operating systems, was developed in a research and academic environment. In universities, research laboratories, data centers, and enterprises, UNIX is the system most often used. Its development has paralleled the entire computer and communications revolution over the past several decades. Computer professionals often developed new computer technologies on UNIX, such as those developed for the Internet. Although a sophisticated system, UNIX was designed from the beginning to be flexible. The UNIX system itself can be easily modified to create different versions. In fact, many different vendors maintain different official versions of UNIX. IBM, Sun, and Hewlett-Packard all sell and maintain their own versions of UNIX.

The unique demands of research programs often require that UNIX be tailored to their own special needs. This inherent flexibility in the UNIX design in no way detracts from its quality. In fact, this flexibility attests to the ruggedness of UNIX, allowing it to adapt to practically any environment. This is the context in which Linux was developed. Linux is, in this sense, one other version of UNIX—a version for the PC. The development of Linux by computer professionals working in a research-like environment reflects the way UNIX versions have usually been developed. Linux is publicly licensed and free and reflects the deep roots UNIX has in academic institutions, with their sense of public service and support. Linux is a top-rate operating system accessible to everyone, free of charge.

EXERCISES

1. Judge whether the following given statements are true or false. If correct, write T in parentheses; otherwise, write F.

(1)　(　) Linux is an operating system anyone can use.

(2)　(　) Linux systems are limited to the Internet.

(3)　(　) KDE and GNOME have become the standard GUI interface for Linux systems.

(4)　(　) Linux is not a fully functional UNIX operating system.

2. Complete the following note-taking with the information mentioned in the text.

(1)　Computer professionals often developed new computer technologies on _____, such as those developed for the Internet.

(2)　Linux consists of the operating system program, referred to as the kernel, which is the part originally developed by _____.

(3)　However, a _____ public license has much the same effect as the software's being in the public domain.

(4)　Linux is, in fact, a PC, _____workstation, and server version of UNIX.

READING MATERIALS

Product Description: Red Hat and Fedora Linux(Figure 15-1)

Figure 15-1　Red Hat and Fedora Linux

Red Hat Linux is currently the most popular Linux distribution. As a company, Red Hat provides software and services to implement and support professional and commercial Linux systems. Red Hat has split its Linux development into two lines, Red Hat Enterprise Linux and the Fedora Project. Red Hat Enterprise Linux features commercial enterprise products for servers and workstations, with controlled releases issued every two years or so. The Fedora Project is an Open Source initiative whose Fedora release will be issued every six months on average, incorporating the most recent development in Linux operating system features as well as supported applications. Red Hat freely distributes its Fedora version of Linux under the GNU General Public License; the company generates income by providing professional-level support, consulting services, and training services.

The Red Hat Certified Engineers (RHCE) training and certification program is designed to provide reliable and highly capable administrators and developers to maintain and customize professional-level Red Hat systems. Red Hat has forged software alliances with major companies like Oracle, IBM, Dell, and Sun. Currently, Red Hat provides several commercial products, known as Red Hat Enterprise Linux. These include the Red Hat Enterprise Advanced Server for intensive enterprise-level tasks; Red Hat Enterprise ES, which is a version of Linux designed for small businesses and networks; and Red Hat Enterprise Workstation. Red Hat also maintains for its customers the Red Hat Network, which provides automatic updating of the operating system and software packages on your system. Specialized products include the Stronghold secure Web server, versions of Linux tailored for IBM-and Itanium-based servers, and GNUPro development tools (www.redhat.com/software/gnupro).

Red Hat also maintains a strong commitment to open source Linux applications. Red Hat originated the RPM package system used on several distributions, which automatically installs and removes software packages. Red Hat is also providing much of the software development for the GNOME desktop, and it is a strong supporter of KDE.

Red Hat provides an extensive set of configuration tools designed to manage tasks such as adding users, starting servers, accessing remote directories, and configuring devices such as your monitor or printer. These tools are accessible on the System Settings and Server Settings menus and windows, as well as by their names, all beginning with the term "system-config".

The new release of Fedora features key updates to critical applications as well as new tools replacing former ones. Fedora includes the GNOME desktop, the Apache Web server, the GNU Compiler Collection (GCC), and the GNU Java Compiler (GJC). Configuration tools, including Program Manager and the PUP updater for managing software and system-config-cluster for configuring your distribution, are included and others have been updated.

The extensive collection of Fedora-compliant software that was held in the Fedora Extras repository has been merged into one large Fedora repository. The former Fedora Core and Fedora Extras repositories have been merged into a single Fedora repository.

Installing Fedora has been significantly simplified. A core set of applications are installed, and you add to them as you wish. Following installation, added software is taken from online repositories, not the disk. Install screens have been reduced to just a few screens, moving quickly through default partitioning, network detection, and time settings, to the package selection. Firewall and SELinux configuration are part of the post-install configuration procedure.

The Fedora distribution of Linux is available online at numerous FTP sites. Fedora maintains its own FTP site at download.fedora.redhat.com along with mirrors at fedoraproject. org/Download/mirrors.html, where you can download the entire current release of Fedora Linux, as well as updates and additional software. Red Hat was designed from its inception to work on numerous hardware platforms. Currently, Red Hat Enterprise supports the Sparc, Intel, and Alpha platforms.See www.redhat.com for more information including extensive documentation such as Red Hat manuals, FAQs, and links to other Linux sites.

If you purchase Red Hat Enterprise Linux from Red Hat, you are entitled to online support services. Although Linux is free, Red Hat as a company specializes in support services, providing customers with its expertise in developing solutions to problems that may arise or using Linux to perform any of several possible tasks, such as e-commerce or database operations.

The Fedora release is maintained and developed by an Open Source project called the Fedora Project. The release consists entirely of open source software. Development is carried out using contributions from Linux developers, allowing them free rein to promote enhancements and new features. The project is designed to work much like other open source projects, with releases keeping pace with the course of rapid online development. The Fedora project features detailed documentation of certain topics like Installation and desktop user guides at doc.fedoraproject.org.

The Fedora versions of Linux are entirely free. You can download the most current version, including betas, from www.fedoraproject.org or fedoraproject.org/Download/mirrors.html. You can update Fedora using the Package Updater (PUP) to access the Fedora Yum repository. Updating can be supported by any one of several Yum Fedora repositories.

Access is automatically configured during installation. The Fedora Project release replaces the original standard Red Hat Linux version that consisted of the entry-level Red Hat release. In addition to the Fedora software, the Fedora Project will also provide popular compatible packages.

The Red Hat Enterprise line of products are designed for corporate, research, and business applications (www.redhat.com). These products focus on reliability and stability. They are released on a much more controlled schedule than the Fedora Project versions. What was once the low-cost consumer version of Red Hat Linux is replaced by a scaled-down commercial desktoop version for consumers and small business. Red Hat provides both desktop and server versions of Red Hat Enterprise Linux. The desktop versions are offered as a simple desktop, a full workstation, or either a simple desktop or workstation with virtualization support (multi-OS). Keep in mind that the lowest level product, the simple desktop, does not include certain networking features like Samba and NFS servers, limiting the ability to share data. The workstation desktop versions have no system memory limit, provides software development support, and include Samba and NFS servers. The workstation virtualization version features unlimited guest OS support. Red Hat offers two Enterprise server versions, Red Hat Enterprise Linux and the Advanced Platform version. The Red Hat Enterprise version provides less server capability limiting both servers and virtual guests. The Advanced Platform includes storage cluster support (GFS) as well as unlimited servers and virtual guests. Both Red Hat Linux Enterprise server versions have standard and premium editions which vary in their level of customer support. A basic edition is also provided for the standard server version which provides minimal support.

All versions, both desktop and server, feature automatic software updating with the Red Hat Network (RHN).

Red Hat Enterprise Linux is valued for its stability, often providing more stable implementations than Fedora. It is licensed as an open source GPL product, so is technically available to anyone. The versions that Red Hat sells include commercial products and support that are not open source. Red Hat does, however, freely provide its open source enterprise versions for download from its FTP site, ftp.redhat.com/pub/redhat/linux/enterprise. Earlier Enterprise versions are available in binary and ISO formats, though without any commercial features. The current Enterprise version is available as source files only.

Unit 16   Windows CE

WORDS AND EXPRESSIONS

embedded [im'bedid]   嵌入式的

terminals ['tə:minlz]   终端机

microprocessor [ˌmaikrəu'prəusesə]   微处理器

release [ri'li:s]   发布

minor ['mainə]   较小的

simultaneously [saiməl'teiniəsli]   同时地

kernel ['kə:nəl]   核心

accessibility [əkˌsesə'biləti]   易接近

implement ['implimənt, 'impliment]   实施

overhead ['əuvəhed,ˌəuvə'hed]   开销

telephony [ti'lefəni, tə-, 'telifəu-]   电话

unify ['ju:nifai]   统一

component [kəm'pəunənt]   组件

megabyte ['megəbait]   兆字节

MIPS [mips]   每秒百万条指令

non-personal-computer   非个人电脑

Universal Disc File System (UDFS)   通用磁盘文件系统

Simple Object Access Protocol (SOAP)   简单对象存取协议

IPv6   互联网协议第六版

Voice over Internet Protocol (VoIP)   互联网语音协议

Transaction-safe FAT (TFAT)   事务安全文件系统

Universal Serial Bus (USB)   通用串行总线

Secure Digital Input/Output (SDIO)   安全数据输入/输出

Dynamic-Link Libraries (DLLs)   动态链接库

Application Programming Interface (API)   应用编程接口

filesystem   文件系统

VM   虚拟存储器

be integrated into   与…相结合

QUESTIONS AND ANSWERS

1. what is the Windows Embedded CE designed for?

2. When did the history of Windows Embedded CE begin?

3. What did contain about the Windows Embedded CE 4.0?

4. What did release in 2006 with the Microsoft?

5. Can you tell us the effects about Windows Embedded CE 6.0 to system architecture?

6. What is the difference between Windows Embedded CE version 6.0 and previous versions?

7. When does a developer can load drivers into kernel space and also be able to create drivers that load in a special user process?

8. When did Microsoft release the Windows Embedded CE 6.0 R2 upgrade?

9. What did Windows Embedded CE 6.0 target to?

10. What is the major feature of the Windows CE 6.0? Why?

TEXT

Windows Embedded CE (Figure 16-1) is designed for mobile devices, terminals, cell phones and IP phones, multimedia devices, TV/video consoles, industrial automation equipment, and other devices that require a minimum size, integration of multiple microprocessor architectures, and support for real-time operations.

The history of Windows Embedded CE began in 1996, when Microsoft released its first operating system (CE 1.0) for non-personal-computer devices, which was originally positioned for the pocket PC market. In 1997, the system (2.0 CE) became componentized and was designed for a wide range of devices and more processor types. Following that, there were two more minor releases (2.11 and 2.12), which expanded and enlarged the functionality of the operating system. Version CE 3.0, released in 2000, contains support for real-time operation and advanced multimedia technologies such as DirectDraw, DirectShow, and Windows Media Player.

http://www.computerhope.com

Figure 16-1   Windows CE

The next version (CE 4.0) came out in 2001. It contained support for advanced technologies such as Direct3D, Universal Disc File System (UDFS), Simple Object Access Protocol (SOAP), advanced power management, and SQL Server CE database. Minor releases 4.1 and 4.2 provided developers with expanded accessibility functionality by adding support for viewing files, Bluetooth profiles, and IPv6, as well as support for Voice over Internet Protocol (VoIP) telephony, transaction-safe FAT (TFAT), and .NET Compact Framework 1.0.

In 2005, Microsoft released the next version of the system (CE 5.0, see Figure 16-2), which provided developers with support for new technologies, such as Universal Serial Bus (USB) 2.0, Secure Digital Input/Output (SDIO), Windows Media 9, and Microsoft Internet Explorer 6, as well as a unified build system, release-quality drivers. In response to the demands of today's embedded devices market, Microsoft released a Network Multimedia Feature Pack in 2006.

Figure 16-2   Windows CE 5.0

With Windows Embedded CE version 6.0 (Figure 16-3), released in the fall of 2006, the system architecture has undergone substantial changes. Now every process has 2GB of virtual memory (previously 32 MB), and the number of possible simultaneously running processes increased to 32,000 (previously 32). In previous versions, parts of the system kernel were implemented as a set of separate processes, whereas in Windows Embedded 6.0, they are combined into one kernel. System processes have become dynamic-link libraries (DLLs) that are loaded into kernel space. This increases the performance of the operating system, reduces overhead for system application programming interface (API) calls, and unifies the kernel interface. Now a developer can load drivers into kernel space and also be able to create drivers that load in a special user process.

In November 2007, Microsoft released the Windows Embedded CE 6.0 R2 upgrade, which adds new components and BSP packages to the CE 6.0 operating system.

Figure 16-3   Windows Embedded CE 6.0

Windows Embedded CE 6.0 is the sixth major release of Windows Embedded Operating System targeted to enterprise specific tools such as industrial controllers and consumer electronics devices like digital cameras. CE 6.0 features a completely redesigned kernel, which supports over 32,768 processes, up from 32 process support of the previous versions. Each process receives 2GB of virtual address space. The features of the Windows CE 6.0 includes:

- Some System components (such as filesystem, GWES (Graphics, Windowing, and

Events Server) , device driver manager) have been moved to the kernel space.

- The system components which now run in kernel have been converted from EXEs to DLLs, which get loaded into kernel space.
- New Virtual memory model. The lower 2GB is the process VM space and is private per process. The upper 2GB is the kernel VM space.
- New device driver model that supports both User mode and Kernel mode drivers.
- The 32 processes limit has been raised to 32,768 processes.
- The 32 megabyte virtual memory limit has been raised to the total virtual memory (Up to 2GB of private VM).
- The Platform Builder IDE is integrated into Microsoft Visual Studio 2005 as plugin, allowing a single development environment for both platform and application development.
- Read-only support for UDF 2.5 filesystem.
- Support for Microsoft's exFAT filesystem.
- 802.11i (WPA2) and 802.11e (QoS) wireless standards, and multiple radio support.
- CE 6.0 works with x86, ARM, SH4 and MIPS based processor architectures.
- New Cellcore components to enable devices to easily make data connections and initiate voice calls through cellular networks.

EXERCISES

1. Judge whether the following given statements are true or false. If correct, write T in parentheses; otherwise, write F.

(1) (   ) The history of Windows Embedded CE began in 1996.

(2) (   ) The next version (CE 4.0) came out in 2002.

(3) (   ) This reduces the performance of the operating system, increases overhead for system application programming interface (API) calls, and unifies the kernel interface.

(4) (   ) The lower 2GB is the process VM space and is private per process. The upper 2GB is the kernel VM space.

2. Complete the following note-taking with the information mentioned in the text.

(1) The history of Windows Embedded CE began in _____, when Microsoft released its first operating system (CE 1.0) for non-personal-computer devices, which was originally positioned for the pocket PC market.

(2) In response to the demands of today's _____ devices market, Microsoft released a Network Multimedia Feature Pack in 2006.

(3) With Windows Embedded CE version 6.0, _____ in the fall of 2006, the system architecture has undergone substantial changes.

(4)   The Platform Builder IDE is integrated into Microsoft Visual Studio 2005 as _____,
allowing a single development environment for both platform and application development.

READING MATERIALS

Product Description: Windows Embedded CE 6.0 R3 (Figure 16-4)

Figure 16-4   Windows Embedded CE

Microsoft Corp. announced on Tuesday the release to manufacturing (RTM) of Windows
Embedded CE 6.0 R3, enhanced with Microsoft Silverlight, which should provide a rich
application experience through Silverlight for Windows Embedded user interface (UI)
framework. The new release is expected to enable designers and developers to make
improvements to the UI capabilities of their Windows Embedded CE 6.0 R3-based devices, and
also to deliver their products faster and with less associated costs.

Advantech, the global leading ePlatform service provider, has announced their continued
support for the new release of Windows Embedded CE 6.0 R3. There are several powerful
functions added into this release, including Microsoft Office & PDF viewers, and Adobe Flash
Lite 3.1.0. Release 3 gives power to differentiated devices with advanced technologies that
deliver better user experiences—all on a solid platform to efficiently bring devices to market.

Windows Embedded CE 6.0 R3 is a powerful new release since CE 6.0 R2 was released in
Nov 2007. Microsoft has collected all the feedback from customers and integrated new
functions.

CE 6.0 R3 New Functions

Silverlight UI Framework: This helps developers to quickly build UI to reduce development
time.

Connection Manager: This manages connections for General Packet Radio Service (GPRS),
Wireless LAN (WLAN), Bluetooth DUN, etc.

Office & PDF Viewers: This includes Office viewers for Word, Excel and Powerpoint. They
support file formats based on 97-2003. The PDF viewer supports version 1.3; equivalent to
Acrobat 4 and later.

Adobe Flash Lite 3.1.0: The Adobe Flash Lite plug-in enables Internet Explorer to show content created with Adobe Flash; equivalent to Adobe Flash 9.

Runtime SKUs

In Windows Embedded CE 6.0 R3, all new functions are supported in the CE Pro version. This means that customers don't need to pay additional money to benefit from them.

Advantech CE 6.0 Supported Platforms

Advantech integrates standard Windows CE into many popular hardware platforms. An embedded software API is developed to enhance control in Windows CE. Customers benefit from reduced project development effort and enhanced hardware platform reliability.

Database and Data Warehouse

Unit 17　An Introduction to Database

WORDS AND EXPRESSIONS

database ['deitəbeis]　数据库

hierarchical [,haiə'rɑːkikəl]　层次的

graph [grɑːf]　图（一种比线性表和树更为复杂的数据结构）

tree [triː]　树（数据结构中的一种简单的非线性结构）

attribute [ə'tribju(ː)t]　属性

index ['indeks]　索引

multiuser [mʌlti'juːzə(r)]　多用户

individual [,indi'vidjuəl]　个人，个人的

infrastructure ['infrə'strʌktʃə]　基础结构

conceptualized [kən'septjuəlaiz]　使有概念

pioneer [,paiə'niə]　先驱

low-end ['ləuend]　低档的

constraint [kən'streint]　约束

row [rau]　行

column ['kɔləm]　列

airline ['ɛəlain]　航线

reservation [,rezə'veiʃən]　预定

pottery ['pɔtəri]　陶器

shard [ʃɑːd]　（瓷）碎片

novel ['nɔvəl]　新颖的

schema ['skiːmə]　计划

log [lɔg]　进行、运行

archaeological [,ɑːkiə'lɔdʒikəl]　考古学的

Pennsylvania [pensil'veinjə]　宾夕法尼亚州

two-dimensional　二维的

government-funded　政府资助的

UNIVAC ['juːnivæk] (Universal Automatic Computer)　通用自动计算机

DNA(DeoxyriboNucleic [diː'ɔksi,raibəu'njuːkliːik] Acid ['æsid])　脱氧核糖核酸

DBMS (Data Base Management System)　数据库管理系统

SQL (Structured Query Language)　结构化查询语言

punched-card machines　纸片打孔机

EDVAC (Electronic Discrete Variable Automatic Computer)　电子数据计算机

ACM (Association for Computing Machinery)　美国计算机协会

ACM SIGPLAN (Special Interest Group on Programming Languages)　美国计算机学会程序设计语言专业组

IDS (Integrated Data Store)　综合数据存储

DBTG (Database Base Task Group)　数据库任务组

Social Security Act　社会安全法案，社会保障法

CODASYL (Conference on Data System Languages)　数据系统语言会议

U.S. Department of Defense (DOD)　美国国防部

Bureau of the Census　联邦人口普查办公署

University of California at Berkeley (UC-Berkeley)　加州大学伯克利分校

Informix　美国数据库产品软件商（已被 IBM 公司收购）

Sybase　美国数据库产品软件商

NCR (National Cash Register Company)　全美现金出纳机公司

Teradate　美国数据库产品软件商（已被 NCR 公司收购）

GE (General Electric Company)　美国通用电气公司

DEC (Digital Equipment Corporation)　美国数字设备公司

Honeywell　美国霍尼韦尔国际公司

Siemens AG ['siːmənz]　德国西门子公司

QUESTIONS AND ANSWERS

1. Why do implementing object databases undo the benefits of relational model by introducing pointers and making queries more difficult?

2. What is the most useful way of classifying database?

3. What is the Background of the development of database?

4. Did you have ever used database technologies? Can you tell us something about it?

TEXT

A database is information set with a regular structure. A database is usually but not necessarily stored in some machine readable format accessed by a computer. There are a wide variety of databases, from simple tables stored in a single file to very large databases with many millions of records, stored in rooms full of disk drives.

Databases resembling modern versions were first developed in the 1960s. A pioneer in the field was Charles Bachman. The most useful way of classifying database is by the programming model associated with the database. Several models have been in wide use for some time. Historically, the relational model overcame with the so-called flat model accompanying it for low-end usage. They were never theorized and were deemed as data models only as a contrast to the relational model, not having conceptual underpinnings of their own; they have arisen simply out of the realization of physical constraints and programming, not data models.

The flat (or table) model consists of a single, two-dimensional array of data elements where all members of a given column are assumed to be similar values, and all members of a row are assumed to be related to one another. For instance, columns for name and password might be used as a part of a system security database. Each row would have the specific password associated with a specific user. Columns of the table often have a type associated with them, defining them as character data, date or time information, integers, or floating point numbers. This model is the basis of the spreadsheet.

The network model allows multiple tables to be used together through the use of pointers (or references). Some columns contain pointers to different tables instead of data. Thus, the tables are related by references, which can be viewed as a network structure. A particular subset of the network model, the hierarchical, limits the relationship to a tree structure, instead of the more general directed graph structure implied by the full network model.

Relational databases consist not of tables, but of three components: a collection of data structures, namely relations, sometimes incorrectly identified with tables; a collection of operators, the relational algebra and calculus; and a collection of integrity constraints, defining the set of consistent database states and changes of state. The integrity constraints can be of four types: domain (AKA type), attribute, relation and database constraints.

Unlike the hierarchical and network models, there are no pointers whatsoever, according to the Information Principle; all information must be represented as data values; attributes of any type represent relationships between relations. Relational databases allow users (including programmers) to write queries that were not anticipated by the database designer. As a result, relational databases can be used by multiple applications in ways the original designers did not foresee, which is especially important for databases that might be used for decades. This has made relational databases very popular with businesses.

The relational model is a mathematical theory developed by Ted Codd to describe how relational databases should work. Although this theory is the basis for relational database software, very few database management systems actually follow the model very closely and all have features violating the theory, thus increasing complexity and subtracting power. Therefore they should not be called relational DBMSs, but SQL (or some other language) ones.

Implementations and Indexing

All of these kinds of databases can take advantage of indexing to increase their speed. The most common kind of index is a sorted list of the contents of some particular table column, with pointers to the row associated with the value. An index allows a set of table rows matching some criterion to be located quickly. Various methods of indexing are commonly used, including b-tree, hashes, and linked lists are all common indexing techniques.

Relational and SQL DBMS have the advantage that indexes can be created or dropped without changing existing applications, because applications don't use the indexes directly.

Instead, the database software decides on behalf of the application which indexes to use. The database chooses between many different strategies based on which one it estimates will run the fastest.

Mapping Objects into Databases

In recent years, the object-oriented paradigm has been applied to databases as well, creating a new programming model known as object databases. These databases attempt to overcome some of the difficulties of using objects with the SQL DBMSs. An object-oriented program allows objects of the same type to have different implementations and behave differently, so long as they have the same interface (polymorphism). This doesn't fit well with an SQL database where user-defined types are difficult to define and use, and where the Two Great Blunders prevail: the identification of classes with tables (the correct identification is of classes with types, and of objects with values), and the usage of pointers.

Application of Databases

Databases are used in many applications, spanning virtually the entire range of computer software. Databases are the preferred method of storage for large multiuser applications, where coordination between many users is needed. Even individual users find them convenient, though, and many electronic mail programs and personal organizers are based on standard database technology.

The Rise of Relational Databases

Large-scale computer applications require rapid access to large amounts of data. A computerized checkout system in a supermarket must track the entire product line of the market. Airline reservation systems are used at many locations simultaneously to place passengers on numerous flights on different dates. Library computers store millions of entries and access citations from hundreds of publications. Transaction processing systems in banks and brokerage houses keep the accounts that generate international flows of capital. World Wide Web search engines scan thousands of Web pages to produce quantitative responses to queries almost instantly. Thousands of small businesses and organizations use databases to track everything from inventory and personnel to DNA sequences and pottery shards from archaeological digs.

Thus, databases not only represent significant infrastructure for computer applications, but they also process the transactions and exchanges that drive the U.S. economy. A significant and growing segment of the software industry, known as the database industry, generates about $8 billion in annual revenue. The U.S. companies—including IBM Corporation, Oracle Corporation, Informix Corporation, Sybase Incorporated, Teradata Corporation (now owned by NCR Corporation), and Microsoft Corporation—dominate the world market. This dominance stems from a serendipitous combination of industrial research, government-funded academic work, and commercial competition.

Much of today's market consists of relational databases based on the model proposed in the late 1960's and early 1970's. It highlights the critical role of the government in advancing this technology. For instance, although the relational model was originally proposed and developed at

IBM, it was a government-funded effort at the University of California at Berkeley (UC-Berkeley) that disseminated the idea widely and gave it the intellectual legitimacy required for broad acceptance and commercialization.

Background

The U.S. government has always had significant requirements for the collection, sorting, and reporting of large volume of data. In 1980, the Bureau of the Census encouraged a former employee, Herman Hollerith, to develop the world's first automated information processing equipment. The resulting punched-card machines processed the censuses of 1980 and of 1900. In 1911, Hollerith's company merged with another, also founded with Census support; the resulting company soon became known as International Business (Anderson, 1988), now IBM.

During World War Ⅰ, the government used new punched-card technology to process the various data sets required to control industrial production, collect the new income tax, and classify draftees. The Social Security Act of 1935 made it necessary to keep continuous records on the employment of 26 million individuals. For this, "the world's biggest bookkeeping job", IBM developed special collating equipment. The Census Bureau purchased the first model of the first digital computer on the commercial market, the UNIVAC I (itself based on the government-funded Electronic Discrete Variable Automatic Computer (EDVAC) project at the University of Pennsylvania). In 1959, the Pentagon alone had more than 200 computers just for its business needs (e.g., tracking expenses, personnel, spare parts), with annual costs exceeding $70 million. U.S. dominance of the punched-card data processing industry, initially established with government support, was a major factor in U.S. companies' later dominance in electronic computing.

By the early 1960s, substantial progress had been made in removing hardware-specific constraints from the tasks of programmers. The term "database" emerged to capture the sense that the information stored within a computer could be conceptualized, structured, and manipulated independently of the specific machine on which it resided. Most of the earliest database applications were developed in military command and intelligence environments, but the concept was quickly adopted by commercial users (System Development Corporation, 1964; Fry and Sibley, 1974).

Early Efforts at Standardization

As computing entered the mainstream commercial market, a number of techniques emerged to facilitate data access, ensure quality, maintain privacy, and allow for managerial control of data. In 1960, the Conference on Data Systems Languages (CODASYL), set up by the U.S. Department of Defense (DOD) to standardize software applications, established the common business-oriented language (COBOL) for programming (ACM SIGPLAN, 1978), incorporating a number of prior data at random, began to replace magnetic tape drives, which required serial data access, for online storage. In 1961, Charles Bachman at General Electric Company introduced the integrated data store (IDS) system, a pioneering database management system that took advantage of the new storage technology and included novel schemas and logging, among other features.

During these early years, innovations in the practice-oriented field tended to be made by user groups and industrial researchers. In the mid-1960s, Bachman and others, largely from industry and manufacturing, set up the Database Base Task Group (DBTG) under Codasyl to bring some unity to the varied field. The group published a set of specifications for how computer languages, COBOL in particular, might navigate databases. In 1971, it published a formal standard, known colloquially in the industry as the Codasyl approach to database management. A number of Codasyl-based products were introduced for mainframe computers by Eckert-Mauchly Computer Corporation (the maker of Univac), Honeywell Incorporated, and Siemens AG, and, for minicomputers, by Digital Equipment Corporation (DEC) and Prime Computer Corporation.

EXERCISES

1. Judge whether the following given statements are true or false. If correct, write T in parentheses; otherwise, write F.

(1) 　(　) The flat model overcame with the so-called relational model.

(2) 　(　) The network model allows only one table to be used through the use of pointers.

(3) 　(　) Relational databases allow users to write queries that were not anticipated by the database designer.

(4) 　(　) An object-oriented program forbids objects of the same type to have different implementations.

2. Complete the following note-taking with the information mentioned in the text.

(1) 　The hierarchical model limits the relationship to a tree structure, instead of the more general directed _____ implied by the full network model.

(2) 　_____ databases allow users to write queries that were not anticipated by the database designer.

(3) 　IBM originally proposed and developed _____, which was a government-funded effort at the University of California at Berkeley (UC-Berkeley).

(4) 　The _____ system was introduced at General Electric Company in 1961.

READING MATERIALS

Product Description: Oracle

Oracle Database 11g delivers the benefits of grid computing with more self-management and automation, making it easier to:

- Change IT systems without risk using Real Application Testing;
- Partition and compress tables to store more data and run queries faster;
- Securely protect and audit data, and enable total recall of data;

- Integrate and manage the lifecycle of all enterprise information;
- Run your business 24×7 with unique maximum availability architecture.

In its January 2008 report, "Oracle Real Application Testing—Business agility through superior testing", research firm, Ovum Summit, praised the new Oracle Database option as a way for businesses to achieve a new level of "adaptability to change".

"Oracle Real Application Testing, a key feature of Oracle Database 11g, allows rapid and safe adoption of infrastructure technology changes by reducing the testing effort and time required to ensure the robustness and quality of the changes before they go into production," says the report. "Feedback from participants in the Oracle Database 11g early adopter program indicates that tasks that previously took many weeks can be reduced to a few days." Ovum Summit noted the following benefits.

> Greater agility. Oracle Real Application Testing allows for greater business agility by reducing the time required to test and QA system changes by as much as 80%.

> Lower costs. Oracle Real Application Testing capabilities can lower infrastructure testing costs by as much as 70% for some customers.

> Reduced risk. By improving the ability to accurately assess the effects of changes, the new features will allow companies to mitigate risks by reducing the number of unexpected outages and by improving the service quality of their IT operations.

> Enhanced efficiency. By intelligently automating many manual and complex testing tasks, Oracle Real Application Testing capabilities allow junior DBAs to perform tasks that currently demand the attention of senior DBAs and enhance the overall efficiency of IT engineers.

Oracle has been named the leader in the data warehouse management category by the analyst firm IDC who found that Oracle had nearly 41 percent (40.9 percent) market share and close to $1.8 billion in revenues for 2006. IDC's report, "Worldwide Data Warehouse Platform Tools 2006 Vendor Shares", also notes that Oracle was the leading data warehouse platform tools vendor based on 2006 software. Oracle extended its lead in this market with nearly 33% market share and almost $1.87 billion in software revenue. In addition, Oracle's data warehouse platform tools software revenue grew at 13.1% —faster than the overall category growth rate of 12.5%.

"The future of the data warehouse market remains strong as companies look to integrate and analyze structured, and increasingly. unstructured, content across the enterprise," said Dan Vesset, Vice President of Business Analytics Research at IDC. "Oracle is well positioned to deliver the platform tools and new capabilities such as Spatial Information Management that companies need in order to drive better visibility within their organizations."

The overall RDBMS(Relational Data Base Management Systems) market continued to be dominated by the top-tier vendors, as the top three vendors (Oracle, IBM, and Microsoft) accounted for 85.6 percent of worldwide RDBMS revenue. Oracle and Microsoft experienced growth rates above the industry average at 14.9 percent and 28 percent, respectively, while IBM trailed in terms of growth with an 8.8 percent revenue increase in 2006.

"As the popularity of the data-intensive initiative continues to grow, the relational database management system is receiving ongoing attention," said Colleen Graham, research director at Gartner. "We expect this to continue as organizations show no sign of flagging in their pursuit of performance management and overarching enterprise information management initiatives."

"Organizations are looking to gain insight into the business to make better decisions and identify new opportunities. This is forcing them to invest in their data assets, purchasing new technology and tools that increase operational efficiency, and enable better use of data management resources," Ms. Graham said.

Each of the major three vendors continues to dominate their particular platform: Oracle on UNIX and Linux, Microsoft on Windows, and IBM on the zSeries. UNIX and Windows Servers were still the leading RDBMS operating system (OS) in 2006 with 34.8 percent and 34.5 percent market share. Linux was the No. 3 RDBMS OS with 15.5 percent market share, but it continued to dominate in terms of OS growth, with 67 percent growth over 2005.

Gartner defines RDBMS as a database management system that incorporates the relational data model, normally including a Structured Query Language (SQL) application programming interface. It is a DBMS in which the database is organized and accessed according to the relationships between data items. In a relational database, relationships between data items are expressed by means of tables. Interdependencies among these tables are expressed by data values rather than by pointers. This allows a high degree of data independence.

Gartner's Software research group has traditionally measured market share in terms of new license revenue. However, due to the emergence and increasing popularity of open-source software and buyer consumption models such as hosted and subscription offerings, Gartner has moved to measure market share in terms of total software revenue which includes revenue generated from new license, updates, subscriptions and hosting, technical support and maintenance. Professional services and hardware revenue are not included in total software revenue.

Oracle leads the industry delivering the most advanced support technologies. We continue to automate and engineer the support process to include industry best practices, advanced support capabilities, and the highest level of collaborative support. We embed supportability into our products and we have built over 250 support tools to help you diagnose and resolve issues before they become critical.

Faster Problem Resolution

Our advanced support technologies help you run your systems more efficiently by providing faster problem resolution, faster updates and faster system performance. Ultimately, this lowers your total cost of ownership while minimizing IT risk.

Capabilities

These are a few examples of the proactive, automated support capabilities available to Oracle E-Business Suite and Oracle technology customers.

> ➢ Software Configuration Manager. A simpler way to track, manage, and support your
>   Oracle configurations.

> HealthChecks. Proactive recommendations to help you improve the performance of your Oracle systems.

> Product Alerts. Proactive notification of potential configuration performance risks by providing environment security and general alerts.

> Maintenance Wizard. Simplifies your upgrade process, saves time, and allows you to use fewer IT resources to transition quickly and effectively to the latest Oracle products and technology.

> Diagnostic Tools. Tools that help you configure, install, and maintain your solutions for optimal performance.

With Oracle Support, you get a simpler way to support your Oracle configurations. Software Configuration Manager, a proactive automated support capability, included in Oracle Premier Support, offers you a simpler way to track, manage, and support your Oracle configurations while reducing the risk of unplanned system downtime.

Software Configuration Manager gives you a complete, dynamic view of your current configurations—including application, middleware, and database versions, plus operating system and hardware platform details—in a new, customizable, easy-to-use dashboard. You define the filters and views to track the configuration information that matters most to your business.

Software Configuration Manager customers have reported 40% faster issue resolution, a 30% reduction in the time it takes to log a Service Request, and 25% problem avoidance with Alerts and HealthChecks.

Benefits

Simplified configuration management—A simpler and more intelligent way to track, manage and support even the most complex, multi-component test, development, and production environments through configuration capture and viewing.

> Faster problem resolution. Accelerated information exchange between your systems and Oracle support analysts, leading to faster problem diagnosis and reduced time to resolution.

> Proactive issue notification. Product Alerts inform you of potential configuration performance risks by providing you with both General Alerts and Security Alerts—automated, secure notifications about issues that could have an impact on your business.

> Optimized performance. HealthChecks identify potential issues that may affect the overall stability, performance, and scalability of your Oracle environment and inform you of the risks and recommendations associated with these issues.

Oracle Maintenance Wizard

Transition quickly and effectively to the latest Oracle product and technology enhancements with the help of Maintenance Wizard. This powerful upgrade assistance tool saves time and avoids the challenges associated with upgrading as it guides you through the entire maintenance and upgrade process.

Tasks are presented in a step-by-step order to guide you through the activities and to prevent accidental "out of order" mistakes, and critical patches that you require are already defined to prevent accidental omissions. Each step of your maintenance and upgrade is tracked: the time required to complete a task is recorded, the completion status is monitored, and project reporting is provided. And since it is a multi-user tool, the system administrator can give different users assignments based on any combination of category, product family or task level.

And if you do run into trouble while upgrading, the Maintenance Wizard has several built-in features to assist you with your issue, including its own Trouble Shooting page, helpful log files, user notepad and automated generation of .zip files to send into Support.

Unit 18　SQL Fundamentals

WORDS AND EXPRESSIONS

create [kri'eit]　创建
use [ju:s]　使用
alter ['ɔ:ltə]　修改
drop [drɔp]　移除
insert [in'sə:t]　插入
update [ʌp'deit]　更新
delete [di' li:t]　删除
bulk [bʌlk]分批
permanently ['pɜ:məntli]　永久地
employee [ˌemplɔi'i:]　雇员
stellar ['stelə]　一流的
DDL (The Data Definition Language)　数据定义语言
DML (Data Manipulation Language)　数据操作语言

QUESTIONS AND ANSWERS

1. SQL commands can be divided into two main sublanguages, what are they?
2. How to establish a table titled "student" in the "college" database with the SQL?
3. How to select all the students whose grade are more than 85 with SELECT command?

TEXT

SQL is short for Structured Query Language, which comprises one of the fundamental building blocks of modern database architecture. SQL defines the methods used to create and manipulate relational database on all major platforms.

SQL commands can be divided into two main sublanguages. The Data Definition Language (DDL) contains the commands used to create and destroy databases and database objects. After the database structure is defined with DDL, database administrators and users can utilize the Data Manipulation Language (DML) to insert, retrieve and modify the data contained within it.

These commands will primarily be used by database administrators during the setup and removal phases of a database project. Let's take a look at the structure and usage of four basic

DDL commands.

CREATE

Once you've installed a database management system (DBMS) on your computer, you can create and manage many independent databases. For example, you may want to maintain a database of customer contacts for your sales department and a personnel database for your HR department. The CREATE command can be used to establish each of these databases on your platform. For example, the command:

CREATE DATABASE employees

creates an empty database named "employees" on your DBMS. After creating the database, your next step is to create tables that will contain data. Another variant of the CREATE command can be used for this purpose. The command:

CREATE TABLE personalinfo

(firstname char(20) not null, lastname char(20) not null, employeeid int not null)

establishes a table titled "personalinfo" in the current database. In our example, the table contains three attributes: firstname, lastname and employeeid.

USE

The USE command allows you to specify the database you wish to work with within your DBMS. For example, if we're currently working in the sales database and want to issue some commands that will affect the employees' database. We would preface them with the following SQL command:

USE employees

It's important to always be conscious of the database you are working in before issuing SQL commands that manipulate data.

ALTER

Once you've created a table within a database, you may wish to modify the definition of it. The ALTER command allows you to make changes to the structure of a table without deleting and recreating it. Take a look at the following command:

ALTER TABLE personalinfo

ADD salary money null

This example adds a new attribute to the personalinfo table—an employee's salary. The "money" argument specifies that an employee's salary will be stored using a dollars and cents format. Finally, the "null" keyword tells the database that it's OK for this field to contain no value for any given employee.

DROP

The final command of the Data Definition Language, DROP, allows us to remove entire database objects from our DBMS. For example, if we want to permanently remove the personalinfo table that we created, we'd use the following command:

DROP TABLE personalinfo

Similarly, the command below would be used to remove the entire employees' database:

DROP DATABASE employees

Use this command with care! Remember that the DROP command removes entire data structures from your database. If you want to remove individual records, use the DELETE command of the Data Manipulation Language.

Different from DDL, the Data Manipulation Language (DML) is used to retrieve, insert and modify database information. These commands will be used by all database users during the routine operation of the database. Let's take a brief look at the basic DML commands.

INSERT

The INSERT command in SQL is used to add records to an existing table. Returning to the previous personalinfo example, let's imagine that our HR department needs to add a new employee to their database. They could use a command similar to the one shown below:

INSERT INTO personalinfo

VALUES('bart', 'simpson',12345,$45000)

Note that there are four values specified for the record. These correspond to the table attributes in the order they were defined: firstname, lastname,employeeid, and salary.

SELECT

The SELECT command is the most commonly used command in SQL. It allows database users to retrieve the specific information they desire from an operational database. Let's take a look at a few examples, again using the personalinfo table. Note that the asterisk is used as a wildcard in SQL. This literally means "Select everything from the personalinfo table".

SELECT *

FROM personalinfo

Alternatively, users may want to limit the attributes that are retrieved from the database. For example, the Human Resources Department may require a list of the last names of all employees in the company. The following SQL command would retrieve only that information:

SELECT lastname

FROM personalinfo

Finally, the WHERE clause can be used to limit the records that are retrieved to those that meet specified criteria. The CEO might be interested in reviewing the personal records of all highly paid employees. The following command retrieves all of the data contained within personalinfo for records that have a salary value greater than $50,000:

SELECT *

FROM personalinfo

WHERE salary>$50000

UPDATE

The UPDATE command can be used to modify information contained within a table, either in bulk or individually. Each year, our company gives all employees a 3% cost-of-living increase in their salary. The following SQL command could be used to quickly apply this to all of the employees stored in the database:

UPDATE personalinfo

SET salary=salary * 1.03

On the other hand, our new employee Bart Simpson has demonstrated performance above and beyond the call of duty. Management wishes to recognize his stellar accomplishments with a 55,000 raise. The WHERE clause could be used to single our Bart for this raise:

UPDATE personalinfo

SET salary=salary+$50000

WHERE employeeid=12345

DELETE

Finally, let's take a look at the DELETE command. You'll find that the syntax of this command is similar to that of the other DML commands. Unfortunately, our latest corporate earnings report didn't quite meet expectations and poor Bart has been laid off. The DELETE command with a WHERE clause can be used to remove his record from the personalinfo table:

DELETE FROM personalinfo

WHERE employeeid=12345

EXERCISES

1. Judge whether the following given statements are true or false. If correct, write T in parentheses; otherwise, write F.

(1)　(　) Users can utilize the DDL to insert, retrieve and modify the data contained within it.

(2)　(　) The USE command can be used to establish each of these databases on your platform.

(3)　(　) The DROP command removes entire data structures from your database.

(4)　(　) Users can limit the attributes that are retrieved from the database.

2. Complete the following note-taking with the information mentioned in the text.

(1)　SQL commands can be divided into two main sublanguages: DDL and _____.

(2)　The _____ command allows you to make changes to the structure of a table without deleting and recreating it.

(3)　The _____ command allows database users to retrieve the specific information they desire from an operational database.

(4)　The _____ command can be used to remove his record from a certain table.

READING MATERIALS

Product Description: IBM DB2

DB2 9.5 for Linux UNIX and Windows

DB2 9.5 further extends the value clients have experienced in the first year of DB2 Viper.

The deep compression capability in DB2 Viper offered a unique capability for clients to drive down the costs associated with an ever growing quantity of data. Beyond the concrete storage cost savings deep compression offered, it also simplified administration of large databases and lead to welcome performance gains for many clients.

> Reflex Response. Today's environments require the data server to be able to react immediately to ensure availability, optimal performance and lower cost. Innovation in this area has long been a focus for DB2. This latest release continues this trend with additional capabilities in the areas of install, manage, and maintain combine to give DB2 the ability to respond as if by reflex to take the right action at the right time to make the best use of system and personnel resources without sacrificing any of the robustness of DB2. Examples include the ability to automatically start compressing data once there's enough data to create a meaningful dictionary and full integration of Tivoli System Automation easily automate the failover process. These benefits are a direct extension of our work with key ISVs like SAP to make DB2 a hands free component of the business solution.

> Confident Compliance. The ability to keep ahead of the ever changing threats and government or internal regulations to ensure fully protection of information assets is a growing concern. DB2 9.5 offers a number of new or enhanced capabilities designed to make clients confident of their ability to meet these objectives. This includes a number of changes to the audit facility of DB2 to both simplify the administration of enabling audits, provide greater flexibility in delivering the right level of information required for auditing, and delivering a new set of tooling for both administrators and auditors to facilitate the audit process and better integrate DB2 into an enterprise-wide audit strategy.

The new capabilities are not limited to keeping track of what happens, but also ensuring that only the desired access happens. To this end we've expanded the depth of the role based security model, enabled trusted context in three-tier environments like WebSphere to be easily and efficiently propagated to the data server to provide more control on when privileges are available to users. The ability to use advanced encryption throughout the data lifecycle further minimizes the potential for unintended access to sensitive data.

> Transactional XML. Many DB2 customers have leveraged the unique XML capabilities provided by this hybrid data server to transform their use of XML from a convenient way of representing data to a true business asset. DB2 9.5 extends the extremely efficient management & querying capabilities of pureXML with the performance and efficiency required to leverage XML in a large scale transaction environment. To accomplish this, we first streamlined the management of small XML documents to minimize I/O and conserve storage space. In fact, pureXML can store these XML documents in about half the space required for restoring them in flat files or LOBs. The result is additional performance gains as much as 2x for a general transaction processing workload and as

much as 5x for bulk inserts with shema validation. DB2 9.5 is also the FIRST major database to support the XQuery update standard. With this comes the ability for sub-document updates that can significantly improve performance when changing only a piece of the XML document.

➤ Dynamic Warehousing. InfoSphere Warehouse is a complete, multipurpose environment that allows you to access, analyze and act on real-time historical and operational information so you can get the insight and agility that you and your people need to consistently generate new opportunities, contain costs and satisfy customers.

IBM DB2 for i 6.1 — Sophistication Simplified

The IBM DB2 for i 6.1 enhancements provide a great foundation for taking your business solutions to new levels. In this article, discover how IBM has delivered the new, sophisticated technology while still maintaining the easy-to-use nature of DB2 for i that has spoiled developers and administrators through the years.

➤ What's with the i Name? With the announcement of the new IBM Power System platform in April, IBM unified the integrated IBM System iTM with the IBM System pTM product line. The integrated operating system that has served IBM AS/400, iSeries, and System i clients for over two decades was also renamed from i5/OS to IBM i. As a result, IBM DB2 for i is now the official name of the integrated database replacing DB2 for i5/OS — or more simply known as DB2 for i.

➤ Introduction. Keeping ahead of the competition is a top priority in today's ever-changing business environment. From an IT and database perspective, this means that you need to be able to access and present business data in new, insightful ways to your user, and deliver these capabilities yesterday!

Ease of use is a key aspect of the integrated database IBM DB2 for i, which has attracted and spoiled System i and AS/400 customers for a long time. As the complexities and requirements of IBM System i applications have increased in recent years, IBM has significantly enhanced the SQL functionality and performance of DB2 for i, while keeping it easy to use and manage. As you will discover in this article, the V6R1 release delivers another round of sophisticated SQL features, paired with self-managing and self-learning features.

Unit 19　Foundation of Database

WORDS AND EXPRESSIONS

collection [kəˈlekʃən]　集合

subscriber [sʌbsˈkraibə]　订户

table [ˈteibl]　表

form [fɔ:m]　表格

report [riˈpɔ:t]　报表

query [ˈkwiəri]　查询

script [skript]　文稿

retrieval [riˈtri:vəl]　查询，检索

data integrity　数据完整性

front-end　前端程序

back-end　后端程序

client/server　客户/服务器结构模型（C/S 结构）

zip code　邮递区号

QUESTIONS AND ANSWERS

1. Could you tell me in which aspects the database system is mainly used?

2. Can you talk about the difference between data and information?

3. What is the database management system?

4. What is data?

TEXT

Database System Application

Database System is now used in various aspects of society, such as government apparatus, universities, airlines, banking, telecommunication and manufacturing. In government apparatus, database can be used to know information resources of human affairs. In banking, database can be used for customer information, accounts, loans, and banking transactions. In airlines, database can be used for reservations and schedule information. In universities, database can be used for student information, course registrations and grades. In the management of economy, database can proceed at statistic data and analysis, and obtain a result so as to guide the enterprises to develop rapidly. Previously, very few people interacted directly with the database system. Till the late 1990s, the assessment to database for users increased with the development of Internet work. For example, when you access a network station and look through the contents on it, in fact, you are accessing the data stored in database. When you access an online shopping website, information about your order for goods may be retrieved from a database. Database plays an important role in most enterprises today.

Basic Database Conceptions

➢ Data are a collection of facts made up of numbers, characters and symbols, stored on a computer in such a way that the computer can process it. Data are different from information in that they are formed of facts stored in machine-readable form. When the facts are processed by the computer into a form, which can be understood by people, the data become information.

➢ Database is a collection of related objects, including tables, forms, reports, queries, and scripts, created and organized by a database management system (DBMS). A database can contain information of almost any type, such as a list of magazine subscribers, personal data on the space shuttle astronauts, or a collection of graphical images and video clips.

➢ Database management system is a software that controls the data in a database, including overall organization, storage, retrieval, security, and data integrity. A DBMS can also format reports for printed output and can import and export data from other applications using standard file formats. A data-manipulation language is usually provided to support database queries.

➢ Database model is the method used by a database management system (DBMS) to organize the structure of the database. The most common database model is the relational database.

➢ Database Server. It is any database application that follows the client/server architecture model, which divides the application into two parts: a front-end running on the user's workstation and a back-end running on a server or host computer. The front-end interacts with the user, collects and displays the data. The back-end performs all the computer-intensive tasks, including data analysis, storage, and manipulation.

➢ Relational database is a database model in which the data always appear from the point of view of the user to be a set of two-dimensional tables, with the data presented in rows and columns. The rows in a table represent records, which are collections of information about a specific topic; such as the entries in a doctor's patient list. The columns represent fields, which are the items that make up a record, such as the name, address, city, state, and zip code in an address list database.

EXERCISES

1. Judge whether the following given statements are true or false. If correct, write T in parentheses; otherwise, write F.

(1)　(　) In government apparatus, database can be used to know information resources of human affairs.

(2)　(　) The assessment to database for users decreased with the development of Internet in 1990s.

(3)　(　) Information about your order for goods may be retrieved from a database.

(4)　(　) The rows in a table represent records, which are collections of information about a specific topic.

2. Complete the following note-taking with the information mentioned in the text.

(1)　Database can proceed at statistic _____ and analysis to guide the enterprises to develop rapidly.

(2)　Data are formed of facts stored in _____ form.

(3)　The most common database model is the _____.

(4)　Database application divides into two parts: a front-end and _____.

READING MATERIALS

Product Description: Visual FoxPro 9.0 SP2

SQL Language Improvements

The SELECT-SQL Command and other SQL commands have been substantially enhanced in Visual FoxPro 9.0. This topic describes the enhancements made to these commands, and new commands that affect SQL performance.

Subquery Enhancements

Visual FoxPro 9.0 provides more flexibility in subqueries. For example, multiple subqueries are now supported. The following describes the enhancements to subqueries in Visual FoxPro 9.0.

➢ Multiple Subqueries. Visual FoxPro 9.0 supports multiple subquery nesting, with correlation allowed to the immediate parent. There is no limit to the nesting depth. In Visual FoxPro 8.0, error 1842 (SQL: Subquery nesting is too deep) was generated when more than one level of subquery nesting occurred. The following is the general syntax for multiple subqueries: SELECT...WHERE...(SELECT...WHERE ... (SELECT...)...)...

Example:

The following example queries, which will generate an error in Visual FoxPro 8.0, are now supported in Visual FoxPro 9.0.

```
CREATE CURSOR MyCursor (field1 I)
INSERT INTO MyCursor VALUES (0)
CREATE CURSOR MyCursor1 (field1 I)
INSERT INTO MyCursor1 VALUES (1)
CREATE CURSOR MyCursor2 (field1 I)
INSERT INTO MyCursor2 VALUES (2)
SELECT * FROM MyCursor T1 WHERE EXISTS ;
    (SELECT * FROM MyCursor1 T2 WHERE NOT EXISTS ;
    (SELECT * FROM MyCursor2 T3))
*** Another multiple subquery nesting example ***
SELECT * FROM table1 WHERE table1.iid IN ;
    (SELECT table2.itable1id FROM table2 WHERE table2.iID IN ;
    (SELECT table3.itable2id FROM table3 WHERE table3.cValue = "value"))
```

➢ GROUP BY in a Correlated Subquery. Many queries can be evaluated by executing a subquery once and substituting the resulting value or values into the WHERE clause of the outer query. In queries that include a correlated subquery (also known as a repeating subquery), the subquery depends on the outer query for its values. This means that the subquery is executed repeatedly, once for each row that might be selected by the outer query.

Visual FoxPro 8.0 does not allow using GROUP BY in correlated subquery, and generates error 1828 (SQL: Illegal GROUP BY in subquery). Visual FoxPro 9.0 removes this limitation and supports GROUP BY for correlated subqueries allowed to return more than one record.

The following is the general syntax for the GROUP BY clause in a correlated subquery:
```
SELECT ... WHERE ... (SELECT ... WHERE ... GROUP BY ...) ...
```
Example:

The following example, which will generate an error in Visual FoxPro 8.0, is now supported in Visual FoxPro 9.0.

```
CLOSE DATABASES ALL
CREATE CURSOR MyCursor1 (field1 I, field2 I, field3 I)
INSERT INTO MyCursor1 VALUES(1,2,3)
CREATE CURSOR MyCursor2 (field1 I, field2 I, field3 I)
INSERT INTO MyCursor2 VALUES(1,2,3)
SELECT * FROM MyCursor1 T1 WHERE field1;
    IN (SELECT MAX(field1) FROM MyCursor2 T2 ;
    WHERE T2.field2=T1.field2 GROUP BY field3)
```

➢ TOP N in a Non-correlated Subquery. Visual FoxPro 9.0 supports the TOP N clause in a non-correlated subquery. The ORDER BY clause should be present if the TOP N clause is used, and this is the only case where it is allowed in subquery.

The following is the general syntax for the TOP N clause in a non-correlated subquery:

SELECT ... WHERE ... (SELECT TOP nExpr [PERCENT] ... FROM ... ORDER BY ...) ...

Example:

The following example, which will generate an error in Visual FoxPro 8.0, is now supported in Visual FoxPro 9.0.

CLOSE DATABASES ALL

CREATE CURSOR MyCursor1 (field1 I, field2 I, field3 I)

INSERT INTO MyCursor1 VALUES(1,2,3)

CREATE CURSOR MyCursor2 (field1 I, field2 I, field3 I)

INSERT INTO MyCursor2 VALUES(1,2,3)

SELECT * FROM MyCursor1 WHERE field1 ;

    IN (SELECT TOP 5 field2 FROM MyCursor2 ORDER BY field2)

➢ Subqueries in a SELECT List. Visual FoxPro 9.0 allows a subquery as a column or a part of expression in a projection. A subquery in a projection has exactly the same requirements as a subquery used in a comparison operation. If a subquery does not return any records, NULL value is returned.

In Visual FoxPro 8.0, an attempt to use a subquery as a column or a part of expression in a projection would generate error 1810 (SQL: Invalid use of subquery).

The following is the general syntax for a subquery in a SELECT list: SELECT ... (SELECT ...) ... FROM ...

Example:

The following example, which will generate an error in Visual FoxPro 8.0, is now supported in Visual FoxPro 9.0.

SELECT T1.field1, (SELECT field2 FROM MyCursor2 T2;

    WHERE T2.field1=T1.field1) FROM MyCursor1 T1

➢ Aggregate Functions in a SELECT List of a Subquery. In Visual FoxPro 9.0, aggregate functions are now supported in a SELECT list of a subquery compared using the comparison operators <, <=, >, >= followed by ALL, ANY, or SOME.

Example:

The following example demonstrates the use of an aggregate function (the COUNT( ) function) in a SELECT list of a subquery.

CLOSE DATABASES ALL

CREATE CURSOR MyCursor (field1 i)

INSERT INTO MyCursor VALUES (6)

INSERT INTO MyCursor VALUES (0)

INSERT INTO MyCursor VALUES (1)

INSERT INTO MyCursor VALUES (2)

INSERT INTO MyCursor VALUES (3)

INSERT INTO MyCursor VALUES (4)

INSERT INTO MyCursor VALUES (5)

```
INSERT INTO MyCursor VALUES (–1)
CREATE CURSOR MyCursor2 (field2 i)
INSERT INTO MyCursor2 VALUES (1)
INSERT INTO MyCursor2 VALUES (2)
INSERT INTO MyCursor2 VALUES (2)
INSERT INTO MyCursor2 VALUES (3)
INSERT INTO MyCursor2 VALUES (3)
INSERT INTO MyCursor2 VALUES (3)
INSERT INTO MyCursor2 VALUES (4)
INSERT INTO MyCursor2 VALUES (4)
INSERT INTO MyCursor2 VALUES (4)
INSERT INTO MyCursor2 VALUES (4)
SELECT * FROM MyCursor WHERE field1;
    < ALL (SELECT count(*) FROM MyCursor2 GROUP BY field2) ;
    INTO CURSOR MyCursor3
BROWSE
```

➢ Correlated Subqueries Allow Complex Expressions to Be Compared with Correlated Field.

In Visual FoxPro 8.0, correlated fields can only be referenced in the following forms:

correlated field <comparison> local field

-or-

local field <comparison> correlated field

In Visual FoxPro 9.0, correlated fields support comparison to local expressions, as shown in the following forms:

correlated field <comparison> local expression

-or-

local expression <comparison> correlated field

A local expression must use at least one local field and cannot reference any outer (correlated) field.

Example:

In the following example, a local expression (MyCursor2.field2/2) is compared to a correlated field (MyCursor.field1).

```
SELECT * FROM MyCursor ;
WHERE EXISTS(SELECT * FROM MyCursor2;
WHERE MyCursor2.field2 / 2 > MyCursor.field1)
```

➢ Changes for Expressions Compared with Subqueries. In Visual FoxPro 8.0, the left part of a comparison using the comparison operators [NOT] IN, <, <=, =, ==, <>, !=, >=, >, ALL, ANY, or SOME with a subquery must reference one and only one table from the FROM clause. In case of a comparison with correlated subquery, the table must also be the correlated table.

In Visual FoxPro 9.0, comparisons work in the following ways.

- The expression on the left side of an IN comparison must reference at least one table from the FROM clause.
- The left part for the conditions =, ==, <>, != followed by ALL, SOME, or ANY must reference at least one table from the FROM clause.
- The left part for the condition >, >=, <, <= followed by ALL, SOME, or ANY (SELECT TOP...) must reference at least one table from the FROM clause.
- The left part for the condition >, >=, <, <= followed by ALL, SOME, or ANY (SELECT <aggregate function>...) must reference at least one table from the FROM clause.
- The left part for the condition >, >=, <, <= followed by ALL, SOME, or ANY (subquery with GROUP BY and/or HAVING) must reference at least one table from the FROM clause.

In Visual FoxPro 9.0, the left part of a comparison that does not come from the list (for example, ALL, SOME, or ANY are not included) doesn't have to reference any table from the FROM clause.

In all cases, the left part of the comparison is allowed to reference more than one table from the FROM clause. For a correlated subquery, the left part of the comparison does not have to reference the correlated table.

Subquery in an UPDATE-SQL Command SET List

In Visual FoxPro 9.0, the UPDATE-SQL Command now supports a subquery in the SET clause.

A subquery in a SET clause has exactly the same requirements as a subquery used in a comparison operation. If the subquery does not return any records, the NULL value is returned.

Only one subquery is allowed in a SET clause. If there is a subquery in the SET clause, subqueries in the WHERE clause are not allowed.

The following is the general syntax for a subquery in the SET clause: UPDATE ... SET ... (SELECT ...) ...

Example:

The following example demonstrates the use of a subquery in the SET clause.

```
CLOSE DATA
CREATE CURSOR MyCursor1 (field1 I , field2 I NULL)
INSERT INTO MyCursor1 VALUES (1,1)
INSERT INTO MyCursor1 VALUES (2,2)
INSERT INTO MyCursor1 VALUES (5,5)
INSERT INTO MyCursor1 VALUES (6,6)
INSERT INTO MyCursor1 VALUES (7,7)
INSERT INTO MyCursor1 VALUES (8,8)
```

```
INSERT INTO MyCursor1 VALUES (9,9)
CREATE CURSOR MyCursor2 (field1 I , field2 I)
INSERT INTO MyCursor2 VALUES (1,10)
INSERT INTO MyCursor2 VALUES (2,20)
INSERT INTO MyCursor2 VALUES (3,30)
INSERT INTO MyCursor2 VALUES (4,40)
INSERT INTO MyCursor2 VALUES (5,50)
INSERT INTO MyCursor2 VALUES (6,60)
INSERT INTO MyCursor2 VALUES (7,70)
INSERT INTO MyCursor2 VALUES (8,80)
UPDATE MyCursor1 SET field2=100+(SELECT field2 FROM MyCursor2;
WHERE MyCursor2.field1=MyCursor1.field1) WHERE field1>5
    SELECT MyCursor1
LIST
```

Unit 20　Microsoft SQL Server 2000

WORDS AND EXPRESSIONS

scalability [ˌskeiləˈbiliti]　可伸缩性

reliability [riˌlaiəˈbiliti]　可靠性

availability [əˌveiləˈbiliti]　可用性

security [siˈkjuəriti]　安全性

multiprocessor [ˈmʌltiˈprəusesə]　多处理器

overhead [ˈəuvəhed]　企业管理费用

login [lɔgˈin]　登录

user [ˈjuːzə]　用户

permission [pə(ː)ˈmiʃən]　权限

statement [ˈsteitmənt]　语句

batche [bætʃ]　批处理

execute [ˈeksikjuːt]　执行

customize [kʌstəmaiz]　自定义

domain [dəuˈmein]　域名

predefined script　预定义脚本

SQL Query Analyzer SQL　查询分析器

Windows DNA (Windows Distributed interNet Applications Architecture) Windows　分布式集成网络应用体系结构

user-friendly　用户界面友好的

Enterprise-level　企业级

Microsoft Management Console (MMC) Microsoft　管理控制台

T-SQL (Transact-Structured Query Language) Debugger T-SQL　调试器

Execution Plan　执行计划

Server Trace　服务器跟踪

Index Tuning Wizard　索引优化向导

Client Statistics　客户统计

Microsoft SQL Server Desktop Engine (MSDE)　基于 SQL Server 核心技术面向小型应用程序桌面扩展的可靠的存储引擎和查询处理器

Vulnerability [vʌlnərəˈbiləti]　受感染文件，漏洞

slammer.worm 针对 Microsoft SQL Server 2000 和 MSDE 2000 的一种蠕虫病毒

SP (service pack)　软件补丁包

QUESTIONS AND ANSWERS

1. What are the features of Microsoft SQL Server 2000?
2. What are the utility tools of Microsoft SQL Server 2000?
3. What is the meaning of "SQL Critical Update"?
4. What is the meaning of "SQL Scan"?
5. What is the meaning of "SQL Check"?
6. Do you have a plan to learn Microsoft SQL Server 2000? What's it?

TEXT

Microsoft SQL Server 2000 is a full-featured relational database management system (RDBMS) that offers a variety of administrative tools to ease the burdens of database development, maintenance and administration.

There are eight different editions of SQL Server 2000. Whether you are a developer, IT professional, or a database administrator, whether you are just developing and testing or are ready to deploy in production, there is a SQL Server 2000 edition for you and your organization. SQL Server 2000 is more than a relational database management system; it is a complete database and analysis product that meets the scalability and reliability requirements of the most demanding enterprises.

Microsoft SQL Server 2000 Features

Internet Integration

Microsoft SQL Server 2000 database engine includes integrated XML support. It also has the scalability, availability, and security features required to operate as the data storage component of the largest Web sites. The SQL Server 2000 programming model is integrated with the Windows DNA architecture for developing Web applications, and SQL Server 2000 supports features such as English Query and the Microsoft Search Service to incorporate user-friendly queries and powerful search capabilities in Web applications.

Scalability and Availability

The same database engine can be used across platforms ranging from laptop computers running Microsoft Windows 98 through large, multiprocessor servers running Microsoft Window 2000 Data Center Edition. SQL Server 2000 Enterprise Edition supports features such as federated servers, indexed views, and large memory support that allow it to scale to the performance levels required by the largest Web sites.

Enterprise-level Database Features

The SQL Server 2000 relational database engine supports the feature required to support demanding data processing environments. The database engine protects data integrity while minimizing the overhead of managing thousands of users concurrently modifying the database. SQL Server 2000 distributed queries allow you to reference data from multiple sources as if it were a part of a SQL Server 2000 database, while at the same time, the distributed transaction support protects the integrity of any updates of the distributed data. Replication allows you to also maintain multiple copies of data, while ensuring that the separate copies remain synchronized. You can replicate a set of data to multiple, mobile, disconnected users, have them work autonomously, and then merge their modifications back to the publisher.

Ease of Installation, Deployment, and Use

SQL Server 2000 includes a set of administrative and development tools that improve upon the process of installing, deploying, managing, and using SQL Server across several sites. These features allow you to rapidly deliver SQL Server applications that customers can implement with a minimum of installation and administrative overhead.

SQL Server 2000 Utility Tools

SQL Server 2000 includes tools for extracting and analyzing summary data for online analytical processing. SQL Server also includes tools for visually designing databases and analyzing data using English-based questions.

SQL Server 2000 has several utility tools, such as Enterprise Manager, Query Analyzer, service Manager, Data Transformation Services and Books Online and so on. Enterprise Manager and Query Analyzer are the most important and constant used tools.

SQL Server Enterprise Manager

SQL Server Enterprise Manager is the primary administrative tool for Microsoft SQL Server 2000 and provides a Microsoft Management Console (MMC)—compliant user interface that allows users to:

- Define groups of servers running SQL Server.
- Register individual servers in a group.
- Configure all SQL Server options for each registered server.
- Create and administer all SQL Server databases, objects, logins, users, and permissions in each registered server.
- Define and execute all SQL Server administrative tasks on each registered server.
- Design and test SQL statements, batches, and scripts interactively by invoking SQL Query Analyzer.
- Invoke the various wizards defined for SQL Server.

MMC is a tool that presents a common interface for managing different server applications in a Microsoft Windows network. Server applications provide a component called an MMC snap-in that presents MMC users with a user interface for managing the server application. SQL Server Enterprise Manager is the Microsoft SQL Server 2000 MMC snap-in.

SQL Query Analyzer

Microsoft SQL Server 2000 SQL Query Analyzer is a graphical tool that allows you to:

- Create queries and other SQL scripts and execute them against SQL Server databases.
- Quickly create commonly used database objects from predefined scripts. (Templates)
- Quickly copy existing database objects. (Object Browser scripting feature)
- Execute stored procedures without knowing the parameters.(Object Browser procedure execution feature)
- Debug stored procedures. (T-SQL Debugger)
- Debug query performance problems. (Show Execution Plan, Show Server Trace, Show Client Statistics, Index Tuning Wizard)
- Locate objects within databases (object search feature), or view and work with objects. (Object Browser)
- Quickly insert, update, or delete rows in a table. (Open Table window)
- Create keyboard shortcuts for frequently used queries. (Custom query shortcuts feature)
- Add frequently used commands to the Tools menu. (Customized Tools menu feature)

SQL Server 2000 Security Tools

SQL Server 2000 security tools are used to scan instances of Microsoft SQL Server 2000 and Microsoft SQL Server Desktop Engine (MSDE) 2000. The tools help detect instances vulnerable to the "Slammer" worm, and then apply update to the affected files. There are three tools, namely SQL Scan, SQL Check, and SQL Critical Update.

SQL Critical Update

SQL Critical Update scans the computer on which it is running for instances of SQL Server 2000 and MSDE 2000 that are vulnerable to the "Slammer" worm, and updates the affected files. SQL Critical Update runs on Windows 98, Windows ME, Windows NT 4.0, Windows 2000 and Windows XP, and is supported in a clustered environment.

Instances of SQL Server 2000 with Service Pack2 (SP2) and security patch MS02-039, MS02-043, MS02-056, or MS02-061, or instances with SP3 or later, are not vulnerable to the Slammer worm.

Restrictions:

- SQL Critical Update must be run on the local machine.
- SQL Critical Update will fix vulnerabilities that it discovers; it cannot be used to simply disable an instance of SQL Server.
- SQL Critical Update does not install SP3. It only updates vulnerable files.
- SQL Critical Update will fix only MSDE installations that are the same language as the SQL Critical Update language you are running.
- The user running SQL Critical Update must have permission to replace SQL Server files in the Program Directory.
- SQL Critical Update works only if the ssnetlib.dll file exists for each instance of SQL server being patched.

- SQL Critical Update must target the active node in order to work in a clustered environment.

SQL Scan

SQL Scan (sqlscan.exe) scans an individual computer, a Windows domain, or a range of IP addresses for instances of SQL Server 2000 and MSDE 2000, and identifies instances that may be vulnerable to the Slammer worm. SQL Scan runs on Windows 2000 or higher and can identify instances of SQL Server 2000 and MSDE 2000 running on Windows NT 4.0, Windows 2000, or Windows XP (Professional).Computers running SQL Server 7.0 and earlier are not vulnerable.

SQL Scan does not locate instances of SQL Server that are running on Windows 98, Windows ME, or Windows XP (Home). SQL Scan does not detect instances of SQL Server that were started from the command prompt.

NOTE: In some circumstances, shutdown of an infected SQL Server instance may not complete successfully. You may need to use system management tools to terminate an infected process.

SQL Scan requires one of the following items as input:

(1)   A domain;

(2)   A range of IP addresses;

(3)   A single machine name.

SQL Scan must be run with domain administrator privileges when it is used to scan remote machines. Otherwise, you must be an administrator on the local machines.

SQL Scan will not return a conclusive result if either the ssnetlib.dll or sqlservr.exe file has been renamed. If these files have been renamed, you should change the names back to their original names.

SQL Scan identifies vulnerable SQL server instances on clustered machines, but does not disable them. Disabling and shutting down of SQL Server instances must be managed manually.

SQL Check

SQL Check scans the computer on which it is running for instances of SQL Server 2000 and MSDE 2000 that is vulnerable to the Slammer worm.SQL Check identifies vulnerable SQL Server 2000 clusters, but does not disable them. SQL Check runs on Windows 98, Windows ME, Windows NT 4.0, Windows 2000 and Windows XP. On computers running Windows NT 4.0, Windows 2000 and Windows XP, it stops and disables the SQL Server and SQL Agent services. On computers running Windows 98 and Windows ME, it identifies vulnerable instances but does not stop or disable any services.

SMS Deployment Tool

This tool provides a SQLFIX.SMS file that you can use to create a package in SMS to deploy SQL Server Critical Update.

- Servpriv.exe. If you are running SQL Server 2000 Service Pack2 (SP2) or MSDE 2000 SP2 and have already applied SQL Critical Update, you must also run the servpriv.exe utility that is included in this package to set the appropriate user rights on the corresponding service registry keys. This utility was first released in the Microsoft Security Bulletin MS02-043. Servpriv.exe automatically runs with SQL Critical Update 3.0 and the new SQL Critical Update Wizard available in the latest SQL Critical Update Kit. If you are applying SQL Critical Update for the first time, you do not need to run servpriv.exe separately. See the readme-Servpriv.txt file for additional details.

- SQL Server Critical Update Wizard. The SQL Critical Update Wizard will walk you through the steps of detecting the vulnerability and updating the affected files. The SQL Critical Update Wizard runs on Windows 98, Windows ME, Windows NT 4.0, Windows 2000 and Windows XP. If you want to install SQL Critical Update on a cluster, use the SQL Critical Update tool instead of the Wizard.

EXERCISES

1. Judge whether the following given statements are true or false. If correct, write T in parentheses; otherwise, write F.

(1)　(　) SQL Server 2000 is only a relational database management system, not a complete database and analysis product.

(2)　(　) SQL Server 2000 supports the Microsoft Search Service.

(3)　(　) SQL Server 2000 distributed queries forbid you to reference data from multiple sources.

(4)　(　) Shutdown of an infected SQL Server instance may not complete successfully.

2. Complete the following note-taking with the information mentioned in the text.

(1)　The SQL Server 2000 is integrated with the _____ architecture to develop Web applications.

(2)　The SQL Server 2000 allows you to also maintain multiple copies of data, while ensuring that the separate copies remain _____.

(3)　SQL Server 2000 includes a set of administrative and development tools that improve upon the process of installing, deploying, managing, and using SQL Server across _____.

(4)　SQL Scan runs on Windows 2000 or _____.

READING MATERIALS

Product Description: SQL Server 2008

SQL Server 2008 delivers on Microsoft's Data Platform vision by helping your organization manage any data, any place, any time. It enables you to store data from structured, semi-structured, and unstructured documents, such as images and music, directly within the database. SQL Server 2008 delivers a rich set of integrated services that enable you to do more with your data such as query, search, synchronize, report, and analyze. Your data can be stored and accessed in your largest servers within the data center all the way down to desktops and mobile devices, enabling you to have control over your data no matter where it is stored.

SQL Server 2008 enables you to consume your data within custom applications developed using Microsoft .NET and Visual Studio and within your service-oriented architecture (SOA) and business process through Microsoft BizTalk Server while information workers can access data directly in the tools they use every day, such as the 2007 Microsoft Office system. SQL Server 2008 delivers a trusted, productive, and intelligent data platform for all your data needs.

SQL Server 2008 New Features

SQL Server provides the highest levels of security, reliability, and scalability for your business-critical applications.

Transparent Data Encryption

Enable encryption of an entire database, data files, or log files, without the need for application changes. Benefits of this include: search encrypted data using both range and fuzzy searches, search secure data from unauthorized users, and data encryption without any required changes in existing applications.

Extensible Key Management

SQL Server 2005 provides a comprehensive solution for encryption and key management. SQL Server 2008 delivers an excellent solution to this growing need by supporting third-party key management and HSM products.

Auditing

Create and manage auditing via DDL, while simplifying compliance by providing more comprehensive data auditing. This enables organizations to answer common questions, such as, "What data was retrieved?"

Learn More About SQL Server 2008 Security

Enhanced Database Mirroring

SQL Server 2008 builds on SQL Server 2005 by providing a more reliable platform that has enhanced database mirroring, including automatic page repair, improved performance, and enhanced supportability.

Automatic Recovery of Data Pages

SQL Server 2008 enables the principal and mirror machines to transparently recover from 823/824 types of data page errors by requesting a fresh copy of the suspect page from the mirroring partner transparently to end users and applications.

Log Stream Compression

Database mirroring requires data transmissions between the participants of the mirroring implementations. With SQL Server 2008, compression of the outgoing log stream between the participants delivers optimal performance and minimizes the network bandwidth used by database mirroring.

Learn More About SQL Server 2008 High Availability

Resource Governor

Provide a consistent and predictable response to end users with the introduction of Resource Governor, allowing organizations to define resource limits and priorities for different workloads, which enable concurrent workloads to provide consistent performance to their end users.

Predictable Query Performance

Enable greater query performance stability and predictability by providing functionality to lock down query plans, enabling organizations to promote stable query plans across hardware server replacements, server upgrades, and production deployments.

Data Compression

Enable data to be stored more effectively, and reduce the storage requirements for your data. Data compression also provides significant performance improvements for large I/O bound workloads, like data warehousing.

Hot Add CPU

Dynamically scale a database on demand by allowing CPU resources to be added to SQL Server 2008 on supported hardware platforms without forcing any downtime on applications. Note that SQL Server already supports the ability to add memory resources online.

Learn More About SQL Server 2008 Performance and Scale

To take advantage of new opportunities in today's fast-moving business world, companies need the ability to create and deploy data-driven solutions quickly. SQL Server 2008 reduces time and cost of management and development of applications.

Policy-based Management

Policy-based Management is a policy-based system for managing one or more instances of SQL Server 2008. Use this with SQL Server Management Studio to create policies that manage entities on the server, such as the instance of SQL Server, databases, and other SQL Server objects.

Streamlined Installation

SQL Server 2008 introduces significant improvements to the service life cycle for SQL Server through the re-engineering of the installation, setup, and configuration architecture. These improvements separate the installation of the physical bits on the hardware from the configuration of the SQL Server software, enabling organizations and software partners to provide recommended installation configurations.

Performance Data Collection

Performance tuning and troubleshooting are time-consuming tasks for the administrator. To provide actionable performance insights to administrators, SQL Server 2008 includes more extensive performance data collection, a new centralized data repository for storing performance data, and new tools for reporting and monitoring.

Learn More About SQL Server 2008 Manageability

Language Integrated Query (LINQ)

Enable developers to issue queries against data, using a managed programming language, such as C# or VB.NET, instead of SQL statements. Enable seamless, strongly typed, set-oriented queries written in .NET languages to run against ADO.NET (LINQ to SQL), ADO.NET DataSets (LINQ to DataSets), the ADO.NET Entity Framework (LINQ to Entities), and to the Entity Data Service Mapping provider. Use the new LINQ to SQL provider that enables developers to use LINQ directly on SQL Server 2008 tables and columns.

ADO.NET Object Services

The Object Services layer of ADO.NET enables the materialization, change tracking, and persistence of data as CLR objects. Developers using the ADO.NET framework can program against a database, using CLR objects that are managed by ADO.NET. SQL Server 2008 introduces more efficient, optimized support that improves performance and simplifies development.

Learn More About SQL Server 2008 ADO.NET

Object Services and LINQ

SQL Server 2008 introduces new date and time data types:

- DATE—A date-only type;
- TIME—A time-only type;
- DATETIME OFFSET—A time-zone-aware datetime type;
- DATETIME2—A datetime type with larger fractional seconds and year range than the existing DATETIME type.

The new data types enable applications to have separate data and time types while providing large data ranges or user defined precision for time values.

HIERARCHY ID

Enable database applications to model tree structures in a more efficient way than currently possible. New system type HIERARCHY ID can store values that represent nodes in a hierarchy tree. This new type will be implemented as a CLR UDT, and will expose several efficient and useful built-in methods for creating and operating on hierarchy nodes with a flexible programming model.

FILESTREAM Data

Allow large binary data to be stored directly in an NTFS file system, while preserving an integral part of the database and maintaining transactional consistency. Enable the scale-out of large binary data traditionally managed by the database to be stored outside the database on more cost-effective storage without compromise.

Integrated Full Text Search

Integrated Full Text Search makes the transition between Text Search and relational data seamless, while enabling users to use the Text Indexes to perform high-speed text searches on large text columns.

Sparse Columns

NULL data consumes no physical space, providing a highly efficient way of managing empty data in a database. For example, Sparse Columns allows object models that typically have numerous null values to be stored in a SQL Server 2008 database without experiencing large space costs.

Large User-Defined Types

SQL Server 2008 eliminates the 8-kB limit for User-Defined Types (UDTs), allowing users to dramatically expand the size of their UDTs.

Spatial Data Types

Build spatial capabilities into your applications by using the support for spatial data.

Implement Round Earth solutions with the geography data type. Use latitude and longitude coordinates to define areas on the Earth's surface.

Implement Flat Earth solutions with the geometry data type. Store polygons, points, and lines that are associated with projected planar surfaces and naturally planar data, such as interior spaces.

Learn More About SQL Server 2008 Programmability and Spatial Data

SQL Server 2008 provides a comprehensive platform, delivering intelligence where users want it.

Backup Compression

Keeping disk-based backups online is expensive and time-consuming. With SQL Server 2008 backup compression, less storage is required to keep backups online, and backups run significantly faster since less disk I/O is required.

Partitioned Table Parallelism

Partitions enable organizations to manage large growing tables more effectively by transparently breaking them into manageable blocks of data. SQL Server 2008 builds on the advances of partitioning in SQL Server 2005 by improving the performance on large partitioned tables.

Star Join Query Optimizations

SQL Server 2008 provides improved query performance for common data warehouse scenarios. Star Join Query optimizations reduce query response time by recognizing data warehouse join patterns.

Grouping Sets

Grouping Sets is an extension to the GROUP BY clause that lets users define multiple groupings in the same query. Grouping Sets produces a single result set that is equivalent to a

UNION ALL of differently grouped rows, making aggregation querying and reporting easier and faster.

Change Data Capture

With Change Data Capture, changes are captured and placed in change tables. It captures complete content of changes, maintains cross-table consistency, and even works across schema changes. This enables organizations to integrate the latest information into the data warehouse.

MERGE SQL Statement

With the introduction of the MERGE SQL Statement, developers can more effectively handle common data warehousing scenarios, like checking whether a row exists, and then executing an insert or update.

SQL Server Integration Services (SSIS) Pipeline Improvements

Data Integration packages can now scale more effectively, making use of available resources and managing the largest enterprise-scale workloads. The new design improves the scalability of runtime into multiple processors.

SQL Server Integration Services (SSIS) Persistent Lookups

The need to perform lookups is one of the most common ETL operations. This is especially prevalent in data warehousing, where fact records need to use lookups to transform business keys to their corresponding surrogates. SSIS increases the performance of lookups to support the largest tables.

Learn More About SQL Server 2008 Integration Services and Data Warehousing

Analysis Scale and Performance

SQL Server 2008 drives broader analysis with enhanced analytical capabilities and with more complex computations and aggregations. New cube design tools help users streamline the development of the analysis infrastructure enabling them to build solutions for optimized performance.

Block Computations

Block Computations provides a significant improvement in processing performance enabling users to increase the depth of their hierarchies and complexity of the computations.

Writeback

New MOLAP enabled writeback capabilities in SQL Server 2008 Analysis Services removes the need to query ROLAP partitions. This provides users with enhanced writeback scenarios from within analytical applications without sacrificing the traditional OLAP performance.

Learn More About SQL Server 2008 Analysis Services

Enterprise Reporting Engine

Reports can easily be delivered throughout the organization, both internally and externally, with simplified deployment and configuration. This enables users to easily create and share reports of any size and complexity.

Internet Report Deployment

Customers and suppliers can effortlessly be reached by deploying reports over the Internet.

Manage Reporting Infrastructure

Increase supportability and the ability to control server behavior with memory management, infrastructure consolidation, and easier configuration through a centralized store and API for all configuration settings.

Report Builder Enhancements

Easily build ad-hoc and author reports with any structure through Report Designer.

Built-in Forms Authentication

Built-in forms authentication enables users to easily switch between Windows and Forms.

Report Server Application Embedding

Report Server application embedding enables the URLs in reports and subscriptions to point back to front-end applications.

Microsoft Office Integration

SQL Server 2008 provides new Word rendering that enables users to consume reports directly from within Microsoft Office Word. In addition, the existing Excel renderer has been greatly enhanced to accommodate the support of features, like nested data regions, sub-reports, as well as merged cell improvements. This lets users maintain layout fidelity and improves the overall consumption of reports from Microsoft Office applications.

Predictive Analysis

SQL Server Analysis Services continues to deliver advanced data mining technologies. Better Time Series support extends forecasting capabilities. Enhanced Mining Structures deliver more flexibility to perform focused analysis through filtering as well as to deliver complete information in reports beyond the scope of the mining model. New cross-validation enables confirmation of both accuracy and stability for results that you can trust. Furthermore, the new features delivered with SQL Server 2008 Data Mining Add-ins for Office 2007 empower every user in the organization with even more actionable insight at the desktop.

Computer Networks

Unit 21　The Network Component

WORDS AND EXPRESSIONS

discipline ['disiplin]　纪律，学科

communication ['kə,mju:ni'keiʃn]　传达，信息，交通，通讯

router ['ru:tə(r)]　路由器

destination [,desti'neiʃən]　目的地

MAC　Media Access Control　介质访问控制

preclude [pri'klu:d]　排除

segment ['segmənt]　段，节，片断

dedicate ['dedikeit]　献（身），致力

amplify ['æmplifai]　放大，增强

regenerate [ri'dʒenərit]　使新生，重建，改革，革新

span [spæn]　跨度，跨距，范围

relatively ['relətivli]　相关地

deploy [di'plɔi]　展开，配置

domestic [də'mestik]　家庭的，国内的

PSTN　Public Switched Telephone Network　公共开关电话网络

converge [əkən'və:dʒ]　聚合，集中于一点

transceiver [ətræn'si:və]　无线电收发机，收发器

topology [tə'pɔlədʒi]　拓扑，布局

terminator ['tə:mineitə]　终结器

bounce [bauns]　（使）反跳，弹起

recipient [ri'sipiənt]　容纳者，容器

alternatively [ɔ:l'tɜ:nətivli]　作为选择，二者择一地

offset ['ɔ:fset]　弥补，抵消，

mesh [meʃ]　网孔，网丝，网眼

propagate ['prɔpəgeit]　传播

hierarchy ['haiərɑ:ki]　层次

QUESTIONS AND ANSWERS

1. What is difference between switch and hub?

2. What are the capacities of the server?

3. Why do we call the internet is the largest WLAN?

4. What kind of way is that the wireless network transfers the data?

5. What does the network topology refer to?

6. Can you tell us something about physical and logical topology?

7. Which kind of topology is one of the most common?

8. What are the advantages and disadvantages of the star topology?

9. What is another name of the tree topology?

10. Could you talk about network device and topology?

TEXT

Computer networking is the engineering discipline concerned with the communication between computer systems or devices. A computer network is any set of computers or devices connected to each other with the ability to exchange data.

Common basic networking devices

- Router: a specialized network device that determines the next network point to which it can forward a data packet towards the destination of the packet. A Router checks the data packet for its destination address and protocol format details. If the router microprocessor finds a match in its address tables, it routes it to that destination address.

- Bridge: a forwarding technique used in packet-switched computer networks. Unlike routing, it depends on flooding and examination of source addresses in received packet headers to locate unknown devices. Once a device has been located, its location is recorded in a table where the MAC address is stored so as to preclude the need for further broadcasting.

- Switch: a device that allocates traffic from one network segment to certain lines (intended destination(s)) which connect the segment to another network segment. So unlike a hub a switch splits the network traffic and sends it to different destinations rather than to all systems on the network.

- Hub: connects multiple Ethernet segments together making them act as a single segment. When using a hub, every attached all the objects, compared to switches, which provide a dedicated connection between individual nodes.

- Repeater: a device to amplify or regenerate digital signals received while sending them from one part of a network into another.

The network types

Local area network (LAN)

A local area network is a network that spans a relatively small space and provides services to a small number of people. A peer-to-peer or client-server method of networking may be used. A peer-to-peer network is where each client shares their resources with other workstations in the network. Examples of peer-to-peer networks are: Small office networks where resource use is minimal and a home network. A client-server network is where every client is connected to the server and each other. Client-server networks use servers in different capacities. The server performs one task such as file server, while other servers can not only perform in the capacity of file servers and print servers, but also can conduct calculations and use them to provide information to clients.

Wide Area Network (WAN)

A wide area network is a network where a wide variety of resources are deployed across a large domestic area or internationally. An example of this is a multinational business that uses a WAN to interconnect their offices in different countries. The largest and best example of a WAN is the Internet, which is a network composed of many smaller networks. The Internet is considered the largest network in the world. The PSTN (Public Switched Telephone Network) also is an extremely large network that is converging to use Internet technologies, although not necessarily through the public Internet.

Wireless networks (WLAN, WWAN)

A wireless network is basically the same as a LAN or a WAN but there are no wires between hosts and servers. The data is transferred over sets of radio transceivers. These types of networks are beneficial when it is too costly or inconvenient to run the necessary cables.

Network topology

Network topology is the layout pattern of interconnections of the various elements (links, nodes, etc.) of a computer network. Network topologies may be physical or logical. Physical topology means the physical design of a network including the devices, location and cable installation. Logical topology refers to how data is actually transferred in a network as opposed to its physical design.

Topology can be considered as a virtual shape or structure of a network. This shape does not correspond to the actual physical design of the devices on the computer network. The computers on a home network can be arranged in a circle but it does not necessarily mean that it represents a ring topology.

Classification of physical topologies

Bus

In local area networks where bus topology is used, each machine is connected to a single cable. Each computer or server is connected to the single bus cable through some kind of connector. A terminator is required at each end of the bus cable to prevent the signal from bouncing back and forth on the bus cable. A signal from the source travels in both directions to all machines connected on the bus cable until it finds the MAC address or IP address on the network that is the intended recipient. If the machine address does not match the intended address for the data, the machine ignores the data. Alternatively, if the data does match the machine address, the data is accepted. Since the bus topology consists of only one wire, it is rather inexpensive to implement when compared to other topologies. However, the low cost of implementing the technology is offset by the high cost of managing the network. Additionally, since only one cable is utilized, it can be the single point of failure. If the network cable breaks, the entire network will be down.

Star

In local area networks with a star topology, each network host is connected to a central hub. In contrast to the bus topology, the star topology connects each node to the hub with a point-to-point connection. All traffic that traverses the network passes through the central hub. The hub acts as a signal booster or repeater. The star topology is considered the easiest topology to design and implement. An advantage of the star topology is the simplicity of adding additional nodes. The primary disadvantage of the star topology is that the hub represents a single point of failure.

Ring

A network topology that is set up in a circular fashion in which data travels around the ring in one direction and each device on the right acts as a repeater to keep the signal strong as it travels. Each device incorporates a receiver for the incoming signal and a transmitter to send the data on to the next device in the ring. The network is dependent on the ability of the signal to travel around the ring.

Mesh

Mesh networking is a type of networking where each node must not only capture and disseminate its own data, but also serve as a relay for other sensor nodes, that is, it must collaborate to propagate the data in the network.

Tree

It is also known as a hierarchy network. This type of network topology in which a central'root' node (the top level of the hierarchy) is connected to one or more other nodes that are one level lower in the hierarchy (i.e., the second level) with a point-to-point link between each of the second level nodes and the top level central 'root' node, while each of the second level nodes that are connected to the top level central 'root' node will also have one or more other nodes that are one level lower in the hierarchy (i.e., the third level) connected to it, also with a point-to-point link, the top level central 'root' node being the only node that has no other node above it in the hierarchy.

EXERCISES

1. Judge whether the following given statements are true or false. If correct, write T in parentheses; otherwise, write F.

(1)　(　) Internet is the biggest network in the world.

(2)　(　) The router checks the addresses from other network devices.

(3)　(　) Distances between nodes, physical interconnections, transmission rates, and/or signal types may differ in two networks and yet their topologies may be identical.

(4)　(　) The wireless LAN is not popular at present.

2. Complete the following note-taking with the information mentioned in the text.

(1)　_____ select the best path to translates information from one network to another, based on the destination address and origin.

(2)　_____ connects network segments and does not generally encompass unintelligent or passive network devices.

(3)　Any particular network topology is determined only by the graphical mapping of the configuration of _____ and/or _____ connections between nodes.

(4)　The defining characteristics of LANs, in contrast to _____, include their usually higher data-transfer rates, smaller geographic area, and lack of a need for leased telecommunication lines.

READING MATERIALS

How to set up a wireless LAN?

A wireless local area network is usually restricted to a relatively small area such as a house, office or public place, such as a library, coffee shop or even a park. A wireless network has many distinct advantages over a wired network, namely a lower set-up cost. Setting up a wireless LAN is moderately easy because of the plug-and-play nature of today's wireless routers.

➢ Buy a wireless router(Figure 21-1). The most popular models are from Linksys, Belkin and D-Link. Which brand you use isn't important; what is important is the ability to allow users with all types of wireless cards in their computers to easily connect. Virtually every wireless router sold today is backwards compatible, so even laptop users with older wireless protocols can easily connect.

➢ Attach your router to your cable or DSL modem using an Ethernet RJ-45 cable(Figure 21-2). One end plugs into the modem in the RJ-45 port (be careful not to force it into the RJ-11 port on a DSL modem) and the other into the Internet or WAN port on your router.

➢ Connect a computer to your router to configure it, either using an Ethernet RJ-45 cable or with a computer with wireless capabilities. To connect wirelessly with a Windows-based computer, click on the "Start" menu and select "Connect To" to see the list of available wireless networks. The default name of the wireless network is usually the same name as the router.

➢ Open a Web browser to configure your router. Each model has its own default address (such as 192.168.0.1), so check the documentation that came with your router. The same goes with the default logon.

➢ Change some settings once you've logged on to your router following the user manual.

➢ Test the network to make sure the signal is strong everywhere it needs to be. Long distances, chimneys and built-in appliances are signal killers, so consider using a repeater in areas where the signal is deficient.

Figure 21-1 Wireless Router

Figure 21-2 Network Cable

Unit 22 Network Architecture

WORDS AND EXPRESSIONS

architecture ['ɑ:kitektʃə] 体系结构

framework ['freimwə:k] 构架，框架，结构

configuration [kən,figju'reiʃən] 构造，结构，配置

conceptual [kən'septʃuəl,-tjuəl] 概念上的

reasonably ['ri:zənəbli] 适度地，相当地

adverse ['ædvə:s] 方向相反的，敌对的

characteristic [ə,kæriktə'ristik] 特性，特征

specifications [,spesifi'keiʃən] 详述，规格，说明书，规范

entity ['entiti] 实体

synchronization [,siŋkrənai'zeiʃən] 同步

congestion [kən'dʒestʃən] 拥塞

reliability [ri,laiə'biliti] 可靠性

sequence ['si:kwəns] 次序，顺序，序列

segmentation [, segmən'teiʃən] 分割

retransmit [,ri:trænz'mit] 转播，转发，中继站发送

duplex ['dju:pleks] 双方的

adjournment [ə'dʒ3:nmənt] 休会，延期

graceful ['greisful] 优美的

explicit [iks'plisit] 明白的，明确的

syntax ['sintæks] 语法，有秩序的排列

encapsulate [in'kæpsjuleit] 压缩

encryption [in'kripʃən] 加密

sufficient [sə'fiʃənt] 充分的，足够的

FTP File Transfer Protocol 文件传送[输]协议

QUESTIONS AND ANSWERS

1. What does network architecture refer to?

2. Who did develop the OSI model?

3. What service does each layer provide?

4. Is each layer implemented independently in OSI model?

5. Which layer has sub layers?

6. What is difference between upper layer and lower layers?

7. Which layer dose the routers operate at?

8. Who does provide controls the dialogues between computers?

9. What is the main function of the presentation layer?

10. Could you talk about the application layer?

TEXT

Network architecture is the design of a communications network. It is a framework for the specification of a network's physical components and their functional organization and configuration, its operational principles and procedures, as well as data formats used in its operation.

OSI Model

Open Systems Interconnection (OSI) model is a reference model developed by ISO (International Organization for Standardization) in 1984, as a conceptual framework of standards for communication in the network across different equipment and applications by different vendors. It is now considered the primary architectural model for inter-computing and internetworking communications. It is a way of sub-dividing a communications system into smaller parts called layers. A layer is a collection of similar functions that provide services to the layer above it and receives services from the layer below it. On each layer, an instance provides services to the instances at the layer above and requests service from the layer below.

Each layer is reasonably self-contained so that the tasks assigned to each layer can be implemented independently. This enables the solutions offered by one layer to be updated without adversely affecting the other layers. The OSI 7 layers model has clear characteristics. Layers 7 through 4 deal with end to end communications between data source and destinations. Layers 3 to 1 deal with communications between network devices. On the other hand, the seven layers of the OSI model can be divided into two groups: upper layers (layers 7, 6 & 5) and lower layers (layers 4, 3, 2, 1). The upper layers of the OSI model deal with application issues and generally are implemented only in software. The highest layer, the application layer, is closest to the end user. The lower layers of the OSI model handle data transport issues. The physical layer and the data link layer are implemented in hardware and software. The lowest layer, the physical layer, is closest to the physical network medium (the wires, for example) and is responsible for placing data on the medium.

Layer 1: Physical Layer

The Physical Layer defines the electrical and physical specifications for devices. In particular, it defines the relationship between a device and a transmission medium, such as a copper or optical cable. This layer conveys the bit stream - electrical impulse, light or radio signal—through the network at the electrical and mechanical level. It provides the hardware means of sending and receiving data on a carrier, including defining cables, cards and physical aspects.

Layer 2: Data Link Layer

The Data Link Layer provides the functional and procedural means to transfer data between network entities and to detect and possibly correct errors that may occur in the Physical Layer. At this layer, data packets are encoded and decoded into bits. It furnishes transmission protocol knowledge and management and handles errors in the physical layer, flow control and frame synchronization. The data link layer is divided into two sub layers: The Media Access Control (MAC) layer and the Logical Link Control (LLC) layer. The MAC sub layer controls how a computer on the network gains access to the data and permission to transmit it. The LLC layer controls frame synchronization, flow control and error checking.

Layer 3: Network Layer

The Network Layer provides the functional and procedural means of transferring variable length data sequences from a source host on one network to a destination host on a different network, while maintaining the quality of service requested by the Transport Layer. This layer provides switching and routing technologies, creating logical paths, known as virtual circuits, for transmitting data from node to node. Routing and forwarding are functions of this layer, as well as addressing, internetworking, error handling, congestion control and packet sequencing. Routers operate at this layer—sending data throughout the extended network and making the Internet possible.

Layer 4: Transport Layer

The Transport Layer provides transparent transfer of data between end users, providing reliable data transfer services to the upper layers. The Transport Layer controls the reliability of a given link through flow control, segmentation/desegmentation, and error control. Some protocols are state and connection oriented. This means that the Transport Layer can keep track of the segments and retransmit those that fail. The Transport layer also provides the acknowledgement of the successful data transmission and sends the next data if no errors occurred. This layer ensures complete data transfer.

Layer 5: Session Layer

The Session Layer controls the dialogues (connections) between computers. It establishes, manages and terminates the connections between the local and remote application. It provides for full-duplex, half-duplex, or simplex operation, and establishes checkpointing, adjournment, termination, and restart procedures. The OSI model made this layer responsible for graceful close of sessions, which is a property of the Transmission Control Protocol, and also for session checkpointing and recovery, which is not usually used in the Internet Protocol Suite. The Session Layer is commonly implemented explicitly in application environments that use remote procedure calls.

Layer 6: Presentation Layer

The Presentation Layer establishes context between Application Layer entities, in which the higher-layer entities may use different syntax and semantics if the presentation service provides a mapping between them. If a mapping is available, presentation service data units are encapsulated into session protocol data units, and passed down the stack. This layer provides independence from data representation (e.g., encryption) by translating between application and network formats. The presentation layer transforms data into the form that the application accepts. This layer formats and encrypts data to be sent across a network.

Layer 7: Application Layer

The Application Layer is the OSI layer closest to the end user, which means that both the OSI application layer and the user interact directly with the software application. This layer interacts with software applications that implement a communicating component. Such application programs fall outside the scope of the OSI model. Application layer functions typically include identifying communication partners, determining resource availability, and synchronizing communication. When identifying communication partners, the application layer determines the identity and availability of communication partners for an application with data to transmit. When determining resource availability, the application layer must decide whether sufficient network or the requested communication exists.

Everything at this layer is application-specific. This layer provides application services for file transfers, E-mail, and other network software services. Telnet and FTP are applications that exist entirely in the application level.

EXERCISES

1. Judge whether the following given statements are true or false. If correct, write T in parentheses; otherwise, write F.

(1)　(　) OSI model developed by ISO in 1982.

(2)　(　) Each OSI layer has clear characteristics.

(3)　(　) Physical layer deals with hardware and software.

(4)　(　) Reliable data transfer services provide by transport layer.

2. Complete the following note-taking with the information mentioned in the text.

(1)　OSI model is a way of sub-dividing a communications system into smaller parts called _____.

(2)　The Physical Layer defines the means of transmitting raw bits rather than logical data_____over a physical link connecting network nodes.

(3)　The _____ Layer is responsible for routing packets delivery including routing through intermediate routers.

(4)　In computer networking, the Transport Layer provides _____ communication services for applications.

READING MATERIALS

Product Description:TCP/IP Model and OSI Model(Figure 22-1)

OSI reference model came into existence way before TCP/IP model was created. Advance research project agency (ARPA) created OSI reference model so that they can logically group the similarly working components of the network into various layers of the protocol. But after the advent of the Internet, there arose the need for a streamlined protocol suite, which would address the need of the ever growing Internet. So the Defense Advanced Research Project Agency (DARPA), decided to create TCP/IP protocol suite. This was going to address many, if not all the issues that had arisen with OSI reference model.

TCP/IP is based on a four-layer reference model. All protocols that belong to the TCP/IP protocol suite are located in the top three layers of this model.As shown in the following illustration, each layer of the TCP/IP model corresponds to one or more layers of the seven-layer Open Systems Interconnection (OSI) reference model proposed by the International Standards Organization (ISO).

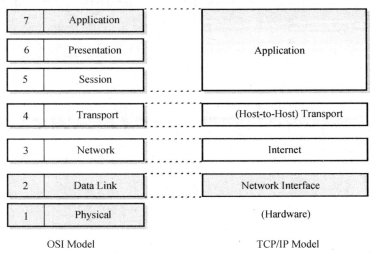

Figure 22-1   OSI Model and TCP/IP Model

The TCP/IP architectural model has four layers that approximately match six of the seven layers in the OSI Reference Model. The TCP/IP model does not address the physical layer, which is where hardware devices reside. The next three layers—network interface, internet and (host-to-host) transport—correspond to layers 2, 3 and 4 of the OSI model. The TCP/IP application layer conceptually "blurs" the top three OSI layers. It's also worth noting that some people consider certain aspects of the OSI session layer to be arguably part of the TCP/IP host-to-host transport layer.

There are a number of reasons for the success of the TCP/IP model over the OSI model:

➢ Internet is built on the foundation of the TCP/IP suite. The tentacles of the Internet and the World Wide Web have spread throughout the world and that is the main reason for the success of TCP/IP model over the OSI model.

➢ TCP/IP protocols were initially researched under a project in the Department of Defense (DOD). DOD was committed to international standards and most of its operational requirements couldn't be met by the OSI model. So it started to develop the TCP/IP. Since the DOD is the largest consumer of software products in the world, the vendors were encouraged to develop TCP/IP based products.

The three top layers in the OSI model—the Application Layer, the Presentation Layer and the Session Layer—are not distinguished separately in the TCP/IP model where it is just the Application Layer. While some pure OSI protocol applications also combined them, there is no requirement that a TCP/IP protocol stack needs to impose monolithic architecture above the Transport Layer. While basic OSI documents do not consider tunneling, there is some concept of tunneling in yet another extension to the OSI architecture, specifically the transport layer gateways within the International Standardized Profile framework. The associated OSI development effort, however, has been abandoned given the overwhelming adoption of TCP/IP protocols.

Unit 23　Protocol

WORDS AND EXPRESSIONS

description [disˈkripʃən]　描写，描述

format [ˈfɔːmæt]　版式，形式，格式

mechanism [ˈmekənizəm]　机构，机制

compression [kəmˈpreʃ(ə)n]　压缩

daemon [ˈdiːmən]　Internet 中用于邮件收发的后台程序

widespread [ˈwaidspred]　普遍的

prerequisite [ˈpriːˈrekwizit]　先决条件

conceptual [kənˈseptʃuəl]　概念上的

proxy [ˈprɔksi]　代理服务器

gateway [ˈgeitwei]　网关

initialize [iˈniʃəlaiz]　初始化

Transmission Control Protocol (TCP)　传输控制协议

synthesis [ˈsinθisis]　综合，合成

namely [ˈneimli]　即，也就是

abstraction [æbˈstrækʃən]　提取

scope [skəup]　范围

reflect [riˈflekt]　反射，反映

loosely [ˈluːsli]　宽松地，松散地

relevant [ˈrelivənt]　有关的，相应的

facilitate [fəˈsiliteit]）　使容易，使便利

User Datagram Protocol (UDP)　用户数据报协议

Post Office Protocol　邮局协议，用于电子邮件的接收

Simple Mail Transfer Protocol　简单邮件传送协议

recipient [riˈsipiənt]　容纳者，容器

Telnet　远程登录

utility [juːˈtiliti]　效用，有用

port [pɔːt]　端口

QUESTIONS AND ANSWERS

1. What will happen if network has no protocol? Why?

2. Where can we find some network protocol?

3. Which protocols are the most important internet communication protocols?

4. Where do we use the HTTP? What can it do?

5. What is a most commonly communication protocol for transferring the files over the internet?

6. What should the client computer do before it perform a number of the operations like downloading the files?

7. Who does define the fundamental addressing namespaces?

8. Which layer does handle direct host-to-host communication tasks in TCP/IP?

9. Why do we use the POP3 and SMTP?

10. Which default TCP port does the SMPT use?

TEXT

A communications protocol is a formal description of digital message formats and the rules for exchanging those messages in or between computing systems and in telecommunications. Protocols include mechanisms for devices to identify and make connections with each other, as well as formatting rules that specify how data is packaged into messages sent and received. Some protocols also support message acknowledgement and data compression designed for reliable and/or high-performance network communication. Hundreds of different computer network protocols have been developed each designed for specific purposes and environments.

Modern operating systems like Microsoft Windows contain built-in services or daemons that implement support for some network protocols. Applications like Web browsers contain software libraries that support the high level protocols necessary for that application to function. For some lower level TCP/IP and routing protocols, support is implemented in directly hardware (silicon chipsets) for improved performance.

Protocols exist at the several levels of the OSI (open system interconnectivity) layers model. In the telecommunication system, there are one more protocols at each layer of the telephone exchange. The widespread use of the communication protocols is a prerequisite to the internet. The term TCP/IP refers to the protocols suite and a pair of the TCP and IP protocols are the most important internet communication protocols. Most protocols in communication are layered together where the various tasks listed above are divided. Protocols stacks refer to the combination of the different protocols. The OSI reference model is the conceptual model that is used to represent the protocols stacks. There are different network protocols that perform different functions. Following is the description of the some of the most commonly used protocols.

HTTP (Hyper Text Transfer Protocol)

Hypertext transfer protocol is a method of transmitting the information on the web. HTTP basically publishes and retrieves the HTTP pages on the World Wide Web. HTTP is a language that is used to communicate between the browser and web server. The information that is transferred using HTTP can be plain text, audio, video, images, and hypertext. HTTP is a request/response protocol between the client and server. Many proxies, tunnels, and gateways can be existing between the web browser (client) and server (web server). An HTTP client initializes a request by establishing a TCP connection to a particular port on the remote host (typically 80 or 8080). An HTTP server listens to that port and receives a request message from the client. Upon receiving the request, server sends back 200 OK messages, its own message, an error message or other message.

FTP (File Transfer Protocol)

FTP or file transfer protocol is used to transfer (upload/download) data from one computer to another over the internet or through or computer network. FTP is a most commonly communication protocol for transferring the files over the internet. Typically, there are two computers are involved in the transferring the files a server and a client. The client computer that is running FTP client software such as Cuteftp and AceFTP etc initiates a connection with the remote computer (server). After successfully connected with the server, the client computer can perform a number of the operations like downloading the files, uploading, renaming and deleting the files, creating the new folders etc. Virtually operating system supports FTP protocols.

TCP/IP

The Internet Protocol Suite is the set of communications protocols used for the Internet and other similar networks. It is commonly also known as TCP/IP, named from two of the most important protocols in it: the Transmission Control Protocol (TCP) and the Internet Protocol (IP), which were the first two networking protocols defined in this standard. Modern IP networking represents a synthesis of several developments that began to evolve in the 1960s and 1970s, namely the Internet and local area networks, which emerged during the 1980s, together with the advent of the World Wide Web in the early 1990s.

The Internet Protocol Suite consists of four abstraction layers. From the lowest to the highest layer, these are the Link Layer, the Internet Layer, the Transport Layer, and the Application Layer. The layers define the operational scope or reach of the protocols in each layer, reflected loosely in the layer names. Each layer has functionality that solves a set of problems relevant in its scope.

The Link Layer contains communication technologies for the local network the host is connected to directly, the link. It provides the basic connectivity functions interacting with the networking hardware of the computer and the associated management of interface-to-interface messaging. The Internet Layer provides communication methods between multiple links of a computer and facilitates the interconnection of networks. As such, this layer establishes the Internet. It contains primarily the Internet Protocol, which defines the fundamental addressing namespaces, Internet Protocol Version 4 (IPv4) and Internet Protocol Version 6 (IPv6) used to identify and locate hosts on the network. Direct host-to-host communication tasks are handled in the Transport Layer, which provides a general framework to transmit data between hosts using protocols like the Transmission Control Protocol and the User Datagram Protocol (UDP). Finally, the highest-level Application Layer contains all protocols that are defined each specifically for the functioning of the vast array of data communications services. This layer handles application-based interaction on a process-to-process level between communicating Internet hosts.

POP3 (Post Office Protocol)

In computing, E-mail clients such as (MS outlook, outlook express and thunderbird) use Post office Protocol to retrieve emails from the remote server over the TCP/IP connection. Nearly all the users of the Internet service providers use POP 3 in the email clients to retrieve the emails from the email servers. Most email applications use POP protocol.

SMTP (Simple Mail Transfer Protocol)

Simple Mail Transfer Protocol is a protocol that is used to send the email messages between the servers. Most email systems and email clients use the SMTP protocol to send messages to one server to another. In configuring an email application, you need to configure POP, SMTP and IMAP protocols in your email software. SMTP is a simple, text based protocol and one or more recipient of the message is specified and then the message is transferred. SMTP connection is easily tested by the Telnet utility. SMTP uses the by default TCP port number 25.

EXERCISES

1. Judge whether the following given statements are true or false. If correct, write T in parentheses; otherwise, write F.

(1) ( ) Every operating system has no network protocol.

(2) ( ) Protocols exist at the several levels of the OSI layers model.

(3) ( ) TCP/IP has only two protocols.

(4) ( ) FTP is a most commonly communication protocol for transferring the files over the internet.

2. Complete the following note-taking with the information mentioned in the text.

(1) In computer protocols means a set of _____, a communication language or set of standards between two or more computing devices.

(2) _____ and _____ used to identify and locate hosts on the network.

(3) SMTP is a standard network protocol used for _____ email messages to a mail server on the Internet.

(4) The Internet Protocol is the principal component of the Internet Layer, and it defines two addressing systems to _____ network hosts computers, and to locate them on the network.

READING MATERIALS

Product Description：IPv4 and IPv6

Internet Protocol version 4 (IPv4) is the fourth revision in the development of the Internet

Protocol (IP) and it is the first version of the protocol to be widely deployed.

IPv4 uses 32-bit (four-byte) addresses, which limits the address space to 4,294,967,296 (2^{32}) possible unique addresses. However, some are reserved for special purposes such as private networks (~18 million addresses) or multicast addresses (~270 million addresses). This reduces the number of addresses that can potentially be allocated for routing on the public Internet. As addresses are being incrementally delegated to end users, an IPv4 address shortage has been developing. Network addressing architecture redesign via classful network design, Classless Inter-Domain Routing, and network address translation (NAT) have contributed to delay significantly the inevitable exhaustion; but on February 3, 2011, IANA's primary address pool was exhausted when the last 5 blocks were allocated to the 5 regional Internet registries (RIRs).

IPv4 addresses may simply be written in any notation expressing a 32-bit integer value. IPv4 reserves some addresses for special purposes such as private networks (~18 million addresses) or multicast addresses (~270 million addresses).

IPv4 addresses are canonically represented in dot-decimal notation, which consists of four decimal numbers, each ranging from 0 to 255, separated by dots, e.g., 172.16.254.1. Each part represents a group of 8 bits (octet) of the address. In some cases of technical writing, IPv4 addresses may be presented in various hexadecimal, octal, or binary representations. Three classes (A, B, and C) were defined for universal unicast addressing(Table 23-1). Depending on the class derived, the network identification was based on octet boundary segments of the entire address. Each class used successively additional octets in the network identifier, thus reducing the possible number of hosts in the higher order classes (B and C). The following table gives an overview of this now obsolete system.

Table 23-1   IP Address Class

Class	Leading address bits	Range of firse octet	Network ID format	Host ID format	Number of networks	Number of addresses
A	0	0~127	a	b.c.d	2^7=128	2^{24}=16 777 216
B	10	128~191	a.b	c.d	2^{14}=16 384	2^{16}=65 536
C	110	192~223	a.b.c	d	2^{21}=2 097 152	2^8=256

Internet Protocol version 6 (IPv6) is a version of the Internet Protocol (IP) that is designed to succeed Internet Protocol version 4 (IPv4). The Internet's growth has created a need for more addresses than IPv4 has. IPv6 allows for vastly more numerical addresses, but switching from IPv4 to IPv6 may be a difficult process.

IPv6 was developed by the Internet Engineering Task Force (IETF) to deal with the long-anticipated IPv4 address exhaustion. Like IPv4, IPv6 is an Internet Layer protocol for packet-switched internetworking and provides end-to-end datagram transmission across multiple IP networks. While IPv4 allows 32 bits for an Internet Protocol address, IPv6 uses 128-bit addresses, so the new address space supports 2^{128} (approximately 340 undecillion or 3.4×10^{38}) addresses. This expansion allows for many more devices and users on the internet as well as extra flexibility in allocating addresses and efficiency for routing traffic. It also eliminates the primary need for network address translation (NAT), which gained widespread deployment as an effort to alleviate IPv4 address exhaustion.

IPv6 specifies a new packet format, designed to minimize packet header processing by routers. Because the headers of IPv4 packets and IPv6 packets are significantly different, the two protocols are not interoperable. However, in most respects, IPv6 is a conservative extension of IPv4. Most transport and application-layer protocols need little or no change to operate over IPv6; exceptions are application protocols that embed internet-layer addresses, such as FTP.

Unit 24　Network Security

WORDS AND EXPRESSIONS

malicious [mə'liʃəs]　怀恶意的，恶毒的

hacker ['hækə]　电脑黑客

vulnerable ['vʌlnərəb(ə)l]　易受攻击的，易受…的攻击

vigilance ['vidʒiləns]　警戒，警惕

unauthorized ['ʌn'ɔːθəraizd]　未被授权的，未经认可的

intruders [in'truːʒən]　闯入，侵扰

authenticate [ɔː'θentikeit]　鉴别

fingerprint ['fiŋgəprint]　指纹，手印

retinal ['retinəl]　视网膜的

Worms [wɜːmz]　计算机网络 "蠕虫"

Trojan ['trəudʒən]　特洛伊

inhibit [in'hibit]　抑制，约束

anomaly [ə'nɔməli]　不规则，异常的人或物

suspicious [səs'piʃəs]　可疑的，怀疑的

audit ['ɔːdit]　审计，稽核

drawback ['drɔːˌbæk]　缺点，障碍

impair [im'pɛə]　削弱

breach [briːʃ]　违背，破坏，破裂，裂口

heuristic [hjuə'ristik]　启发式的

destructive [dis'trʌktiv]　破坏（性）的

frequently ['friːkwəntli]　频繁地，经常地

legitimate [li'dʒitimit]　合法的，合理的

unsolicited ['ʌnsə'lisitid]　未被恳求的，主动提供的

harvest ['hɑːvist]　收获，收成，结果，成果

embedded [em'bedid]　植入的

QUESTIONS AND ANSWERS

1. What is the network security?

2. What will happen if we do not protect our computer network?

3. What is the function of detection in the network security?

4. How does the network security authenticate the user commonly?

5. Are there some other ways to authenticate the user except username and password?

6. Could you say something about the malware?

7. Is the security management same in all kinds of network?

8. Is there any side-effect when antivirus run in the computer? What is it?

9. What is firewall?

10. What should we do if we encounter spam?

TEXT

Network security is one of the most talked-about subjects on the internet, but what is it and why is it important? Network security guard the computers in a network, business, school, or even home, against malicious software and viruses. An unprotected or under protected network will often run slowly and have errors, and occasionally will be knocked out entirely by hackers or malware. Fortunately, there exist solutions to vulnerable networks. Anti-virus software and vigilance on the part of administrators can protect a network and keep it functioning.

Computer security is the process of preventing and detecting unauthorized use of your computer. Prevention measures help you to stop unauthorized users (also known as "intruders") from accessing any part of your computer system. Detection helps you to determine whether or not someone attempted to break into your system, if they were successful, and what they may have done.

Network security starts from authenticating the user, commonly with a username and a password. Since this requires just one thing besides the user name, i.e. the password which is something you know, this is sometimes termed one factor authentication. With two factor authentication something you have is also used, or with three factors authentication something you are is also used (e.g. a fingerprint or retinal scan).

Once authenticated, a firewall enforces access policies such as what services are allowed to be accessed by the network users. Though effective to prevent unauthorized access, this component may fail to check potentially harmful content such as computer worms or Trojans being transmitted over the network. Anti-virus software or intrusion prevention system (IPS) helps detect and inhibit the action of such malware. An anomaly-based intrusion detection system may also monitor the network and traffic for unexpected (i.e. suspicious) content or behavior and other anomalies to protect resources, e.g. from denial of service attacks or an employee accessing files at strange times. Individual events occurring on the network may be logged for audit purposes and for later high level analysis.

Security Management for networks is different for all kinds of situations. A small home or an office would only require basic security while large businesses will require high maintenance and advanced software and hardware to prevent malicious attacks from hacking and spamming.

Antivirus

Antivirus or anti-virus software is used to prevent, detect, and remove malware, including but not limited to computer viruses, computer worm, trojan horses, spyware and adware. This page talks about the software used for the prevention and removal of such threats, rather than computer security implemented by software methods.

No matter how useful antivirus software can be, it can sometimes have drawbacks. Antivirus software can impair a computer's performance. Inexperienced users may also have trouble understanding the prompts and decisions that antivirus software presents them with. An incorrect decision may lead to a security breach. If the antivirus software employs heuristic detection, success depends on achieving the right balance between false positives and false negatives. False positives can be as destructive as false negatives. Finally, antivirus software generally runs at the highly trusted kernel level of the operating system, creating a potential avenue of attack.

Firewall

A firewall is a device or set of devices designed to permit or deny network transmissions based upon a set of rules and is frequently used to protect networks from unauthorized access while permitting legitimate communications to pass. The term firewall originally referred to a wall intended to confine a fire or potential fire within a building. Later uses refer to similar structures, such as the metal sheet separating the engine compartment of a vehicle or aircraft from the passenger compartment.

Many personal computer operating systems include software-based firewalls to protect against threats from the public Internet. Many routers that pass data between networks contain firewall components and, conversely, many firewalls can perform basic routing functions.

Anti-spam

E-mail spam, also known as junk E-mail or unsolicited bulk E-mail (UBE), is a subset of spam that involves nearly identical messages sent to numerous recipients by E-mail. Definitions of spam usually include the aspects that E-mail is unsolicited and sent in bulk. Spammers collect E-mail addresses from chat rooms, websites, customer lists, newsgroups, and viruses which harvest users' address books, and are sold to other spammers. They also use a practice known as "E-mail appending" in which they use known information about their target (such as a postal address) to search for the target's E-mail address.

To prevent E-mail spam, both end users and administrators of E-mail systems use various anti-spam techniques. Some of these techniques have been embedded in products, services and software to ease the burden on users and administrators. No one technique is a complete solution to the spam problem, and each has trade-offs between incorrectly rejecting legitimate E-mail and not rejecting all spam, and the associated costs in time and effort.

EXERCISES

1. Judge whether the following given statements are true or false. If correct, write T in parentheses; otherwise, write F.

(1)　(　) The network which under the protection will be have no problems.

(2)　(　) Security Management for networks is different for all kinds of situations.

(3)　(　) The computer would be kept safe if the antivirus software has been installed.

(4)　(　) Firewall is just a type of software.

2. Complete the following note-taking with the information mentioned in the text.

(1)　Network security is generally taken as providing protection at the boundaries of an organization by keeping out _____.

(2)　_____ means identify the users who use the computer resources.

(3)　Most of the computer _____ written in the early and mid 1980s was (were) limited to self-reproduction and had no specific damage routine built into the code.

(4)　Unauthorized users is also known as _____ in the network security.

READING MATERIALS

How to protect your wireless LAN

So you have joined the revolution and set up a wireless network in your office or home. Congratulations! But along with the freedom that wireless brings comes responsibility —protecting your wireless network against intrusion. Wireless networks are great because they let you connect from anywhere in your office or home. But that same principle is what makes them vulnerable; hackers do not need to be physically connected (wired) to your network to access it.

Unsecured wireless LANs are easy targets for hackers, both over the Internet and via "wardriving." Wardrivers are hackers armed with laptops and scanner programs who drive around until they detect an unsecured wireless Ethernet connection. They can then log on and do most anything an authorized user could do, just as if they were sitting at the computer. They can, quite literally, snatch your information out of thin air. Think it couldn't happen to your business?

Snatching information is known as "packet sniffing," and can be used to devastating effect over wireless connections. If your wireless network is unsecured, hackers could have access to everything you send and receive over your network. To guarantee that you don't end up a victim, take these steps:

➢ Change the default settings on your router. Routers come with usernames, passwords, and other information installed by the manufacturer. As soon as you install your router, change these values. If you don't, you may as well ask to be hacked.

➢ Use the security measures your wireless devices already have. Wireless encryption protocol, or WEP, is an older security standard, and can be breached by determined hackers. Wi-Fi protected access, or WPA, is newer and much stronger. No matter which encryption standard your devices have, use it. If your system has WPA and offers shared key encryption, enable it.

➤ Install firewalls. Every computer connected to the Internet should be protected by a firewall, and that goes double or triples for computers on wireless networks. You can either install software firewalls on each computer, or install a hardware firewall on your entire network.

E-commerce

Unit 25　Electronic Commerce Concept

WORDS AND EXPRESSIONS

extraordinarily [ikˈstrɔːdənərili]　纪律，学科

spur [spəː]　鞭策，刺激

innovation [ˌinəuˈveiʃən]　改革，创新

Electronic Data Interchange (EDI)　电子数据交换

inventory [ˈinvəntri]　详细目录，存货

transaction [trænˈzækʃən]　办理，处理

encompass [inˈkʌmpəs]　包围，环绕

convenient [kənˈviːnjənt]　便利的，方便的

regionally [ˈriːdʒənəli]　地方的，地域性的

retailer [riˈteilə]　零售商人，传播的人

strategy [ˈstrætidʒi]　策略，军略

wholesaler [ˈhəulseilə]　批发商

popularity [ˌpɔpjuˈlæriti]　普及，流行

catalog [ˈkætəlɔg]　目录，目录册

lucrative [ˈluːkrətiv]　有利的

can [kæn]　罐头，铁罐

nozzle [ˈnɔzl]　管口，喷嘴

investment [inˈvestmənt]　投资

alliance [əˈlaiəns]　联盟，联合

extreme [iksˈtriːm]　极端的，极度的，偏激的

overhead [ˈəuvəhed]　企业一般管理费用

utilize [juːˈtilaiz]　利用

auction [ˈɔːkʃən]　拍卖

bid [bid]　出价，投标

intermediary [ˌintəˈmiːdiəri]　中间者，媒介

barter [ˈbɑːtə]　物品交换，实物交易

swap [swɔp]　交换

disadvantage [ˌdisədˈvɑːntidʒ]　缺点，劣势

QUESTIONS AND ANSWERS

1. What is meaning of the electronic commerce?

2. What is the foundation of electronic commerce?

3. Why do we say the e-commerce marketplace become the virtual main street of the world?

4. What is the main reason for the popularity of B2B sales?

5. Why do many companies provide B2B options at their website?

6. What else are B2B communications do except exchange traditional products?

7. What kind of transaction do we usually consider the sale of the product from the manufacture to the retailer?

8. What is the problem to retailers and manufactures in a B2C online selling environment?

9. Could you talk something about search engine?

10. What are disadvantages of the C2C model?

TEXT

Electronic commerce, commonly known as e-commerce, consists of the buying and selling of products or services over electronic systems such as the Internet and other computer networks. The amount of trade conducted electronically has grown extraordinarily with widespread Internet usage. The use of commerce is conducted in this way, spurring and drawing on innovations in electronic funds transfer, supply chain management, Internet marketing, online transaction processing, Electronic Data Interchange (EDI), inventory management systems, and automated data collection systems. Modern electronic commerce typically uses the World Wide Web at least at some point in the transaction's lifecycle, although it can encompass a wider range of technologies such as E-mail, mobile devices and telephones as well.

The e-commerce marketplace has become the virtual main street of the world. Providing a quick and convenient way of exchanging goods and services both regionally and globally, e-commerce has boomed. In the last decade, many startup e-commerce companies have rapidly stolen market share from traditional retailers and service providers, pressuring these established traditional players to deploy their own commerce websites or to alter company strategy.

Business-to-Business (B2B)

Business-to-business (B2B) describes commerce transactions between businesses, such as between a manufacturer and a wholesaler, or between a wholesaler and a retailer. One major reason for the popularity of B2B sales and services is sheer volume. An individual customer may visit a clothing manufacturer's website catalog and order two pairs of shoes or a sweater. The buyer for a national chain of clothing stores, however, may order 5,000 pairs of shoes and 2,000 sweaters. Without a B2B component, the manufacturer would have lost out on a very lucrative sale. This is why many companies provide B2B options alongside the B2C offerings at their websites and other outlets.

B2B sales are also generated by providing a specialized product line or service not available to the general public. This form of B2B transaction is very common in the manufacturing world. A company which produces shaving cream in cans, for example, may need a specific plastic nozzle. Several plastic injection molding companies would send sales representatives to pitch their particular designs. These nozzles would be useless for individual customers, but a manufacturer may order thousands of them.

With the growth in electronic communications, B2B has taken on even more importance. Instead of simply focusing on business-to-business sales, modern corporations are conducting other financial transactions online. B2B communications are now being used to promote investment, trade stocks and form financial alliances.

Business-to-Consumer (B2C)

B2C is an electronic Internet-facilitated medium where products or services are sold from a company to a consumer. Today, B2C often refers to the online selling of products, which is known as e-tailing. E-tailing products to consumers may be conducted by either manufacturers or retailers. An example of a B2C transaction would be a person buying a pair of shoes from a retailer. However, the sale of the shoe from the shoemaker to the retailer would be considered a B2B transaction.

Virtually any product can be e-tailed. The challenge for retailers and manufactures in a B2C online selling environment is to get consumer traffic to their website marketplace. This need makes search engine marketing (SEM) of extreme importance in business to consumer selling. SEM promotes a website by making the site highly visible on search engines.

When most people think of B2C e-commerce, they think of Amazon, the online bookseller that launched its site in 1995 and quickly took on the nation's major retailers. In addition to online retailers, B2C has grown to include services such as online banking, travel services, online auctions, health information and real estate sites.

Providing on-site security is a must for B2C. Consumers must feel secure in entering credit card and bank information when ordering and paying for items. In spite of its challenges, the business to consumer online model can greatly benefit both consumers and businesses. Consumers get the convenience of shopping online in their own home, while businesses enjoy a low overhead since a storefront and a large inventory aren't necessary. Business can offer good prices to consumers and provide free or low cost shipping in many cases.

Consumer-to-Consumer (C2C)

C2C is an electronic Internet-facilitated medium that involves transactions between consumers utilizing a third-party. A common example is the online auction, in which a consumer posts an item for sale and other consumers bid to purchase it. The third party generally charges a flat fee or commission. The sites are only intermediaries, just there to match consumers. They do not have to check quality of the products being offered. C2C is a modern day form of barter, flea markets, yard sales and swap meets, among others. The C2C model is convenient, because products are there whenever consumers are ready to find and buy them. Yet, C2C does have some disadvantages such as limited payment options and lack of quality control.

EXERCISES

1. Judge whether the following given statements are true or false. If correct, write T in parentheses; otherwise, write F.

(1)　(　) Electronic commerce grows rapidly because of the widespread Internet usage.

(2)　(　) E-commerce company stolen market share from traditional retailers and service providers slowly.

(3)　(　) All the manufacturers can be sale well without a B2B component.

(4)　(　) B2B transaction is very common in the manufacturing world.

(5)　(　) Product quality is not a problem in C2C transaction.

2. Complete the following note-taking with the information mentioned in the text.

(1)　Often referred to as simply e-commerce the phrase is used to describe business that is conducted over the _____ using any of the applications.

(2)　An automobile manufacturer makes several _____ transactions such as buying tires, glass for windscreens, and rubber hoses for its vehicles.

(3)　By using B2C commerce they can instead showcase all of their products on the internet which____ the cost of transaction.

(4)　Electronic commerce can be between two businesses _____ funds, goods, services and/or data or between a business and a customer.

(5)　C2C is characterized by the growth of electronic marketplaces and online _____.

READING MATERIALS

Product Description: Taobao(Figure 25-1)

Figure 25-1　Tabao

Taobao is the largest online retail website and one-stop platform for shopping, socializing and information sharing in china. It is wholly owned by Alibaba Group. Launched in 2003, Taobao (www.taobao.com) is the largest online retail website in China. With more than 800 million product listings and more than 370 million registered users currently, Taobao is the primary online shopping destination for the largest online population in the world. Taobao receives more than 50 million unique visitors daily and is one of the world's top 20 most visited websites.

Taobao Mall (www.tmall.com), a dedicated B2C platform featuring more than 30,000 local and global brands, was introduced in 2008 to complement Taobao's C2C marketplace. Several product verticals were launched on Taobao Mall in 2010, including Consumer Electronics Mall, Hong Kong Design Gallery Mall, Designer Footwear Mall, Home Furnishing Mall and Beauty Mall.

Features and services that serve to enhance the Taobao user experience include Taojianghu, a social networking service; Taobao Open Platform, a resource for third-party software developers; Taobao Data Cube, an aggregate data sharing service; Taobao Mobile app; Taobao Tianxia, a consumer-focused magazine; HiTao, a television show on Hunan Television Network; TaoJapan, a cross-border shopping initiative; and interactive digital television shopping in cooperation with Wasu Digital Television Media Group. Alimama (www.alimama.com), an online advertising exchange and affiliate network for millions of publishers in China, and Koubei.com (www.koubei.com), China's leading classified listing website, are both also part of the Taobao platform.

Unit 26　Electronic Commerce Security

WORDS AND EXPRESSIONS

tremendous [tri'mendəs]　极大的，巨大的

exploitation [ˌeksplɔi'teiʃən]　开发，开采

vulnerability [ˌvʌlnərə'biləti]　弱点，攻击

disclosure [dis'kləuʒə]　揭发，败露

injection [in'dʒekʃən]　注射，注射剂

manipulation [mənipulation]　处理，操作，操纵

cripple ['kripl]　削弱

compromise ['kɔmprəmaiz]　危及…的安全

exaggerate [ig'zædʒəreit]　夸大，夸张

PKI　Public Key Infrastructure　公钥基础设施

RSA　美国 RSA 实验室，以研究加密算法而著名

PGP　Pretty Good Privacy　基于 RSA 公匙加密体系的邮件加密软件

symmetric [si'metrik]　相称性的，均衡的

generate ['dʒenə,reit]　产生，发生

lapse [læps]　失误，下降，丧失

signature ['signitʃə]　签名，署名

reliability [ri,laiə'biliti]　可靠性

integrity [in'tegriti]　完整，完全，完整性

hash [əhæʃ]　无用信息

digest [di'dʒest]　分类，摘要

tamper ['tæmpə]　篡改

repudiation [ri,pju:di'eiʃən]　批判

CA certification authority　认证授权

SSL Secure Socket Layers　加密套接字协议层

negotiate [ni'gəuʃieit]　商议，谈判，磋商

SET　Secure Electronic Transaction　安全电子交易协议

QUESTIONS AND ANSWERS

1. What is the beginning that will lead to further exploitation in e-commerce?

2. Why do we say information security and privacy are very important in e-commerce?

3. What should we protect in the commerce chain of E-Commerce?

4. What is the measure used to protect our privacy in e-commerce?

5. What is difference between public key and private key in PKI?

6. Who can decide the key when sender and recipient transmit large amounts of information?

7. Why is a plain text message run through a hash function?

8. How do we ensure the message digest value remains unchanged?

9. How is the information sent over the Internet?

10. Who did develop the SET?

TEXT

The tremendous increase in online transactions has been accompanied by an equal rise in the number and type of attacks against the security of online payment systems. Some of these attacks have utilized vulnerabilities that have been published in reusable third-party components utilized by websites, such as shopping cart software. Other attacks have used vulnerabilities that are common in any web application, such as SQL injection or cross-site scripting. Successful exploitation of vulnerabilities can lead to a wide range of results. Information and path disclosure vulnerabilities will typically act as initial stages leading to further exploitation. SQL injection or price manipulation attacks could cripple the website, compromise confidentiality, and in worst cases cause the e-commerce business to shut down completely. Since large public money is involved in the transactions, the role of information security and privacy is not exaggerated in this kind of business.

E-Commerce security requirements can be studied by examining the overall process, beginning with the consumer and ending with the commerce server. Considering each logical link in the "commerce chain", the assets that must be protected to ensure secure e-commerce include client computers, the messages travelling on the communication channel, and the web and commerce servers – including any hardware attached to the servers. While telecommunications are certainly one of the major assets to be protected, the telecommunications links are not the only concern in computer and e-commerce security. For instance, if the telecommunications links were made secure but no security measures were implemented for either client computers or commerce and web-servers, then no communications security would exist at all.

Privacy is handled by encryption. In PKI (public key infrastructure) a message is encrypted by a public key, and decrypted by a private key. The public key is widely distributed, but only the recipient has the private key. For authentication (proving the identity of the sender, since only the sender has the particular key) the encrypted message is encrypted again, but this time with a private key. Such procedures form the basis of RSA (used by banks and governments) and PGP

(Pretty Good Privacy, used to encrypt emails).

Unfortunately, PKI is not an efficient way of sending large amounts of information, and is often used only as a first step — to allow two parties to agree upon a key for symmetric secret key encryption. Here sender and recipient use keys that are generated for the particular message by a third body: a key distribution center. The keys are not identical, but each is shared with the key distribution center, which allows the message to be read. Then the symmetric keys are encrypted in the RSA manner, and rules set under various protocols. Naturally, the private keys have to be kept secret, and most security lapses indeed arise here.

Digital Signatures and Certificates

Digital signatures meet the need for authentication and integrity. To vastly simplify matters, a plain text message is run through a hash function and so given a value: the message digest. This digest, the hash function and the plain text encrypted with the recipient's public key is sent to the recipient. The recipient decodes the message with their private key, and runs the message through the supplied hash function to that the message digest value remains unchanged (message has not been tampered with). Very often, the message is also times tamped by a third party agency, which provides non-repudiation.

What about authentication? How does a customer know that the website receiving sensitive information is not set up by some other party posing as the e-merchant? They check the digital certificate. This is a digital document issued by the CA (certification authority) that uniquely identifies the merchant. Digital certificates are sold for emails, e-merchants and web-servers.

Secure Socket Layers (SSL)

Information sent over the Internet commonly uses the set of rules called TCP/IP. The information is broken into packets, numbered sequentially, and an error control attached. Individual packets are sent by different routes. TCP/IP reassembles them in order and resubmits any packet showing errors. SSL uses PKI and digital certificates to ensure privacy and authentication. The procedure is something like this: the client sends a message to the server, which replies with a digital certificate. Using PKI, server and client negotiate to create session keys, which are symmetrical secret keys specially created for that particular transmission. Once the session keys are agreed, communication continues with these session keys and the digital certificates.

PCI, SET

Credit card details can be safely sent with SSL, but once stored on the server they are vulnerable to outsiders hacking into the server and accompanying network. A PCI (peripheral component interconnect: hardware) card is often added for protection, therefore, or another approach altogether is adopted: SET (Secure Electronic Transaction). Developed by Visa and MasterCard, SET uses PKI for privacy, and digital certificates to authenticate the three parties: merchant, customer and bank. More importantly, sensitive information is not seen by the merchant, and is not kept on the merchant's server.

EXERCISES

1. Judge whether the following given statements are true or false. If correct, write T in parentheses; otherwise, write F.

(1)　(　) E-Commerce security requirements are necessary only in some stage of the transaction process.

(2)　(　) PKI is an efficient way of sending large amounts of information.

(3)　(　) The private keys have to be kept secret.

(4)　(　) A digital document issued by the CA that uniquely identifies the merchant.

(5)　(　) PCI is a type of encrypt arithmetic.

2. Complete the following note-taking with the information mentioned in the text.

(1)　The term _____ refers to message must not be altered or tampered with.

(2)　Information security and _____ are very important in E-commerce because a lot of money involves in this transaction.

(3)　In PKI a message will _____ by a public key, and decrypted by a private key.

(4)　I f there are no _____ the message would be often times tamped by a third party agency.

(5)　The digital certificates authenticate the three parties in SET: _____, customer and bank.

READING MATERIALS

Product Description:SSL: Your Key to E-commerce Security

What is SSL?

Since its introduction in 1994, SSL has been the standard for e-commerce transaction security, and it's likely to remain so well into the future.

SSL is all about encryption. SSL encrypts data, like credit cards numbers (as well other personally identifiable information), which prevents the "bad guys" from stealing your information for malicious intent. You know that you're on an SSL protected page when the address begins with "https" and there is a padlock icon at the bottom of the page (and in the case of Mozilla Firefox in the address bar as well).

Your browser encrypts the data and sends to the receiving Web site using either 40-bit or 128-bit encryption. Your browser alone cannot secure the whole transaction and that's why it's incumbent upon e-commerce site builders to do their part.

SSL Certificates

At the other end of the equation, and of greatest importance to e-commerce site builders, is the SSL certificate. The SSL certificate sits on a secure server and is used to encrypt the data and to identify the Web site. The SSL certificate helps to prove the site belongs to who it says it belongs to and contains information about the certificate holder, the domain that the certificate was issued to, the name of the Certificate Authority who issued the certificate, the root and the country it was issued in.

SSL certificates come in 40-bit and 128-bit varieties, though 40-bit encryption has been hacked. As such, you definitely should be looking at getting a 128-bit certificate. Though there a wide variety of ways in which you could potentially acquire a 128-bit certificate, there is one key element that is often overlooked in order for full two-way 128-bit encryption to occur. According to SSL certificate vendor VeriSign, in order to have 128-bit encryption you need a certificate that has SGC (Server Grade Cryptography) capabilities.

Unit 27　Electronic Payment

WORDS AND EXPRESSIONS

payment ['peimənt]　付款，支付

facilitate [fə'siliteit]　使便利，推动，使容易，促进

increasingly [in'kri:siŋli]　日益，愈加

debit ['debit]　借方，借

PSP Payment Service Providers　支付服务提供商

currency ['kʌrənsi]　流通，货币

scrip [skrip]　纸片，凭证

deposit [di'pɔzit]　存款，押金，保证金

cryptography [krip'tɔgrəfi]　密码使用法，密码系统

contactless ['kɔntæktlis]　不接触的，遥控的

payee [pei'i:]　收款人，领款人

payroll ['peirəul]　薪水册

mortgage ['mɔ:gidʒ]　抵押

envelope ['enviləup]　信封，封套，封袋

stem [stem]　滋生，阻止

confidential [kɔnfi'denʃəl]　秘密的，机密的

constant ['kɔnstənt]　不变的，持续的

regardless [ri'ga:dlis]　不管，不顾

institution [,insti'tju:ʃən]　公共机构，协会

QUESTIONS AND ANSWERS

1. What kind of currency do we use in electronic payment?

2. Why does electronic payment become increasingly popular?

3. Who is the third party to help to complete the online transaction in payment system?

4. What will you do when you choose electronic payment in e-commerce?

5. Could you say something about electronic money?

6. Why do some electronic money systems use contactless payment transfer?

7. What is the influence of the growing popularity of EFT?

8. What are advantages of EFT?

9. What is the problem along with the growing popularity of electronic payment?

10. How do we making sure that the online transaction is being done over a secure server?

TEXT

Electronic payment is the term used for any kind of payment processed without using cash or paper checks. An e-commerce payment system facilitates the acceptance of electronic payment for online transactions. Also known as a sample of Electronic Data Interchange (EDI), e-commerce payment systems have become increasingly popular due to the widespread use of the internet-based shopping and banking. There are numerous different payments systems available for online merchants. These include the traditional credit, debit and charge card but also new technologies such as digital wallets, e-cash, mobile payment and e-checks. Another form of payment system is allowing a third party to complete the online transaction for you. These companies are called Payment Service Providers (PSP).

When it comes to payment options in Ecommerce, nothing is more convenient than electronic payment. You don't have to write a check, swipe a credit card or handle any paper money; all you have to do is enter some information into your Web browser and click your mouse. It's no wonder that more and more people are turning to electronic payment — or e-payment — as an alternative to sending checks through the Internet.

Electronic money

Electronic money (also known as e-currency, e-money, electronic cash, electronic currency, digital money, digital cash, digital currency, cyber currency) refers to money or scrip which is only exchanged electronically. Typically, this involves the use of computer networks, the Internet and digital stored value systems. Electronic Funds Transfer (EFT), direct deposit, digital gold currency and virtual currency are all examples of electronic money. Also, it is a collective term for financial cryptography and technologies enabling it. A number of electronic money systems use contactless payment transfer in order to facilitate easy payment and give the payee more confidence in not letting go of their electronic wallet during the transaction.

Electronic Funds Transfer (EFT)

EFT is a system of transferring money from one bank account directly to another without any paper money changing hands. One of the most widely-used EFT programs is Direct Deposit, in which payroll is deposited straight into an employee's bank account, although EFT refers to any transfer of funds initiated through an electronic terminal, including credit card, ATM and point-of-sale (POS) transactions. It is used for both credit transfers, such as payroll payments, and for debit transfers, such as mortgage payments.

The growing popularity of EFT for online bill payment is paving the way for a paperless universe where checks, stamps, envelopes, and paper bills are obsolete. The benefits of EFT include reduced administrative costs, increased efficiency, simplified bookkeeping, and greater security. However, the number of companies who send and receive bills through the Internet is still relatively small.

Electronic Payment Security

Questions have been raised regarding the security of electronic payments and most of these stem from the fear of having confidential and private information compromised. Identity theft is a valid concern, and this has cast some doubts on the security of electronic payments.

However, there are some basic security measures that can be taken to greatly minimize the risks involved. Some of these include the installation and constant updating of anti-virus and anti-spyware programs. Installation of firewalls, awareness of new threats online, and knowledge about how best to deal with these threats would also help. Making sure that the online transaction is being done over a secure server can also greatly minimize the risk of compromising your credit card and financial information. This can be done by looking for the lock or key icon in your browser and for "https" instead of "http" in the address bar.

Regardless of the security risks, online or electronic payments are here to stay. Moreover, more and more banks and financial institutions are providing this method of payment to their customers.

EXERCISES

1. Judge whether the following given statements are true or false. If correct, write T in parentheses; otherwise, write F.

(1)　(　) EDI is the only one payments system available for online merchants in E-commerce.

(2)　(　) Traditional credit cannot be used in online transactions.

(3)　(　) Electronic money involves the use of computer networks, the Internet and digital stored value systems.

(4)　(　) Paper money will not been changed hands in EFT for transfer money.

(5)　(　) The risk of electronic payment can be avoided completely.

2.　Complete the following note-taking with the information mentioned in the text.

(1)　The main drawbacks to electronic payments are concerns over privacy and the possibility of _____ theft.

(2)　You can minimize the risks of electronic payment by using _____ protection software and a firewall on your computer.

(3)　Your Internet _____ will notify you when a server is secure by showing a lock or key icon.

(4)　When a customer enters his or her information on a e-commerce site, the payment service authorizes the transaction and transfers _____ to your account.

(5)　With electronic payments, all you have to do is input your account and shipping information and the _____ can proceed.

READING MATERIALS

Praduct Description: What is online banking?

If you're like most people, you've heard a lot about online banking but probably haven't tried it yourself. You still pay your bills by mail and deposit checks at your bank branch, much the way your parents did. You might shop online for a loan, life insurance or a home mortgage, but when it comes time to commit, you feel more comfortable working with your banker or an agent you know and trust.

Online banking isn't out to change your money habits. Instead, it uses today's computer technology to give you the option of bypassing the time-consuming, paper-based aspects of traditional banking in order to manage your finances more quickly and efficiently.

The advent of the Internet and the popularity of personal computers presented both an opportunity and a challenge for the banking industry.

For years, financial institutions have used powerful computer networks to automate millions of daily transactions; today, often the only paper record is the customer's receipt at the point of sale. Now that its customers are connected to the Internet via personal computers, banks envision similar economic advantages by adapting those same internal electronic processes to home use.

Banks view online banking as a powerful value added tool to attract and retain new customers, while helping to eliminate costly paper handling and teller interactions in an increasingly competitive banking environment.

If you don't mind foregoing the teller window, lobby cookie and kindly bank president, a "virtual" or e-bank, such as Virtual Bank or Giant Bank, may save you very real money. Virtual banks are banks without bricks; from the customer's perspective, they exist entirely on the Internet, where they offer pretty much the same range of services and adhere to the same federal regulations as your corner bank.

Virtual banks pass the money they save on overhead like buildings and tellers along to you in the form of higher yields, lower fees and more generous account thresholds.

The major disadvantage of virtual banks revolves around ATMs. Because they have no ATM machines, virtual banks typically charge the same surcharge that your brick-and-mortar bank would if you used another bank's automated teller. Likewise, many virtual banks won't accept deposits via ATM; you'll have to either deposit the check by mail or transfer money from another account.

Unit 28　Internet of Things

WORDS AND EXPRESSIONS

sensor ['sensə]　传感器

metabolism [me'tæbəlizəm]　新陈代谢，变形

kitchen ['kitʃin]　厨房

vigilance ['vidʒiləns]　警戒，警惕

scenario [si'nɑːriəu]　某一特定情节

peek [piːk]　一瞥

RFID Radio Frequency IDdentification　无线射频识别

fridge [fridʒ]　电冰箱

quote [kwəut]　引用，引证

recipe ['resipi]　处方

ingredient [in'griːdiənt]　成分，因素

minuscule [mi'nʌskjuːl]　极小的

tag [tæg]　标签

revolution [ˌrevə'luːʃən]　革命，旋转

nanotechnology　纳米技术

tremendous [tri'mendəs]　极大的，巨大的

crucial ['kruːʃiəl]　至关紧要的

MEMS　Micro Electro Mechanical Systems　微电子机械系统

ETC　Electronic Toll Collection　电子不停车收费系统

pharmaceutical [ˌfɑːmə'sjuːtikəl]　药物

essential [i'senʃəl]　本质的，实质的，基本的

artificial [ˌɑːti'fiʃəl]　人造的

QUESTIONS AND ANSWERS

1. What is the Internet of Things on earth?

2. What can the Internet fridge do?

3. How does the bed detect you in the scenario of the future life in the Internet of Things era?

4. How does the network security authenticate the user commonly?

5. Why do we say the Internet of Things application is difficult?

6. What should we do to the object of daily life to realize the Internet of Things?

7. What is the function of the radio tags in the objects in Internet of Things?

8. What is the key to connect everyday objects and manage them? Who can do it?

9. How does the RFID identify items?

10. What is the function of the sensors in Internet of Things?

TEXT

It was 7:00 am in a winter morning, 2018. You were still sleeping in bed when your sensor enabled bed detected that you were about to wake up through your metabolism activities. You bed notified your kitchen management center, car, PDA, alarm clock and etc. Then your kitchen started to heat the milk up for you, your car started to deice and preheat, your PDA download your personal schedule for today from your calendar account in the internet, and your alarm clock started the beep to wake you up.

The scenario descript above is a peek at the future life in the Internet of Things era. Nowadays the Internet of Things becomes not only a very hot topic but is also considered to be the next biggest technology trend after Internet. However, it is very hard for people to understand or conduct a research on it since the "Internet of Things" concept is not only very wide but also has many industries include. Moreover, the related investment opportunities of the Internet of things are not very obvious.

The Internet of Things is a network of Internet-enabled objects, together with web services that interact with these objects. Underlying the Internet of Things are technologies such as RFID (Radio Frequency IDentification), sensors, and smart phones. The Internet fridge is probably the most often quoted example of what the Internet of Things will enable. Imagine a refrigerator that monitors the food inside it and notifies you when you're low on milk. It also perhaps monitors all of the best food websites, gathering recipes for your dinners and adding the ingredients automatically to your shopping list. This fridge knows what kinds of foods you like to eat, and based on the ratings you have given to your dinners. Indeed the fridge helps you take care of your health, because it knows which foods are good for you.

Although the idea is simple, its application is difficult. If all objects in the world were equipped with minuscule identifying devices, daily life on our planet could undergo a transformation. If all objects of daily life were equipped with radio tags, they could be identified and inventoried by computers. The next generation of Internet applications using Internet Protocol Version 6 (IPv6) would be able to communicate with devices attached to virtually all human-made objects because of the extremely large address space of IPv6. This system would therefore be able to identify any kind of object.

The Internet of Things is a technological revolution that represents the future of computing and communications, and its development depends on development of a series of advanced technologies, such as wireless, sensor, nanotechnology, and etc.

First, in order to connect tremendous amount of everyday objects and devices and manage them in large database and network, identification is crucial. Then data can be collected from them and be processed. RFID offers this functionality. Second, using advanced sensor technology to detect sorts of changes in the status of things and the environment helps data collection. Embedded chips in the things themselves can further provide the intelligent information to the networks. Finally, advanced in nanotechnologies and MEMS (Micro Electro Mechanical Systems) mean that smaller and smaller things will have the ability to interact, connect and execute. Combine all those technology development together, an intelligent planet which can function in both a sensory and smart way emerges.

RFID technology, which uses radio waves to identify items, is one of the early technologic enablers of the Internet of Things. Early applications of RFID include automatic highway toll collection (ETC), pharmaceuticals, supply chain management and e-health. Although it has sometimes been labeled as the next generation of bar code, RFDI changes not only the tagging system or identification, but also the business models.

In addition to RFDI, sensors play a critical role to detect changes in the physical status and surrounding environment of things is also essential for communicating between things themselves and bridging the gap between the physical and virtual worlds. Sensors collected data, process it, and turn it into decision. Embedded chips in things themselves will distribute processing power to the edges of the network, offering basic data processing and artificial intelligence. Independent decision can be made by those smart things to adjust themselves or take actions.

The Internet of Things will draw on the functionality offered by all of these technologies to realize the vision of a fully interactive and responsive network environment.

EXERCISES

1. Judge whether the following given statements are true or false. If correct, write T in parentheses; otherwise, write F.

(1) (　) The Internet of Things is already popular in our life.

(2) (　) The Internet of Things covers many industries and underlying technologies.

(3) (　) IPv6 can help to realize the Internet of Things.

(4) (　) RFID is only collecting the data in the interconnection of tremendous amount of everyday objects and devices.

(5) (　) The sensor is very important between the physical and virtual worlds.

2. Complete the following note-taking with the information mentioned in the text.

(1) Everyday objects and things will be added into the internet by ＿＿＿＿ chips and sensors into them in Internet of Things.

(2) All the things can send and receive data, ＿＿＿＿＿ information and extract wisdom out of that information.

(3) The Internet of Things will be able to ＿＿＿＿ and monitor changes in the physical status of connected things in real-time.

　　(4)　RFID consist a(n) _____ which is located on the object to be identified.

　　(5)　A sensor is a device that measures a _____ quantity and converts it into a signal which can be read by an observer or by an instrument.

READING MATERIALS

Artificial Intelligence

　　Artificial Intelligence, or AI for short, is a combination of computer science, physiology, and philosophy. AI is a broad topic, consisting of different fields, from machine vision to expert systems. The element that the fields of AI have in common is the creation of machines that can "think".

　　In order to classify machines as "thinking", it is necessary to define intelligence. To what degree does intelligence consist of, for example, solving complex problems, or making generalizations and relationships? What about perception and comprehension? Research into the areas of learning, of language, and of sensory perception has aided scientists in building intelligent machines. One of the most challenging approaches facing experts is building systems that mimic the behavior of the human brain, made up of billions of neurons, and arguably the most complex matter in the universe. Perhaps the best way to gauge the intelligence of a machine is British computer scientist Alan Turing's test. He stated that a computer would deserve to be called intelligent if it could deceive a human into believing that it was human.

Alan Turing

　　Artificial Intelligence has come a long way from its early roots, driven by dedicated researchers. The beginnings of AI reach back before

George Boole

electronics, and to philosophers and mathematicians such as Boole and others theorizing on principles that were used as the foundation of AI Logic. AI really began to intrigue researchers with the invention of the computer in 1943. The technology was finally available, or so it seemed, to simulate intelligent behavior. Over the next four decades, despite many stumbling blocks, AI has grown from a dozen researchers, to thousands of engineers and specialists; and from programs capable of playing checkers, to systems designed to diagnose disease.

　　AI has always been on the pioneering end of computer science. Advanced-level computer languages, as well as computer interfaces and word-processors owe their existence to the research into artificial intelligence. The theory and insights brought about by AI research will set the trend in the future of computing. The products available today are only bits and pieces of what are soon to follow, but they are a movement towards the future of artificial intelligence. The advancements in the quest for artificial intelligence have, and will continue to affect our jobs, our education, and our lives.

Embedded Technology

Unit 29　Microcontroller

WORDS AND EXPRESSIONS

single ['siŋgl]　n.一个；单打，单程票；adj. 单一的；单身的；单程的；vt. 选出；vi. 击出一垒安打

chip [tʃip]　n. [电子]　芯片；筹码；碎片；vt.削，凿；削成碎片；vi. 剥落；碎裂

feature in　（使）在中起重要作用；（使）在中占重要位置

internal [in'tə:nəl]　adj.国内的；内部的；内在的

external [ik'stə:nəl]　adj. 外部的；表面的，外面的；[药]外用的；外国的；n. 外部；外面；外观

integrated ['intigreitid]　adj. 综合的；完整的；互相协调的；v. 整合；使…成整体

communication [kə,mju:ni'keiʃən]　n . 通讯，通信；交流

peripheral [pə'rifərəl]　adj. 外围的；次要的

microcomputer [,maikrəukəm'pju:tə]　n. [计]微型计算机；[计]微电脑

complex ['kɔmpleks]　adj. 复杂的；合成的；n. 复合体；综合设施

integration [,inti'greiʃən]　n. 综合；集成

dedicated ['dedikeitid]　adj. 专注的；献身的；专用的；　v. 以…奉献；把…用于（dedicate 的过去式和过去分词）

processor ['prəusesə, 'prɔ-]　n. 处理器；加工者；[计算机]处理程序

volume ['vɔlju:m]　n. 体积；卷；册；音量；大量；量；adj. 大量的；vi. 成团卷起；vt. 把…收集成卷

performance [pə'fɔ:məns]　n. 性能；表演；执行；绩效

electronics [,ilek'trɔniks]　n. 电子学；电子工业

mainstream ['meinstri:m]　n. 主流

replaced　v. 取代；替换；放回（replace 的过去分词）；adj. 被替换的

suitable ['sju:təbl]　adj. 适当的；相配的

accessories　n. 辅助程序；[计]附件（accessory 的复数形式）

department [di'pɑ:tmənt]　n. 部门；系；科；部；局

complex ['kɔmpleks]　adj. 复杂的；合成的；　n. 复合体；综合设施

exceed [ik'si:d]　vt. 胜过；超过；vi. 超过其他

QUESTIONS AND ANSWERS

1. Is single-chip an integrated on a single chip a complete computer system.

2. Do you think that single-chip has become one of the most important helpful "partners" of human beings?

3. What did microcontroller?

4. What is microcontroller?

5. Is it usually microcontroller as a part of a complete device including hardware and mechanical parts?

6. Can microcontroller do many different task?

7. 16-bit single-chips has not been very widely used, Why?

8. At present, the high-end 32-bit single-chip frequency over 300MHz, is it?

TEXT

Single-chip is an integrated on a single chip a complete computer system. Even though most of his features in a small chip, but it has a need to complete the majority of computer components: CPU, memory, internal and external bus system, most will have the Core. At the same time, such as integrated communication interfaces, timers, real-time clock and other peripheral equipment. And now the most powerful single-chip microcomputer system can even voice, image, networking, input and output complex system integration on a single chip.

Also known as single-chip MCU (Microcontroller), because it was first used in the field of industrial control. Only by the single-chip CPU chip developed from the dedicated processor. The design concept is the first by a large number of peripherals and CPU in a single chip, the computer system so that smaller, more easily integrated into the complex and demanding on the volume control devices. INTEL the Z80 is one of the first design in accordance with the idea of the processor, From then on, the MCU and the development of a dedicated processor parted ways.

Early single-chip 8-bit or all of the four. One of the most successful is INTEL's 8031, because the performance of a simple and reliable access to a lot of good praise. Since then in 8031 to develop a single-chip microcomputer system MCS51 series. Based on single-chip microcomputer system of the system is still widely used until now. As the field of industrial control requirements increase in the beginning of a 16-bit single-chip, but not ideal because the price has not been very widely used. After the 90's with the big consumer electronics product development, single-chip technology is a huge improvement. INTEL i960 Series with subsequent ARM in particular, a broad range of applications, quickly replaced by 32-bit single-chip 16-bit single-chip high-end status, and enter the mainstream market. Traditional 8-bit single-chip performance has been the rapid increase in processing power compared to the 80's to raise a few hundred times. At present, the high-end 32-bit single-chip frequency over 300MHz, the performance of the mid-90's close on the heels of a special processor, while the ordinary price of the model dropped to one U.S. dollars, the most high-end models, only 10 U.S. dollars. Contemporary single-chip microcomputer system is no longer only the bare-metal environment in the development and use of a large number of dedicated embedded operating system is widely used in the full range of single-chip microcomputer. In PDAs and cell phones as the core processing of high-end single-chip or even a dedicated direct access to Windows and Linux operating systems.

More than a dedicated single-chip processor suitable for embedded systems, so it was up to the application. In fact the number of single-chip is the world's largest computer. Modern human life used in almost every piece of electronic and mechanical products will have a single-chip integration. Phone, telephone, calculator, home appliances, electronic toys, handheld computers and computer accessories such as a mouse in the Department are equipped with 1-2 single chip. And personal computers also have a large number of single-chip microcomputer in the workplace. Vehicles equipped with more than 40 Department of the general single-chip, complex industrial control systems and even single-chip may have hundreds of work at the same time! SCM is not only far exceeds the number of PC and other integrated computing, even more than the number of human beings.

EXERCISES

1．Judge whether the following given statements are true or false. If correct, write T in parentheses; otherwise, write F.

(1)   (   ) Also known as single-chip MCU (Microcontroller), because it was first used in the field of industrial control.

(2)   (   ) Early single-chip 16-bit or all of the four.

(3)   (   ) As the field of industrial control requirements increase in the beginning of a 32-bit single-chip, but not ideal because the price has not been very widely used.

(4)   (   ) At present, the high-end 64-bit single-chip frequency over 300MHz.

2. Complete the following note-taking with the information mentioned in the text.

(1)   Single-chip is an integrated_____   a single chip a complete computer system. .

(2)   More than a dedicated single-chip processor suitable for_____ systems, so it was up to the application.

(3)   Personal computers also have a large number of single-chip _____in the workplace.

(4)   SCM is not only far_____ the number of PC and other integrated computing, even more than the number of human beings.

READING MATERIALS

Product Description:About common single chip

STC microcontroller

STC's mainly based on the 8051 microcontroller core is a new generation of enhanced MCU, the instruction code is fully compatible with the traditional 8051, 8 to 12 times faster, with ADC, 4 Road, PWM, dual serial ports, a global unique ID, encryption of good, strong anti-interference.

PIC Microcontroller: MICROCHIP's products is its prominent feature is a small, low power consumption, reduced instruction set, interference, reliability, strong analog interface, the code of confidentiality is good, most of the chip has its compatible FLASH program memory chips.

EMC SCM: Elan's products in Taiwan, with much of the PIC 8-bit microcontroller compatible, and compatible products, resources, compared to the PIC's more, cheap, there are many series of options, but less interference.

ATMEL microcontroller (MCU 51)

ATMEl company's 8-bit microcontroller with AT89, AT90 two series, AT89 series is the 8-bit Flash microcontroller 8051 is compatible with the static clock mode; AT90 RISC MCU is to enhance the structure, all static methods of work, containing the line can be Flash MCU programming, also known AVR microcontroller.

PHLIPIS 51PLC Microcontroller (MCU 51): PHILIPS company's MCU is based on the 80C51 microcontroller core, embedded power-down detection, simulation and on-chip RC oscillator and other functions, which makes 51LPC in highly integrated, low cost, low power design to meet various applications performance requirements.

HOLTEK SCM

Sheng Yang, Taiwan Semiconductor's single chip, cheap more categories, but less interference for consumer products.

TI company microcontroller (MCU 51)

Texas Instruments MSP430 provides the TMS370 and two series of general-purpose microcontroller. TMS370 MCU is the 8-bit CMOS MCU with a variety of storage mode, a variety of external interface mode, suitable for real-time control of complex situations; MSP430 MCU is a low power, high functionality integrated 16-bit low-power microcontroller, especially for applications that require low power consumption occasions.

Taiwan Sonix's single, mostly 8-bit machines, some with PIC 8-bit microcontroller compatible, cheap, the system clock frequency may be more options there PMW ADC internal noise filtering within the vibration. Shortcomings RAM space is too small, better anti-interference.

Unit 30　Embedded System

WORDS AND EXPRESSIONS

embedded system　[计] 嵌入式系统；预埋系统
special-purpose computer　[计算机]专用计算机
perform [pə'fɔːm]　*vt.* 执行；完成；演奏；*vi.* 执行，机器运转；表演
real time　实时；同时
mechanical parts　机械零件
in contrast　与此相反；比较起来
general-purpose ['dʒenərəl'pəːpəs]　*adj.* 多用途的；一般用途的
programming ['prəugræmiŋ, -grə-]　*n.* 设计，规划；编制程序，[计] 程序编制
economies of scale　规模经济
be dedicated to　奉献；从事于；献身于
mass-produced [,mæsprə'djuːst]　*adj.* 大量生产的，大批生产的
portable ['pɔːtəbl, 'pəu-]　*adj.* 手提的，便携式的；轻便的；*n.* 手提式打字机
stationary ['steiʃənəri]　*n.* 不动的人；驻军；adj. 固定的；静止的；定居的；常备军的
programmability ['prəu,græmə'biləti, -grə-]　[计] 可编程性
microprocessor [,maikrəu'prəusesə, -'prɔ-]　[计] 微处理器
application to　用于；应用到
optimize ['ɔptimaiz]　*vt.* 使最优化，使完善；*vi.* 优化；持乐观态度
peripherals [pə'rifərəls]　*n.* 周边设备；外围设备
nuclear power plant　核电站（nuclear power plant 的复数形式）
albeit [ɔːl'biːit]　*conj.* 虽然；即使
stepper motor　步进马达，步进电机
level converter　[电子学]电平变换器
electronic [,ilek'trɔnik]　*adj.* 电子的

QUESTIONS AND ANSWERS

1. Do you think that embedded system s have become one of the most important helpful "partners" of human beings?

2. What did embedded system?

3. What is embedded system?

4. Is it usually embedded as a part of a complete device including hardware and mechanical

parts?

    5. Can embedded system do many different?

    6. Can embedded system reduce the size and cost of the product?

    7. Can you tell us something about embedded system?

    8. Do Embedded Systems led the entire electronics industry?

TEXT

Embedded System

An embedded system is a special-purpose computer system designed to perform one or a few dedicated functions, often with real time computing constrains. It is usually embedded as a part of a complete device including hardware and mechanical parts.In contrast, a general-purpose computer, such as a personal computer, can do many different tasks depending on progrAmming. Embedded systems control many of the common devices in use today.

Since the embedded system is dedicated to specific tasks, design engineers can optimize it, reducing the size and cost of the product, or increasing the reliability and performance. Some embedded systems are mass-produced, benefiting form economies of scale.

Physically, embedded systems range from portable devices such as digital watches and MP3 players, to large stationary installations like traffic lights, factory controllers, or the systems controlling nuclear power plants. Complexity varies from economies of scale.

In general, "embedded system" is not an exactly defined term, as many systems have some element of programmability. For example, handheld computers share some elements with embedded systems –such as the operating systems and microprocessors which power them –but are not truly embedded systems, because they allow different applications to be loaded and peripherals to be connected.

Current electronic components industry, in addition to microprocessors, embedded system devices, the most modern electronic systems around the supporting components industries, such as keys used to meet the human-computer interaction, LED / LCD display drivers, LED / LCD display units, voice integrated device, etc., to meet the requirements of data acquisition channel digital sensor, ADC, data acquisition module, signal conditioning modules to meet the servo drive control in the DAC, solid state relays, stepper motor controller, frequency control unit, etc., to meet the communication requirements various bus driver, level converters.

Electronic components in the embedded systems world, driven by embedded applications along fully meet requirements of modern electronic systems development. This makes the original classic world of increasingly small electronic systems. Practitioners in the various electronic systems to modern electronic systems as early as possible to stay.

EXERCISES

1. Judge whether the following given statements are true or false. If correct, write T in parentheses; otherwise, write F.

(1) ( ) In general, "embedded system" is an exactly defined term, as many systems have some element of programmability.

(2) ( ) Embedded systems can do many different tasks depending on programming.

(3) ( ) Embedded systems can increase the reliability and performance.

(4) ( ) Embedded systems control many of the common devices in use today.

2. Complete the following note-taking with the information mentioned in the text.

(1) Embedded systems _____ many of the common devices in use today.

(2) Some embedded systems are _____, benefiting form economies of scale.

(3) Handheld computers share some elements with _____, because they allow different applications to be loaded and peripherals to be connected.

(4) Electronic components in the embedded systems world are driven by _____.

READING MATERIALS

Fujitsu Semiconductor and ARM Sign Comprehensive License Agreement

A strategic partnership using cutting-edge IP such as Cortex-A15 and Mali graphics to expand global business.

CAMBRIDGE, UK & YOKOHAMA, JAPAN-Feb. 28, 2011-Fujitsu Semiconductor Limited and ARM today announced that they have signed a comprehensive license agreement for ARM IP products. Through this strategic agreement, Fujitsu Semiconductor will offer platforms featuring the latest ARM technology including the Cortex™-A15 processor, Mali™ graphics and CoreLink™ systems IP, in order to help accelerate its customers' product development.

The two companies have been collaborating for more than a decade. More recently, Fujitsu Semiconductor launched sales of its FM3 family of general-purpose microcomputers equipped with the Cortex-M3 processor last November.

The agreement will enhance and deepen the companies' partnership, and Fujitsu Semiconductor will provide its customers with cutting-edge ARM technology at an early stage as it develops new products in order to accelerate its customers' product development.

The combination of compatible and scalable low-power processor IP, including the recently launched Cortex-A15 processor, graphics and fabric IP, will enable Fujitsu Semiconductor to continuously provide its customers with complete, full function SoC platforms featuring ARM technology, while significantly reducing time-to-market.

"Fujitsu Semiconductor is working to enhance its product appeal and boost its IP lineup," said Corporate Senior Vice President Haruyoshi Yagi of Fujitsu Semiconductor. "One of the major ways in which we are doing this is with this comprehensive license agreement we have signed with ARM. This will allow our customers to select the ARM technology most suited for their application, and use a platform that combines it with other IP provided by us. These platforms will use our proven design and authentication technology, meaning we will be able to achieve high levels of quality and functionality, as well as a dramatic reduction in LSI development time.

"Fujitsu Semiconductor provides products that meet its customers' needs in a timely manner over a wide range of applications. We are already moving ahead with the provision of IP to ASIC customers and the development of our ASSP, which are scheduled to be rolled out sequentially in the second half of 2011.

"In addition, we will share the Fujitsu Semiconductor product roadmap with ARM, and closely collaborate in the development of future ARM technologies, from the specification setting stage and up. As a strategic partner, we look forward to an even closer relationship with ARM."

"In a constantly evolving marketplace, ARM is committed to empowering its Partners with the resources they need to not only remain competitive today, but to meet future technology challenges head-on," said Tudor Brown, President, ARM. "The combination of ARM's advanced processor, system and graphics technology and Fujitsu's leadership in advanced SoC development forms a solid foundation for the development of pioneering semiconductor products."

About Fujitsu Semiconductor

Fujitsu Semiconductor Limited designs, manufactures, and sells semiconductors, providing highly reliable, optimal solutions and support to meet the varying needs of its customers. Products and services include microcontrollers, ASICs, ASSPs, and power management ICs, with wide-ranging expertise focusing on mobile, ecological, automotive, imaging, security, and high-performance applications. Fujitsu Semiconductor also drives power efficiency and environmental initiatives. Headquartered in Yokohama, Fujitsu Semiconductor Limited (formerly named Fujitsu Microelectronics Limited) was established as a subsidiary of Fujitsu Limited on March 21, 2008. Through its global sales and development network, with sites in Japan and throughout Asia, Europe, and the Americas, Fujitsu Semiconductor offers semiconductor solutions to the global marketplace.

About ARM

ARM designs the technology that lies at the heart of advanced digital products, from wireless, networking and consumer entertainment solutions to imaging, automotive, security and storage devices. ARM's comprehensive product offering includes 32-bit RISC microprocessors, graphics processors, video engines, enabling software, cell libraries, embedded memories, high-speed connectivity products, peripherals and development tools. Combined with comprehensive design services, training, support and maintenance, and the company's broad Partner community, they provide a total system solution that offers a fast, reliable path to market for leading electronics companies.

ARM is a registered trademark of ARM Limited. Cortex, Mali, CoreLink and MPCore are trademarks of ARM Limited. All other brands or product names are the property of their respective holders. "ARM" is used to represent ARM Holdings plc; its operating company ARM Limited; and the regional subsidiaries ARM Inc.; ARM KK; ARM Korea Limited.; ARM Taiwan Limited; ARM France SAS; ARM Consulting (Shanghai) Co. Ltd.; ARM Belgium Services BVBA; ARM Germany GmbH; ARM Embedded Technologies Pvt. Ltd.; ARM Norway, AS and ARM Sweden AB.

Unit 31　An Introduction to Windows CE and Linux

WORDS AND EXPRESSIONS

operating system　[计] 操作系统

multitasking ['mʌlti,tɑ:skiŋ,-,tæsk-]　*n.* 多重任务处理；多重任务执行

typically ['tipikəli]　*adv.* 代表性地；作为特色地

consists of　包含；由组成；充斥着

function call　[计]函数调用；函数引用

interrupt [,intə'rʌpt]　*n.* 中断；*vt.* 中断；打断；插嘴；妨碍；*vi.* 打断；打扰

be responsible for　对负责；是的原因

embedded [im'bedid]　*v.* 嵌入（embed 的过去式和过去分词形式）；*adj.* 嵌入式的；植入的

Windows Embedded　微软的一个研发部门（微软的嵌入式系列产品家族）

pocket PC　掌上电脑；袖珍型电脑

Pocket PC 2002　操作系统为微软发布的一种类似于 Windows XP 台式机的操作系统，其增加了 802.11b 无线联网功能和 VPN 软件，代码名为 Merlin

VxWorks 操作系统　美国温瑞尔（WindRiver）公司于 1983 年设计开发的一种嵌入式实时操作系统（RTOS），是嵌入式开发环境的关键组成部分

pSOS　一种实时的嵌入式操作系统（pSOS 是 ISI 公司研发的产品，该产品推出时间比较早，因此比较成熟，可以支持多种处理器，曾是国际上应用最广泛的产品，主要应用领域是远程通信，航天，信息家电等领域）

Linux ['lainʌks]　*n.* 一个个人电脑上免费的 UNIX 操作系统

application [,æpli'keiʃən]　*n.* 应用；申请；应用程序；敷用

commercially [kə'mə:ʃəli]　*adv.* 商业上；通商上

substitute for　代替，取代

amazed [ə'meizd]　*v.* 使吃惊；把弄糊涂（amaze 的过去分词）；*adj.* 惊奇的，吃惊的

typically ['tipikəli]　*adv.* 代表性地；作为特色地

gamut ['gæmət]　*n.* 全音阶；全音域；整个范围

cellular phone　移动电话；便携式电话

API　the Application Programming Interface　应用程序界面

Windows API　视窗操作系统应用程序接口（Windows API）（有非正式的简称法为 WinAPI，是微软对于 Windows 操作系统中可用的内核应用程序编程接口的称法）

robustness [rəu'bʌstnis]　*n.* [自] 鲁棒性；[计] 稳健性；健壮性

compatibility [kəm,pætə'biləti]　*n.* [计] 兼容性

secondary ['sekəndəri]   *adj.* 第二的；中等的；次要的；中级的；*n.* 副手；代理人

multithreaded   多重线串的

optional ['ɔpʃənəl]   *adj.* 可选择的，随意的；*n.* 选修科目

graphical user interface   图形用户界面

runtime [rʌn'taim]   *n.* 执行时间，运行时间

from scratch   白手起家；从头做起

copy-on-write   *n.* 写时拷贝；写入时复制；写时备份

executable ['eksikju:təbl]   *adj.* 可执行的；可实行的

kernel ['kə:nəl]   *n.* 核心，要点；[计] 内核；仁；麦粒，谷粒；精髓

communication protocol   [通信]通信协议

QUESTIONS AND ANSWERS

1. Is operating system a piece of software that makes multitasking possible？

2. Why shall we use Linux?

3. What did microcontroller?

4. What is microcontroller?

5. Can we port our Linux kernel and root file system to the Flash ROM?

6. What is an Embedded OS?

7. What is embedded Linux?Explain the feature of embedded Linux.

8. What is ARM Linux?

TEXT

Operating system is a piece of software that makes multitasking possible. An operating system typically consists of a set of function calls, or software interrupts, and a periodic clock tick. The operating system is responsible for deciding which task the processor should be using at a given time and for controlling access to shared resources.

What is an Embedded OS? Embedded system OS include:

➢ (1) Windows Embedded(Microsoft).

  ● Embedded NT/XP:"Real-time" control.

  ● Windows CE (CE.NET):Internet devices.

  ● Pocket PC 2002:Handheld PC's and PDA's.

➢ (2) Wind River Systems:

  ● VxWorks;

  ● pSOS.

➢ (3) Embedded Linux.

An embedded system is any computer system or computing device that performs a dedicated function or is designed for use with a specific embedded software application.Embedded systems may use a ROM-based operating system or they may use a disk-based system, like a PC. But an embedded system is not usable as a commercially viable substitute for general purpose computers or devices.

I've been working with Microsoft Windows CE for almost as long as it's been in existence. A Windows programmer for many years, I'm amazed by the number of different, typically quite small, systems to which I can apply my Windows programming experience. These Windows CE systems run the gamut from PC-like mini-laptops to cellular phones to embedded devices buried deep in some large piece of industrial equipment. The use of the Win32 API in Windows CE enables tens of thousands of Windows programmers to write applications for an entirely new class of systems. The subtle differences, however, make writing Windows CE code somewhat different from writing for the desktop versions of Windows.

Just What Is Windows CE?

Windows CE is the smallest and arguably the most interesting of the Microsoft Windows operating systems. Windows CE was designed from the ground up to be a small ROM-based operating system with a Win32 subset API. Windows CE extends the Windows API into the markets and machines that can't support the larger footprints of the Windows XP kernel.

The now-defunct Windows 95/98/Me line was a great operating system for users who needed backward compatibility with MS-DOS and Windows 2.x and 3.x programs. Although it had shortcomings, Windows Me succeeded amazingly well at this difficult task. The Windows NT/2000/XP line, on the other hand, is written for the enterprise. It sacrifices compatibility and size to achieve its high level of reliability and robustness. Windows XP Home Edition is a version of Windows XP built for the home user that does strive for compatibility, but this is secondary to its primary goal of stability.

Windows CE isn't backward compatible with MS-DOS or Windows. Nor is it an all-powerful operating system designed for enterprise computing. Instead, Windows CE is a lightweight, multithreaded operating system with an optional graphical user interface. Its strength lies in its small size, its Win32 subset API, and its multiplatform support.

Windows CE also forms the foundation for the initial version of the .NET Compact Framework, a version of the .NET runtime for mobile and embedded devices. The Compact Framework provides the same powerful .NET runtime environment with a smaller class library so that it fits in small battery-powered devices.

What Is Linux?

Linux is a UNIX clone written from scratch by Linus Torvalds with assistance from a loosely-knit team of hackers across the Net. It aims towards POSIX compliance.

It has all the features you would expect in a modern fully-fledged UNIX, including true multitasking, virtual memory, shared libraries, demand loading, shared copy-on-write executables, proper memory management and TCP/IP networking.

It is distributed under the GNU General Public License.

Okay, but what is ARM Linux?

ARM Linux is a port of the successful Linux Kernel to ARM processor based machines, led mainly by Russell King, with contributions from many others. ARM Linux is under almost constant development by various people and organizations around the world.

The ARM Linux kernel is being ported, or has been ported to more than 500 different machine variations, including complete computers, network computers, handheld devices and evaluation boards.

Why Shall Use Linux?

- Open source.
- Reliability.
- Salability.
- Secure.
- Supports virtually all network communication protocols.

What Components Are in Our Embedded Linux?

- Linux kernel.
- Root file system.
- /bin, /usr, /dev, etc.

We can port our Linux kernel and root file system to the Flash ROM so that they can be permanently stored on the board.

EXERCISES

1. Judge whether the following given statements are true or false. If correct, write T in parentheses; otherwise, write F.

(1)　(　) An operating system typically consists of a set of function calls, or software interrupts, and a periodic clock tick.

(2)　(　) Embedded systems may use a ROM-based operating system or they may use a disk-based system, like a PC.

(3)　(　) Linux is not a UNIX clone written from scratch by Linus Torvalds with assistance from a loosely-knit team of hackers across the Net.

(4)　(　) The ARM Linux kernel is being ported, or has been ported to more than 500 different machine variations, including complete computers, network computers, handheld devices and evaluation boards.

2. Complete the following note-taking with the information mentioned in the text.

(1)　Operating system is a piece of software _____ makes multitasking possible.

(2)　An embedded system is any computer system _____ computing device that performs a dedicated function _____ is designed for use with a specific embedded software.

(3)　The use of the _____ in Windows CE enables tens of thousands of Windows programmers to write applications for an entirely new class of systems.

(4) Windows CE _____ backward compatible with MS-DOS or Windows. Nor is it an all-powerful operating system designed for enterprise computing.

READING MATERIALS

Product Description: A Little Windows CE History

To understand the history of Windows CE, you need to understand the differences between the operating system and the products that use it. The operating system is developed by a core group of programmers inside Microsoft. Their product is the operating system itself. Other groups, who develop devices such as the Pocket PC, use the newest version of the operating system that's available at the time their product is to be released. This dichotomy has created some confusion about how Windows CE has evolved. Let's examine the history of each, the devices and the operating system itself.

The Devices

The first products designed for Windows CE were handheld "organizer" devices with 480-by-240 or 640-by-240 screens and chiclet keyboards. These devices, dubbed Handheld PCs, were first introduced in late 1996. Fall Comdex 97 saw the release of a dramatically upgraded version of the operating system, Windows CE 2.0, with newer hardware in a familiar form—this time the box came with a 640-by-240 landscape screen, sometimes in color, and a somewhat larger keyboard.

In January 1998 at the Consumer Electronics Show, Microsoft announced two new platforms, the Palm-size PC and the Auto PC. The Palm-size PC was aimed directly at the pen-based organizer market dominated by Palm OS–based systems. The Palm-size PC featured a portrait mode and a 240-by-320 screen, and it used stylus-based input. Unfortunately for Windows CE fans, the public reception of the original Palm-size PC was less than enthusiastic.

Later that year, a new class of mini-laptop–style Windows CE machines with touch-typable keyboards and VGA or Super VGA screens made their appearance. These machines, called H/PC Professionals, provided 10 hours of battery life combined with improved versions of Microsoft's Pocket Office applications. Many of these machines had built-in modems, and some even diverged from the then-standard touch screen, sporting track pads or IBM's TrackPoint devices.

In April 2000, Microsoft introduced the Pocket PC, a greatly enhanced version of the old Palm-size PC. The original Pocket PC used a prerelease of the more full-featured Windows CE 3.0 operating system under the covers. The user interface of the Pocket PC was also different, with a cleaner, 2D, look and a revised home page, the Today screen. The most important feature of the Pocket PC, however, was the greatly improved performance of Windows CE. Much work had been done to tune Windows CE for better performance. That improvement, coupled with faster CPUs, allowed the system to run with the zip expected from a pocket organizer. With the

Pocket PC, the inevitability of Moore's Law enabled Windows CE devices to cross over the line: the hardware at this point was now capable of providing the computing power that Windows CE required.

The Handheld PC was updated in 2000 to use Windows CE 3.0. Although these systems (now called the Handheld PC 2000) haven't been a consumer success, they have found a home in the industrial market, where their relative low cost, large screens, and great battery life satisfy a unique niche market.

The Pocket PC was updated in late 2001 with a release named Pocket PC 2002. This release was based on the final released version of Windows CE 3.0 and contained some user interface improvements. An exciting development was the addition of the Pocket PC Phone Edition, which integrated cellular phone support into a Pocket PC device. These devices combined the functionality of a Pocket PC with the connectivity of a cellular phone, enabling a new generation of mobile but always connected software.

Another group within Microsoft released the Smart Display, a Windows CE .NET 4.1–based system that integrated a tablet form factor device with wireless networking and a base connected to a PC. When the Smart Display is in its base, it's a second monitor; when removed, it becomes a mobile display for the PC.

In the spring of 2003, the Pocket PC team released an update of the Pocket PC called the Pocket PC 2003. This system, while not providing much of a change to the user interface, did provide a huge increase in stability and performance because it was based on Windows CE .NET 4.2. The Pocket PC 2003 also added integrated Bluetooth support for those OEMs that chose to include it.

Microsoft has also been working with OEMs to produce cellular phones based on Windows CE. A smattering of these phones, called Smartphones, were released in late 2002 and were initially based on Windows CE 3.0. An upgrade in 2003 moved the Smartphone to Windows CE 4.2 and increased the feature set of the device to include the .NET runtime.

New devices are being introduced all the time. An example are the Media to Go devices, which are mobile video players using a hard disk for storage. The power of the Windows CE operating system enables applications that are beyond the capability of systems with simpler operating systems to run on these devices.

The Operating System

Although these consumer-oriented products made the news, more important development work was going on in the operating system itself. The Windows CE operating system has evolved from the days of 1.0, when it was a simple organizer operating system with high hopes. Starting with Windows CE 2.0 and continuing to this day, Microsoft has released embedded versions of Windows CE that developers can use on their custom hardware. Although consumer platforms such as the Pocket PC get most of the publicity, the improvements to the base operating system are what enable devices such as the Pocket PC and the Smartphone.

Windows CE 2.0 was released with the introduction of the Handheld PC 2.0 at Fall Comdex

1997. Windows CE 2.0 added networking support, including Windows standard network functions, a Network Driver Interface Specification (NDIS) miniport driver model, and a generic NE2000 network card driver. Added COM support allowed scripting, although the support was limited to in-proc servers. A display driver model was also introduced that allowed for pixel depths other than the original 2-bits-per-pixel displays of Windows CE 1.0. Windows CE 2.0 was also the first version of the operating system to be released separately from a product such as the H/PC. Developers could purchase the Windows CE Embedded Toolkit (ETK), which allowed them to customize Windows CE to unique hardware platforms. Developers who used the ETK, however, soon found that the goal of the product exceeded its functionality.

With the release of the original Palm-size PC in early 1998, Windows CE was improved yet again. Although Windows CE 2.01 wasn't released in an ETK form, it was notable for its effort to reduce the size of the operating system and applications. In Windows CE 2.01, the C runtime library, which includes functions such as strcpy to copy strings, was moved from a statically linked library attached to each EXE and DLL into the operating system itself. This change dramatically reduced the size of both the operating system and the applications themselves.

In August 1998, Microsoft introduced the H/PC Professional with a new version of the operating system, 2.11. Windows CE 2.11 was a service pack update to Windows CE 2.1, which was never formally released. Later in the year, Windows CE 2.11 was released to the embedded community as Microsoft Windows CE Platform Builder version 2.11. This release included support for an improved object store that allowed files in the object store to be larger than 4MB. This release also added support for a console and a Windows CE version of CMD.exe, the classic MS-DOS–style command shell. Windows CE 2.11 also included Fast IR to support IrDA's 4-MB infrared standard, as well as some specialized functions for IP multicast. An initial hint of security was introduced in Windows CE 2.11: a device could now examine and reject the loading of unrecognized modules.

Windows CE 2.12 was also a service pack release to the 2.1, or Birch, release of Windows CE. The big news in this release was a greatly enhanced set of Platform Builder tools that included a graphical front end. The operating system was tweaked with a new notification interface that combined the disparate notification functions. The notification user interface was exposed in the Platform Builder to allow embedded developers to customize the notification dialog boxes. A version of Microsoft's PC-based Internet Explorer 4.0 was also ported to Windows CE as the Genie, or Generic IE control. This HTML browser control complements the simpler but smaller Pocket Internet Explorer. Microsoft Message Queue support was added as well. The "go/no go" security of Windows CE 2.11 was enhanced to include a "go, but don't trust" option. Untrusted modules can run—but not call—a set of critical functions, nor can they modify parts of the registry.

The long-awaited Windows CE 3.0 was finally released in mid-2000. This release followed the April release of the Pocket PC, which used a slightly earlier internal build of Windows CE 3.0. The big news for Windows CE 3.0 was its kernel, which was optimized for better real-time support. The enhanced kernel support includes 256 thread priorities (up from 8 in earlier versions of Windows CE), an adjustable thread quantum, nested interrupt service routines, and reduced latencies within the kernel.

The improvements in Windows CE 3.0 didn't stop at the kernel. A new COM component was added to complement the in-proc COM support available since Windows CE 2.0. This new component included full COM out-of-proc and DCOM support. The object store was also improved to support up to 256MB of RAM. File size limits within the object store were increased to 32MB per file. An Add-On Pack for the Platform Builder 3.0 added even more features, including improved multimedia support though a media player control; improved networking support (and XML support) with PPTP, ICS, and remote desktop display support; and a formal introduction of the DirectX API.

The next release of Windows CE involved more than just new features; the name of the product was also changed. Windows CE .NET 4.0, released in early 2001, changed the way virtual memory was organized, effectively doubling the virtual memory space per application. Windows CE .NET 4.0 also added a new driver loading model, services support, a new file-based registry option, Bluetooth, 802.11, and 1394 support. Ironically, while .NET was added to the name, Windows CE .NET 4.0 didn't support the .NET Compact Framework.

Late in 2001, Windows CE 4.1 was a follow-on to Windows CE 4.0, adding IPv6, Winsock 2, a bunch of new supporting applets, and an example Power Manager. Windows CE 4.1 also supports the .NET Compact Framework. The final bits of the .NET runtime were released as a quick fix engineering (QFE) package after the operating system shipped.

The second quarter of 2003 saw the release of Windows CE .NET 4.2. This update provided cool new features for OEMs wanting to support Pocket PC applications on embedded systems. The Pocket PC–specific APIs that support menu bars, the soft input panel (SIP), and other shell features were moved to the base operating system. The Explorer shell was rewritten to support namespace extensions. The performance of the kernel was improved by directly supporting hardware paging tables on some CPUs.

Because Windows CE is a work in progress, the next version of Windows CE is being developed. I'll be updating my Web site, www.bolingconsulting.com, with information about this release as it becomes available.

Unit 32　Embedded Processor Based Automatic Temperature Control of VLSI Chips

WORDS AND EXPRESSIONS

phenomenal [fi'nɔminəl, fə-]　*adj.* 现象的；显著的；异常的；能知觉的

ambitious [æm'biʃəs]　*adj.* 野心勃勃的；有雄心的；热望的；炫耀的

power dissipation　功耗；功率损耗

power dissipation：　电力分散、功耗、功率耗散

degrade by　因而丢脸（或丢面子）

package ['pækidʒ]　*n.* 包，包裹；套装软件，[计] 程序包；*adj.* 一揽子的；*vt.* 打包；将包装

thermal ['θəːməl]　*adj.* 热的，热量的；*n.* 上升暖气流

climbing ['klaimiŋ]　*adj.* 上升的；攀缘而登的；*n.* 攀登；*v.* 爬（climb 的 ing 形式）

performance [pə'fɔːməns]　*n.* 性能；绩效；表演；执行

parameter [pə'ræmitə]　*n.* 参数；系数；参量

parametric [ˌpærə'metrik]　*adj.* [数][物] 参数的；[数][物] 参量的

environmental conditions　环境条件；周围条件

maintain [mein'tein]　*vt.* 维持；继续；维修；主张；供养

allowable [ə'lauəbl]　*adj.* 许可的；正当的；可承认的；可获宽免

significantly [sig'nifəkəntli]　*adv.* 意味深长地；值得注目地

speed up　加速；使加速

prominent ['prɔminənt]　*adj.* 突出的，显著的；杰出的；卓越的

throttling ['θrɔtliŋ]　*n.* 节气，节流；油门调节

functionality [ˌfʌŋkʃə'næliti]　*n.* 功能；[数] 泛函性，函数性

consisting of　包含；组成元素为

sensor ['sensə, -sɔː]　*n.* 传感器（接收信号或刺激并反应的器件，能将待测物理量或化学量转换成另一对应输出的装置，用于自动化控制、安防设备等）

precise [pri'sais]　*adj.* 精确的；明确的；严格的

trimming ['trimiŋ]　*n.* 整理；装饰品；配料；修剪下来的东西

calibration [ˌkæli'breiʃən]　*n.* 校准；刻度；标度

heat sink　散热器；吸热部件；冷源

alternative [ɔːl'təːnətiv]　*n.* 二中择一；供替代的选择；*adj.* 供选择的；选择性的；交替的

remote [ri'məut]　*adj.* 遥远的；偏僻的；疏远的；*n.* 远程

be assured　保证；我敢担保；请放心；勿疑

bipolar transistor [电子] 双极型晶体管

thermal ['θə:məl]   *adj.* 热的，热量的；*n.* 上升暖气流

diode ['daiəud]   *n.* [电子]二极管

excellent ['eksələnt]   *adj.* 卓越的；极好的；杰出的

accuracy ['ækjurəsi]   *n.* [数]精确度，准确性

plastic ['plæstik,'plɑːs-]   *n.* 塑料制品；整形；可塑体；*adj.* 塑料的；（外科）造型的；可塑的

to monitor   监督

automatic [,ɔːtə'mætik]   *n.* 自动机械；自动手枪；*adj.* 自动的；无意识的；必然的

overheating [,əuvər'hiːtiŋ]   *n.* [热]过热；*v.* [热] 过热（overheat 的 ing 形式）

QUESTIONS AND ANSWERS

1. Are nowadays the CPU chips   becoming smaller and smaller?

2. Why the high speed chips must to maintain good performance for the longest possible operating time and over the widest possible range of environmental conditions?

3. Do you think that sensor has become one of the most important helpful "partners" of human beings?

4. What does depend on the process and how the chip is designed?

5. What is the LM35?

6. Can the LM3 be used with single power supplies?

7. What is the drawback in fan speed control?

TEXT

With the phenomenal developments in VLSI technology, the ambitious IC designers are trying to put more transistors in to smaller packages. So, the ICs run at higher speeds and produce large amount of heat which creates the problem of thermal management. For example, nowadays the CPU chips are becoming smaller and smaller with almost no room for the heat to escape. The total power dissipation levels now reside on the order of 100 W with a peak power density of 400-500 W/Cm2, and are still steadily climbing.

As the chip temperature increases its performance is very much degraded by parameters shift, decrease in operating frequencies and out-of specification of timings. So the high speed chips must be cooled to maintain good performance for the longest possible operating time and over the widest possible range of environmental conditions. The maximum allowable temperature for a high speed chip to meet its parametric specifications depends on the process and how the chip is designed.

Among the various cooling techniques, heat sinks, heat pipes, fans and clock throttling are usually employed. Among these techniques, fans can dramatically reduce the temperature of a high speed chip, but they also generate a great deal of acoustic noise. This noise can be reduced significantly by varying, the fans speed based on temperature i.e. the fan can turn slowly when the temperature is low and can speed up as the temperature increases.The other prominent method is clock throttling i.e. reducing the clock speed to reduce power dissipation. But it also reduces the system performance and the systems functionality is lost.So, the objective of the present work is, to design a hardware system consisting of a brushless DC motor fan whose speed is controlled based on the temperature of the chip, sensed by the sensor LM35. The LM35 series are precision integrated-circuit temperature sensors, whose output voltage is linearly proportional to the Celsius (Centigrade) temperature. The LM35 thus has an advantage over linear temperature sensors calibrated in Kelvin, as the user is not required to subtract a large constant voltage from its output to obtain convenient Centigrade scaling. The LM35 does not require any external calibration or trimming to provide typical accuracies of $\pm 1/4°C$ at room temperature and $\pm 3/4°C$ over a full -55 to $+150°C$ temperature range. Low cost is assured by trimming and calibration at the wafer level. The LM35's low output impedance, linear output, and precise inherent calibration make interfacing to readout or control circuitry especially easy. It can be used with single power supplies, or with plus and minus supplies. As it draws only 60 μA from its supply, it has very low selfheating, less than 0.1°C in still air. The LM35 is rated to operate over a $-55°$ to $+150°C$ temperature range, while the LM35C is rated for a $-40°$ to $+110°C$ range ($-10°$ with improved accuracy). The LM35 series is available packaged in hermetic TO-46 transistor packages, while the LM35C, LM35CA, and LM35D are also available in the plastic TO-92 transistor package. The LM35D is also available in an 8-lead surface mount small outline package and a plastic TO-220 package. To monitor the voltage at the terminals of the DC motor fan, the PWM signal is generated by the ARM7TDMI processor. This PWM signal is changed in accordance to the output of the LM35temperature sensor. So the important component of this entire project is the temperature sensor.

In ARM processor based automatic temperature control system, the output of the temperature sensor is fed to the on chip ADC and the output of the ADC is given to the L293D driver IC which in turn is fed to DC motor fan as shown in the block diagram in Figure 32-1. A graphic LCD (128X64 pixels) is inter faced to the ARM LPC 2378 processor to display the temperature of the IC and the speed of the fan. A buzzer is also connected to the processor which gives an indication, in case of the failure of the fan or overheating of the chip beyond some level. The entire circuit diagram is shown in Figure 32-2.

Normally, controlling fan speed or clock throttling based on temperature requires that the temperature of the high speed chip should be first measured. This is done by placing a temperature sensor close to the target chip either directly next to it or in some cases, under it or on the heat sink. The temperature measured in this way corresponds to that of the high speed chip, but can be significantly lower and the difference between measured temperature and the actual die temperature increases as the power dissipation increases. So, the temperature of the circuit board or heat sink must be correlated to the die temperature of the high speed chip. Of course a better alternative is possible with a number of high speed chips. Many CPUs, FPGAs and other high speed ICs include a thermal diode which is actually a diode connected bipolar transistor, on the die. Using a remote diode temperature sensor connected to this thermal diode, the temperature of the high speed IC's die can be measured directly with an excellent accuracy. This not only eliminates the large temperature gradients involved in measuring temperature outside the target IC's package, but it also eliminates the long thermal time constants,from several seconds to minutes, that cause delays in responding to die temperature changes.

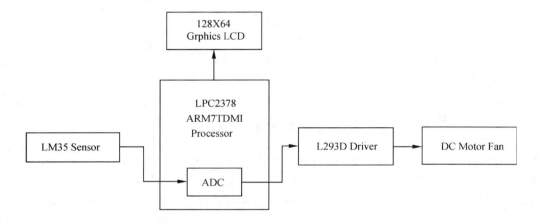

Figure 32-1   Block diagram

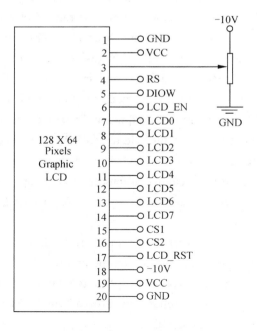

Figure 32-2   Circuit Diagram

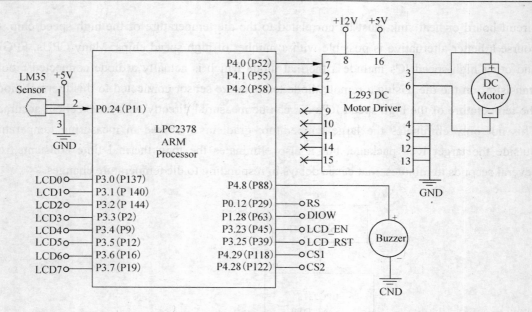

Figure 32-2　Continue

There is also a drawback in fan speed control. Normally the fan speed is controlled by adjusting the power supply voltage of the fan. This is done by a low-frequency PWM signal, usually in the range of about 50Hz, whose duty cycle is varied to adjust the fan's speed. This is inexpensive and also efficient. But the disadvantage of this method is that it makes the fan somewhat nosier because of the pulsed nature of the power supply. The PWM waveforms fast edges cause the fans mechanical structure to move, which is easily audible.

In some systems, it is also important to limit the rate of change of the fan speed. This is critical when the system is in close proximity to users. Simply switching a fan on and off or changing speed immediately as temperature changes is acceptable in some environments. But when users are in nearby, the sudden changes in fans noise are highly annoying. So to avoid these effects the fan's drive signal must be limited to an acceptable level.

In the present work temperature is sensed using the temperature sensor LM35 and the speed of the motor is controlled by varying the width of PWM generated by the processor. But the temperature sensed by the IC LM35 is not very accurate even though we keep the IC very near to the processor or VLSI chip. So, we can use a remote diode temperature sensor connected to the thermal diode which measures the temperature of the high speed ICs directly with excellent accuracy.

Another important aspect is a variety of remote temperature sensors with up to five sensing channels is available that can detect the die temperature of the high speed chip and transmit temperature data to a microcontroller. Fan speed regulators with multiple channels of fan tachometer monitoring can provide reliable control of fan RPM or supply voltage based on commands from an external microcontroller.

EXERCISES

1. Judge whether the following given statements are true or false. If correct, write T in parentheses; otherwise, write F.

(1) (   ) The total power dissipation levels now reside on the order of 100W with a peak power density of 400-500W/Cm2, and are still steadily climbing.

(2) (   ) The maximum allowable temperature for a high speed chip to meet its parametric specifications depends on the process and how the chip is designed.

(3) (   ) Among the various cooling techniques, heat sinks, heat pipes, fans and clock throttling are not usually employed.

(4) (   ) There is not any drawback in fan speed control.

2. Complete the following note-taking with the information mentioned in the text.

(1) Simply switching a fan on and off or changing speed immediately_____ temperature changes is acceptable in some environments.

(2) A better alternative is possible _____ a number of high speed chips.

(3) The temperature of the circuit board or heat sink must _____ the die temperature of the high speed chip.

(4) In the present work temperature is sensed using the temperature sensor LM35 and the speed of the motor is controlled_____varying the width of PWM generated by the processor.

READING MATERIALS

Product Description:Product Overview Introduction

This manual describes SAMSUNG's S3C2410A 16/32-bit RISC microprocessor. This product is designed to provide hand-held devices and general applications with cost-effective, low-power, and high-performance micro-controller,solution in small die size. To reduce total system cost, the S3C2410A includes the following components: separate 16kB Instruction and 16kB Data Cache, MMU to handle virtual memory management, LCD Controller (STN & TFT),NAND Flash Boot Loader, System Manager (chip select logic and SDRAM Controller), 3-ch UART, 4-ch DMA, 4-ch timers with PWM, I/O Ports, RTC, 8-ch 10-bit ADC and Touch Screen Interface, IIC-BUS Interface, USB Host, USB Device, SD Host & Multi-Media Card Interface, 2-ch SPI and PLL for clock generation.

The S3C2410A was developed using an ARM920T core, 0.18μm CMOS standard cells and a memory complier. Its low-power, simple, elegant and fully static design is particularly suitable for cost- and power-sensitive applications. It adopts a new bus architecture called Advanced Microcontroller Bus Architecture (AMBA).

The S3C2410A offers outstanding features with its CPU core, a 16/32-bit ARM920T RISC processor designed by Advanced RISC Machines, Ltd. The ARM920T implements MMU, AMBA BUS, and Harvard cache architecture with separate 16kB instruction and 16kB data caches, each with an 8-word line length.By providing a complete set of common system peripherals, the S3C2410A minimizes overall system costs and eliminates the need to configure additional components. The integrated on-chip functions that are described in this document include:

- 1.8V/2.0V int., 3.3V memory, 3.3V external I/O microprocessor with 16kB I-Cache/16 kB D-Cache/MMU;
- External memory controller (SDRAM Control and Chip Select logic);
- LCD controller (up to 4k color STN and 256k color TFT) with 1-ch LCD-dedicated DMA;
- 4-ch DMAs with external request pins;
- 3-ch UART (IrDA1.0, 16-byte Tx FIFO, and 16-byte Rx FIFO) / 2-ch SPI;
- SD Host interface version 1.0 & Multimedia Card Protocol version 2.11 compatible;
- Watch Dog Timer;
- 117-bit general purpose I/O ports / 24-ch external interrupt source;
- Power control: Normal, Slow, Idle and Power-off mode;
- 8-ch 10-bit ADC and Touch screen interface;
- RTC with calendar function;
- On-chip clock generator with PLL.

➢ Architecture
- Integrated system for hand-held devices and general embedded applications.
- 16/32-bit RISC architecture and powerful instruction set with ARM920T CPU core.
- Enhanced ARM architecture MMU to support WinCE, EPOC 32 and Linux.
- Instruction cache, data cache, write buffer and Physical address TAG RAM to reduce the effect of main memory bandwidth and latency on performance.
- ARM920T CPU core supports the ARM debug architecture.
- Internal Advanced Microcontroller Bus Architecture (AMBA) (AMBA2.0, AHB/APB).

➢ System Manager
- Little/Big endian support.
- Address space: 128M bytes for each bank (total 1G bytes).
- Supports programmable 8/16/32-bit data bus width for each bank.
- Fixed bank start address from bank 0 to bank 6.
- Programmable bank start address and bank size for bank 7.
- Eight memory banks.
- Fully Programmable access cycles for all memory banks.
- Supports external wait signals to expend the bus cycle.
- Supports self-refresh mode in SDRAM for power-down.

- Supports various types of ROM for booting (NOR/NAND Flash, EEPROM, and others).
➢ NAND Flash Boot Loader
  - Supports booting from NAND flash memory.
  - 4KB internal buffer for booting.
  - Supports storage memory for NAND flash memory after booting.
➢ Cache Memory
  - 64-way set-associative cache with I-Cache (16KB) and D-Cache (16KB).
  - 8 words length per line with one valid bit and two dirty bits per line.
  - Pseudo random or round robin replacement algorithm.
  - Write-through or write-back cache operation to update the main memory.
  - The write buffer can hold 16 words of data and four addresses.
➢ Clock & Power Manager
  - On-chip MPLL and UPLL:
    UPLL generates the clock to operate USB Host/Device;
    MPLL generates the clock to operate MCU at maximum 266MHz @ 2.0V.
  - Clock can be fed selectively to each function block by software.
  - Power mode: Normal, Slow, Idle, and Power-off mode.
  - Normal mode: Normal operating mode.
  - Slow mode: Low frequency clock without PLL.
  - Idle mode: The clock for only CPU is stopped.
  - Power-off mode: The Core power including all peripherals is shut down.
  - Woken up by EINT[15:0] or RTC alarm interrupt from Power-off mode.
➢ Interrupt Controller
  - 55 Interrupt sources(One Watch dog timer, 5 timers, 9 UARTs, 24 external interrupts, 4 DMA, 2 RTC, 2 ADC, 1 IIC, 2SPI, 1 SDI, 2 USB, 1 LCD, and 1 Battery Fault).
  - Level/Edge mode on external interrupt source.
  - Programmable polarity of edge and level.
  - Supports Fast Interrupt request (FIQ) for very urgent interrupt request.
➢ Timer with Pulse Width Modulation (PWM)
  - 4-ch 16-bit Timer with PWM / 1-ch 16-bit internal timer with DMA-based or interrupt-based operation.
  - Programmable duty cycle, frequency, and polarity.
  - Dead-zone generation.
  - Supports external clock sources.
➢ RTC (Real Time Clock)
  - Full clock feature: second, minute, hour, date, day, month, and year.
  - 32.768kHz operation.
  - Alarm interrupt.

- Time tick interrupt.
- General Purpose Input/Output Ports
  - 24 external interrupt ports.
  - Multiplexed input/output ports.
- UART
  - 3-channel UART with DMA-based or interrupt-based operation.
  - Supports 5-bit, 6-bit, 7-bit, or 8-bit serial data transmit/receive (Tx/Rx).
  - Supports external clocks for the UART operation (UEXTCLK).
  - Programmable baud rate.
  - Supports IrDA 1.0.
  - Loopback mode for testing.
  - Each channel has internal 16-byte Tx FIFO and 16-byte Rx FIFO.
- DMA Controller
  - 4-ch DMA controller.
  - Supports memory to memory, I/O to memory, memory to I/O, and I/O to I/O transfers.
  - Burst transfer mode to enhance the transfer rate.
- A/D Converter & Touch Screen Interface
  - 8-ch multiplexed ADC.
  - Max. 500kSPS and 10-bit Resolution.
- LCD Controller STN LCD Displays Feature
  - Supports 3 types of STN LCD panels: 4-bit dual scan, 4-bit single scan, 8-bit single scan display type.
  - Supports monochrome mode, 4 gray levels, 16 gray levels, 256 colors and 4096 colors for STN LCD.
  - Supports multiple screen size.
    Typical actual screen size: 640×480, 320×240, 160×160, and others.
    Maximum virtual screen size is 4M bytes.
    Maximum virtual screen size in 256 color.
    Mode: 4096×1024, 2048×2048, 1024×4096, and others.
- TFT(Thin Film Transistor) Color Displays Feature
  - Supports 1, 2, 4 or 8 bpp (bit-per-pixel) palette color displays for color TFT.
  - Supports 16 bpp non-palette true-color displays for color TFT.
  - Supports maximum 16M color TFT at 24 bpp mode.
  - Supports multiple screen size.
    Typical actual screen size: 640×480, 320×240, 160×160, and others.
    Maximum virtual screen size is 4M bytes.
    Maximum virtual screen size in 64k color mode: 2048×1024, and others.
- Watchdog Timer
  - 16-bit Watchdog Timer.

- Interrupt request or system reset at time-out.
➢ IIC-Bus Interface
  - 1-ch Multi-Master IIC-Bus.
  - Serial, 8-bit oriented and bi-directional data transfers can be made at up to 100kbit/s in Standard mode or up to 400kbit/s in Fast mode.
➢ IIS-Bus Interface
  - 1-ch IIS-bus for audio interface with DMA-based operation.
  - Serial, 8-/16-bit per channel data transfers.
  - 128 Bytes (64-Byte + 64-Byte) FIFO for Tx/Rx.
  - Supports IIS format and MSB-justified data format.
➢ USB Host
  - 2-port USB Host.
  - Complies with OHCI Rev. 1.0.
  - Compatible with USB Specification version 1.1.
➢ USB Device
  - 1-port USB Device.
  - 5 Endpoints for USB Device.
  - Compatible with USB Specification version 1.1.
➢ SD Host Interface
  - Compatible with SD Memory Card Protocol version 1.0.
  - Compatible with SDIO Card Protocol version 1.0.
  - Bytes FIFO for Tx/Rx.
  - DMA-based or Interrupt-based operation.
  - Compatible with Multimedia Card Protocol version 2.11.
➢ SPI Interface
  - Compatible with 2-ch Serial Peripheral Interface Protocol version 2.11.
  - 2×8 bits Shift register for Tx/Rx.
  - DMA-based or Interrupt-based operation.
➢ Operating Voltage Range
  - Core: 1.8V for 200MHz (S3C2410A-20); 2.0V for 266MHz (S3C2410A-26).
  - Memory & I/O: 3.3V.
➢ Operating Frequency
  - Up to 266MHz.
➢ Package
  - 272-FBGA.

References

[1] 孙建中. 电子商务专业英语[M]. 北京：中国水利水电出版社，2003.

[2] 张凤生，卢川英. 计算机专业英语[M]. 大连：大连理工大学出版社，2006.

[3] 卜艳萍，周伟. 计算机专业英语[M]. 北京：清华大学出版社，2004.

[4] 赵俊荣. 计算机专业英语[M]. 北京：中国铁道出版社，2008.

[5] 王国超，王玉律，任煜昌. 计算机专业英语[M]. 北京：冶金工业出版社，2005.

[6] 司爱侠，张强华. 计算机英语教程[M]. 第 2 版. 北京：人民邮电出版社，2007.

[7] 盛时竹，丁秀芹，殷树友. 计算机专业英语[M]. 北京：清华大学出版社，2006.

[8] 支丽平. 计算机专业英语[M]. 北京：中国水利出版社，2010.

[9] 卜艳萍，周伟. 计算机专业英语[M]. 北京：清华大学出版社，2010.

[10] 朱一伦. 电子技术专业英语. 北京：电子工业出版社，2010.

[11] 冯新宇. 电子技术专业英语教程. 北京：电子工业出版社，2009.

[12] 张筱华. 计算机网络专业英语[M]. 北京：人民邮电出版社，2002.

[13] 赵俊荣. 计算机专业英语[M]. 北京：中国铁道出版社，2009.

[14] [美]Timothy J.O. 计算机专业英语[M]. 北京：高等教育出版社，2009.

[15] 王晓刚. 计算机专业英语[M]. 北京：电子工业出版社，2000.

[16] 张政. 计算机专业英语教程[M]. 北京：北京大学出版社，2007.

[17] 潘维琴，张健. 电子商务专业英语[M]. 北京：机械工业出版社，2008.

[18] 孙建忠，王斌. 电子商务专业英语[M]. 北京：中国水利水电出版社，2004.

[19] 姚国章. 电子商务英语[M]. 北京：北京大学出版社，2007.

[20] 王翔. 实用 IT 英语[M]. 天津：天津大学出版社，2009.

[21] Stanislav Pavlov, Pavel Belevsky. Windows® Embedded CE 6.0 Fundamentals[M]: Publisher: Microsoft Press,2008.

[22] Richard Petersen. Red Hat—The Complete Reference Enterprise Linux & Fedora Edition[M]. Publisher: Brandon A. Nordin, 2003.

[23] David Pogue. Switching to the Mac: The Missing Manual, Leopard Edition [M]. Publisher: O'Reilly, 2008.